Everything We Thought Was True

LISA MONTANARO

Everything We Thought Was True
Red Adept Publishing, LLC
104 Bugenfield Court
Garner, NC 27529
https://RedAdeptPublishing.com/

This is a work of fiction. Names, characters, places, and incidents either are the product of the author's imagination or are used fictitiously, and any resemblance to locales, events, business establishments, or actual persons—living or dead—is entirely coincidental.

---

1.   http://StreetlightGraphics.com

The story of Frank and Teresa is lovingly dedicated to my parents, Joseph and Carol.

"To be nobody—but yourself—in a world which is doing its best day and night to make you like everybody else means to fight the hardest battle which any human being can fight and never stop fighting."
~ e.e. cummings

"It takes courage to grow up and become who you really are."
~ e.e. cummings

"For whatever we lose (like a you or a me), it's always our self we find in the sea."
~ e.e. cummings

OVERTURE

LENA – NEW ROCHELLE, NY
1983

When my family sat down for dinner, the last thing I expected was my typically unruffled Italian American mom to hurl a plate of spaghetti and peas against the wall. Even worse—she was aiming for my father.

To officially kick off summer and celebrate the end of school, Mom had made one of our favorite dishes, *pasta e piselli*—spaghetti with peas in red gravy. She spent hours making it from scratch, holed up in the cramped kitchen, which grew hot as an inferno on this sticky summer night. Every time my older brother, Anthony, still whining at fifteen, asked when dinner was, she'd say, "When your goddamn father gets home," and then under her breath, "Whenever that will be."

My father's absence from the dinner table had become the norm lately—he was often out late after work—yet my mother still held out hope for his arrival that night. He graced us with his presence a half hour later, waltzing in and washing up, while my mom motioned for us to sit down at the dining room table of the duplex my family rented in a New York City suburb. Mom served my father's spaghetti and peas with more force than necessary, hitting the serving spoon against the side of the bowl with a clank that made me jump in my seat.

Dad spread his napkin on his lap as though nothing was amiss. "Sorry I'm late. I had to swing by the boatyard after work and check on something."

Mom raised her eyebrows and didn't make eye contact with him. "I don't remember you telling me you had to stop by the boatyard. Are you sure that's where you were?"

"Of course. I told you. Where else would I be?"

Mom put down the serving spoon and looked up at him. "Well, I don't know, Frank. I hardly ever know where you are these days, do I?"

I looked from my mother to my father, trying to make sense of what was happening. Anthony was oblivious, heartily eating, already on his second helping. I'd heard my parents fight many times, but this time felt different. Mom's jaw was set, and steely resolve shone in her eyes. Electricity buzzed around the table, so strong I could almost hear it. My parents' roles were reversed, with my mother appearing to have the upper hand and my father looking like a petulant teenager who'd been caught coming home past curfew.

I had a sinking feeling her change in attitude had something to do with what I'd said to her about Dad a few nights before at McDonald's. I'd told her that I knew his secret, though I hadn't understood the full weight of it. One Saturday afternoon four summers earlier, on my dad's boat, I'd caught my dad and his friend Henry in the midst of an intimate moment. Henry's hand was on my father's arm, and my father had his head bent toward his friend, a satisfied smile on his face, a look of tenderness on Henry's. My mother looked at my father that way, but I'd never seen someone else with that exact look on their face directed at my father. Burned into my brain was the image of my father and this man huddled close together in the captain's seat of the boat, a tableau framed by the bright-blue sky and sea. And I'd come to a conclusion: my dad and Henry were more than friends.

"I said I was at the boatyard. That's it."

"That's it? No, Frank, I don't think that's it. There's a lot more going on than *that's it*, and you know it. And so do I."

"Oh, come on, Teresa. Stop with the theatrics."

She snatched her plate of spaghetti and peas and hurled it in my father's direction. He ducked just in time. The plate flew past him and crashed against the dining room wall. Shards of china skidded across the gold linoleum floor. Red streaks dripped down the wall onto the sideboard that held the stereo system with an eight-track tape of Barry Manilow sticking out. My father stood up, wide-eyed, his hands tightly grasping the sides of the table. His face and knuckles turned white, like they'd been drained of color.

Mom's face was red, and her voice was quivering. "These are your theatrics, Frank! You created them."

I held my breath. *What is she going to do? And, oh my God, what is she going to say? Will she tell him what I know?* I realized my family was precarious, teetering on a cliff, about to fall over.

"No, Frank, I'm not hysterical or a drama queen or whatever else you've accused me of in the past to avoid the real subject—the one we never talk about but is always there. You think it's hidden. Well, it's not." She glanced over at me then back at my father. It seemed once the words poured out, Mom couldn't dam the rest. "Your own daughter knows what's going on—a thirteen-year-old! So don't tell me to stop with the theatrics. If anyone needs to stop with the theatrics, it's you."

She told him. I couldn't believe this was happening.

Dad looked over at me questioningly. I couldn't meet his eyes. I turned away and looked at Anthony, who by this time had stopped eating and was watching the scene unfold with wide-open eyes, holding his forgotten fork in midair. The two of us were like a Greek chorus—there to witness the tragedy and comment on it but not control it. And I knew the truth. Anthony was clueless. I envied him at that moment. I didn't want to be in the know.

"Teresa, I don't know what you're talking about, but this is not the time. That's enough." Dad looked around wildly, like he was trying to find an escape route. But he stayed glued to his spot. His face registered an expression unfamiliar to me, and I realized with horror that it was fear.

The same refrain repeated over and over in my head like a needle stuck on a scratch on one of my worn-out records. *Oh my God, oh my God, oh my God.*

"Yes, I agree. It's enough! I'm tired of you going out and doing what you want while I cover for you." She glanced at me again. "While we all cover for you. We've been dancing around this secret long enough, Frank. I'm not having any more of it. I'm done."

Mom shot to her feet and this time threw the entire serving bowl across the table. It shattered against the wall. The sound was deafening, like something had cracked that could never be repaired. The spaghetti trailed down like an army of caterpillars, inching slowly toward the floor and mixing with the red gravy. The wall looked as if millions of tiny bugs had been squashed all over it, leaving their blood behind like evidence of a crime. The crime, in this case, was the unraveling of my parents' marriage and the breaking apart of our family.

"Mom!" I pleaded.

She stared at my father, her eyes boring into him, her glare seething. "Get out of this house."

Anthony jumped to his feet, scraping his chair against the floor. "Mom, no. What do you mean, get out?"

"I mean, I want your father to leave. Right now."

My father flinched but remained immobile. "Teresa, calm down. No one is going anywhere."

"Oh yeah?" She said it like it was a dare. "Well, if you won't leave, I will."

Stunned silence. I looked at Anthony, who was frozen in place.

Mom swiftly moved into the kitchen and grabbed her purse and keys from the counter. I bolted up from the table, following her, crying, "Mom, no! Don't go!"

A moment of affection flashed across my mother's face as she glanced back at me and then Anthony. She gave my shoulder a quick squeeze and then marched forward, a determined look on her face. She went through the back door and stepped outside. The screen door slammed shut behind her, like the period at the end of a long sentence. I heard her big yellow Cadillac back out of the driveway with a mechanical whine and then growl away.

ACT 1: A SECRET IS LURKING

Chapter One
LENA - LOS ANGELES, CA
June 2015
THIRTY-TWO YEARS LATER

I hit Ignore on my cell phone, sending my dad's call to voicemail and feeling guilty. We often chatted in the morning before work. I would ring him later, but at the moment, I needed to focus. I'd come to the office early so I could be totally prepared to practice my opening statement with Marcus by the time he arrived.

As if on cue, Marcus appeared in my office doorway, trench coat still on, a briefcase in one hand and a cardboard coffee holder with two cups in the other. "You ready, kid?"

It cracked me up that Marcus referred to me as "kid." He was only twelve years my senior but still used that affectionate term often. It didn't rankle me. I secretly enjoyed it.

"Absolutely," I said. "Be right there. Just printing out a clean copy."

"Of course you are." He snickered. "Wouldn't want a dirty, marked-up opening statement. So messy." He shuddered, making fun of me.

He glanced around my office, which was a study in minimalism with no visible clutter. My desk held only the multitiered inbox system I used for active cases, meticulously color coded and labeled. My credenza contained the few law books I consulted, organized alpha-

9

betically by title. It was a stark contrast to the other attorneys' offices, with their papers, books, and files haphazardly strewn all over surfaces, along with the occasional used coffee mug with contents that looked like a leftover science experiment. Although the chief liked to chide me about my anal behavior, I credited it as one reason I'd moved up in the division so quickly. I was Ms. Organized before anyone had even heard of Marie Kondo, thank you very much.

"See you in five in the conference room. Oh, and I brought you one of those lattes you love." Marcus raised the cardboard coffee holder as proof.

Shit. The chief drank his coffee black. Nothing fancier than that. He only brought me a latte when he wanted to butter me up or cheer me up. *Which one is it?*

"I've got to talk to you about another case," he added. "Bring that planner of yours."

"Okay," I said, sounding noncommittal even to my own ears.

I was already mentally scanning my docket to see if I could squeeze in another case. I had two upcoming trials, settlement negotiations for two other cases, and a handful of depositions. But my biggest commitment, by far, was the behemoth Hawke Health Care case that could make or break my career. The case scared the shit out of me. Marcus had made me first chair, and I needed to nail it. I was thrilled that a significant case like this had landed in my lap. We were taking on the Southern California health care system for its unfair treatment of female physicians. I'd been waiting years for a case like this to come along—one that could be a game changer and make a big statement about gender discrimination.

I stood up and smoothed down my skirt. I wanted to strike the right note to practice my opening statement and get myself in court mode—confident, approachable, and intelligent. I was wearing my favorite suit, a gorgeous cobalt blue from Nordstrom Rack. Power blue, the saleswoman had called it. Not navy blue—that was so New

York financial district. This was Los Angeles—lighter and brighter, less serious but still formidable. It was the suit I'd worn when I won the Randall case the previous year. I also wore three-inch leather heels, a splurge from a recent trip to Florence with my husband, Kevin. Though five feet, nine inches tall—thanks to my mother—I stood at six feet with the heels on, the same height as Marcus.

May as well be eye to eye with the chief while going toe to toe over my opening statement. I knew he'd be putting me through the paces. He always did.

When I walked into the conference room a few minutes later, Marcus was already seated, papers laid out, coffees on the table. The flip chart was on the easel, ready for us to jot down notes as we stopped along the way. A podium was waiting for me across the room. The chief was ready to go.

Many of my law school friends complained incessantly about their supervisors. I felt like the universe had given me something special when I'd been assigned to work with Marcus. He was my boss, my mentor, and a legend. He'd seen everything and then some. He was about as close as a lawyer could get to being a superhero, in my book. He made me believe in the concept of a true counselor at law—he was dedicated, humble, and a tremendous supporter of his team. Born and bred in downtown LA, he'd gone east to attend the first historically black university law school in the United States—Howard University—then boomeranged back to the West Coast to clerk for the Ninth Circuit Court of Appeals and then entered the US Attorney's Office. He worked his way up the ranks until he took his seat at the top, in the 1980s, as the first African American Civil Rights Division chief.

When I attended NYU School of Law in the '90s, I read some cases Marcus had argued in federal court and developed a bit of a professional crush on him. I worked my ass off in law school and was rewarded with an offer for my dream job after graduation. The only catch was that it was across the country in California, far from my mother. It was so hard leaving her.

"Lena, before we begin, I wanted to ask if you could handle that sexual orientation case that just came in, for the town of Fletcher school district. Can I add it to your cases?"

I froze. I'd heard about the case and knew it was coming down the pipeline. They'd fired a gay teacher from his public school position in a Central Valley agricultural town, and he was claiming sexual orientation discrimination. It had the potential to explode with media coverage. Typically, I liked to act as first or second chair in high-profile cases for the division. But I didn't have time for this one. Not at the moment.

"I heard about that case. Good one for the division. But I'm slammed with first chairing the Hawke case and overseeing my other cases." *Is that true?* I'd managed heavier caseloads in the past.

I ran through the short list of attorneys at the division I thought could do justice to this case and, grudgingly, came up with only one—Bradley Hanford III, the other deputy in the division besides me. Brad was a good litigator, even if he was a pompous ass. It drove him crazy when he didn't get to sit at the attorney's table with Marcus because I was taking up the second-chair seat. And I had to admit to a certain amount of satisfaction at Brad's irritation.

"Can you give it to Brad?" The words came out of my mouth and made me cringe inside. I couldn't believe I was giving this case away. *Am I really feeling that overwhelmed with my work, or is something else going on?* I couldn't put my finger on it. I just knew in my gut that I didn't want to say yes to this case.

"You sure you don't want this one? You're perfect for it. I'm surprised you're not jumping at it. Heavy dockets never stopped you before."

"I know. But I want to nail this Hawke case and really focus my attention on it." I hesitated. "I think Brad can handle the Fletcher one. And you know he'll jump at the chance." I rolled my eyes.

"Oh, he'll jump at it—that's for sure." Marcus snickered. "But I really think the Fletcher case should be yours. Besides, I think we'll be in good shape for the Hawke case. What gives?"

Damn, he's not letting this go. "I just think I should focus on the cases I already have. The Hawke case is consuming me more than I thought it would. Why don't we give Fletcher to Brad? I can provide backup if he needs it."

Ugh. That was the last thing I wanted—to help Brad shine. But I could also tell I didn't want to take on the Fletcher case.

Marcus nodded slowly, hand to his forehead, processing my request. It was a gesture he often made when he was thinking, almost like he was trying to access his brain waves. He then nodded more vigorously, and I knew I'd won. "Okay, that'll work. But let me know soon if you change your mind, before Brad digs in."

Yes. I felt relieved but didn't want that to show on my face. "Will do. Thanks, Marcus. I appreciate it." I left it at that. He didn't like when his attorneys harped on issues and offered unnecessary explanation.

"One other thing," Marcus added. "The Los Angeles Bar Association dinner is next month on July 15. Unfortunately, I can't make it, as I'm already booked as the keynote speaker for the UCLA Black Law Students Association event. Can I put you down for the bar dinner in my place?"

I cringed. I hated schmoozing at legal events, but it was an honor to be asked to go on behalf of our division.

"I know you hate these shindigs, but I can't be in two places at once. Besides, you're good at them once you get there and stop worrying about it."

"I wouldn't go that far," I said.

"It's a free meal," he added.

"If you call rubber chicken a meal," I said. He mockingly stared at me, waiting for me to give in. "Fine, I'll go. But I'd much rather be at your event, listening to you give that keynote, to be honest."

"Nothing you haven't heard before," he said dismissively. "Okay, enough admin crap. You ready to go? Take your place, counselor." Marcus gestured to the podium.

"Aye-aye, Chief," I said, saluting him. I walked across the room, stood behind the podium, stared out at my imaginary courtroom, and began. "May it please the court, my name is Lena Antinori, and I am the deputy United States attorney for the central district of California, representing the plaintiffs in this case."

No matter how many times I went to court and got to recite that opening, it still made my skin tingle with excitement. I loved hearing my name next to that title, although I'd shortened my first name to spare the judge and jury the religious association that *Magdalena* conjured. My father was always so proud that I'd kept my maiden name when I married Kevin. Dad liked to remind me it was his last name, after all. I mostly kept it because I loved my Italian heritage. And since Kevin and I had decided not to have children, I didn't see the need to have the same last name as my husband. Also, Magdalena Ryan? It didn't exactly roll off the tongue. A complete mismatch.

I stirred my concoction of *pasta e piselli* and watched the peas bobbing like little green buoys in the pot. I'd always made my mother's signature dish on June 29, even though it came with a huge serving of one very bad childhood memory, being the anniversary of that fateful night when the spaghetti flew and our family's story was forever split into *before* and *after*. If someone had told me, when I was a child, that a plate of spaghetti and peas splattering against the dining room wall would be the defining moment in my family's life, I would have called them crazy. But my family was anything but typical. Loving? Yes. Honest with each other? Sometimes. Crazy? Most of the time. But typical? Definitely not.

Sometimes, I thought I was a masochist. No matter how many times I told myself I wouldn't make this dish on this day, I always did. It comforted me and reminded me of my mother and of the *before*.

My mom used to say, "You can never really know what's going on inside someone else's marriage." Yet at thirteen, I'd known exactly what was going on in the sham of my parents' marriage.

My phone buzzed with a text message from Kevin: *Hey, babe. Won't be home before you hit the sack. Save me a plate of that infamous pasta dish. Team is ordering Domino's—I know you'd kill me for eating that crap. Night night. Love you.*

My tech-geek husband was working on a big special effects project with his team at Disney Studios that I couldn't even wrap my head around. He loved his work, which made it much easier for me to be as career focused as I was. Ambition was something we had in common, fortunately. Our mutual understanding that spending time in fulfilling careers didn't amount to spousal neglect made our marriage one without a ton of drama. Well, that and not having children, another pretty important decision to agree on for a successful relationship. It was probably for the best that Kevin was working late and couldn't point out that I was being melodramatic in resurrecting the dish that included family trauma among its ingredients. I could wallow in self-pity with a glass of Chianti.

Cheers, Mom, I thought as I took a sip of wine.

Our black Lab, Atticus, whined and stuck his wet nose under my elbow, trying to get me to pet him. I absentmindedly rubbed under his chin and sighed. Atticus echoed the sentiment, letting out a satisfied groan.

Yeah, buddy, you get it, don't you?

It had been a long workday of opening-statement prep, and I felt depleted from Marcus's constant interruptions. There was a lot more to do before I would feel confident delivering that opening statement in court. I was relieved to have more than a month before the trial. I still had to prep my witnesses, compile exhibits, and review hundreds of pages of depositions. The prep would be relentless.

Speaking of relentless... Dad. I had to call him back. He'd called a second time, and I'd let it go to voicemail. He would call again if I didn't call him back. Kevin always wondered why I didn't just pick up the phone.

"You know he's just going to call you again. Besides, he's a man of few words. Just rip off the Band-Aid, and call him."

Kevin was right. My dad was very much a get-to-the-point kind of person. Sometimes to a fault. I lowered the temperature on the stove so the gravy didn't overcook.

"Lena, my love," he said, greeting me with his signature New York Italian accent.

My dad had relocated from New York to the LA area a few years before me, making us both West Coast transplants—something I never could have predicted years ago. His accent still lingered, like a badge of pride, while I worked hard to erase any trace of that telltale sound from my voice. But apparently not with total success—Kevin liked to tease, "You can take the girl out of New York, but you can't take the New York out of the girl," when the *New Yawk* dialect crept back into my speech.

"Hi, Dad."

"Where've you been?" I could hear the annoyance in his voice. I hadn't been calling him as much for the last few weeks because I'd been so busy with work. He always hated when I went radio silent. I immediately felt guilty, like a little girl who'd skipped school and gotten caught.

"Working. Big case going on that I'm heading up for the division. Trial is going to be later this summer."

"You'll do great. You always do. We still on for Sunday on the boat?"

The boat, his pride and joy. When I was a kid, it seemed like Dad had loved that boat more than he loved our family. He'd certainly spent a lot of time on it—and not always alone. My mom resented his boat as if it were his mistress. And alongside Mom, I'd resented it too. But that was years ago. Nowadays, when we weren't stuck working on the weekends, Kevin and I enjoyed hitting the water for some sunshine and ocean breeze.

"Yup, we're on," I said.

"Listen," he said. A slight note of hesitation in Dad's voice made me press the phone closer to my ear. "You know how happy Oliver and I have been, right? Well, we've been thinking of doing something about it. Something more permanent."

"Um..." *What does he mean by 'more permanent'?* "You two live together. That's pretty permanent." My voice was quiet. "And... you're committed to each other..." I stopped talking. This was feeling awkward, like I was my dad's therapist or something.

"Yes, we're committed. But we want to make it official."

Official. What the heck does that mean? Have they been having an unofficial relationship until now?

"We want to get married!" He said it like it was the punch line of a great joke.

"Married?" I asked with a jolt.

My legs felt wobbly. I stumbled back and sat on a kitchen stool. Everything went still—my father's voice, the electric buzzing on the phone line, and my breath. Even the air in the room seemed like it had skidded to a stop. All I heard was the gurgling of the gravy boiling.

"Yes, Oliver and I want to get married," he said.

My heartbeat thumped inside my chest in a staccato pattern like horses' hooves galloping around a track. Dad and his partner had been together for several years now and got along great. He was the happiest I'd seen him in a long time. He could finally be free to live the life he'd always wanted. The rest of us were still picking up the pieces of our life that had been strewn around years ago, like the shards of that plate bouncing off the walls of our dining room.

My dad's words snapped me back into the conversation. "And now we can, and it will be recognized in the whole damn country."

I could hear the smile in his voice. He'd posted on Facebook about the recent Supreme Court decision that legalized same-sex marriage, placing a photo of him and Oliver against the rainbow pride flag, but I didn't think he considered it for himself. After all, he was nearing his seventieth birthday.

"That's..." I stopped, not sure what I wanted to say. That it was great news? That I was happy for them?

I couldn't bring myself to speak. I didn't trust what would come out. There was something bubbling under the surface. My jumbled thoughts matched the tomatoes boiling in the pot, one idea popping up and bursting, followed by another. I was thirteen again, sitting in that dining room with my family frozen around the table, spaghetti trailing down the wall. It seemed like my father was taking something from me all these years later. But what? My parents had been divorced for so many years. We'd all moved on. Still, I couldn't shake the feeling my father was betraying my mom, cheating on her again. How absurd. I knew that was ridiculous. But I couldn't persuade my heart otherwise.

"Tell me what you have in mind," I said, shifting gears to focus on details. Getting lost in the minutiae and steering away from the emotions—that was a skill I'd mastered in my legal training and reverted to when it served me.

As my father talked about his ideas for the wedding, my mother came to mind. *Was he this excited about his wedding to her? Did he know, even before he said, "I do," that he would break her heart and his kids' too?*

"Lena, this is important to me. I want to do this. I'm ready."

He's ready? Well, that's nice. It had only taken sixty-seven years and a lot of pain and suffering of everyone around him for him to be ready. He'd left a lot of broken hearts in his wake. *But that's old news. Why am I thinking about this now?*

"Why not do something simple?" I asked. "Maybe go to City Hall and just get married there? Or do it in Palm Springs or Las Vegas over one of your weekend trips?"

Surely, he didn't plan to have a big wedding and invite a ton of people. He had a handful of close friends in the LA area, many of whom were also gay. I figured he'd ask them to attend. As for me, besides Kevin, I'd told no one my dad was gay, not even my work colleagues, who'd spent their careers fighting for social justice issues. I kept my personal and professional lives very separate. I preferred it that way.

"Hmm, I'll ask Oliver. But I think he wants a real wedding. And I want to give it to him. It's something to celebrate. We'll do it here in LA and keep it small. Just some family and close friends. I'm hoping Anthony will come out with Donna and the kids. And I want Henry there too."

Henry. Of course he'd want Henry there. I could never really understand their relationship. They'd cheated on their wives with each other, betraying their children and their families. They'd broken their marriage vows, eventually broken up their tryst, and then broken apart their families. Yet they'd stayed the closest of friends all these years. Now my dad wanted Henry at his wedding. To his current lover.

I swear you can't make this shit up.

"Lena, if you could research places for the ceremony and reception, that would be a big help. I know you're good at that. Someplace by the water."

I couldn't believe this. "Dad, I don't know. I have a case at work that's going to demand a ton of time over the next few months. Besides, wouldn't you and Oliver like to do the planning for yourselves? I mean, it's going to be your big day after all."

"Yeah, but we want you to be involved. We thought this would be a good role for you."

A good role. *What an accurate phrase*, I thought. I would certainly play a role. Many of them. The role of a civil rights attorney championing equality on all levels—including LGBTQ rights—who couldn't be happier to support diversity in my family. The role of the loyal daughter ready and willing to plan her gay father's second wedding to his partner.

But where was the loyalty he was supposed to show to my mother when they were married? To his kids?

I shook my head, trying to snap out of this funk. That was a long time ago. I was an adult now. I should be happy for my father.

"And, honey, I want you to be one of our witnesses for the ceremony. Kind of like a best man."

"Oh, don't you want to ask Anthony?"

"Yes, he'll be the other witness. The two of you."

"Have you talked to him yet?"

"No, I'll call him as soon as we hang up, because it's getting late in New York."

"Got it."

Fine, let him break the news to Anthony himself. One less awkward thing for me to deal with. Oh man, do I have to talk to Anthony about this?

"When were you thinking of having the wedding?" I asked.

"October."

Is he kidding me? How am I supposed to plan a wedding in only four months with this big trial coming up and everything else on my docket? But I didn't protest. When my dad made up his mind, that was it. No use fighting him on it. He was always so impulsive. I just wished he'd been able to tame some of his impulses over the years.

"That's only four months away," I said.

Four months to process that my father was marrying again after all these years. Four months to figure out how to accept that. Four months to convince myself I wasn't stabbing Mom in the back. We both said nothing. The silence was thick between us.

"Well, at least you aren't planning on doing it this summer," I finally said, giving in.

I was always trying to solve the issues, be the perfect hostess, make it all happen. My perfectionism clung to me like an extra layer of skin I couldn't shed. It was my way of dealing with the messy family dynamics I grew up with. It didn't matter how grown up I was, how accomplished I was at my career, or how happy I was in my marriage. With my family, I often became exactly who I'd always been—the dutiful daughter trying to manage the wreckage. I stepped right back into that role as if it were carved for me in stone. If I were going to plan this event, at least I could somewhat control it. I'd plan the wedding in a secluded place, where there was no chance of meeting anyone I knew.

"I'm so happy," my dad said, his voice quivering.

"Good, I'm happy for you." I wasn't nearly as emotional. I sounded like someone trying to encourage herself to be happy. Which then made me feel guilty. I wanted him to be happy. I wanted to be happy for him. "Dad, I have to run. It's been a long workday, and I'm finally about to eat dinner."

"This late? Okay, get going. You work too hard. Go eat."

"I will. Congratulations, Dad. And pass on my congrats to Oliver too."

"I will. Thanks, Lena. I really appreciate it. Love you."

He always said that before we hung up, a habit he'd started when I was eighteen, when we came together after years of estrangement. Dad 2.0 wasn't afraid to show his emotions. You always knew how he felt and where you stood. I wished he'd been that much of an open book when I was younger. I'd spent most of my childhood trying to read him and figure out who he was, what he'd been hiding, and why.

"Love you too, Dad. See you Sunday." I felt like I'd just finished one of my long runs—depleted—though I was at the beginning of this race. The details of the next few months loomed before me like tall hurdles to leap. But logistics were where I excelled.

"Bye, honey."

I hung up. Hearing my dad's voice excitedly announcing he was getting married again felt like a tidal wave knocking me over. *Why didn't I see this coming?*

My dad and Oliver seemed to be a great match. But I hadn't thought my dad would ever get married again. He was a divorced man who'd been married a long time ago to my mother. Now he was the groom-to-be. Engaged. I couldn't help worrying that my father remarrying, especially to his same-sex partner, would somehow erase my parents' marriage and our family.

My stomach growled, reminding me of my dinner. I served my plate of spaghetti and peas and poured some more wine. Atticus sat at my feet, partly under the table and partly sticking out because of his large girth. I placed my bare feet on his fur and rubbed back and forth. He leaned into me to get a firmer massage along his back. I twirled a big wad of spaghetti around my fork the way my mother had taught me then stared at the pasta coated with red gravy and a few stray peas, my appetite gone. I dropped the fork onto the plate with a clatter. Atticus flinched.

"Sorry, buddy," I cooed. I pushed the plate away, grabbed my wine, and took a long, slow sip.

Oh, the irony. Of course Dad had to go and select the date that our family had fallen apart to announce that he was getting married again. I was sure he didn't remember that this was the anniversary of the incident. But still... the fact that he'd picked this day, of all days, to drop this bomb on me felt like an omen.

I signed onto Facebook to distract myself. I hadn't been on social media for a few days, since posts about the Supreme Court decision had flooded my feeds—most celebratory, some ugly. When social media was blowing up with news of the decision, I'd chimed in, posting about the historic weight of it. I was thrilled about the legal strides made in recent years. Heck, I was part of making those strides as a deputy US attorney, but that was my professional life, not my personal one.

Despite the upbeat mood online, I saw the seed of hatred like a spot staining my retina from looking directly at the sun. It was still there, lurking in the shadows, ready to pounce, gaining momentum, becoming angrier and bolder. It was like the decision bestowing rights was oil thrown on an open flame, sparking an even bigger fire. That was what was going through my mind—and it made me sick to be focusing on the negativity, unable to bask in the glow of such a momentous occasion and see past the ugliness. When I saw those hateful comments, a wave of protectiveness toward my father spread through me, which surprised and gladdened me. I didn't know how to explain to others my fear that my father was different, stood out, and was a target of the hateful people of the world.

I checked my Facebook wall and froze. *Oh my God.* My father had already posted about his engagement and tagged me. I had no idea how the hell that had happened—my privacy settings on social media were airtight. I had made sure of that. *Dammit.* Facebook must have done yet another update that canceled out my privacy selections. I quickly went into the post and untagged myself, praying that, in the short time between my conversation with my dad and this post, none of my connections had seen it. I scrolled through the reactions and comments. Fortunately, all of them were from my dad's connections, none from mine. I felt instant relief—and then guilt over my reaction.

My life had been shaped by this one fact—that I was the daughter of a gay father. Yet I still hid it. That was the Antinori family way. My mother had instituted a gag order, forbidding us from revealing that Dad was gay. And I loved my mom, so I'd done just that my entire life, religiously adhering to the Don't Ask, Don't Tell policy long before the US military instituted it. It was our way of trying to maintain a peaceful existence.

My mom's familiar mantra ran through my mind—"No reason to air your dirty laundry"—a phrase that had ruled my childhood as we navigated our family secret.

Chapter Two
TERESA - NEW ROCHELLE, NY
1968

Teresa pushed the baby carriage up the hill the last few steps toward home, cursing the slight incline that never looked that bad in the distance. It was a killer on her calves but worth it. Walking Anthony to the park and back had finally stopped his crying and made him fall asleep. *Thank goodness.*

She glanced at her watch, thankful that she still had enough time to set her hair in rollers, do her makeup, and get dressed up. That night, she and Frank were going to the Drifters Boat Club summer party. It felt like months since they'd been out together. She'd been busy caring for five-month-old Anthony, which often left her exhausted. When Anthony was first born, Frank had come home directly after work to see the baby before Teresa put him to bed. But lately, Frank was working later hours at the Cadillac dealership, hoping to get promoted from auto mechanic to a position in the parts department. Teresa really hoped the promotion would happen soon, so they could get a bigger apartment with more than just three rooms in an attic. On top of that, Frank was working a second job at the Drifters Boat Club, taking weekend shifts to make extra money, which meant more time away from her and Anthony. Fortunately, they still had mornings when Frank sat with her in the kitchen, bouncing Anthony on his lap, feeding him a bottle. And that night,

Frank's mother, Eva, was coming over to watch Anthony so she and Frank could enjoy some alone time.

She parked the baby carriage on the front porch and stared up at the haunted-looking Victorian house. Not the most welcoming of homes, but it was the first place she'd lived other than her parents' house, so she cherished it. She hadn't gone very far. This house was walking distance from where she and Frank had both grown up, in the west end of New Rochelle, a New York City suburb filled with Italians.

Teresa reached their attic apartment, stopping to catch her breath after climbing all three flights of stairs with Anthony asleep in her arms. She settled the baby into his crib and paused to watch him sleep. He was so cherubic with those fat cheeks she loved to nuzzle. It felt strange to be only nineteen years old with a baby. She'd married at eighteen. The two years she and Frank dated had felt like an eternity—she'd been eager to start their "real life" together and be his wife. On Valentine's Day 1967, Teresa Marchesi had worn a white dress and ballet flats so she wouldn't be taller than the groom and officially became Teresa Antinori in a Catholic ceremony at St. Bartholomew Church, her family's local parish.

Frank looked so handsome on their wedding day. When he smiled directly at her, Teresa felt as though the gods had bestowed a gift upon her. It wasn't uncommon for Teresa to catch other women sneaking glances at Frank when they were out together, which always made her feel discomfort mixed with a sense of pride. It didn't hurt that Frank looked like he came from a long line of handsome Italian American Franks—Frankie Avalon, Frank Sinatra, and Frankie Valli.

Teresa opened the door to the small closet she and Frank shared and picked out a shift in lavender, her favorite color. *Perfect match for a summer party.* Yes, that night, she was going on a date with her husband. And she couldn't wait.

Teresa took a bite of her hors d'oeuvre, swaying to the music, watching the pulsating dance floor. The band started playing "I Got You Babe," by Sonny and Cher, and the crowd erupted in excitement. Frank grabbed Teresa's hand and pulled her onto the dance floor, with a big grin on his face.

Frank led Teresa around the floor like a pro. He had a natural rhythm to his movements. He also had years of formal dance classes under his belt, thanks to his mother, who'd seen his interest and talent in dance and enrolled him in ballroom classes from a young age. Teresa was a good dancer but not on a par with Frank. No matter. She loved being in his arms and following his lead. Her hips sashayed as he twirled her away from him and back. They danced song after song, and Teresa was grateful she'd worn flats.

She felt her face flushing and beads of sweat forming on her forehead. A stickiness lingered in the evening, leftover from the humid day, but she didn't care. She couldn't remember the last time they'd danced together for this long. It had probably been before Anthony was born. She and Frank used to go to Glen Island Casino together, a beautiful spot in the southern part of New Rochelle with expansive views over Long Island Sound, which featured big band music on Friday nights.

She thought back to their first date there and smiled to herself, reliving the exchange. "Wow, you dance like Fred Astaire—so smooth on your feet," she'd said.

"So, you've danced with Fred Astaire?" Frank teased.

"Ha ha. No... but I've seen him in the movies. I bet you bring lots of girls here, don't you?"

"Lots of girls? No. Just the ones I really like." Frank winked.

"I've passed the test, then?"

"Oh, you are definitely on your way to passing the test."

"And what else is involved in this test of yours?" she asked.

"Well, the night is still young, isn't it?"

Frank then pulled her closer, pressing her against him in a tight embrace as they danced. He touched a piece of her hair that had fallen out of her chignon and twirled it between his fingers. He'd nuzzled his head into the crook of her neck, and she'd felt his lips lightly brush against her skin as they swayed together in time with the music. Her body had felt electrified with excitement. She remembered thinking she'd never felt like that in her entire life.

She brought her attention back to the present, where the song had changed to Frankie Valli and the Four Seasons' "Can't Take My Eyes Off of You," one of their favorites. She smiled at Frank, and they both started singing along. Frank twirled her again, and when she rolled back into his arms, he dipped her backward. She threw her head back, a yelp of laughter escaping her lips. Frank popped her back up, and she noticed their new friends, Henry and Joanie, dancing nearby. They had a boat on the same dock as Frank's.

Henry leaned in to be heard over the music. "Want to grab something to drink after this song?"

Frank looked at Teresa, and she nodded. "Sure," he said.

Even with flats on, Teresa knew she would need a break from dancing soon. Her calves were going to be so sore in the morning. But it was deliciously worth it.

Hours later, a ringing phone awakened Teresa from a deep sleep. She glanced at the bedside clock. Two o'clock in the morning. She groggily leaned over to reach for the phone, praying it didn't wake Anthony, but Frank had beaten her to it.

"Hello?" he said. Through the glow of the streetlight coming through the window, she watched his face. "Rosa, what's wrong?"

Teresa heard alarm in his voice. She sat bolt upright in bed. Frank listened intently, cradling the phone and looking at her.

"It's Marco. He's missing," he mouthed.

Not again. Teresa hadn't heard from her little brother in the last few days and knew when he was radio silent, it was never good news. He almost always surfaced in some kind of trouble.

After her father, Sergio, passed away of a heart attack at the age of fifty-two, Teresa had worried about her mother, Rosa. Even though Sergio was a difficult man to live with, prone to bouts of drinking and treating Rosa as a second-class citizen, she didn't know any other life than the one she had with him. Teresa worried her mother would find it a challenge to navigate life alone after so many years of being part of a couple, even one with glaring imperfections.

Teresa and her two brothers had still been living at home after Sergio died. Then, one by one, they'd moved on. First, Teresa's big brother, Sal, went to college in Pennsylvania on a scholarship, met his wife, got a great job in the area, and settled there, to Rosa's dismay. Teresa married Frank a few years later—a joyous occasion for her mother but one that meant Teresa left home. That left only her younger brother, Marco, at home, which had proved to be a burden rather than a comfort. Ever since Sergio died, Marco had struggled with alcohol and drug addiction, often going on benders where he was drunk or stoned—or both—for days or weeks at a time and failing to come home. The task of roaming the streets, looking for him before and after work or in the wee hours of the morning, usually fell to Frank, who'd dragged a disheveled Marco back to their apartment too many times for Teresa to count, letting him sober up before bringing him home to a worried-sick Rosa. On those occasions, Teresa would try to reason with Marco, begging him to keep it together for their mother's sake. He would make promises he couldn't keep—to get help, to make a new start, to really try this time. But then the drama would happen all over again, like a well-choreographed play they couldn't stop acting out.

"I'll go canvass the usual spots," Frank said. "Try not to worry, Rosa. I'll find him." He nodded, listening. "You're welcome."

Teresa's heart hurt for her mother, who'd had to put up with her father all those years and now had to deal with Marco. She never got a break.

Frank hung up and got out of bed. He pulled on a pair of jeans, grabbed his keys from his nightstand, and kissed Teresa.

"Thank you," she said. "I'm sorry—"

Frank gently placed a finger to her lips. "Don't apologize—it's not your fault." He shook his head. "Damn kid. I swear, I could kill him sometimes." Frank clenched his fist. "Although he's doing a damn good job heading in that direction on his own."

"I know," Teresa said, releasing an enormous sigh.

Teresa worried Marco would get so high one day that he would overdose. She'd spent years trying to save him and eventually realized he didn't want to be saved. So she'd given up trying to change him and instead just loved him for who he was—her lost little brother wasting his life away on drugs.

She loved her family, but they were never easy. Thank goodness for Frank. He was her family now—along with their precious baby. Teresa thought for the thousandth time about how lucky she was to have Frank in her corner. It was the two of them against the world.

Chapter Three
FRANK - NEW ROCHELLE, NY
1968

Driving along Shore Road, Frank smelled the grease frying from the burger joint, Greasy Nick's, where families sat outside on picnic tables, eating fried clams, french fries, and of course, the signature burgers. Over the soundtrack of opera on his radio, the engines of the muscle cars roared, driven by guidos in undershirts, with thick gold chains around their necks and cigarettes dangling out of the corners of their mouths, staring out with sly smiles and daring you to mess with them. To make the grade, a car had to be a Corvette or a Camaro. No self-respecting west-ender guido would be caught dead driving anything else. And if it was a Z-28 with the T-tops off to let the sun in and the music out, even better.

Yet Frank proudly drove a Cadillac, which he'd gotten as part of his job at the dealership. He didn't want to be one of the guidos, who were stuck in the old world even though most of them had never set foot on actual Italian soil. They seemed low-class. Sure, he was friendly with some of them—he'd gone to school with them and even worked with a few of them now. His hands and nails were just as dirty from working on cars as theirs were. But he longed to make a better life for himself and his family.

The town of New Rochelle was situated on Long Island Sound, atop a rocky shoreline that signified its tough interior. New Rochelle was for the rough-and-tumble—those who worked hard and could shed their blood, sweat, and tears, all the while striving for a better life for their kids. Only one slice of town was far from typical New Rochelle in class and style—Davenport Neck.

As he approached Davenport Neck, Frank smelled the sea air, its briny pungency pulling him toward it like a siren. He rolled down the window and breathed in a unique mixture of diesel fumes and sea. It invigorated him and made his senses come alive. Seagulls flew overhead, squawking as they dove into the water before arching back up to the sky. This was a different world, on the edge of the sea. It felt freer, more open, brighter. Even though Davenport Neck was a mere ten-minute drive from where he and Teresa lived, as soon as he crossed the little bridge that arched over the inlet, he had arrived someplace special.

Compared to most of New Rochelle, with its modest working-class homes, fast-food joints, and pizza places, Davenport Neck stood out like Cinderella at the ball. The wide streets were filled with mansion after mansion, with expansive green lawns reaching down to the water's edge, bikini-clad women lying on chaise lounges, champagne glasses in hand, private docks with boats waiting to be taken out for a spin, and Rolls-Royces parked in the circular driveways. There was yacht club after yacht club, with a few beach and tennis clubs thrown in for good measure. Davenport Neck was made for those born with a silver spoon in their mouths, who'd never had to toil away a day in their lives. When Frank dreamed of a perfect place to live, he always pictured Davenport Neck—on the water but a step up from the New Rochelle he'd grown up in.

At the very tip of Davenport Neck sat the Drifters Boat Club, a place that signaled success to Frank. Two years ago, when his boss at the Cadillac dealership had said he could get Frank a boat slip for free in exchange for Frank working part-time at the boat yard, Frank had jumped at the chance. And even though he'd heard that the owner of the Drifters, Jim Butler, was a real hard-ass, so far, the man had been pretty easy to get along with. It was a dream come true, an invitation to a better life that he couldn't pass up.

Ever since he was a boy, Frank had lusted after boats. He bought boating and yachting magazines and would sit at the kitchen table, flipping through them, daydreaming that someday he would own one of those beauties. Frank had saved money for years until he had enough to buy a thirteen-foot Boston Whaler. It was a small entry-level boat, but it was his, and he hoped it would be the start of a long line of boats he would own throughout his lifetime. He'd named it *Horizon* so it would always remind him of where he was heading when steering it.

Frank pulled into the Drifters' parking lot. Even though it was already six o'clock, he would still have several more hours of light on this summer evening. He'd been glad when Teresa had told him she planned to bring Anthony to see her mother, Rosa, that night, encouraging Frank to take the boat out for a spin and burn off some steam. Knowing his wife, she also wanted to check up on her little brother, Marco, and make sure he wasn't straying too far from his latest drug-treatment plan. Frank doubted this attempt would differ from the last hundred times Marco had tried to get clean. But that was his Teresa—loyal to those she loved, sometimes to a fault.

He walked down the dock and broke into a huge smile when he saw *Horizon*. There she was, sitting next to his friend Henry's boat. He pulled back the cover and folded it up. Then he started the engine, untied the ropes, and slowly maneuvered out of the slip, through the harbor, past the buoy, and into the open water of the sound.

Work at the car dealership had been stressful lately. He was hoping for a promotion soon, but it was taking longer than expected. He wanted to make more money so he and Teresa could move to a bigger apartment—maybe even get a house someday. And they wanted to have another baby, hoping for at least two children. He needed to provide for them without constantly worrying about making ends meet. For the time being, he would continue to prove himself at the dealership, while also taking weekend shifts at Drifters. But he was feeling restless. He worried it wasn't just work stuff nagging at him but that something was resurfacing—a shadow from his past trying to creep back in.

Frank looked out over the bow at the offing in the distance, that part of the sea visible between the boat and the horizon. It held promise and mystery, luring him like a beacon of light. Frank didn't know if he was running toward the horizon or running away from what he tried to conceal. He realized he'd been running for years. He'd always thought he could outrun what haunted him, but now he wasn't so sure.

Because of Henry. Henry was married with kids, just like Frank. But something had shifted recently, and Frank felt there was something more between them. It scared and excited him. He'd only really felt this once, years before, or at least, he'd only *allowed* himself to feel it once. Since then, he'd desperately tried to push it out of his mind, but lately, it had come crashing back like a large wave cresting on the beach.

Frank would never forget the first time he'd touched another boy. He'd been fifteen years old, and his friend Eddie had come over after school so they could do homework together. Frank's mother was in the kitchen, making dinner. The neighbor's dog started barking loudly, and Eddie and Frank went to the window to investigate, laughing when they saw the dog chasing a squirrel. Standing side by side, Frank glanced at Eddie's profile, admiring his long eyelashes. Eddie positioned himself closer to Frank until their arms were touching. Frank didn't know if it was intentional, but he hoped so. Unable to control the yearning he'd felt for months, Frank reached over and brushed his fingers lightly against the back of Eddie's hand. There was mystery in that first touch, as wondrous as the first time Frank had felt the ocean breeze on his skin. Eddie didn't pull away but was still looking straight ahead out the window, as if immobilized. Frank's heart jumped, hoping he hadn't misread the cues. After what seemed like an eternity but was probably only a few seconds, Eddie turned to look at Frank and smiled. That smile melted Frank and made him bolder. He lightly caressed Eddie's hand and let his fingers trail up his forearm. Eddie leaned his head onto Frank's shoulder and closed his eyes. Frank felt electrified, every cell standing at attention. He kept going, moving his fingers up to Eddie's neck, slowly turning Eddie's chin to face him. Eddie opened his eyes, and they stared at each other, neither moving any closer. Frank felt his breath coming faster as he stared at Eddie's lips. There was the tiniest distance left between them, and he wanted to close it. He bent his head toward Eddie—

"Frank, what are you doing?" His mother's voice exploded through the room.

Frank's hand dropped to his side with a thump. Eddie jumped back. A chill ran down Frank's body. He wanted to shrink into himself and fade into the background. But he couldn't. His mother's stare bored into him. He felt exposed. He looked away, not answering her. Eddie coughed but remained silent. Frank's mother marched over and stared at him without saying a word, her wide eyes glaring and questioning.

Frank took a deep breath while maintaining eye contact with her. "Nothing," he said quietly. "We were just watching Coco chase a squirrel."

He knew that wasn't what she was referring to. His mother kept watching him while his heart thundered in his chest. The silence stretched and filled the room like a thick smoke.

Then she turned to his friend. "Eddie, I think it's time for you to leave now. Frank needs to wash up for dinner."

Eddie coughed nervously again, gathered up his books, and without saying a word or making eye contact with Frank, hurriedly left the room. Eva gave Frank one last lingering look and walked away. And in that moment, he knew she knew.

She knew, and her look had told him she thought those feelings were unnatural. Frank never hung out with Eddie again after that day. The experience had tainted their friendship. What had been pure and loving and tender had become twisted and perverted when exposed to the outside world.

Lately, Henry had awoken similar feelings in Frank and made every nerve ending in his body feel on fire. Frank assured himself he could resist this. He'd experienced attraction to men before and never acted on it. He would make sure this wasn't any different.

He increased the speed of the boat and felt the bow lift and slam down on the waves over and over in a constant, soothing rhythm. He wanted to feel the ocean spray on his face and wash away any trace of these confusing thoughts. Frank breathed in the sea and felt instantly lighter, like a window had opened and fresh air had rushed in. His body relaxed. He was always at peace on the water—feeling at home.

The only other place he'd ever truly felt at home was with Teresa. When they'd met in the summer of 1965, he'd felt like he'd been saved. She was only sixteen years old to his eighteen but possessed maturity beyond her years. Yet she also had a carefree way about her that was appealing to Frank, who carried an immense burden within him. Teresa was loving and kind and believed not only in him but in their future together as well. She was his horizon. He couldn't lose sight of that. With Teresa at his side, he'd be able to weather any storm.

Chapter Four
TERESA - NEW ROCHELLE, NY
1968

Teresa tried to look nonchalant, smiling at a few club members as she walked by, keeping her eyes glued to the spot where she'd last seen Frank. *Where is he?*

The evening had been lovely at the start. She and Frank had come to the club for an adult game night and barbecue, and Teresa was thrilled to have another chance to go out, just the two of them. Eva had offered to watch Anthony again—she was a godsend—and Teresa had looked forward to being baby free for the evening so she could play rummy cube, one of her favorite games. While Frank chatted with club members, uninterested in games, she happily played multiple rounds, unaware of the time. At one point, she spotted their friends Henry and Joanie milling about and waved at them. The last time she saw Frank, he was by the pool, chatting with Carmen, a bombshell of a woman who flirted a little too much for Teresa's taste. When she'd looked back about fifteen minutes later, she'd lost sight of him.

It was getting late, and she wanted to head home soon to relieve Eva of babysitting. Teresa stood at the poolside, scanning the crowd for Frank. *Where the heck is he?* She walked around the perimeter of the pool. Still no sign of him. She fought a nagging feeling of doubt.

She approached a pleasant couple she'd seen at club events be-fore. "Have you seen my husband, Frank? I was playing rummy cube for so long that I lost track of time." She laughed, and it came out high-pitched, sounding fake even to her ears.

They glanced around then shook their heads. "No," the husband said. "Sorry, haven't seen him."

"I saw him earlier, but it's been a while now," the wife added. "I'm sure he's around here somewhere."

"Thank you," Teresa said, feeling foolish standing there alone, hunting for her husband.

She walked away from them and closed her eyes, feeling woozy. She took a deep breath to steady herself. She felt overtired and couldn't think straight. Those few sips of wine, mixed with lack of sleep from taking care of Anthony, must have gone to her head. She was a lightweight since she hardly ever drank.

Of course Frank was here somewhere. He wouldn't just abandon her. Teresa fought her way back through the crowd to reach the place she'd last seen Henry and Joanie, thinking maybe Frank was chatting with them, but they weren't there. *Where else could he be?*

She realized she hadn't checked their boat yet. Teresa headed down the dock and noticed the boat was missing. That was it. Frank had taken the boat out.

But why wouldn't he tell me and include me? Why would he leave and take the boat out alone? Unless he wasn't alone. Teresa stood there, staring at the empty spot where the boat should be, and felt panic rising. *He wouldn't go out on the boat with that woman, would he? Nonsense. He's not having an affair. And if he were, he wouldn't be so obvious about it, would he?*

An image flashed before Teresa's vision—Carmen flipping her hair back as she laughed and leaning forward to expose generous cleavage. Teresa stood up straighter, sucking in her stomach and taking in a big gulp of air. *Breathe. He'll be back any minute. It will all be okay.*

She returned to the pool and snack bar area. The crowd had grown thinner. A few people walked by on their way to the parking lot and nodded, smiled, or waved. She tried to appear normal even though her heart was beating hard and tears threatened to fall.

Another image flashed in her mind—Frank kissing Carmen, his arms around her small waist, pulling her against him. Teresa's eyes stung from holding back tears. Her hands shook as she waited, praying to be wrong. Praying for Frank to come.

The Liebers, a kind elderly couple she'd met at the club multiple times, walked by. They waved as they made their way to the parking lot. Mrs. Lieber called out, "Teresa, honey, do you need a lift home?"

Teresa hesitated, shifting her weight from one foot to the other. If she took the ride home, Frank might come back and worry that she wasn't here. But Frank had abandoned her. Anger rose within her.

She turned to Mrs. Lieber. "That would be great, thanks. Frank got caught up with something and won't be heading home until much later."

How quickly and easily the lie had sprung from her mouth. It shocked her. Yet she had a strange premonition this would be the first of many lies she would have to tell about her marriage.

Teresa followed the Liebers to their car, hoping this wouldn't be how the night ended. She kept her eye out for Frank coming up from the dock. Nothing. She climbed into the back seat, feeling like she was moving in slow motion. As the car pulled out of the Drifters' parking lot and the pool became smaller in the distance, she realized Frank had bailed on her, leaving her alone and ruining their night out. She sat back against the seat, silently crying, sobs racking her body, but not letting a single wail out—just as she'd hidden the truth of Frank's abandonment from the Liebers.

Fifteen minutes later, Teresa thanked them for the ride and made her way up the long flights of stairs, stopping to wipe the mascara smeared under her eyes. She dreaded facing her mother-in-law. It was hard enough to hide her despair from acquaintances. Now she had to figure out what to say to Eva.

She entered the apartment quietly and saw Eva sitting at the kitchen table. Teresa gave her a half-hearted smile. "Anthony okay?"

"Yes, yes, he's fine. He was a good boy," Eva said in her singsong Italian accent. She stared at Teresa, who felt like she was under a microscope. Eva looked past Teresa. "Frank parking the car?"

"No." Teresa took in a deep breath and exhaled raggedly. "He... we got separated at the boat club. I got a ride home with some friends."

Eva pursed her lips. "He didn't drive you home?"

Teresa shook her head, not trusting herself to speak for fear that the tears would start again.

Eva got up and gently touched Teresa's arm. "Do you know where he is?"

Teresa shook her head again, feeling like a puppet with only one motion.

"*Va bene*," Eva said, squeezing Teresa's arm.

Teresa resisted the urge to lean, like a sinuous, arching cat, into the warmth of Eva's touch. She didn't want to alarm her mother-in-law by crying in her arms. Eva gave another squeeze and then released her.

Eva gathered her purse and started walking to the door. "He'll be home soon. Try not to worry."

"I know," Teresa croaked, not feeling confident at all in that knowledge.

Eva hesitated. "You know if you ever need me, Teresa, for anything, I'll be there. For you. And for Anthony." Eva pointed her finger, emphasizing each phrase. Teresa watched it move back and forth, as if in a trance.

"Thank you," Teresa whispered.

Eva put her hand on the doorknob, looked back at Teresa, gave a curt nod, and left.

Teresa lay in bed for over an hour, unable to sleep. She heard the apartment door open and looked at the bedside clock. It read *11:36*. The sound of Frank washing up in the bathroom drifted toward her. She felt him cautiously climb into bed.

Teresa turned over and faced him. "You're finally home."

"You're awake?" Frank asked, sitting upright, startled.

Teresa sat up also, supporting herself with her elbows. "I couldn't find you, Frank. You just disappeared. I had to get a ride home from the Liebers." Her voice trembled.

"I know. I'm sorry. I took the boat out for a spin with Henry, and we lost track of time."

"Henry?" Teresa asked, surprised. "I figured he went home with Joanie. I looked for the two of them when I couldn't find you, and they were both gone."

"No, Joanie left earlier. So I had to give him a ride home after we got back to the club. That's why I'm later than I thought I'd be. Sorry."

Teresa's voice caught. "Why didn't you tell me you were going?"

"I thought it would be a quick spin, but we wound up stopping at City Island. He'd never docked there before with the boat, and I wanted to show it to him. I didn't think we'd be so late."

"Oh..." Teresa said, a bit confused. She should have been relieved Frank was with Henry, especially compared to the farfetched scenarios she'd been concocting with her imagination on overdrive. Yet an uneasy feeling still nagged at her.

"You can't do that—just disappear," she whispered.

Frank took her lead and whispered too. "I'm sorry. I should've told you."

"Yes, you should have. I couldn't find you..." Teresa looked at the wall, making out shadows from the streetlight. She wasn't sure she believed him. "I need you to be honest with me, Frank. Were you really with Henry? Or were you with... someone else?"

"Yes, I was with Henry. There was no one else there, I swear. I should've told you, and I'm sorry we were out for so long. God, I feel so bad I made you worry and left you without a ride. Please forgive me."

She tried not to raise her voice again. "Honestly, I can't shake this off. When I came home alone, I had hours to think about what might have happened to you. I was afraid you went off with a woman."

Teresa felt embarrassed to admit that she'd felt abandoned and that this night had triggered every insecurity she had ever known. Her parents' marriage wasn't one to aspire to, and so many of her extended family members had husbands who strayed. She didn't want to be next in a long line of marriages riddled with infidelity.

"Why would I do that?" Frank asked.

"Because you could. You could disappear and go off with another woman." She sounded insecure. And maybe that was justified. But she didn't want her insecurity to create a chasm between them.

"I'm sorry I didn't tell you Henry and I were taking the boat out and that I'm so late. I didn't know it would make you worry this much."

"Don't do it again—disappear and not tell me where you're going and then not come home for hours, knowing I'm sitting here, worried."

"Okay," said Frank, stroking her hair. "I won't. But please, Teresa, don't worry. You're my wife." He lifted her chin, and she could see the streetlight reflected in his eyes. "I love you." He said each word slowly.

"That doesn't make what I went through tonight hurt any less or make me feel any better about it."

"Fair enough. That's true. But I do love you. Don't forget that."

Frank leaned over, kissed her good night, and then settled himself on the pillow. Teresa leaned back and stared up at the ceiling, bone-tired. She heard the baby cry. *Great.*

"I'll get him," Frank said, jumping back up from bed. He walked over to the crib and picked Anthony up.

As Frank rocked the baby to soothe him, one thought kept tumbling over in her mind: *Will he be able to keep his promise?*

Chapter Five
FRANK - NEW ROCHELLE, NY
1968

Frank tried to focus on steering the boat around the buoys in the harbor, but his mind was racing. He felt horrible about the way he'd treated Teresa last weekend—abandoning her, forcing her to get a ride home, making her worry about him. *What is wrong with me?* He'd never done anything like that before. But it was almost like he couldn't help himself. Lately, feelings from Frank's past were resurfacing. God, was he confused. And he wondered if it showed. He pictured the expression on Teresa's face after he got home. He'd never seen her look at him that way before. The uncertainty. The way she held him in her gaze, like she was trying to decipher clues.

I thought I could keep this at bay. Why is this happening again? Images from Saturday night flickered through his mind—Henry laughing, the wind whipping back his hair, his profile silhouetted against the late-evening sky. He worried that Henry would be his downfall. Two competing emotions tore at Frank—desire and fear. He was dying to see Henry alone again. Curiosity was teeming inside him, and he wanted to see whether there was anything there or if it was only in his imagination. But acting on his attraction wasn't worth the risk. He'd made his choice a long time ago. Nothing was worth losing his family over. With Teresa by his side, he'd always been able to drown out the desires he'd been trying to deny.

And now, as he was steering his boat to meet Henry—who had ⋅ awoken these instincts in him in such a powerful way that it often took his breath away—Frank tried to convince himself that he could resist. That he wasn't putting himself and his family at risk. That he wasn't being unfaithful to Teresa just by spending time with Henry, knowing how he felt about him.

Frank pulled up to the dock at the City Island Marina, where they'd arranged to meet after Henry finished a work appointment there. It was en route to Manhasset Bay, one of Frank's favorite spots that he was going to show Henry that evening, giving them a reason to be alone together on the boat. They were just two friends out for a sunset spin without their wives and kids, blowing off steam after a long day of work. But as much as he tried to convince himself that this was an innocent joy ride with a friend, Frank knew deep down that he was looking for an excuse to spend time with his crush, dangerous though that was. Frank felt like a masochist, torturing himself by being around Henry. But it also felt like torture to stay away.

Henry stood, one hand lifted to his forehead to shade his eyes from the sun, the other waving to Frank. "Hey, you." He gave Frank a wide smile, which made Frank's stomach flip-flop.

"Gorgeous night," Frank said. "Hop on."

"I thought you'd never ask," Henry said, winking.

Frank looked away to steer the boat closer to the dock—and to hide the effect Henry's gesture had on him. He felt undone by it, like his attempts to keep a cool demeanor would crumble at any moment, and he'd give away his true feelings to Henry with just one look.

Henry grabbed the side of the boat and helped pull it to the dock, taking out the side buoy to avoid a collision. When the boat was close enough, he hopped inside. Frank watched Henry push the boat away from the dock, taking in his muscular arms and the curve of his back. Henry turned toward Frank and stared back intently for a second longer than was comfortable, a small smile playing upon his lips. Frank realized he might have been caught admiring him.

Henry walked over, and instead of taking the passenger seat of the boat, as the cocaptain, he sat down next to Frank behind the wheel. Henry's leg was squeezed up against his, and Frank could feel the heat of the man's body through his shorts. He shuddered, startled by the strength of his own desire. Frank thought about moving his leg, but there was a tremor running through his body, so delicious he wanted to freeze the moment and enjoy it forever. He waited a few beats, relishing the closeness. Then he shifted his leg to the right, breaking contact.

Frank couldn't turn and look at Henry. But he didn't have to. For months, he'd been observing those brown eyes, and he'd become well acquainted with them. He knew the way Henry's eyes twinkled when their conversation moved from harmless banter to outright flirtation.

When they pulled up to the area of the bay where he wanted to anchor, Henry went up to the bow and threw the anchor out. It sank to the bottom, securing their spot. Frank cut the engine, and silence descended. There was a charge in the air, and Frank suddenly felt giddy with nerves, like he was that high school boy from six years earlier, who had wanted to kiss Eddie.

Henry walked up to Frank, an intense look in his eyes. He reached out and cupped his hand around the back of Frank's neck. Frank leaned into Henry's hand and slowly rubbed against it. He felt a deep tingling throughout his body and became lightheaded.

"We can't," he heard himself say. Frank had buried his true feelings for so many years that it had become a part of him. Denial was in his blood.

"Yes, we can," Henry whispered. "No one has to know. We both want it. I know that, Frank, and so do you."

Henry moved even closer and pulled him slowly into the cabin, staring into his eyes, a determined look on his face. Frank vibrated with lust as he followed Henry. He couldn't focus when the man was this close. Frank felt his body ignite, like it was radiating heat. His thoughts were churning and jumbled, his breath heaving in his chest.

"But... our wives. Our kids—" Frank didn't finish because Henry put his finger to Frank's lips.

"Shhh." Henry's voice lingered in the sea air, encircling them. "We're not going to talk about them now. That's not what matters here. We're what matters." He gestured to the two of them and laid his hand over Frank's chest. Frank felt his skin glow underneath. "We've both wanted this for a long time."

Henry's eyes were soft, searching Frank's, their lips only inches apart. He leaned over, closing the space between them, and lightly brushed his lips against Frank's. At the first touch of Henry's mouth, Frank's body went into a kind of shock. It surprised him how soft Henry's lips—a man's lips—were.

He'd never kissed a man, although he'd dreamed of it many times before—yearned for it. So many times, Frank had wanted to feel what this was like, to see if his estimate of himself was accurate. These longings, which he'd suppressed for years, now came bubbling to the surface, irrepressible, relentless. He couldn't deny them anymore.

Frank felt a wave overtake him as he grabbed Henry's face and kissed him back, giving in completely. Henry ran his hands through Frank's hair and then slid his arms around his shoulders, pulling Frank tight against him with a suggestion of overwhelming strength. Everything about Henry was alien—he smelled different, his lips were softer than expected, his chest was hard against Frank's.

His whole body felt as if it had become molten, melded to Henry's, long-dormant synapses springing to life. Their kisses grew deeper, more urgent, his breath rapid. Frank wanted to feel Henry's skin against his, smooth and warm, hard and strong. He wanted to wrap himself completely around Henry.

Frank had tried being what everyone expected of him, so-called normal. But here in the boat cabin, with Henry's lips on his, with their bodies touching, that was just what struck him—how normal it felt. How effortless and right.

Time stalled. Frank let everything fade into the background. He gave in to what he knew he wanted, and all those other thoughts vanished, and it was just Henry.

The next morning at work, Frank crouched down next to the car he was repairing, hoping he'd find some answers underneath its hood. He gazed absentmindedly at his toolbox, unsure which tool to grab. His hands were shaking. Man, he needed to pull it together. To focus. But he couldn't get the previous night out of his head. Henry had kissed him. And oh my God, he had kissed Henry back. And Frank wanted to do a lot more than just kiss Henry. He could still feel Henry's mouth on his. Henry's tough, sinewy body pressed against his. He thought of Henry's lips with a flush of heat that might be pleasure or shame. He didn't want to interrogate himself as to which.

Then he thought of Teresa, and his stomach churned. He worried she could read guilt all over his face and he wouldn't be able to hide such a monumental shift from her. Because something had altered in the foundation of Frank's being. He'd finally claimed a piece of himself he'd always suspected was missing but never had the courage to reach for, a piece of the puzzle that made him who he truly was. But that puzzle took him further away from Teresa and his children and the life he'd built and loved. How could he be the man who'd chosen that life, lived it, and kept choosing it because it brought him joy—and stability and safety—yet still be true to who he was at his core? He couldn't reconcile it. It was too big. Too much.

He let out a shuddering breath. *What on earth have I done? Who have I become?*

Frank glanced around guiltily to see if anyone had noticed something different about him and could sense that he, Frank Antinori, was sneaking around with a man. Everyone went about their business as usual, with heads bowed, bodies hidden under cars, music playing, and work continuing. Yet Frank felt like the earth had shifted and he'd entered an alternate universe. And he had a feeling there would be no turning back.

Chapter Six
LENA - ORANGE, CA
June 2015

It was pitch-black in our bedroom, but I was wide-awake. I glanced at the alarm clock on my nightstand and saw the digital display: 4:45 a.m. *Fuck.* My thoughts somersaulted over each other, competing for the number-one spot. Cases at work normally occupied my mind, but now I had a litany of other items to add to my typical mental clutter. And all of them had to do with my father's wedding—filling in Kevin, talking to Anthony, wondering what my mom would have thought of it, and of course, planning the actual event.

Kevin slept peacefully beside me. I tried not to resent him for it, but sometimes, I couldn't help feeling annoyed at his ability to sleep through the night without interruption. Insomnia and I were old friends, and during the hours of sleep deprivation, Kevin's blissful slumber made me want to jump out of my skin. Not the best recipe for catching some z's.

Instead of tossing and turning, I went for my morning run earlier than usual. I harnessed Atticus, and he yawned but obliged, thumping his tail rhythmically on the terracotta tiled floor. When Kevin and I bought our home in Orange, I'd used running to acquaint myself with the new neighborhood. I memorized landmarks, learning my way around the antique shops of Old Towne, the Chapman University campus, and the old Sunkist Exchange Building. I ran in the early morning, when the air was cool and full of the promise of a new day. The sound of my sneakers hitting the ground would measure my progress, while Atticus's frequent urination marked his.

I ran, craving a release. Two miles, three miles, four. My brain spun. I pushed harder, pumping my arms, my hands in tight fists. I looked at the pearl ring on my right hand—my mother's ring. A powerful sense of longing hit me. What I really wanted to do was pick up the phone and call her to vent about my father throwing me this curve ball and about how I didn't want him to make a big to-do of the wedding. If anyone deserved to have gotten married again, it should have been her, not the one who'd screwed up the marriage because he couldn't stay faithful. I wanted to hear her familiar voice telling me it would all be okay, that yes, my father was being ridiculous by having a wedding at his age, that I was justified for being annoyed, and that helping my father plan his second wedding to his boyfriend was not stabbing her in the back. But the hole in my heart reminded me that there'd be no such phone call.

I sighed, rounding the corner, and our house came into view. I'd hoped the soothing sunrise and meditative sound of my footfalls on the pavement would calm my nerves, but they didn't. That familiar revved-up feeling was still taking up precious real estate in my body—like blood coursing through my veins in overdrive. *Great. Now I'm sleep-deprived and stressed.*

I entered the house and unharnessed Atticus, setting him free to drink. While he lapped at his water bowl, I filled a huge glass with water and started downing it at the sink. Kevin strode into the kitchen, saw Atticus and me drinking, and smirked. He always made fun of me for not bringing water on my runs, but I hated carrying anything or wearing a silly-looking fanny pack. I came up for air, taking a break from rehydrating. Kevin planted a good-morning kiss on my lips, and I breathed in his freshly showered scent. He was dressed for work in the crisp blue-and-white-striped button-down shirt I'd bought him for Christmas. His shirt sleeves were pushed up, revealing the golden hairs of his forearms set against his tanned skin. Kevin exuded a Southern California beach vibe that my dark features, thick mane of unruly curls, and olive-toned skin could never naturally achieve.

I knew I had to fill him in on the news, though it felt surreal to even think of telling Kevin about my father's upcoming nuptials. *No time like the present.*

"Okay, are you ready for this?" I asked.

He nodded and leaned forward.

I had to just spit it out. "My dad called last night. He wants to get married. To Oliver. This October."

"What? Wow, that's amazing," Kevin said.

"It's many things. It's crazy, it's weird, it's rushed..." I huffed. "Oh, and to make matters worse, he wants me to help plan it. Do you believe it?"

"I think it's great. And yes, I believe it. Of course he wants you to be involved."

"Kevin, my father has no right to get married again."

He looked at me, surprise registering on his face. "Why?"

"Seriously? It's not like he was any good at it the first time. He screwed up his marriage to my mom, remember?"

"Lena, hon, come on. There's no rule that says someone who screwed up their first marriage can't get married again. If that were the case, there'd be a lot less second marriages."

He laughed, which rattled me. This wasn't the time to make jokes.

"My mom didn't get married again."

"That was her choice. She had to do what was right for her after what she went through. You made it sound like that was kind of her way of asserting her independence."

I bit my lip. He was right. My mom had had no interest in being married again, partly because she'd been burned so badly the first time around and partly because it made her feel strong to stand on her own two feet. She'd told her live-in boyfriend, Larry, right at the start that marriage was off-limits.

"It's hard to explain. You don't know what it was like. You weren't there. You didn't have to live it. You don't have to live it."

"Hey, my father-in-law is gay, right? It's not the same as you, of course." He paused. "Not that you let me talk about it or anything."

"It's not the same. Sorry. You didn't grow up with it or go through it."

I wondered how I could explain it to Kevin. The ugliness of the 1970s and '80s. Bullies who would make fun of a boy for wearing a pink Izod polo shirt to school and call him a faggot. The AIDS crisis and how society had responded with fear and blame of the gay community. The senseless murder of Matthew Shepard. When I rented the movie *Boys Don't Cry* while Kevin was away on business, I'd heaved sobs, unable to move off the couch for a solid half hour after the credits. All those images and experiences were part of my DNA.

Sweat beaded at the back of my neck, and there was that old familiar feeling of mild nausea and tingling in my hands. *No, no, no.* The beginnings of a panic attack. I went over to the sink and put cold water on the inside of my wrists and back of my neck, trying to ward it off. I took a few deep breaths.

Kevin jumped up and came over to me. He grabbed my hand. "You okay?"

I nodded. I could feel my pulse slowing down. He gave me a moment.

Then he lifted my face to his. "Sweetie, maybe your father never got married again because he never thought he could. And now he can finally marry someone of the same sex and have it recognized in the entire country. I mean, the timing makes sense with the recent case. Heck, you know that better than anyone."

I didn't need to be reminded of the current legal landscape. I knew it by heart. That was my career, not my personal life, but now my two worlds were colliding.

"Maybe I'm being unreasonable, but it doesn't seem fair that he gets to do this when he screwed up his first marriage big-time."

I hated admitting this out loud. I felt like I was letting my dad down by even thinking this way. It was an honor that he'd asked me to help plan his big day. I'd committed to it and wouldn't go back on my word. But I had a feeling the wedding planning was going to give me a lot of gray hairs in the coming months.

"Is he planning on a big celebration?" Kevin asked.

"No, they want something small. Nothing extravagant, only about thirty people." *Thank goodness.* "But the next few months will be so busy for me with the case and now the wedding..."

I sounded so whiny. And my jaw hurt. I could feel stress along my jawline where Kevin's hand was. *Probably grinding my teeth in my sleep again. I'll have to wear my mouth guard. So attractive.*

"Okay, so something small, and the wedding isn't for almost four months? You know him... he's not picky. You can put this thing together in no time. Lena, he trusts you. You'll be like the best man." He gave me an encouraging smile.

The best man. How strange. How many adult women are serving as their father's best man for his second wedding? Few, I bet.

"I don't want to be the best man," I said. "Bad enough I'm planning the shindig."

"I'll help you. We'll make it fun," Kevin said, squeezing my hand. "Problem solved."

Problem solved, just like that. Except I didn't need Kevin to solve my problems. I wanted him to sympathize and tell me I was justified in being so rattled by this.

No drama, I reminded myself. *Too messy.* There was so much drama in my parents' marriage that I always tried to keep it out of mine. For the past eighteen years, I'd tried to keep that pledge as seriously as I treated our wedding vows.

"Okay, you're right. I can pull this off." I managed a weak smile.

"And it'll make the old man happy. He loves when you get involved."

"I know," I said like a kid giving in.

"It's your way of showing love. Kind of like your mom used cooking to show love. With you, it's planning for other people."

Planning as a way of showing love? He was giving me way too much credit. *More like my way of being a control freak.*

"You should call Anthony. I'm sure he'll offer some words of wisdom."

"Yeah, I'm planning to on my way to work. And I'm sorry I'm snappy this morning," I said. "I'm just stressed."

"Don't worry about it. I'm sorry if I pushed your buttons. Just trying to cheer you up." Kevin kissed me on the lips, butterfly light, and then grabbed his travel mug. He waved and headed out the door to work.

Fine. I've got this. I can plan a damn wedding.

I couldn't help thinking Kevin's reaction was probably more like what my father would have wanted from me. My husband seemed genuinely pleased for my father and Oliver. *Great.* I could add guilt to my already-boiling-over emotions. Kevin had always had a good relationship with my father, and I was thankful for that. It was childish and unfair to expect him to hold a grudge on my behalf for what my father had done to our family years before Kevin came into the picture. After all, it wasn't his grudge to bear.

My marriage could have gone completely the other way. I could have wound up with a husband unforgiving of my family history, or worse, not accepting. I'd been petrified of that possibility, which was why I'd held back the truth from Kevin the entire first year of our courtship. When Kevin had proposed on a summer night in 1996, he'd done everything right—the romantic setup, the champagne, the beach house, the ring. And then I had to spoil it.

Here goes. I dove in. "I have to tell you something, and it isn't easy." I stopped talking, unsure of how to proceed.

"What? What's wrong?" Kevin furrowed his brow. He'd had a big smile on his face all night long that was now replaced by worry lines and a frown.

"What if I wasn't who you thought I was?" I asked.

"What do you mean? I know who you are." He looked confused and moved closer to me on the couch at his Seal Beach apartment, where we'd been enjoying celebratory champagne minutes before.

I jumped up, needing to put some distance between us to give me courage to continue. Kevin's arms around me, comforting me, might make me chicken out.

"There's something about me you don't know, Kevin. And it's... it's hard to tell you. But you need to know before we get married."

"Okay, now you're scaring me. What's this about?" He dashed his hands through his thick blond hair.

"It's a secret that I haven't shared with many people. I don't intentionally hide it, but it's really none of anyone's business. But it will be your business if you're going to be my husband."

"Lena, there's nothing you can tell me that would make me change my mind about getting married."

My hand went to my mouth as a soft sob escaped. Tears dripped from the corners of my eyes. I wiped them away, trying to stay strong. *Don't break down now. Get it over with.* I wanted it in the past, behind us.

"It's not really about me. It's about my family. About my parents. It will all make sense once you find out, but I'm so scared it's going to freak you out."

"What's freaking me out is you keeping me in suspense. I can handle a family issue. What I can't handle is you not trusting me enough to let me in. Please tell me what this big secret is, Lena."

I cringed. I was making this harder by not blurting it out. By being a coward. Our future was at stake. I needed to trust him. I did trust him. Now was the time to prove it.

"Okay, I'm sorry. I've been so nervous about how to tell you, but here goes. My father..." I sputtered, crying even harder.

Kevin squeezed my arm, encouraging me to continue.

"My father is gay."

There, I'd said it. Out loud. To Kevin.

"Oh..." Kevin said, staring at me. "That's your big secret? Lena, my God, you had me freaked out."

"I'm sorry. It's not something I share. I'm so used to keeping it secret."

Kevin looked like he was processing, his forehead creased in thought. He started pacing back and forth a few feet away. "This explains so much. Holy shit."

He was piecing things together. My intense loyalty toward my mother, which Kevin always thought went beyond the average bond between parent and child—including kids who had experienced the infidelity of one parent. How I always skirted questions of who my father was dating and asked Dad not to bring a plus-one to family events.

"Yeah, we're a strange family. Unconventional for sure." I hiccupped from crying.

He came over to me and took my hands. "But, Lena, why didn't you tell me before? Did you really think I would care? Do you think I'm homophobic or something? Have more faith in me than that."

"I know this will sound strange, but it was less about you and more about me. It was the way I grew up."

"Well, I'm not going anywhere," Kevin said. "This changes nothing about us—you hear me?"

I nodded, relieved and exhausted, and leaned my head against Kevin's.

"We'll have to fill in my family before the wedding, but we'll deal with that together," he said.

His family. Of course they'd have to be told at some point. *Ugh. Why can't I just have a normal family like Kevin's?* I hated that no matter how much time had passed, the secret was still hiding in the closet, festering like a boil.

"Can't we just keep it quiet just for a little while? There will be so much going on with the wedding planning, and our families meeting each other. This will take over."

Dammit—I'm still doing it. I'd poked my head out of my turtle shell only to pull it right back in. I didn't want to crawl out of that shell. What I wanted to do was bask in the glow of being engaged, with nothing tainting it. A marriage proposal should be one of the happiest moments of my life. I wanted to have this moment, not have to face my past head-on. I wanted to get a break from navigating all the twists and turns I'd had to deal with since I was a little girl, censoring what I revealed when and to whom. It was exhausting keeping up the charade, but hiding had become my safe place.

I squeezed Kevin's hand. "For now, can we just focus on us, please? This is our time. Let's not let anything overshadow celebrating our engagement, okay?" I smiled and kissed him, and the past faded away. I was certain it would come back, but for that moment in the summer of '96, I'd kept it at bay.

Chapter Seven
TERESA - NEW ROCHELLE, NY
1969

Teresa heard the phone ring in the distance and wearily realized she'd fallen asleep. She sprang up to answer it, hoping to reach it before it woke Anthony. She felt so tired lately, tending to Anthony's needs and doing the household chores, that when he went down for his afternoon nap, she lay down as well. Glancing at the bedside clock, she saw that she'd been sleeping for over an hour.

"Hello?" she said groggily.

"Teresa, it's me, Eva," her mother-in-law said.

"Oh, Eva, you startled me."

"Startled? Why?"

"I was just lying down while Anthony napped. I must've fallen asleep." Teresa paused, not sure how much she wanted to tell Eva. "I'm just not feeling great, Ma. I'm so... tired."

"You sick?" Eva asked.

"No, just... I'm not feeling like myself."

Teresa hesitated, knowing if she continued, she'd start crying again. She'd had a hard time shaking off the nagging feeling that started the night Frank abandoned her at the club party and had only gotten worse over the ensuing months. She attempted to go about her daily routine but kept breaking into tears, like a faucet that wouldn't stop flowing. *What's wrong with me? Why can't I shake this off?*

She knew why. Marriage was lonelier these days. Frank was coming home later and later from work. But it wasn't just work keeping him away from home. He went out more after work. Sometimes he went to Antonio's Pizzeria for a slice with some guys from Cadillac. Or he took the boat out on Long Island Sound for a spin, alone or with his friend Henry. At first, going out with the guys had been rare, and Teresa had thought it was good for Frank to blow off steam after his long workdays. But it was becoming more of a habit, and she didn't like it. She wanted him home with her and Anthony. More importantly, she wanted him to want to be home. But he now went out a few nights per week, missing dinner and occasionally coming home after she'd gone to bed. Frank sometimes didn't even tell her what he was doing or where he was going. He would just say he was going out. *Out.* Teresa hated that word.

"I'm coming to get you. Both of you," Eva said decisively.

"What? No, Ma, you don't have to do that." A sense of relief washed over her, and a sob escaped from her throat.

"Yes, right now. Get out of bed, and get Anthony ready. I'll be there in a few minutes."

"Okay," Teresa eked out.

Ten minutes later, Eva arrived and, in her typical no-nonsense manner, snatched Teresa up along with Anthony. "*Andiamo.*" She gathered Teresa's and Anthony's things then picked up the kitchen telephone and dialed a number. "Frank," she snapped, "your wife and son are coming to my house for the afternoon. Go there after work for dinner."

Eva put her arm around Teresa's shoulders and ushered her out the door. They went down the three flights of steps and into Eva's waiting car. Teresa slumped down in the passenger seat and wrapped the blanket more snugly around Anthony, on her lap, who was still peacefully napping. Out the window, the houses flashed by like the pages of a comic book turning too quickly. It was all a blur. Teresa couldn't focus on any one thing, so she shifted her gaze to Eva, whose take-charge personality always calmed her. Such a far cry from Teresa's mother, Rosa, who had played the subservient wife to Teresa's often-drunk father, Sergio, before he passed away—*May he rest in peace*—and doted on Teresa's drug-addict brother, Marco.

Sitting ramrod straight behind the wheel, Eva wore a pleated skirt without a wrinkle, a crisp white button-up shirt, nude stockings, and her characteristic Italian leather loafers. Her short brown hair was curled in all the right places, and she had a dusting of make-up on her face. Teresa was envious. Eva wasn't the prettiest woman, but she somehow always looked put together. Neat and clipped and fashionable.

When they arrived at the house, Eva got to work quickly. She put Anthony in his playpen in the living room then turned to Teresa in the kitchen. "Drape this towel over your housedress. Your hair needs washing."

Teresa didn't have the strength to object and wasn't sure she even wanted to. Eva pulled over a kitchen chair, set it with its back against the sink, and motioned for Teresa to sit. Then she tilted Teresa's head back and washed her hair. As the warm water ran over Teresa's head and down her neck, Teresa leaned toward it like she was looking for the beams of the sun. Although petite, Eva had firm hands, and she massaged the shampoo into Teresa's hair and scalp with big sweeping strokes. It felt good to be touched so intimately, and it made Teresa realize how long it had been since Frank had really touched her. She was grateful that Eva said nothing as she washed her hair, letting her relax and enjoy the sensation.

While toweling off Teresa's hair, Eva leaned forward and looked her in the eye. "Teresa, what's going on?"

"I don't know how to explain it."

"You're unhappy. Alone. Crying. Is it Frank?"

"It's fine. I'm just having a hard time adjusting to being a mom, that's all."

"No. I'm not *stupida*, Teresa." Eva looked at Teresa like she was trying to decide how to phrase her next statement, which made Teresa nervous, as the woman was always so sure-footed. "Is Frank not coming home after work? Is he staying out late? Are you and Anthony alone?"

Teresa stared at her wide-eyed, incredulous that someone had guessed exactly what was going on. Even more surprising was that this had come from Frank's own mother. "Yes," Teresa whispered.

Eva put her hands on her hips, her small stature belying her powerful personality. "Teresa, here's what you do. You are busy taking care of a baby. It's not easy. You're a little *musciad*." Eva swung her arms around in search of the English translation. "You're... sad. You're not feeling or looking your best. Frank is probably overwhelmed with being a father and even a husband. He may be straying. You being so upset all the time isn't helping. Pull yourself together. *Capisce?*"

Teresa stared at her with her mouth open slightly, not knowing what to say. *Is she blaming me? Does she know whether Frank is actually cheating?*

Eva wiped her hands on a dishtowel and smoothed down her skirt. She looked up at Teresa and pointed her index finger in the air, like she'd just thought of something. "You can handle this. If you need help with little Antonio, you call me. You can drop him off here."

"Ma, I don't want to bother you—"

"*Far niente*. It's nothing," Eva said, holding up a hand and stopping Teresa. "You call me when you need me, and I'll watch the bambino." She stared at Teresa, waiting.

Teresa slowly nodded.

Eva continued. "At home, you need to take a bath, wash your hair, put some nice clothes on, and let Frank know you're not giving up."

"I'm not giving up," Teresa promised. "I'm just so tired and a little lonely."

Eva shook her head dismissively. "You need to make sure Frank remembers he has a wife and son at home and he should make the choice to be there and not be out gallivanting with Lord knows who. Do you hear me? You need to do this, Teresa."

Teresa could hear an urgency in her mother-in-law's voice. She wondered if Eva knew something more about what was going on with Frank but wasn't telling her. Or maybe Eva had been through something like this when she was first married to Enzo. It didn't seem possible, though. Enzo was devoted to Eva and their family. And he was a devout Catholic.

She nodded slowly, over and over, looking Eva in the eye. Eva gave a firm nod, turned away, and headed into the living room, where Anthony was starting to cry.

Then Teresa mentally recited the tangled mantra of so many women. *He will be happy with just me. I will make him happy. There will be no other women.*

Chapter Eight
TERESA - NEW ROCHELLE, NY
1970

F rank walked over and kissed Teresa on the forehead. "Here are
your keys."

"My keys?" she asked, confused.

"Yeah. I changed the oil in your car. It needed it. Heading out to
go tinker with the boat now. I want to work on the trim tabs."

Trim tabs. Teresa didn't know half the time what Frank was talking about with that damn boat. It had a secret language, one she
didn't understand. What she really resented was that it took up so
much of Frank's time. She couldn't help feeling like he preferred the
boat over his own family lately. She partly blamed herself. She'd been
going to the boat club less and less, mostly because she didn't enjoy it
as much as Frank did. She'd never learned to swim and still harbored
a fear of the water, which was ironic given how much their lives re-
volved around that boat and the sea. At the club, she would sit on the
sidelines and watch the water from a safe distance.

Besides, Teresa had a pretty good reason to stay away from the
boat club that summer, and her name was Magdalena—Lena for
short. Teresa had given birth to her second baby a few months before
and was exhausted from not getting enough sleep and all the extra
chores having two little ones brought—not to mention the constant
stress of worrying about her marriage. She and Frank had been so

excited to learn they were having another child, and for months, he was more attentive and present, giving her hope that things had gone back to the way they used to be. But all the optimism she'd felt during her pregnancy deflated once Lena was born and Frank boomeranged back to his routine of staying out too often.

"Please be home on time for dinner, Frank," she said, hating that she sounded like a nagging wife.

"I'll be home for dinner—promise. And I'll bring bread from Arthur Avenue." He smiled.

She loved that fresh Italian bread. It would go perfectly with the stuffed manicotti she was planning to make.

"Thank you," she said, leaning into him for another kiss on her forehead. He obliged, and she felt her defenses weaken. It was hard to stay annoyed with him.

"Have fun at the beach today with the kids." He headed to the door then added, "And that cousin of yours." He snickered and left.

She knew he wasn't fond of Veronica. Ronnie, as everyone called her, had a sharp tongue and a thick New York accent and was always too quick to speak her mind. Teresa didn't disagree. But she was her cousin, and she loved her. Ronnie had her faults but was loyal to the core. She wasn't only a cousin to Teresa but also a trusted friend and confidante. She would always have Teresa's back, and spending time with Ronnie helped Teresa get a short-lived reprieve from the loneliness caused by Frank's increased absence.

Teresa went to her dresser and grabbed her bathing suit out of the bottom drawer. She looked forward to some time at the beach but knew that meant wearing a bathing suit, which she dreaded. Thank goodness she still had a maillot on hand, left over from years before, when one-piece bathing suits with attached skirts were all the rage. She pulled out the suit, which covered as much skin as possible, and squeezed her body into it, then eyed her reflection in the mirror and sighed.

Lena had measured nine pounds and twenty-one inches at birth. A huge baby. Teresa had gained a lot of weight during the pregnancy. She didn't know how much because she refused to look at the scale when they weighed her at OB-GYN checkups. But it had been several months since Lena was born, and none of the weight had come off. In fact, more of it was piling on. The first number on the scale was most definitely a two.

On the nights when Frank didn't come home for dinner, she'd put the kids to bed and fix herself a salad or cottage cheese and fresh fruit, determined to get her weight down. But as the clock ticked on, another type of hunger would appear. The apartment would fall into an unnatural silence, and she'd catch herself staring at the door for indefinite lengths of time, willing it to open, willing Frank to come home. His absence wormed a hole inside Teresa, an emptiness that resembled hunger but that she couldn't satisfy with anything. Many nights, she'd sit at the window, waiting for the rumble of Frank's Cadillac to end the silence. In the hours since her lean dinner, she'd grow so empty—and so hungry—that she'd sneak back into the kitchen, open the fridge, and stuff down anything she found there. It seemed fitting, almost defiant, to let herself indulge in food despite her growing weight and absent husband. But when morning arrived, shedding light over her sizable curves, her body would ache with a new pain—a new disappointment.

She wiped a tear from the corner of her eye, irritated to find herself crying. *Snap out of it.* There was no reason to sit around wallowing. Loneliness was only a temporary state, one that she could get relief from once Frank wasn't spending so many nights away from home. It was just a phase, she told herself. In the meantime, she would enjoy time at the beach.

Teresa picked up Lena from the crib and finished getting her ready. Anthony trailed in, holding his favorite stuffed animal, a little lamb called Mary, who he'd named after the nursery rhyme Teresa sang to him. He adored that ratty little blue lamb, even though it was missing an eye and the stuffing was coming out in multiple places. Teresa slipped his bathing suit on over his diaper, and he happily waddled away, the pathetic stuffed animal still in hand.

She walked into the kitchen and grabbed the sandwiches and snacks she'd packed for the beach, along with the baby food and bottles from the refrigerator. As she stuffed them inside her beach bag, a thought entered her mind, and she almost let out a gasp. Addiction ran in her family like an insidious disease. Her father had been an alcoholic. Her brother Marco struggled with drugs. *What if food is my drug of choice?*

Teresa relished the role that food and cooking played in her life. She could recall meals from important moments of her life: her grandmother's homemade lentil soup on the day of her Holy Communion, her aunt's homemade gnocchi on her thirteenth birthday, her mother's escarole and beans on Easter. Food was a way to show love. She wondered if her relationship with food would be soured along with her not-so-perfect marriage.

Teresa sat on her beach chair next to Ronnie at Shore Beach in New Rochelle. Ronnie wore a string bikini and was holding a sun reflector under her face. Not that she needed to be any tanner. Ronnie was so dark people often thought she was from a Caribbean island, like Puerto Rico, as opposed to being Italian American. Her fancy suntan oil, Bain de Soleil, smelled like coconut and shea butter. She had long shapely legs, gorgeous black silky hair that fell to the middle of her back, wide hips, and deep-set cleavage. She was what most people called drop-dead gorgeous.

Ronnie was a permanent fixture at Shore Beach. Pretty much on any summer day, she could be found sitting with her chair in the sand, reflector under her face, soaking up the sun, getting tanner and tanner. She would look up now and again to check on her kids, but pretty much everyone at Shore Beach parented the kids in the baby beach area, so Ronnie benefited from a village of onlookers giving her ample time to bake in the sun.

Not Teresa. She sat under an umbrella in her one-piece bathing suit that covered a significant portion of her neck and torso—and even hips and thighs with its attached skirt—and tried not to get too much direct sun. She didn't have the typical olive complexion many Italians were lucky to have been born with. Her skin was very fair, and when she got too much sun, she turned pink.

Teresa leaned over to check on Lena, who was still happily napping under the cover of the umbrella on the towel. Anthony was playing in the sand next to her, and Teresa looked at his drooly smile and melted. It would take extra long to get all the sand off him in the bath that night, but watching how content he was, she knew it would be worth it. She picked up the *Cosmopolitan* Ronnie had brought and flipped through it. Teresa had never been a fan of this magazine. If you'd read one article, you'd read them all. "How to Become a Better Homemaker," "Ten Ways to Make the Man of Your Dreams Fall in Love With You," "How to Tell if Your Husband Is Cheating." The heat rose in her cheeks, and she glanced at Ronnie. Luckily, Ronnie had her eyes closed. Teresa shifted in her seat so Ronnie couldn't see the page and started reading.

He has mood swings. Check. Frank had a temper and had been moody. She chalked it up to his heritage.

He dresses better. Well, Frank always took care with what he wore, so that wouldn't be a clue.

He drops the name of the person he's cheating with into conversation to throw you off course.

She thought a minute. *Hmm, who does he mention often?* There weren't that many women at his workplace. In fact, other than the receptionist, who was a much older woman, Teresa couldn't think of any. There were quite a few ladies Frank flirted with at the boat club, but it seemed innocent enough. At least she hoped so. This one had her stumped.

He doesn't initiate sex as often. As Teresa thought about it, she realized they hadn't been having sex as often as they used to. Frank had turned to her less in bed. It was a gradual sliding away, so subtle as to be almost imperceptible, but it occurred to Teresa that she and Frank hadn't made love in over a month. Sure, they had two babies who took up her time and energy. And Frank wasn't home as much these days. But their infrequent sex wasn't a sure sign he was having sex with someone else.

Frustrated, Teresa threw down the stupid magazine. She thought about it over and over, yet she still felt clueless. She was missing something.

Ronnie took one last drag on her Kool menthol cigarette, blew out the smoke, and put it out in the empty can of Fresca stuck in the sand. Teresa tried not to breathe in the noxious fumes, thankful the wind was blowing in the opposite direction. She hated smoke.

Ronnie glanced over at her with a serious look on her face. "Teresa, honey, I want to tell you something, but please don't get mad, okay?"

Teresa nodded, already worried about what Ronnie might say. Ronnie could shoot her mouth off one moment with a brutal honesty that hurt Teresa's feelings then, in the next second, could be so compassionate. She had a reputation for being quite direct, something Teresa both feared and admired.

"Teresa, you know I love you, honey. But you're getting really big. It's not healthy. And it's not flattering."

Teresa stared at Ronnie, wide-eyed. *Okay, wow. That's definitely blunt.*

Ronnie gave Teresa a gentle smile. "Have you thought about maybe trying Weight Watchers? Lots of women have success with it."

Her voice was kinder and quieter than the biting tone of a moment ago.

Teresa knew how popular Weight Watchers was but doubted that Ronnie had any firsthand experience with it. Ronnie had been born with that lithe body, and Teresa had never seen her struggle with an extra pound a day in her life.

"I know. I'm trying. I really am. But it's difficult. Frank is hardly ever home these days. I try to make a healthy dinner, but when he doesn't come home, I eat more and more."

Teresa bit her lip. The sound of the waves lapped in the background. *Should I tell her more?* She knew she could trust Ronnie. She just wasn't sure she wanted to give voice to her fears. But if she was going to confide in anyone, it would be Ronnie. Besides being cousins, they'd been close friends since they were young girls. They'd attended Catholic school together and were bridesmaids in each other's weddings. Ronnie had been there for Teresa when her father, Sergio, died, and Teresa had been there for Ronnie when her marriage had fallen apart.

She couldn't believe she was going to admit this to Ronnie, given her cousin's rocky marital history, but she had to tell someone. "I'm actually scared Frank may be straying."

Ronnie sat bolt upright in her beach chair and dropped her reflector in her lap. "What? Are you serious? No. That bastard. What makes you think that?"

"He's often going out after work. A few times a week. And even on weekends, he wants to go down to the boat club, and he stays for hours. I'm worried maybe there's a woman there that he's having an affair with." Teresa nervously wrung her hands together in her lap.

"Maybe he's really just out on that boat. You said he's always working on it. I sure hope he's not with another woman there."

"What were the signs—you know, with Charlie?" Teresa asked sheepishly, not sure she wanted to know the answer.

"Oh, the usual. Coming home late from work, not paying enough attention to me, not having as much sex, sneaking in late into the evening, always making excuses to be away from home."

Teresa felt her body stiffen. Ronnie was describing exactly what was going on with Frank. *Stay calm. This doesn't mean he's actually cheating. All of this could be a coincidence.*

"And then the lying started. Looking back now, it was so obvious. I don't know how I missed it. People who lie overcompensate, you know? He started making up shit." Ronnie looked out onto the water as if she were watching a scene unfolding and said with disgust, "Telltale signs of a cheater."

Teresa glanced at the foam left on the sand from the last wave that had washed up on the beach. Her head was swimming with thoughts. *Oh my God. Is my weight driving Frank away?* She didn't think that had anything to do with Frank's behavior. He'd given no indication that her full-size figure mattered to him or made comments about her weight gain. But Teresa wondered if perhaps deep down, it bothered him.

She looked over at Ronnie again and gathered her nerve. "Do you think my getting heavy could make him stray?" Teresa hated asking this.

"I don't know. I hope not, but men are so strange." Ronnie shook her head. "But even more reason to lose the weight, sweetie. Take it from me. Hell, I'm skinny, and Charlie cheated on me and left me. But I'm not comparing Frank to Charlie. My husband was a loser. Left me for one of my friends, and now I'm alone with three friggin' kids. Well, you know the story," she said, lifting her hand and swatting it through the air.

Teresa knew the story. So did everyone else in their extended family, at Shore Beach, and probably in all New Rochelle. Not that Teresa blamed Ronnie. Charlie *was* a loser. Teresa's heart broke for Ronnie and those kids. It did. But Ronnie's grief and loss had hardened her in a way Teresa found even more tragic, in the long run, than Charlie's leaving. It was like Ronnie lost not only her husband but also her optimism and hope. Yes, Ronnie still had her figure, but inside, she seemed broken. Teresa prayed that would never happen to her. She would rather be fat and hopeful than bitter. Of course, what Teresa really wanted was to be happy. And to be happy, she needed to stay hopeful that her marriage wasn't falling apart and she and Frank could find their way back to each other.

On the way home from the beach, Teresa glanced in the rearview mirror at her babies, blissfully napping in the back seat, spent from a day at the beach. With the volume low, she turned on the radio, and Frank Sinatra's "Ebb Tide" filled the car. It hit her straight in the heart, that song she loved so much, the one she and Frank had chosen as their wedding song. Images flooded her memory—Frank and her dancing, his eyes shining as he held her in his arms. The music, Sinatra's soothing voice, the images of Frank. They brought a wave of profound loneliness. She grabbed the steering wheel, biting her lip to not let out a cry.

The song reminded her of a time when they'd been so happy that the world felt like it belonged to them and everyone else just happened to be living in it. As a wedding favor, they gave guests candy-coated almonds in a little linen pouch with Frank and Teresa's initials on it, in keeping with the Italian tradition that life ahead would be both bitter and sweet. Little had she known how fitting that gesture would be and how much it would describe her marriage and life with Frank.

Chapter Nine
FRANK - NEW ROCHELLE, NY
1973

Frank got out of his car and detected Henry's cologne on his skin, musky and spicy. He worried Teresa would detect it. He climbed the three flights of stairs, opened the front door to the apartment, and stood in the kitchen doorway but didn't step inside. The kids sat at the kitchen table, boosted on phone books, while Teresa washed dishes at the sink.

"Well, hello. Look who's home," Teresa said.

Lena registered his presence and jumped up from her seat to greet him. Anthony joined her, squealing, "Daddy!" They threw their arms around his legs, and he bent down to hug them.

"Hey, you two." Frank smiled and kissed Lena on the head. "How's my little Cricket?" She was obsessed with the character of Jiminy Cricket in the children's movie *Pinocchio*. "And what about you, kiddo?" He tousled Anthony's mop of hair, his heart swelling.

But he remained rooted to the spot. He didn't go over to kiss Teresa because he was nervous about the lingering scent of his infidelity, which was making him feel both guilty and aroused. Thank goodness he'd popped a mint into his mouth on the way home. It had become Frank's habit to carry mints to freshen up. He mostly did it to prepare himself to see Henry. But now he realized it also had the opposite effect—to help mask any lingering taste of Henry on his lips and tongue.

"Did you all have a good day?" he asked.

"Yes, we did. And how about you? How was that work event?" Teresa asked. "I bet it felt good to get out of the dealership for the afternoon."

"Yeah, it was a nice change of pace. Good not to be stuck behind the parts counter all day, you know?"

Frank tried to sound as casual as he could muster. He hated how easily the lie fell out of his mouth. There hadn't been any work event that afternoon. He'd made up a fake regional meeting in Queens but had really met up with Henry at a motel, where they'd made love. He'd never taken time off work to meet up with Henry before. It felt risky, yet here he was, getting away with it.

Over the last few years, Frank had kept up this charade, sneaking time with Henry when he could manage it after work and on weekends. He told Teresa he was working late at the car dealership or had to go to Drifters to meet with the owner, Jim, or one of the boat owners, or was going out on his boat. All lies. Frank couldn't bring himself to tell Teresa the truth, afraid that she would see him as he'd always seen himself—an outcast reciting his lines and trying to pass. An impostor. If he told her, he was petrified he would lose everything—his marriage, his kids, his whole life as he knew it. But he suspected he was fighting a losing battle. No matter how many times he'd told Henry they couldn't keep seeing each other and he couldn't keep up this farce, he found himself unable to stop. Frank knew about the terrible things happening to the gay community, like raids, fires, arrests, and violent attacks, even killings. He should lie low for his marriage's sake—and for his safety. But the affair was like a vortex pulling him back, and he felt powerless to resist. He was so attracted to Henry, to being with a man, and to finally giving in to what he'd known all along was his true nature. It was a powerful, but dangerous, elixir.

"After we eat, I thought we'd take the kids to the park since it's still light out. Maybe stop at Carvel for ice cream," Teresa said.

Anthony jumped up and down, chanting, "Ice cream, ice cream," while slapping Frank's leg with excitement.

Frank smiled. Such a sweet, silly boy. Lena giggled at her brother. It was times like this when Frank hated himself and couldn't bear what he was doing to his family.

"Sure, that sounds great. I'm just going to jump in the shower first. I'm still feeling dirty from work earlier this morning." Frank watched Teresa swallow his lie. He headed down the hall, hoping to scrub away any evidence of his infidelity, along with his guilt.

Frank sensed something brewing beneath the surface with Teresa, a kettle about to whistle. He kept waiting for her to question him more and voice her suspicions. But she didn't. Her silence was often louder and more powerful than if she'd screamed those unuttered thoughts at the top of her lungs. Every time she let him get away with his lies, it made him feel even worse, as if he almost wanted to get caught. They kept going around in circles, with him feeding her lies and her accepting them without putting up a fight. He guessed she wanted the lies to be true more than she wanted to know the truth.

As he showered, Frank thought back to the first time he'd met Teresa. It was summer 1965. While driving his Chevy on North Avenue in New Rochelle with his cousin Dino, he spotted Teresa walking with her friend. She'd looked so self-assured, like she was exactly where she was supposed to be, doing exactly what she was supposed to be doing at that moment. Years later, he would think how ironic it was that he'd noticed her maturity, as he would come to find out she was only sixteen years old at the time. She walked with her head held high, periodically laughing and throwing her head back, carefree, like a breath of fresh air.

During their introductions, Frank stole some good, long looks at Teresa. She wore a gray box-pleated skirt and a lavender sweater, with a matching cardigan draped over her shoulders. She was taller than him by about an inch, even with her penny loafers on. Her hair, styled in a bouffant, was a striking black. She had pale, creamy skin, small lips, and a bit of a crooked smile. And her eyes were the color of chocolate with specks of caramel. She had wide hips and full breasts, a long neck, and shapely legs.

He was drawn to her. And the feeling seemed to be mutual, as she kept giving him that crooked little smile. After some mutual flirting, Frank asked her to go dancing the following Friday night at Glen Island Casino, and she said yes.

They danced the night away, and it amazed Frank that for a full-figured girl, she was so light on her feet and graceful. The different expressions moving across her face entranced him as they danced. At one moment, Teresa's face would be a study in determination. Then she would shake her head and smile as if she realized how seriously she'd been concentrating.

Frank wanted to dance with her all night long. She felt soft and comforting. Holding her had made him feel at home in a way he'd never felt before. He'd thought that perhaps with Teresa at his side, he could drown out the feelings he'd been trying to deny.

Entering the kitchen after his shower, Frank felt nauseated when he saw Teresa at the table and remembered how frantic and desperate he and Henry had been, hastily tearing off their clothes to get closer. Even though he'd just showered, he felt dirty. *There's something wrong with me. God in heaven, what have I become?* He reeked of desire and betrayal. He could smell it coming off him no matter how much he'd scrubbed himself.

Teresa looked at him in the doorway and smiled, gesturing with motherly pride at the kids, who were engrossed in a puzzle with pieces scattered all over the table. Frank smiled back and sighed. He longed to see himself through Teresa's eyes—a straight man with a loving wife, working a good job to support his family. He struggled to be that reflection. But he was losing the fight. He hated leaving Teresa alone so much. He still loved her. She was his wife. His *wife*. Frank said the word silently to himself like a talisman, thinking if he repeated it enough, it would help him break free of the spell that he found himself under.

Teresa came over, grabbed his hand, and squeezed it. Surprised, he felt his body relax. Maybe Teresa wasn't really suspicious, trying to catch him in an act of betrayal. But it didn't matter. He felt guilty all on his own. Guilt was a familiar foe, something Frank had grown up with as a Catholic.

He thought of the church with its traditions and rituals. Frank hadn't been to church in ages. Suddenly, he felt a need to go to confession—a powerful pull, like a beacon calling to him.

Frank stood on the steps of a church he'd never set foot inside. He watched three old women walking out with their heads covered in scarves. They reminded him of his mother. He'd chosen this church two towns away, on a Saturday afternoon, because he didn't want to bump into anyone he knew. But everyone looked like they could be someone he knew.

I'm paranoid, he thought.

Frank used to go to Mass regularly but hadn't gotten any comfort from it the way his parents had. He felt trapped by sin and guilt. It had actually begun when he was much younger, while he was an altar boy. He felt like a fraud. Every week, he took the host during communion and wanted to believe his sins were forgiven and he was pure and whole again, but he sensed that was a lie. Even if it was true, he would continue to have blasphemous fantasies about other boys, and the sins would start accumulating again. It was a vicious cycle and not one he cared to repeat week after week, so he stayed away once he and Teresa were married. She sometimes still went to Mass with the kids, while he made excuses such as needing to take an extra weekend shift at Drifters or tinker with something on the boat. But he noticed even she didn't attend church as much as she used to.

Now he was back, and as with riding a bike, he knew exactly what to do. He went through the familiar motions. Frank genuflected as he passed the altar on his way to the confessional. He entered the dark space and could sense the priest on the other side of the screen, more than he could make out the man's shadow.

"Bless me, Father, for I have sinned," Frank said, reciting the words he'd said so many times in the past.

But this time was different. *How can I tell him what I'm really thinking and doing?* He feared his sins were beyond forgiveness. But he didn't feel unforgivable. He felt confused, sad, and flawed. Frank opened his mouth to speak, but only a tiny sound came out. He stopped.

"Yes... go on. Tell me what is heavy on your heart," the priest said soothingly as if he were speaking to a child.

"I'm sorry, Father."

"Yes, I know. What are you sorry for now?" The priest spoke with an Irish lilt that made him sound friendly and approachable.

But Frank couldn't go on. He couldn't tell this priest—this holy man—he was having an affair with another man. Sodomy was a sin in his religion. The thought of telling a priest what he was doing made him cringe with shame.

Frank rose abruptly. "I'm sorry, Father." It was barely audible, a whisper that got lost in the dark, confined space. Frank tore aside the curtain and broke free of the confessional. He hurried down the aisle toward the back of the church. He stopped at the altar, genuflecting one last time, and said quietly, "I really am sorry."

ACT 2: THE CHARADE

Chapter Ten
LENA - ORANGE, CA
June 2015

I pulled my Fiat convertible out of the driveway of our home in Old Towne Orange to brave the traffic to downtown LA. It was a beautiful blue-sky Southern California kind of day, but the Santa Ana winds howled. I remember my dad mentioning the Santa Ana winds to me before I moved out west, but until I experienced them, they'd been a hard concept to grasp. I'd thought, *What's the big deal? It's just wind*, but they took on a life of their own, like an extraterrestrial being that haunted my days.

The cypress trees bent as though leaning in to hear a juicy bit of gossip. A few oranges had fallen off their branches in our front yard, their bright color contrasting starkly with the drab brown of the mulch, announcing that something was amiss—reflecting my mood.

LA traffic crawled on the freeway. *What else is new?* I hit the Bluetooth button on my steering wheel to call Anthony and took a deep breath. This call would make everything more real. Anthony—the other side of the Antinori-sibling coin, a reflection of my upbringing. He was the only other person who had lived through our family drama.

As the phone rang, I wished for the hundredth time that Anthony lived out here. No chance. Anthony didn't fly far from the nest. He was a proud member of the Johnston Police Department, in the town we lived in during our middle school and high school years. As a member of the force, he had to live in proximity to that town. Plus, his wife, Donna, was a schoolteacher there, and their two kids—Christopher, seventeen, and Ella, fifteen—were being raised there.

I had to admit that Anthony's geographical status benefited me as much as his parental one did. Thank goodness he had kids and had stayed in New York, so our mother got to be near her beloved grandchildren, and my extended Italian family stayed off my back. All anybody in our family ever asked was "When are you getting married?" if you were single and "When are you having kids?" if you were married, as if the only purpose in life was to procreate. Anthony and Donna had done me a huge favor by having those kids.

"Hey, Lena. Believe the old man's news?" My brother was a lot like my father. He always got to the point.

"Well, actually, I'm a bit surprised."

"I'm not. Makes sense they'd want to get married at this point."

Amazing. He's not freaked out in the least. So why am I so freaked out? Why can't I just let this play out? Anthony and I had shared so much growing up that I often felt like we should agree with each other about every aspect of our family issues. Yet that had never been the case. He didn't carry around our family secret like an albatross around his neck. For me, it was burden I couldn't escape that often forced me to twist myself into a pretzel as I went through the machinations of hiding in plain sight.

"Really? Because he was so damn good at it the first time around?" I asked.

"That was a long time ago. Different circumstances, different time. He's changed."

I chewed on that. *Has our dad really changed?* He'd become more himself over the years. This time, he was choosing marriage with a person who was the right gender for his sexual identity. But that didn't excuse the many infidelities of his first marriage—and the scars they'd left.

Anthony continued. "The guy spent the first half of his life tortured for who he is. Let's try to be happy for him, okay, Lena?"

"I am happy for him. It just feels... strange. Almost like our past is being erased."

"Nah," Anthony said. "Don't think of it like that. Think of it like his second act."

"You're planning to come out here, right? Don't make me have to go through this alone, Anthony."

"Of course. As soon as they pick a date, I'll put in for the time at work."

I smiled. Anthony was like a big teddy bear wrapped in masculine armor. When he'd started dating in his teenage years, he was so into each girlfriend, thinking she was the one and practically asking her to marry him, even in high school. When he fell from those relationship failures, he fell hard. It was like watching him react to our parents splitting up over and over again. Rinse and repeat. I'd been relieved and happy for him when he found Donna and settled down.

"Good, because I don't think I could face this on my own." I sounded like such the little sister.

"You won't be alone. All of us are coming—me, Donna, and the kids. Come on. Try to be happy for the old man. Christopher and Ella are really excited. This is a big deal for Dad. And our family."

I was happy to hear that my niece and nephew were thrilled about the news. And why shouldn't they be? All they'd ever known was a happy, well-adjusted, out-and-proud gay grandfather. They knew little about the tsunami that had preceded that. Anthony told them snippets here and there but downplayed it for their sake. I certainly didn't want to burst their bubble and tell them about all the indiscretions that had happened in our family years before they were even born.

"I'm glad they're excited." I made a mental note to text my niece, Ella, later if I didn't hear from her first. We were constantly texting each other. My nephew preferred to chat by phone occasionally. A major benefit of serving in the role of cool aunt was that I got to enjoy a close relationship with my niece and nephew—one I treasured.

I shifted gears. "So, get this. Dad wants me to actually plan the wedding."

"Yeah, he mentioned that. It's a compliment. He knows you're good at that stuff. You could whip something together with your eyes closed."

"Yeah, well... that may be the case. But the timing sucks. I have so much going on at work, a big case I'm heading up." I added, "Thank God he's planning to keep it small. He doesn't need some enormous affair. And neither do we."

"Is that what you're worried about—that he's going to have some big wedding and invite the world?"

"He's not," I snapped. "He promised me it would be small. Only close friends and us."

"Well, it's up to him and Oliver. If that's what they want, that's fine. Don't rain on his parade, Lena. Let them have the wedding they want. Don't worry about the size of it or who they invite or... anything else. Okay?"

I rolled my neck, trying to crack a kink. "Okay. But it's going to be small. Tasteful and intimate. If I'm planning this thing, I'll make sure of it."

Come on. You can pull this off and throw something together in a few months. Rally, Lena, rally. In the back of my mind, I could already see a plan formulating. I remembered a beautiful place near the ocean, the Terranea Resort in Rancho Palos Verdes, where Kevin and I had spent a day once with my dad and Oliver. I would call and check on availability later this week.

"Of course you will," he joked.

I lowered my voice, even though I was alone in my car. "I wish she could be there. Isn't that weird?" I didn't say her name. I didn't need to. Anthony knew I meant our mom.

I stole a glance at the pearl ring on my right hand—her ring. I admired its antique setting, the centered gem surrounded by tiny diamonds. It was one of the few valuable pieces of jewelry she'd ever owned. She'd worn it from the day her mother, Rosa, died until she gave it to me for my law school graduation. I thought about her long, elegant fingers, and my mind drifted back to that fateful day when the spaghetti and peas went flying. I recalled seeing the shimmer of that pearl ring on my mom's hand as she jumped out of her chair at the dining room table. The glint of the ring had matched the steely look in her eye. I'd never seen her look like that before—or after.

"Yeah, a little weird. But I know what you mean," he said, audibly letting out a long breath. "Listen, I gotta go. Call me if you need me. I'm here."

Anthony always made himself available to me. Unless he was in the middle of a serious issue at work or at home, he answered when I called. I couldn't remember a time when he hadn't been there. We'd shared a room until I was nine and he was eleven, whispering secrets across the darkness between our beds. When we first saw the house in Johnston, Anthony's face had dropped as he realized he would be sleeping alone on the first floor, far from the rest of us. Far from me. I remember how pleased I was, after years of sharing with Anthony, to move into a room of my own. Filled with the dignity of my nine years, I picked out pink paint and white curtains, reveling in my independence and closet space. But lying alone in bed at night, I would hear Anthony call, "Good night," from the bottom of the stairs below and felt—well, wistful.

He'd taken me everywhere, letting me tag along to the park, the movies, and the pool. His guidance smoothed my way through the awkward parts of childhood. Sure, there were also pillow fights, hair pulling, and the terrifying time when I'd thrown a fork at him and it stuck in his upper arm. I smiled, remembering how I'd hightailed it out of the kitchen, up the stairs, and into my room, behind the safety of a locked door, before he could catch me.

For every major event in my life, my brother had been there—all the boyfriends and breakups, when I went to college and law school, and when I moved away to California. Anthony had been on my side always. The least I could do was let him be happy for Dad with no reservations.

"Stay near the phone for the next few months. I have a feeling I'll be giving you an earful."

He laughed. "You got it. Talk soon. Miss ya."

"Love you, bro. Bye."

"Love ya too. Bye."

I stared at all the brake lights in front of me on the freeway and shook my head. After all these years, I was still sometimes in awe of my brother's carefree attitude about growing up with a closeted gay father. He truly didn't seem to care what others thought or whether they approved, as if it didn't touch him as much or he didn't let himself be defined by it. I wore it like a scar. An ugly scar I always tried to hide.

What was fascinating about my brother was how, when we were kids, his personality was a juxtaposition of different attributes. He'd clearly wanted everyone to know he was as straight as they came—not only heterosexual but very macho as well. He joined the wrestling team, only dated girls with ample breasts, rode a motorcycle, got his first of many tattoos, and vowed to get a rottweiler as his first dog when he was old enough to have an apartment of his own. He'd kept his promise and named the dog Tarzan, as if the dog needed a masculine name to announce to the world that he was a badass. You could say Anthony wore his heterosexuality like armor, sending the message constantly that he chose women and definitely was not gay. Yet he didn't hide the fact that his father was.

I remember the day when Anthony came home from high school and announced to Mom matter-of-factly, "Well, I told Victor, Angelo, and Nicky that Dad is gay. They're all okay with it."

Mom stared at Anthony, blinking repeatedly. She kept opening her mouth to speak, but nothing came out—like a guppy caught on a fishing line. I felt sweat beading on the back of my neck, and my hands tingled. A wave of nausea flooded into my gut. I tried to breathe evenly to calm myself down.

Then Mom exploded into words, like someone had just performed the Heimlich maneuver and dislodged them. "Are you crazy? You can't tell anyone. Least of all a bunch of Italian boys from your Catholic school with off-the-boat parents."

Anthony shrugged, clearly not appreciating the weight of his betrayal in our mom's eyes. "It wasn't a big deal. I told them that my father is gay—but I'm not—and they'd better be okay with it if they still want to be my friend. If they have a problem with it, they can take a hike. They all said they understood and felt bad for you, Mom, but they were okay with it."

"I don't care if they say they're okay with it. It's none of their business. You never talk about what is going on with this family with outsiders, you hear me? Never. How dare you talk about your father to those boys? Their parents are old-fashioned Italians who would crucify your dad for what he is. Don't you get that?"

"They pinky swore, Mom, and said they'd tell no one, including their parents. They don't even get along with their parents."

"I don't care. In a few years, those little shits won't even remember your name. But family? They're forever. You don't talk about family to strangers. You hear me?"

"But they're my friends," he said.

"Your real friends are your family."

I realized Anthony had committed the cardinal sin of disloyalty, but he'd done it out of loyalty to our dad because he worshipped the man. I also recognized that he'd done it out of respect for Mom, as if he was proud of her battle scars and that she—we—were all still standing. The reasons made no difference to Mom. She didn't care about Anthony's intentions, only his impact.

Anthony looked hurt but didn't walk away. He stared at Mom with genuine curiosity. "You're saying we can't tell anybody? Not even someone we trust?"

"That's what I'm saying, yes." Mom's voice had softened a little around the edges. She let out an enormous sigh. "Do I need to remind you that your father could get fired from both his jobs if this comes out—that in the worst-case scenario, he could even be thrown in jail?" Her jaw tightened. "And if that happened, I couldn't support us on my own. Not to mention that we'd be the laughingstock of everyone." She teared up.

Anthony moved toward her. "I'm sorry, Mom. I am. I didn't... I wasn't thinking of all that." As she opened her mouth to speak, he put up his hand. "I heard you. Loud and clear. It won't happen again."

"Please tell those boys not to tell anyone. Not a soul, you hear me, so help you God." She pointed at Anthony like a spectral ghost that had come back from the dead to haunt him.

He raised his hands in surrender. "I will—I promise."

Satisfied that she'd convinced Anthony, she turned her attention to me. "Have you told anyone?" she asked in an accusatory tone.

I shook my head vehemently from side to side.

"Good. Keep it that way."

"What if someone asks us?" Anthony asked. "Kids talk about who their parents are dating and stuff like that."

"If anyone asks, you say your father can't stay with just one girlfriend, that he dates too many women and can't settle down—stuff like that, to use your phrase. Or say nothing at all. It's nobody's business. We don't need to air our dirty laundry for all to see."

After that exchange, I certainly didn't intend to say anything. I was a good rule follower—always had been. Growing up, I'd only broken that rule one time when I confided in a high school guidance counselor about our family secret, only to be shut down. I shuddered and pushed that unpleasant memory out of my mind.

The car in front of me lurched forward, brake lights turning off, and I realized traffic had opened while I was busy chatting with my brother and reliving our family history. *It's about time*, I thought and hit the gas pedal.

As the elevator ascended to the division's offices, I ran through a mental checklist of my day: multiple client appointments, an all-staff division meeting, deposition prep for one of my cases not yet ready for trial, lunch meeting with opposing counsel to discuss a potential settlement, and trial prep for the Hawke Health Care case. Chock full. Thank goodness I'd gotten out of handling that sexual orientation case against the Fletcher School District. *Dodged a bullet.* It would be tough to watch Brad be the one to try that case, knowing I could have said yes to it. But I didn't have the time. That case would be huge, all-encompassing. And public. I felt a sense of relief, but something else was nagging at me. Perhaps my regret for giving it to Brad ran deeper than I'd realized.

"Hey, Lena, come here. I want you to meet someone."

Speak of the devil. Brad gestured to me as I exited the elevator and headed down the hall. He was towering over a man I didn't recognize, who looked like a little kid by comparison. Then again, Brad towered over most people. He was six foot three, with a large, bald, shiny head atop his body, like an ornament adorning a Christmas tree.

As I approached the two of them, I got a better look at the stranger next to Brad. He looked to be in his twenties and was well dressed and good-looking. Fresh-faced and eager—another paralegal probably. Brad hired paralegals and law students for the division. He claimed to love finding new talent and mentoring them. I had a feeling it had more to do with his massive ego.

"Lena, this is Toby, our newest paralegal. Toby, this is the *other* deputy US attorney." He emphasized the word *other*, stressing that he occupied the deputy role as well. In some federal government agencies, there was only one deputy. Ours had two—me and Brad. And he let no one forget it.

I reached my hand out. "Nice to meet you."

Toby shook my hand and smiled at me warmly.

"If you need to know about any discrimination statute, ask Lena. She's like a walking encyclopedia of discrimination laws." Whenever Brad said this, it didn't sound like a compliment.

"Well, that may be a slight exaggeration," I said, giving Brad a sideways smirk. He was always trying to one-up me. Although it irked me, it served the purpose of keeping me on my toes. Not that I would admit that to Brad.

"Hey, you and Toby have something in common," Brad said. "He just moved here from New York. Long Island, right?"

Toby nodded.

"Lena is from New York originally too. In fact, if you get her going, her accent still sometimes comes out to play."

Seething, I forced myself to smile. Brad loved to mention my New York accent, which got stronger every time I spoke to one of my Italian cousins back east—the accent that still lingered in my dad's speech even after he'd been living in Los Angeles for two decades.

"That's cool. Where in Long Island exactly?" I asked, ignoring Brad.

"Manhasset," Toby said.

My stomach lurched. Visual snapshots of time spent on my dad's boat in Manhasset Bay came flooding back to me—not all of them pleasant. One still haunted me, sometimes making me feel like a soldier with PTSD who kept replaying a wartime incident over and over.

"Oh..." I hesitated, not trusting myself to continue. Fortunately, Toby saved me.

"I read about you on the website. Looking forward to working with you." He looked at Brad then added, "Hopefully."

Only here a few minutes, and he can already tell Brad will try to hog him all for himself. Very perceptive.

"And as far as accents, I get it. I've tried hard not to let my Long-guyland accent take over. Not a simple thing to do, as I'm sure you know," Toby teased.

"Yes, I sure do." I smiled, detecting the accent now that he'd mentioned it. "About as hard to keep at bay as an Italian American New York accent. But alas, we can still try." This guy seemed really likable. I might steal him for one of my cases. "What brought you out here to Los Angeles?"

"My partner, David, is from here. We met in law school, and I followed him here after graduation last month. He got a great job offer with O'Melveny & Myers. I'm sort of a romantic stalker, if you will." He laughed.

Well, well. Toby and I had more in common than both being from New York. I always felt a jolt when someone told me he was gay, as if they'd moved the red velvet rope to the side, allowing me to pass into the inner sanctum of a private club. It still shocked me that some people talked about it so openly. I was fully aware it was 2015 and I was living in Los Angeles, a city known to be progressive. And the legal landscape for sexual orientation law was being revolutionized. But to me, it remained a foreign concept to talk about one's sexual orientation—or that of one's parents—so openly and not worry about the consequences. Leftover baggage from my upbringing. The particular luggage I carried around was heavy and persistent.

I spent the bulk of my waking hours in the US Attorney's Office, where every morning I shed my private persona and zipped myself up into my lawyer-as-advocate existence, a role that allowed me to feel like I was staying true to my past while keeping a safe distance from fully owning being the daughter of a gay parent. I told myself I wasn't actually hiding the truth—I just wasn't voluntarily sharing it, so it wasn't so much a lie as an omission. I could spin my logic in almost any way that suited me. *Such a lawyer.*

"That's a great firm," Brad said. "Lena and I had a case against them a few years ago. We won, of course. But they put on a solid case."

For God's sake, shut up, Brad. He always had to go on and on about his wins.

I stared at Toby, curious. In typical lawyer fashion, I wanted to fire off a round of questions: *Have you always been out? Did your family accept you? What was your religious upbringing?* I couldn't help comparing his normal to what my father had endured years before—the secretiveness, the hiding, and the fear of being outed, arrested or killed. And the heavy toll that secret took on our family—before and after we knew.

"Yes, that's a great firm," I managed to say. "But glad you decided on public sector instead and joined us. Looking forward to working with you—if I can pry you out of Brad's claws."

Brad smirked.

"Nice meeting you, Toby," I said.

"Likewise," Toby said.

I walked down the hall the last few feet to my office and stepped inside. I closed the door behind me, and the sound it made, sealing me off from the rest of the world, was satisfying and solid.

Chapter Eleven
TERESA - NEW ROCHELLE, NY
1974

Teresa hunkered down in the boat's cabin to escape the glaring midday sun. She'd agreed to go out on the boat that day, knowing it had been a while since she and the kids had joined Frank at Drifters. When they first arrived, Frank and one of the boat mechanics, Tommy, were putting the finishing touches on an engine repair they'd started before she arrived. Frank assured her they would finish it in only fifteen more minutes—the perfect amount of time to make lunch, which she preferred to do when the boat wasn't moving anyway.

She watched Anthony scarf down the apple slices she'd cut up to tide him over. That kid had some appetite. *Like mother, like son.* Lena was reading a book in the boat's bow, with their new little Yorkie, Libby, curled up beside her. Lena had become quite attached to that dog, insisting they bring Libby on the boat and not leave her at the apartment all day alone. Teresa agreed but could tell Frank wasn't thrilled with the idea. In fact, Frank didn't seem enamored with the new dog at all, even though he didn't need to take care of her. That task was, of course, left for Teresa since he was hardly ever home.

"Tommy, you going to have some lunch with us before we shove off from the dock? I've got Caprese salad and salami and provolone sandwiches that'll be ready in a few. I'm sure you're hungry. Not to mention thirsty. It's scorching out there."

"Yeah, thanks, Teresa. I'd love some," Tommy said, breaking into a big, white-toothed smile.

Teresa smiled back at him. Tommy had thick wavy black hair, crystal-blue eyes, a muscular physique that showed off his athleticism, and one of the best laughs Teresa had ever heard. She remembered Frank saying that Tommy was a hard worker and had gained the respect of the owner, Jim, as well as the boat owners and club members. It didn't hurt that Tommy was distractingly good-looking, Teresa thought.

"Hot as hell," Frank said, climbing out of the engine compartment from the belly of the boat.

Tommy wiped his forehead with his hand. "You're not kidding. Man, it's hot out today."

He grabbed the bottom of his T-shirt, which was tucked into his jeans, and pulled it up over his head, taking it off. Then he used his shirt to wipe his forehead and threw it down on the deck. His well-defined muscles were covered in a light sheen of sweat, glistening in the sun. He didn't have that much hair on his chest, but what he had was well placed, running right down the middle, between his pecs. His stomach rippled, revealing six-pack abs. He had a small line of hair that extended from his navel down past the point of his jeans' zipper. Teresa couldn't help thinking about how sexy that line was.

Stop it. You're staring. She felt herself blush.

Just as she turned away, something caught her eye—Frank. He was staring at Tommy, transfixed, like Tommy's bare chest was the answer to all life's problems or maybe just Frank's prayers. Tommy was oblivious, his eyes fixed on the small engine part in his hands that he was trying to repair. But Teresa wasn't oblivious. Frank was unwilling or unable to tear his eyes from Tommy's skin and physique, paralyzed into stillness. Afraid Frank would catch her watching him,

Teresa looked away, but not before she saw an expression on Frank's face. And it was unmistakable. Lust.

Teresa swiftly turned back to preparing lunch, her mind racing, wondering what she'd just witnessed. *Is he jealous of Tommy's physique?* And then a thought flashed into her mind. *Is Frank attracted to Tommy... in that way?* Teresa gasped, surprised at her thoughts. *Get ahold of yourself.* She had to be wrong.

She snuck a glance at Frank, who had refocused on the engine repair. As if sensing her gaze, he looked up, a quizzical expression on his face. Maybe he knew she'd seen him staring. But she didn't think so.

Teresa swallowed nervously and gave him a small smile. She put on her supportive-wife facade and ignored the thoughts churning in her head. She wondered if this was her special armor—avoiding the truth.

Teresa squinted against the late-afternoon sun, shielding her eyes with her hand. She adjusted the towel draped over her legs to cover the sliver of skin that had been exposed to the sun when she shifted position on the lounge chair. She was sitting by the Drifters pool with Sharon, the wife of the club owner, Jim, making small talk while Frank finished working on some projects on the boat. Anthony and Lena were frolicking around in the shallow end of the pool, where she could keep her eye on them.

"Teresa, it's so good to see you here today. I haven't seen you down at the club much lately," Sharon said.

"I've been spending a lot of time with my family on weekends. They all want to see the kids, and Frank has been busy here at the club," Teresa said.

"Speak of the devil," Sharon said, and Teresa turned to see Frank leaning over the edge of the pool, splashing the kids, who were happily bobbing up and down.

Anthony splashed his dad back, and Frank made a show of jumping back to avoid the water spray, laughing. "You almost got me, kid."

Lena swam closer to her brother, who then turned his attention to her, splashing her silly. She sputtered and yelped, but her wide grin gave away her delight. Teresa smiled at the scene as Frank plopped down on the vacant lounge chair on the other side of her. He leaned over and gave her a peck on the cheek.

"Ready to head home?" she asked, assuming he'd finished up on the boat.

"Change of plans," he said. "I'm heading out to the city with Henry for the night to meet some friends. Have dinner here with the kids. I'll let them know at the snack bar you're going to put in an order and add it to our tab."

"Tonight? I thought we'd go home as a family." *Is it too much to ask that we'll be together as a family for dinner on a weekend night?*

"Sorry, hon. There are some friends we've been trying to meet up with, and they'll be in the city tonight, so Henry and I want to see them." He wouldn't look directly at her. He kept shifting his eyes around, smiling at the kids in the pool or at other people as they walked by.

"Oh, okay..." It wasn't okay. "Who are these friends?"

"No one you know. They live on Long Island, and Henry and I met them once out on the boat when we had dinner on City Island."

"Hmm," she said, feeling her insides knot up. She wanted to open Frank's head and peer inside. *Are they really meeting these unnamed friends, or is it just going to be him and Henry?* She had so many questions and fears but didn't trust herself to voice them.

She no longer felt like the wife who'd believed her husband when he vowed to love and honor her so long as they both shall live. Her heart ached as she realized they'd entered a new phase of their marriage. She'd become cautious and careful around Frank lately—resigned to his actions and not bold enough to question them. She felt nostalgic for a time, years earlier, when things had been more carefree.

Frank glanced toward the parking lot, and she looked in that direction. There was Henry, with his hand blocking the sun from his eyes, sandy-blond hair glowing, crisp linen pants hanging loosely on his lean frame. Frank beamed and waved at Henry, who waved back enthusiastically. She could sense an electric current running under the surface. It was palpable. Teresa felt like an interloper, a third wheel. She felt a catch in her throat and thought she might cry.

Frank turned back to her, brushed his lips lightly against her cheek, and met her eyes. "I'll be back by midnight. Don't wait up." In that instant, she saw a flash of regret.

He went to the edge of the pool and called the kids over then tousled Anthony's hair and gave Lena a kiss on the forehead. They were oblivious to where he was going, probably assuming he was heading back to work, which gave them more time to play. And then Frank was off, heading toward Henry, away from her. She watched his figure get smaller and smaller until he reached Henry in the parking lot. Then they disappeared into Henry's car and drove off.

A growing fright was taking root in her mind, and she couldn't shake it. When she and Frank had become friends with Henry and Joanie a few years ago, they'd gotten together as two families, including wives and kids. But it had been ages since she'd seen Joanie or their kids. Lately, Frank and Henry spent their time alone together. She wondered if there was something between them.

Sharon jumped right back into their conversation from earlier. "Yes, Frank has been here a lot lately. So has Henry. I swear I see them here every weekend together. They're such good pals. Always out on their boats when Frank's not working. It's like they're glued to the hip. You must be jealous!"

Teresa recoiled as if someone had slapped her face. A shiver ran through her. *Is she implying Henry and Frank are...?*

Sharon studied her. "Teresa? Did I upset you?" she asked hesitantly. "I was just teasing." Sharon reached out her hand and put it on Teresa's arm. "Of course, I know you aren't jealous of Frank's friendship with Henry. I just meant they spend so much time together."

Teresa was unnerved but tried to act normal. "Yes, I knew what you meant." She hesitated. "It's just that Frank spends a lot of time at the club and on the boat, and I miss him."

Teresa stopped, afraid she might cry. *No, no, no. Do not cry to Sharon.* That wouldn't be a good idea. It would get back to Jim, and then back to Frank, and she didn't want to make waves.

"Oh, I know. These men and their hobbies and toys. They become a bit obsessed, right?" Sharon smiled at her, squeezed her shoulder, and then gently pulled away.

Teresa gave a little smile and nodded. Sharon nodded back as if the matter was closed. *If she only knew how spot-on she really is.*

Later that night, Teresa couldn't sleep, so she grabbed the Stephen King book she was reading. After a few pages, she gave up, unable to concentrate as thoughts flashed through her mind. She remembered the look that had come over Frank's face when she caught him staring at Tommy and then his reaction when he locked eyes with Henry in the parking lot. *What has he been hiding? Could he be attracted to men? And why is he spending so much time with Henry? Could Frank be interested in Henry?* Teresa gasped for breath and broke out in a sweat that made her forehead bead and her body feel clammy. She lay in bed, waiting for the sound of Frank's car in the driveway.

A little after midnight, Frank turned up. Teresa heard him enter the apartment, tiptoe into the bathroom, and close the door behind him. Teresa listened to him washing his face and brushing his teeth, sounds as familiar to her as the ring of their telephone or the heat coursing through the old radiators of their apartment. And then he was shedding his pants and shirt and climbing in beside her in his underwear, the bedsprings squeaking slightly under his weight. Their little Yorkie, Libby, who'd been curled up sleeping against Teresa's back, growled.

"Shh, you little shit."

Teresa got a sense of satisfaction knowing that Libby had growled at Frank, almost like the dog was sticking up for her. *Serves him right.*

"How was the city?" Teresa asked, trying not to sound like she was pouncing.

"Good."

"Where did you go?"

"We went to Greenwich Village. Had dinner and then went to a bar for a few hours to shoot the breeze."

Teresa's heart raced. "A bar? You never go to bars. You don't even drink," she reminded him, thinking of what he'd told her about Eva's struggles with alcohol years before and how he'd sworn off the stuff, just as she had because of her father's addiction.

"I didn't have a drink—of course not. You know that's not my thing. But they were going there tonight, so I went along." He shrugged.

She didn't know what his *thing* was anymore. "So, it wasn't just you and Henry alone? Who are these other guys again? Do I know them? What are their names?"

"Wow, so many questions. What is this, the inquisition?" She heard a teasing tone in his voice and felt her demeanor soften. "We met up with Mark and Bennie. They're the ones I told you we met that time on City Island, 'member?"

Teresa recognized the names. She nodded slowly, processing Frank's words and attitude. He seemed relaxed, devoid of any sense of wrongdoing. She wondered if she was overreacting.

Frank punched his pillow and flipped over, facing away from her in the bed. For some time now, they'd stopped sleeping facing each other. Despite being annoyed at him for going out, she felt herself wishing he would reach for her. It had been months since they'd made love. Making love used to be the way they could feel like themselves again—not some shadow of what they once were. Teresa missed it. She felt starved for physical contact. She missed being held, touched, desired. She leaned over and pressed herself against his back, wrapping her arms around him, touching his bare chest.

Frank's voice broke across the silence. "Sorry, hon. I'm just so tired tonight. Not really feeling up to it."

It was as if he'd slapped her. She felt stung. His words hung in the darkness of their room. Teresa grew still then slowly untangled her arms from her husband's body. She wiggled back over to her side of the bed and turned away so that she was facing the wall. They lay in silence for a minute, the weight of everything that was unspoken sharing space between them.

Then he spoke again. "Next weekend, I don't have to work a long shift at Drifters. I won't be so beat."

She felt like she no longer existed. She heard herself whisper, "Don't make any promises you can't keep, Frank." They both knew she was talking about a lot more than making love.

She couldn't voice what was really going on in her head—thoughts that felt foreign, unimaginable. *Can it really be? Could my husband, the man I created two children with, be a homosexual?* Teresa wasn't ready to know the truth. She wasn't sure she could handle it. They were playing a charade, and her part was to pretend she was the clueless wife, busy with their children and her life, and didn't notice all the symptoms set before her. She preferred to ignore the signs, on the theory that what wasn't named didn't exist. If she didn't say her suspicions out loud or acknowledge them, it could be like this wasn't really happening. As long as they kept up appearances, there was no need to scratch below the surface.

Teresa felt a nagging pain in her chest. Tears slipped out as she squeezed her eyes shut. She didn't want to jump to conclusions, but her intuition was strong and almost never failed her. She had to face the fact that this could be real. And if it was, she had to brace herself. Once out in the open, some things could not be unknown. Teresa knew in her gut that they would not only change her life but would hurt for a lifetime as well.

Chapter Twelve

FRANK - GREENWICH VILLAGE, NY

1975

"Come on, Frank—stop gawking," Henry teased. Frank moved away from the doorway, where he'd been trying to peek inside and get a view of the club and its inhabitants. He hurried to catch up to Henry, who was a few steps ahead of him.

"I wasn't gawking," Frank said. "I wanted to see what time they close in case the other club sucks and we want to go back there."

Henry threaded his arm around Frank's waist, pulling him close as they walked along Christopher Street. "It will not suck. I spoke to Mark, and he said this is *the* gay club in the Village. They have a new DJ who's supposed to be great. You can dance that little butt off."

He squeezed Frank's butt. Frank lurched forward and laughed. Then he glanced around to see if they were alone on the street. He knew he was being paranoid. The chances of someone outside the gay community seeing him and Henry here were slim. This was their turf, a place they felt safe to be themselves. Fortunately, the cops had backed off on raiding gay clubs in the Village since the Stonewall rebellion six years earlier. And while Frank didn't dare join the extremely public gay pride parades that started the year after Stonewall, he felt comfortable going to a gay club with Henry about once a month when they could slip away from their regular lives and responsibilities.

As much as Frank relished their time together, he was also nervous about what that meant for his marriage. It was becoming tough to balance his desire to be with his family with his desire to be with Henry—and truly be himself. He continued to do things for Teresa he'd always done in the past—fixing things around the apartment, keeping her car running safely, and other domestic responsibilities. And he tried to spend time with the kids but noticed it was mostly Anthony he wound up bringing with him to the boat on weekends, leaving Lena to be with her mother. Lena didn't seem attached to him. He wondered if that was typical of little girls her age. Maybe he was creating a chasm between him and Lena by being away from home so often and not taking her with him when he made time for the kids.

"Here we are," Henry announced, opening the door for Frank.

It was dark inside, and Frank's eyes took a moment to adjust. Once they did, he saw bodies in motion on the dance floor—hips swaying, arms flailing, heads thrown back—and wide smiles. All men. Men in suits, jeans, and shorts and even one or two shirtless, their bare torsos glistening with sweat. He glanced over at the bar. Men had their arms draped over each other's shoulders, laughing and drinking. One gave another a lingering kiss on the lips. Frank's heart skipped a beat. It still took his breath away to see gay men acting so carefree with each other in public. He couldn't believe it.

Frank heard the first notes of a new song he loved, "You Sexy Thing." He started tapping his foot to the beat.

Henry leaned over and whispered in his ear, his breath tickling Frank's cheek. "Let's go, you sexy thing. Show me your moves."

He took Frank's hand and led him onto the dance floor. Frank glanced around, smiling, but felt self-conscious. Whenever they went out like this, it took him time to warm up, not to the dancing but to being fully out with Henry.

Henry snapped his fingers to the music, a satisfied grin on his face. Frank loosened up, moving his hips to the beat, circling Henry and dancing more freely. Henry hooked his arms around Frank's neck, pulling him close and kissing him full on the lips, his tongue darting inside Frank's mouth. A surge charged through Frank's body. There had been many stolen kisses between them over the two years of their affair, but to do this out in the open was still a foreign concept, one that thrilled and terrified him.

Henry seemed so much more at ease with all of this than Frank did. He didn't just act bolder when they were out—he was more relaxed with their entire affair. With being gay. With lying to their wives. Henry came and went as he pleased and said Joanie hardly ever questioned him about where he was. Their life differed from Frank and Teresa's. They were better off, their kids were older, and Joanie was involved in lots of community activities, which kept her schedule booked up. Henry and Joanie didn't really seem married in the traditional sense. It was more of an arrangement.

Frank thought of his own marriage to Teresa. *Is it really that different?* Sure, she questioned him, but she mostly accepted his pathetic excuses. And although they still had sex, it was infrequent and lackluster. His relationship with Teresa felt distant, like they were now on opposite sides, still orbiting each other but not truly a part of each other's worlds.

Henry understood him like no one else could. He saw who Frank was at his core. And that was freeing. Frank confided in Henry about so many things—his goals for his career, what it was like to grow up hiding his true nature, falling for Teresa, his guilt over what he was doing to Anthony and Lena. Henry listened and offered advice and a supportive place to land. Henry told Frank all about his past and the other men. Frank found himself jealous of those who'd come before him, even though he knew he didn't have a right to be.

He felt like he was standing on the edge of a precipice and was about to hoist himself over. On one side stood his family, a safe life. On the other side stood his ability to claim his true self. Which was the truth? Which was a lie? The lines were getting harder for Frank to decipher.

Chapter Thirteen

FRANK - NEW ROCHELLE, NY

1975

F rank was an early riser, often leaving Teresa in bed, sleeping. He liked to get ready in the bathroom before anyone else needed it, get dressed, and then have time to relax before he had to leave for work or the boat club. And to sip his tea. He might be Italian, but he was a tea lover. He knew how uncommon that was. Most Italians drank espresso or maybe a cappuccino or macchiato. He preferred Lipton. Very unassuming. Very American.

His favorite mug was a translucent glass one with a smoky charcoal tint the kids had brought him home from McDonald's. Characters from the fast-food chain were etched into the glass. It had a sturdy handle, was the perfect size, and allowed him to see inside, which he liked. He dunked his anisette biscotti into his tea and loved watching the pieces float around after they'd become soft and broken apart. This comforted him. He had enough mystery in his life. He didn't need his daily tea to be one of them.

Frank rose from the table, rinsed out his mug, and put his plate in the sink. He first went into the kids' room and kissed them both on the forehead gently, trying not to wake them. Then he approached Teresa, who was soundly sleeping. He quietly stood over her. She looked so peaceful with her hair splayed across the pillow.

Young and innocent. He blew her an air kiss, not running the risk of waking her up by touching her.

Frank drove to the Drifters Boat Club slowly, enjoying the ride on a Saturday morning with few cars on the road, listening to his beloved opera and humming along. He was happy to make extra money by picking up more weekend shifts but also was hoping Jim would eventually offer him a full-time position with a higher salary than he made at the car dealership. His dream was to get his captain's license one day and man yachts in the NYC area. He had to work all morning that day but then would take off in the afternoon. Maybe he would take the boat out and try an alternative route to Port Jefferson. Teresa wouldn't want to come. She tolerated the boat but never loved it like he did. She didn't feel comfortable on the water, no matter how much she tried. He wished she would learn to swim, for God's sake. It was ridiculous that they owned a boat and their kids were such skilled swimmers, and she wouldn't even go in the water.

Frank arrived at the club and walked into the main office. Jim was already at his desk, as was typical. No matter how early Frank arrived, Jim always beat him to it. Jim was wearing his tennis whites. *Of course*, Frank thought. *It's Saturday.* Jim and his wife, Sharon, played doubles tennis every Saturday morning with Jerry Leiber and his wife. Frank glanced at his fingernails, suddenly feeling inferior to Jim. He saw the grease he could never fully scrub away and fisted his hands to hide them. Jim served as a constant reminder to Frank that he would never be as wealthy and successful. He seemed so cliché, a typical WASP working on his Studebaker model race car on weekends, parading his two beautiful daughters, who attended private academies instead of public school, and living in his mansion with a circular driveway on Davenport Neck. Frank admired and respected Jim but also resented him. He'd heard the rumors that Jim's in-laws were loaded, and even though Jim had already come from money, he'd married into even more of it. Sharon had supposedly fronted him the money to buy the boat club years before, using the investments her wealthy father had been smart enough to set aside for her. *Lucky bastard*, Frank often thought when he was feeling resentful. There was no fairy godmother waiting to hand Frank a cherished career.

Jim looked up at him now and made eye contact. Frank was glad he was early as he knew Jim ran a tight ship.

"Hey, Frank, how's it going?"

"Good." Frank took a seat at his desk and shuffled through the paperwork for a boat they were taking out of the water that day for repairs.

"I've been meaning to talk to you about something," Jim said, getting up from his desk and walking over to Frank.

Frank swiveled his chair around to face Jim. "Sure, what's up?"

"This isn't easy for me. I'm not sure how to say this, so I'm just going to say it, okay?"

Frank felt himself get warm. He worried he was being fired. But that didn't seem possible. He was such a hard worker. Even though he was only here on weekends, he'd already made a tremendous impact on the Drifters, and Jim knew it. Clients asked for Frank directly, many of them waiting until the weekend to come to the office, knowing Frank would take care of their needs the right way.

What the hell is going on?

Jim nodded as if Frank had told him to go on. "You're a good guy, Frank, and I think maybe you're just confused. I think something is going on with you. And I don't approve of it. Not at all. I want you to really think about this before you do anything stupid and hurt your family. Teresa is a nice girl and a good wife. But I'm mostly worried about your kids. Anthony needs you. He's your boy. So does Lena. They need a strong father figure."

Frank's mind swirled with thoughts, all jumbled together, each one trying to take the lead, like little kids raising their hands to be called on in class. *What the hell? How in the world does Jim know what's going on? And what exactly does he think he knows?* Frank swiveled in his chair, nervously looking at Jim, but not saying anything. He wanted Jim to go first, to show his hand, so Frank could gauge how much he knew.

"You know what I'm talking about, right? Don't play dumb with me." Jim raised his voice slightly, which startled Frank. Jim raised his voice with many workers and even some of the club members but never with him.

"What in the world are you talking about?" Frank was sweating even though it wasn't hot in the office.

Jim bounced on his legs a few times as if he was going to jump or run. He looked like he had so much extra energy. His behavior unsettled Frank. He was usually very calm.

"Think about what you're doing to your kids. Your son is going to be confused. Boys look to their father as a role model to know how to be a man, Frank. And your daughter. You're going to ruin her. How is she ever going to have a normal relationship with a man, when her own father isn't a man himself?"

Frank felt stung. "Hey, I'm a man. And I'm not ruining my kids. Anthony spends a lot of time with me and looks up to me. And Lena is only five years old, for God's sake. She's fine."

Jim shook his head vigorously. "Anthony needs to see what a normal man is like in order to become one himself. That kid is crazy about you. He wants to be you. And that's the problem."

Frank was stunned. *How dare he?* He felt like his blood was boiling, he was so mad.

Jim kept going. "And Lena... I know it may sound strange, but the lack of a father leaves a hole in a girl's heart. A girl needs to feel she's protected. She needs masculine energy to develop trust in men and later to give herself in love. You're going to scar her for life,

Frank, and ruin her chances at a stable relationship. She's going to jump from one guy to another, searching for the security of a father."

"Don't give me that psychology crap," Frank said, exasperated. He stared at Jim to show him he wasn't backing down. "I'm not sure what you're trying to say, Jim, but I don't like it. It's not your place, you hear me?"

"I'm worried about you. And your family. That's all."

"Don't be. Stay out of it. I'm fine. I don't need you prying into my life."

"Here's the thing." Jim raked his hand through his hair quickly. "I know some of your friends are... faggots. I hear talk."

"You son of a bitch! Are you calling me a faggot, Jim? Is that what you're doing?" Frank stood up, facing Jim. He was shocked to find himself there, in front of his boss, yelling the word *faggot*.

It also petrified him. He wondered what Jim knew and how he'd come to know it. He and Henry were always so careful but maybe not as much as they thought. Maybe they'd let their guard down at some point. *And what did Jim mean when he said he heard "talk"? What kind of talk?*

Frank shuddered as he realized that the same rumor mill that had given him intel on Jim over the years might have turned its attention on him and Henry. *My God. I could get fired. And not just from this job but from the dealership as well. Everyone could find out. I could be ruined.*

Jim put his hands up as if he were surrendering. He backed up a few steps and then started walking back to his desk, but he was shaking his head. "Listen, Frank. It's your life. But you work here. For me. And I've noticed some things. And I am telling you to be careful. Don't cross any lines. You understand?"

Frank looked at him and then, in a quick motion, flung open the door and stepped out of the office. He couldn't believe his boss knew. And if he knew, who else did? Frank was scared. Terrified, actually. He had to get to Teresa and talk to her before anyone else did. *What if Jim tells Sharon about his suspicions?* Frank would beat him to it. He would make Teresa understand Jim was totally out of line and having crazy thoughts. That they weren't true. And then, as if a sharp pain had crippled him, Frank realized with stark reality that they were true. Jim wasn't spinning lies—Frank was.

Chapter Fourteen
TERESA - NEW ROCHELLE, NY
1975

The door to their apartment burst open, and Teresa jumped to her feet off the couch.

"That son of a bitch!" Frank thundered, and the door slammed shut behind him.

Teresa glanced at the clock on the side table. Ten thirty in the morning on a Saturday. Frank was never home this early. Afraid to ask him what was going on but also curious, Teresa just stood there, staring.

Frank threw his keys down on the side table, ripped off his jacket, and flung it onto the couch. "That son of a bitch," he repeated even louder this time.

"Shh, lower your voice. The kids will hear you. They're in their room, playing." She gestured for him to come closer and lowered her own voice. "Who are you talking about?"

"Jim. I could kill him right now. He cornered me in his office this morning and said some shit to me I can't believe came out of his mouth. He has some nerve."

"What did he say?" She felt her pulse quicken.

"He told me I'm going to ruin Anthony and Lena. I'm going to ruin my son and daughter. I'm not a good role model for them because I'm not man enough. What the hell does he know? His wife is a cold bitch, and their two daughters are spoiled brats."

Teresa felt every muscle in her body tense up. *Oh no. Could Jim be onto Frank? Is he wondering about Frank the same way I am?* Jim was a bit of a bully, and Teresa wasn't sure what he meant by bringing Anthony and Lena into this, but he was certainly perceptive. She felt heat rise in her neck and butterflies flutter in her stomach. If the truth came out, it could put them on the brink of destruction.

"What does he mean you're not man enough? And what does this have to do with Anthony and Lena?"

"Who the hell knows? I swear he's spinning something in his head. He's nuts. Seriously. You had to hear what he accused me of. He's got this crazy idea that some of my friends are faggots. And because of that, I may be one of them too. Idiot. What the hell does he know?"

Teresa felt her legs turn to jelly beneath her and slowly sat back down on the couch. Her worst nightmare was coming true. Her suspicions about Frank, about who he was, what he was— this truth had been dancing around in her mind for a while now, taunting her with its ugliness and its power to consume her. And her silence had been a denial.

But if others were also suspicious, everything would change. This would ruin their lives and push them past the boundaries of decency. She understood she had to get to the bottom of what was happening in her marriage before other people found out. She would have to decide to keep it a secret or ruin everything. If she kept it a secret, she would live an outright lie. Her silence would graduate from denial to acquiescence. She would be complicit in Frank's lies, a guilty party to his illicit behavior.

But if I confront him, what will happen to our marriage? Our children? She couldn't find a clear path forward. It was like a landscape she couldn't see all at once—like the sky at night, which was so dark she couldn't detect its edges. It was too vast. She had to deal with this issue—but how?

Frank's voice pulled her out of her thoughts. "You know he's nuts, right? He doesn't know what he's talking about. He gets these cockamamie ideas in his head, and then he believes them. I told him how angry I was at him, and then I stormed out."

He sat down next to her on the couch. He grabbed her hand in his, and it felt foreign. They hardly ever held hands anymore. *Where is the man I fell in love with all those years ago?*

"This will blow over, Teresa. He just blurts out stuff, but he doesn't mean it. I'll go in next week, and I'm sure he'll apologize."

Frank kneaded her hand with his, and she wanted to pull it away. She felt smothered by his lies. Disturbing thoughts bobbed to the surface, vying for her attention. The possibility that Frank had been lying to her for years. All the time she spent alone, wondering where he was and who he was with. *Was he with his lover all those times—another man?* The thought disgusted her.

Teresa pulled her hand away and tucked it by her side, and Frank stiffened. "Frank, I don't think Jim is going to drop this. I don't think this is going to blow over." She was talking about more than Jim and wondered if Frank knew it.

"It will, Teresa, I promise. Jim is just being paranoid."

"Perhaps, but I doubt it," she said, unwilling to be pacified so easily anymore.

She didn't think Jim was paranoid or that he'd drop it. This was just the beginning. The first domino had been knocked over, and she felt powerless to stop the remaining ones that were bound to follow.

While the kids were at school on Thursday afternoon, Teresa met her cousin Ronnie at the aptly named Highway Diner. They'd hardly ordered their coffees before Teresa started in about

Frank. She felt like she was going to burst if she didn't confide in someone and voice her concerns aloud. And Ronnie was the only person she could say something this bold to.

"I'm so sick of Frank hanging out with Henry. They go out all the time. Whether it's dinner after work or hanging out on the boat on the weekends, they're constantly together. And I'm left alone. I swear, Ronnie, I'm at my wit's end." Teresa put her head in her hands.

"There's something off about that Henry guy," Ronnie said.

It surprised Teresa to hear this, as Ronnie had only met Henry once or twice at the boat club. All her synapses were on high alert. *Does she sense something about Henry? About Frank? Is the situation more obvious than I thought?*

"What do you mean, 'off'?" she asked.

Ronnie was quiet for a few seconds. "Do you know who Bob Foley is?"

Teresa shook her head.

The server came over with their coffees and placed them on the table. She smiled at both of them. Ronnie lit a cigarette while Teresa wrung her hands in her lap.

"My ex, Charlie, knows him well. They went to Iona Prep together and are still good friends. Play golf together, smoke cigars—guy stuff. Bob's a business owner. He owns a chain of restaurants in New Rochelle, Yonkers, and I think Pelham. Pretty well-connected. And here's the thing—he's crossed paths with Henry."

Teresa nodded, encouraging Ronnie to continue. She added cream to her coffee and took a sip. It was still too hot and burned her lips.

"Charlie played golf with Bob over the weekend at that hoity-toity Wykagyl Country Club. You know the one? I swear he throws money around for things like that, but it was like pulling teeth to get him to pay alimony when we first separated, you know?" She gave Teresa an exasperated look and took a drag of her cigarette.

Teresa tried to keep Ronnie on track. "What does this have to do with Henry?"

Ronnie blew out the smoke. "Charlie asked Bob how things were with work. And Bob started going off about how he interviewed Henry for a job as comptroller for his company and then offered it to him, thinking surely Henry would take it. And apparently, Henry turned him down. Bob was pissed and then told Charlie some things about Henry."

"Like what?" Teresa asked, riveted by what Ronnie was telling her—while simultaneously dreading it.

Ronnie leaned in conspiratorially and looked around the diner then back at Teresa, lowering her voice. "Bob told Charlie that he thinks Henry's light on his feet, cheats on his wife... with men. Now Bob thinks it's Frank who's caught Henry's eye, if you know what I mean."

Heat rose in Teresa's neck, and she put down her coffee mug with a clatter. "I've heard nothing like that about Henry." *Does Henry have a history of having affairs with men? Why does Frank have to get caught up in this?*

"Well, now you have," Ronnie said.

Teresa spoke slowly, trying to form the sentence that was like a neon sign announcing itself, unable to be ignored. "This guy, Bob, thinks Henry's... a homosexual?"

"He said Henry goes both ways." Ronnie hesitated, blew on her coffee to cool it off, and then took a sip. She looked at Teresa. "Oh hon, your neck and face are turning all red. Sorry. I know this is hard." Ronnie put her hand on Teresa's and squeezed it. "But I have to say it. Do you think maybe Frank could too?"

Teresa sipped her coffee. Her head hurt. She felt like she was trying to figure out an impossible math equation. She felt exposed for a fool and wondered if that was what she minded most of all. But Frank wasn't flamboyant in the way he dressed, spoke, and acted.

And he flirted a lot with women, but now Teresa wondered if that was because he was covering up what he really was.

"You should give Frank an ultimatum—his friend Henry or you. Pick." Ronnie gestured wildly, her hands moving so fast they looked like butterflies flapping their wings.

"And if he doesn't choose me, then what do I do? Give up my marriage? Try to raise two kids on my own?"

"I don't know," Ronnie said. "I'm not sure what to tell you. Charlie had money. You know that. I took him to court and got alimony. I don't have to work. My kids were older than Anthony and Lena are now. It wouldn't be easy to be on your own—that's for sure. I'm worried that Frank can't pay enough in alimony and child support."

"I'm his wife. We have a family." Teresa felt tears sting her eyes. "I still love him," she whispered.

"I know you do." Ronnie pouted. "But what good is it, though, if what he really wants is to be with someone else? What if he was born into the wrong life, and now you're paying for that mistake?"

"Do you really think this Bob Foley guy could be telling the truth—about Henry, I mean?" Teresa's voice sounded tired and meek even to her own ears.

"Why would he say it otherwise? I guess the real question is, what're you going to do?"

"I don't know. Hope it's not true. If it is true, hope it runs its course." Teresa felt so defeated. She looked up at Ronnie, embarrassed by the small glimmer of hope already appearing in her mind. "Even if it is true—and I'm not saying it definitely is—it's not like he's cheating on me with another woman, you know? I mean, it's different."

"Oh, honey, stop fooling yourself. Of course it's cheating. Woman, man—makes no difference. Your husband is sleeping with someone else. That's all that matters. In some ways, this is much worse. Think about it. How many married men do you know who cheat with other men?"

A sob broke through Teresa's lips, and she clasped a hand over her mouth.

"Sweetie, I'm not telling you to leave him, but make no mistake—it's cheating."

Teresa thought, *I didn't know about my husband's sex life.* What a strange statement. She'd lived with her husband all this time and never suspected until recently. It was, at the very least, a monumental act of naivete and obliviousness. Even sexually, she'd never guessed. She'd assumed the falling off she and Frank had experienced was simply the normal course of events when the husband was working two jobs and the wife was taking care of two little kids. Or with a wife like Teresa, who had gained so much weight. The gall of him—letting her believe her own inadequacies had been the cause when all along, he'd been having an affair.

Teresa and Frank had a way of making love that was long practiced and differed little from one time to the next. It allowed them to go through the motions in a language of their own, not having to renew their communication, sticking to the protocol. She'd sensed an unmistakable shift recently. But she'd never smelled a trace of another woman or found a smear of lipstick on his shirt. Another man? That hadn't even been on her radar. Not until she caught Frank looking lustfully at Tommy. That had been the first clue. She thought about how much time Frank and Henry spent alone together, seemingly in their own world. How they looked at each other and interacted. The pieces of the puzzle were fitting together.

"All those years," Teresa said, recognition dawning. "It may have all been false." She shook her head. "All those times we made love, I was making love to a man who was having sex with other men."

"Don't beat yourself up. You didn't know. How could you have known?"

"I guess it's better that I know. Better not to live a lie." Teresa couldn't tell who she was trying to convince—herself or Ronnie.

Then she thought of something that filled her with fear. She leaned across the table and tightly gripped Ronnie's wrist. "You can't tell anyone about this, Ronnie. You hear me? No one."

Ronnie flinched. "Of course not. You know I would never do that. For Christ's sake." Teresa released Ronnie's wrist, and Ronnie pulled it back to her side in a protective gesture. "And for your sake too. And the kids."

"I know," Teresa said, already sorry for lashing out at her.

"This isn't something we should shout from the rooftops. I know that." Ronnie looked pleadingly at Teresa. "My heart breaks for you. It does. No matter what you decide, this will not be easy. But I'm most worried about your kids. Thankfully, they're still young enough to be oblivious to their father's... foolishness. The question is whether things will change in time to save them from it."

Teresa swallowed hard. She felt like she was on a merry-go-round. If she confronted Frank head-on, her life would be over either way, whether they stayed together and lived a lie or separated and broke apart their family. She felt trapped. *How long will this charade go on?*

Teresa was desperate—so desperate that on the way home from the diner, she stopped at St. Bartholomew Church, where she and Frank had been married. It felt foreign, like they'd altered it during her absence. Then she realized it was she that had changed, not the church. Teresa had been born a Catholic but had become a convert to spirituality, struggling with religious conviction. Her parents' strict adherence to religious doctrine often felt like a straitjacket during her childhood. But this wasn't a time for splitting hairs. Religion or spirituality—it didn't matter. Teresa needed to call upon all the gods and religions and higher spirits to help her through this.

Seated in a pew, she bowed. Then she raised her head and looked over at the statue of Mother Mary, which had always held a special place to her. She loved the wedding tradition that some Catholics followed of gifting a bouquet to the statue of Mary and asking her to watch over the bride and help her be a strong and loving wife and mother. Teresa remembered the bouquet she'd given. The beautiful lilac flowers.

Mary, I hope you're listening. I could really use your help. Teresa knew a long line of wives had come begging Mary for help before her, but maybe Mary didn't have a quota and could fit in one more bereft wife.

Teresa thought of the other Mary, as many Catholics referred to Mary Magdalene. Perhaps that Mary would help her more than any other saint or deity. Mary Magdalene had always fascinated Teresa, who suspected this Mary had been in love with Jesus but knew she couldn't be with him. Teresa felt empathy for her. This woman might have been hurt by falling in love with the wrong man. She felt blasphemous for comparing her unholy situation with Frank with Jesus and Mary Magdalene. But maybe because so many Catholics shunned Mary Magdalene, she had more room in her docket for Teresa's unconventional prayers.

It certainly couldn't hurt, she thought. *I'll take any help I can get from either Mary. Who cares if it's blasphemous?* Maybe the other Mary could help her get through this with her marriage intact and without hurting her children.

Chapter Fifteen
LENA - LOS ANGELES, CA
July 2015

I looked at my watch. *Four thirty p.m. already. Shit.* If I didn't leave work immediately, I'd hit a ton of traffic and be late. I clicked Send on the email I'd been drafting, slammed my laptop shut, and shoved it into my bag. I grabbed the Hawke case folder and tucked it in there as well. I needed to work on the direct examination of a few of the plaintiffs later that night at home. But at the moment, I needed to hit the road. I was meeting my dad at the Terranea Resort, where the wedding would take place. I thought, for the thousandth time, how surreal it was to be planning my dad's second wedding.

When I stood up to leave, Brad was standing in the doorway. *Oh God, now what?* I had to get out of here and didn't have time for more of Brad's questions. Since he'd taken on the Fletcher case, he'd come to me for advice more often than I liked.

"Where're you heading? You never leave this early."

"I've got an appointment. Family commitment." That was all he was getting. It was none of his business. I walked over to the door.

"Oh, bummer. I wanted to discuss strategy for the Fletcher case."

I shut off the light to my office then gestured to him to back up so I could close the door.

"Walk me to the elevator. That's all I've got time for now." I was losing my patience with his constant comments about the case. *What is this—the third time he's come to me? It might have been easier to handle that goddamn case myself.*

He fell in step alongside me, matching my quick gait. "So, because there's still no federal protection for sexual orientation discrimination, we're using the state statute as our principal argument."

Obviously, I thought, nodding dismissively.

"But we were thinking of adding a different federal claim to the case. Something more creative. I remembered that case you handled years back, when California first passed state protection but it still wasn't well tested in the courts."

Brad had an excellent memory. When I was a new attorney at the division, I worked on a case representing a public school teacher who alleged the district had fired her for telling her students she was a lesbian. We added on an argument that the district violated her First Amendment right of freedom of speech. There was a gaping hole at the federal level, with no protection against sexual orientation employment discrimination, and the new California statute was too weak to hang our entire case on. It had a long, sordid history, including a veto by then Governor Pete Wilson, protests by LGBTQ community members and advocates, and the state legislature then enacting a watered-down version of the original statute. So we'd attempted the creative argument that if the teacher hadn't answered her students' questions about her sexual orientation, she wouldn't have been fired. And we'd won.

I turned and stared at Brad. "I'm surprised you remember that."

"Don't be. It was impressive." He lobbed that compliment to me like a kid who'd been told he had to hand over his favorite toy to a playmate by his parent—reluctantly. But I'd take it. "So I'm taking a page out of your playbook. I reviewed your case file for Deborah Woodside vs. West Covina School District, and we're adding a freedom-of-speech claim."

I shrugged but felt myself smile. "Stop trying to butter me up so you can boast more about your case." Brad loved talking strategy.

"Is it working?" Brad asked, eagerness and smugness playing across his face.

Infuriating. "A little," I admitted, groaning.

"Yes!" Brad said, pumping his fist in the air. "That's the ticket." He looked like he wanted to pick me up and twirl me around.

Please, no.

We'd reached the elevator bank. I hit the button impatiently. "Is that it?" I hoped this would be the last time he came to me about this case.

"Yes, ma'am," he said, saluting me. I rolled my eyes.

He cocked his head, curious. "So, what gives? Why didn't you want this case for yourself? I thought you'd be all over it."

"I'm swamped right now with the Hawke case and a few others I'm handling. Plus, I've got some outside commitments that are going to need my attention for the next few months." I waved my hand in a dismissive gesture, letting Brad know these commitments were not open for discussion.

"Got it. Hey, if you need help, I can assign that new paralegal, Toby, to work with you on the Hawke case."

"No, I'm fine. I don't need his help." My reply came out much more firmly than I'd expected it to.

Brad must have noticed. He put his hands up in a gesture of surrender. "Okay, I was just offering. Marcus wants him to work with as many of us as possible. But no worries. If you've got it covered, that's cool."

I was relieved to see the elevator doors opening. I stepped inside and quickly hit the button to close the doors. "Yup, all good," I said dryly, watching Brad's face disappear as the doors shut.

I was the one who'd passed this case on to Brad. But I couldn't help feeling annoyed that I had more experience with this area of law and he would be the one to try the case. It was hard to sit on the side-lines and watch him gloat.

Why didn't I take that freaking case for myself? The timing was to-tally off. That was what I told Marcus. And that was true. I had my hands full. But I realized it might be more than that.

As the elevator descended to the parking garage, my mind drift-ed back to that 1998 case I'd handled. How jarring to think of it again. It was an important case for me professionally, for sure. But it had also affected me personally. I had a hard time separating myself from the case. It hit too close to home, even though the client was a lesbian, not a gay man.

I sometimes wondered if part of my discomfort was that I had enough knowledge as an antidiscrimination lawyer to be aware of what could go wrong. I saw the ugly side of being *other* daily. You would think being so close to the issue would help. I wondered if it made things worse. My work often served as confirmation that my fears were well founded, as it constantly exposed me to the hatred that still lived in the veins of our supposedly enlightened society. It was a disease that every person who was *other* had to live with and be exposed to.

I remembered the day my dad called to ask me the question that would haunt me for years. It was that same year—1998—and I'd been working at the Civil Rights Division for only a few years.

I'd answered the phone in my office. "Lena Antinori speaking."

"Lena, it's Daddy."

I laughed that my father still referred to himself as Daddy some-times—like I was a little girl. It was embarrassing but also kind of sweet. I was a grown woman with a career, a home, and a husband. That didn't matter to him.

"Hi, Dad."

"Question for you—can I be fired for being gay?" he blurted.

His question stunned me into silence. And that didn't happen often. Then I found my voice.

"Why? Did something happen at work?"

"No. One of my friends told me that, and I thought it was nuts."

"Well, federal law doesn't cover sexual orientation discrimination. And there are only a handful of states that cover it. California is one of them, but the statute is still fairly new, and it's pretty weak in its coverage. It's somewhat untested by the courts, to be honest. So even though technically an employer can't fire you because you're gay, it still may be a tough case to win."

"Wow, even in 1998? You're kidding me," my dad replied.

"Yeah, it's absurd. It's something we're working on changing. We think the landscape is going to get better and better, with more states passing laws that have some real teeth. But right now, it's risky to come out at work. I wouldn't recommend it, Dad."

It was my dad's turn to be silent. I waited, letting him gather his thoughts.

"I wasn't thinking of coming out at work. I guess I'm more concerned someone may find out and tell my boss."

"That could happen," I said. "So I suggest you lie low. I don't mean you should lie exactly, but maybe don't be too open about it. You've heard the phrase, 'Don't ask, don't tell'? Kind of like that. Is your boss the type that may retaliate against you for being gay, even though you're such a great worker?"

"I don't think so. But I don't want to take any chances." My dad sighed.

I felt myself sigh along with him. I was relieved he wouldn't do anything drastic and risk losing his job, but my heart hurt for him having to be silent about who he was. What a messed-up world we lived in that an employer could fire someone just because of who they loved or were attracted to.

"I think this will change someday. We're just not there yet. There are still a lot of bigoted, close-minded people."

"Fuck them! What I do is my business. I don't tell them who to love!"

"I know," I said. "I'm sorry." I felt like the air had been let out of a balloon. "But it's not that bad. Just don't speak about your love life at work."

Opposing forces were pulling at me. My dad was frustrated and had a right to be. But I felt old wounds coming to the surface. The secrecy of my childhood had left so many scars.

"I'm tired of hiding, Lena. Of feeling like some freak. I hate that these bastards force me to hide who I am, and the fact that if I'm honest about it—or God forbid, proud of it—I can be treated like shit at work, overlooked for promotion, or lose my job altogether. And that it would be hard to fight that legally."

"I know, I do. You're preaching to the choir about the law. It's still nowhere near what it should be by now. But it's the reality." I heard someone talking in the background.

"Okay, I gotta go. I'll talk to you in a few days, okay?"

"Okay, Dad. Talk to you later."

"Love you."

"Love you too."

I remember hanging up after our call and feeling a cloud hovering over me. It was like my entire life was staring me in the face. Here was my father, asking me if he could be fired for being gay. And I not only had to answer that yes, maybe he could, but I also had to advise him to keep quiet. It was one thing to give legal advice to a client, prepare a case, argue it in court, and believe in it. Of course I felt invested in those cases. Of course I believed in what I was advocating and zealously represented my client. But I wasn't my client's daughter.

I felt like a fake playing the part of the civil rights attorney by day then not just telling my dad to hide but hiding in that closet with him. There were only a handful of people in my life who knew I had a gay parent—some extended family members and no one at work. For someone open-minded who professed to be an advocate, I was damn good at hiding the truth. Maybe I was my father's daughter after all.

The elevator chimed, and the elevator doors opened to the parking garage, bringing my attention back to the present. I climbed into my Fiat and turned on the radio. Frankie Valli crooned the opening line to "Can't Take My Eyes off You," one of my parents' favorite songs when I was a kid. I could picture my dad singing it to my mom, the two of them laughing. And when the song would crescendo as it reached the chorus, they'd raise their hands and mimic playing the horns with their fingers while singing at the top of their lungs.

I sighed. They loved each other. It just hadn't been enough.

Chapter Sixteen
FRANK - NEW ROCHELLE, NY
1976

Frank looked at Henry and breathed an exasperated sigh. They'd been over this many times before in their eight years together, disagreeing about their affair and about coming out. Their bickering sounded like a broken record. Frank could tell that Henry was more ready than he was, further along on the coming-out spectrum.

Henry tried to reason with Frank. "Not an easy boat we're in, is it?" He wasn't literally talking about his boat. "Always keeping our heads down, watching our backs, covering our tracks."

Frank said nothing. He stared ahead at the whitecaps in the water across Long Island Sound.

"Why do people care? We just want to live our lives. It's none of their business. We're not hurting anyone," Henry continued.

Frank turned and looked at him. He shook his head quickly in disbelief.

"What?" Henry asked.

"We are hurting people. Lots of people. Our wives, our children..."

Henry turned his head back toward the front of the boat, looking pensive. "Okay, okay. You're right. I guess I meant... other people."

"We're not lying to other people," Frank said.

"Yes, we are, Frank. We're lying to everyone. Our families, our jobs, our friends... ourselves."

Frank didn't protest. Henry was right. They were lying to everyone. And Frank hated himself for it.

"I'm just saying that what a man does behind closed doors is his business," Henry said. "Who he sleeps with, who he prefers. That's his inner thoughts. No one else needs to know. It's not a crime, for God's sake."

Frank looked at him and laughed. It was a crime, and Henry knew it. Sodomy was against the law, and homosexuality was against the church. Both Frank and Henry could lose their jobs if someone found out about them. They could end up in jail.

Understanding his laugh, Henry threw up his hands. "Ugh! Well, it shouldn't be. That's what I'm saying. You shouldn't be fired because of who you sleep with or love. What you do in your private time should be private, not something you can be put in jail for or cast out of so-called decent society for."

Frank stayed silent. He agreed with Henry, but he still found it uncomfortable to talk about these things out loud. Henry seemed so much more at ease with it, as if it were the most natural thing in the world to be talking about two men having sex with each other. Henry, a Protestant whose family wasn't devout, didn't wrestle with Catholic guilt over this being a sin. Frank was envious. He tried—he really did—but he still couldn't shake the thought that this was wrong, even though it felt so right. When it was just him and Henry alone, it felt so natural. But when he was back in the world, he was riddled with guilt and often second-guessed their affair. He felt horrible about what he was doing to Teresa and the kids and was often shocked by the sheer betrayal of his actions. He wondered if he would ever fully accept who he was or if he would always be torn between wanting to be this version of himself and hating himself for it.

Henry put his arms around Frank from behind in a conciliatory gesture. He rested his head on Frank's shoulder, and they both looked out at the horizon. Frank nuzzled Henry's neck. He worried that Henry might get impatient and choose not to stick around. Henry loved him, but maybe Henry loved the idea of being openly gay more than sneaking around with Frank.

Frank didn't want to lose Henry. He'd finally found someone he could be himself with after hiding for so many years. He watched the waves fly by as the boat crested and fell over them, wondering if he would ever catch up to Henry.

Chapter Seventeen
TERESA - JOHNSTON, NY
1979

Ronnie leaned against the kitchen counter, looking around and exhaling cigarette smoke, which Teresa tried not to breathe in. Teresa and Frank had moved to a new rental home a few weeks before, in the town of Johnston, and Ronnie was visiting for the first time. As the crow flew, Johnston was only about ten miles from New Rochelle, yet it felt worlds away, with pretty lawns, garages left wide open, and bicycles abandoned on the grass with no chance of being stolen.

"Gorgeous place. I love it," Ronnie said.

One of Frank's coworkers from the Cadillac dealership had moved his family to Johnston a year earlier and raved about the beautiful town and superior school system. Teresa and Frank had longed to expand beyond their cramped attic apartment. When Frank's coworker put them in touch with a landlord with a duplex home they could afford to rent on Frank's salary, they'd jumped at the chance.

Teresa nodded at Ronnie halfheartedly. To leave New Rochelle was both a relief and a disappointment. The relief lay in knowing it would separate Frank from his playmates. Teresa, though, was being torn from the people and places that provided her with a sense of comfort. She sighed and said a silent prayer that the move to Johnston would help change things back to normal. Help change Frank. But she had a feeling that what she was praying for amounted to a miracle. And she no longer believed in miracles.

Ronnie narrowed her eyes at Teresa. "Okay, enough with the house tour, sweetie. Spill the beans. What's going on?"

Teresa went over to the kitchen table, motioning for Ronnie to sit down. "I feel..." She searched for a word or phrase that could adequately describe the mixed emotions churning inside her. She landed on the closest one she could think of. "Stuck."

"I've been thinking about this a lot, Teresa. You should leave him. There's no way he'd get the kids. He's hardly home, and you've always been the hands-on parent. Besides, it's almost the 1980s. No judge is going to take kids from their mother unless she's completely unfit, which you, my dear, are not."

Teresa stared out the kitchen window at their new backyard, wondering why her husband wanted so badly to lead a separate life. She felt like an afterthought. If he couldn't make their family the center of his life, then what she really needed was to be left in peace. It was this anguish of living with a ghost—the uncertainty, the fear of the unknown, the wondering—that was really driving her crazy.

But being left in peace meant being alone. A divorcée. For that, she needed money of her own, more money than anyone in her extended family could afford to give her even if she asked, which she wouldn't. So her only choice for the moment was to stay.

"I can't afford to leave him," Teresa said, but that wasn't the entire truth. "I don't *want* to leave him. I want him to quit being out so much and come home and be with his family."

"You know that won't happen if he's doing what we think he is," Ronnie replied, pouting her lips and tilting her head down.

Doing what we think he is. Ronnie's comment made Teresa recall her exchange with Frank this past weekend. She'd been sitting at the kitchen table, having a cup of coffee, when Frank walked in, dressed for the boat. It was Sunday morning, and he didn't have to work at the boat club.

"Oh, I thought you were going to stay home today. The kids want to go to the mall for lunch, and then I told them we'd take them to the movies. It'll be a great way to escape the heat."

"Sorry. I promised Henry I would take him out on the boat to the sand dunes of Port Jefferson. He's never been all the way out there. I've been promising to do that for a while now, and I knew you wouldn't want to take such a long trip on the water."

Henry again. Teresa sighed.

"Besides," Frank said, "you know it's hard for me to stay away from the boat all weekend."

Stay away from the boat—or Henry?

He grabbed his keys, kissed her on the cheek, and headed out the door. She could smell his cologne and, as he walked away, noticed a spring to his step. *He's happy while I'm sitting here, miserable.*

The old version of Frank was right there. Teresa could clearly see him. His flirtatious banter. His sexy smile. He'd been just like that with her in the early years. And she'd been watching him direct that same behavior to Henry for some time now. How obvious he was. *Doesn't he realize I can see right through him?*

Thinking of Frank going out with Henry conjured up pictures in her mind of them doing things she didn't even want to imagine. She tried to bury the images, but they kept rising like bile—images of Frank being a homosexual. It twisted her up in knots.

How odd that she knew there were lesbian women, and that didn't bother her that much. She had one standard for women and a different one for men. Or maybe it wasn't different for all men. Maybe her standard was just different for the one man who was hers.

Teresa acknowledged she'd been uncurious about others' sexual preferences and habits. In fact, it amazed her to realize she'd just assumed most people—maybe all people—were interested in the opposite sex. *How limiting and closed-minded.* She wondered if sexual attraction was variable for some people and inflexible for others—if it was like a continuum. Maybe some people were one hundred percent heterosexual while others might be less, and most people didn't know exactly where they fell on the continuum. Of course, because she was one hundred percent one way, she found it impossible to imagine there was a continuum at all, because she'd always believed everyone was exactly the same as her. She'd grown up thinking that. She'd been taught that. It was like an unwritten rule she took for granted. And now Teresa realized the rules had changed and what she'd believed to be the absolute truth all along might not be. She wanted to turn back time and unlearn everything she'd learned in the last few years.

What do I do? Sure, she'd confided in Ronnie, whose husband had cheated but with a woman, not a man. And the gender mattered, adding a layer of shame, the sense of something taboo. Even though she wasn't the one who was cheating, she felt as if by staying with Frank, she was guilty by extension, an accomplice to his socially unacceptable lifestyle.

Then she realized there was indeed one person she could talk to who was in the same boat as her—Henry's wife, Joanie. Teresa wondered why she hadn't thought of that earlier. Maybe deep down, she'd been avoiding talking to Joanie. The woman intimidated her. Joanie was in a different league. Teresa had ignored that when they interacted early on, as couples, at the boat club—she'd been able to fool herself that they were somewhat on equal footing. But that wasn't true. Joanie was involved in all sorts of community events, and she and Henry had help with their home and their kids. Teresa had felt inferior to Joanie. But that didn't matter now. What mattered was that when it came to their husbands and what might be going on between them—an affair—Joanie and Teresa, sadly, might indeed be on similar terms. And it was time to get some genuine answers.

She swallowed hard, anxious just thinking about it, not sure she could summon the nerve to approach her about this. *What does Joanie actually know? Will Frank be livid if he finds out?* Teresa decided she needed to chance it.

Before she lost her nerve, Teresa called Joanie to make a date to meet up. She didn't tell her what it was about, and fortunately, Joanie didn't ask. When Joanie accepted, Teresa felt sick to her stomach but also determined to see this idea through.

The following week, while the kids were at school, Teresa met Joanie after lunch at a little trattoria off the thruway in Yonkers. Teresa realized she'd never met Joanie without Frank and Henry being with them. If Joanie was suspicious, she said nothing. She was already sitting at a booth, a martini in front of her, when Teresa arrived. She stood and greeted Teresa, and they briefly hugged. Joanie styled her long blond hair in a high ponytail, which gave her face a tightly pulled effect. Teresa had always thought Joanie resembled Barbara Eden, the actress from the sitcom *I Dream of Jeannie.*

The server came over, and Teresa ordered her signature non-alcoholic drink that looked good next to people drinking cocktails—cranberry juice with seltzer and a twist of lime. When the server left, Teresa inhaled a deep breath and jumped right in, saying the lines she'd rehearsed in the car on the way over.

"I believe your husband and my husband have a very special type of friendship." Teresa paused and then kept going before she lost her nerve. "They're... lovers."

Joanie took a long sip of her martini, a small frown turning down the corners of her mouth. She said nothing. Teresa couldn't tell if she was in shock or just not reacting.

"Wow. I've never said that out loud," Teresa said.

Joanie didn't take her eyes off Teresa while swirling her drink around with her finger. "Yes, I know. Henry and I have talked about it. I've known for a while. Frank is not... the first."

"Oh," said Teresa, feeling flushed. She clenched and unclenched her fists. She hadn't expected this. "I didn't know you knew. I've been so consumed by what this means for Frank, for our family..."

"I've known about Henry for years. I hoped he could change, but he doesn't seem to be able to. He used to want to be different. Now I'm not so sure. I think he's decided to be fully who he is." Joanie shrugged. "It's almost romantic when you think about it," she said with sarcasm. "Well, except for us, of course. You know... the wives."

Joanie slumped against the back of the booth and reached into her pocketbook to pull out a metallic gold cigarette case. She took out a cigarette, lit it, and exhaled the smoke out of her nose. She was slow and methodical in her movements, like she had all the time in the world, while Teresa felt an urgency rising in her chest.

There wasn't much fight left in Joanie. Teresa got the impression she'd come to terms with all this a long time ago and had decided to live with it. Joanie looked like a sad, defeated woman. *Will that be me in time?*

"Do you think they can change?" Teresa asked.

Joanie flipped her ponytail from left to right. "I used to think so but not anymore. It doesn't seem to be a choice. It's something they're just born with or they feel inside. Like it sort of happens to them, and they can't control it."

"Almost like they're trapped," Teresa whispered.

"Well, they could at least try to restrain themselves, even if they can't change their feelings," Joanie said.

"But would you want that—a marriage where your husband is attracted to other men but holds back and restrains himself only for your sake and fakes wanting to be with you?"

"For his wife? For his children? Yes! I don't think that's too much to ask." Joanie was getting angry. "I'm not a perfect wife. Or mother. But at least I'm not a freak. At least I'm normal," she sneered.

Teresa didn't like the sound of that. She knew she should find Frank and Henry's behavior abhorrent, but she just couldn't start down that path. She didn't want to. Yes, she was Frank's wife, and this was happening to her, but she didn't think her role was to judge him. What she needed to do was understand him so she could make a decision with full knowledge of what she was dealing with. God was the only one who could sit in judgment, and although she was aware of the Catholic church's hardline view on homosexuality, it didn't convince her God wouldn't forgive what Frank and Henry were. Teresa had never toed the line with the church anyway. She couldn't help but notice that churchgoing didn't equal goodness and forgiveness. Exhibit A was her father, who'd mistreated her saint of a mother and had bigoted views of anyone outside his limited Italian American community. To Teresa, God was a much more benevolent and forgiving spirit. She had to believe in that kind of God if she, Frank, and their kids were going to figure out their way through this.

"So, you just found out?" Joanie asked, ridicule in her voice, like she thought it was comical Teresa had been in the dark so long. "I assumed you knew."

"I've been suspicious for a while, but I think I'm finally admitting it now."

"I remember when I found out. Confronted Henry. How are you not furious? I was so angry for so long. It started with the occasional dalliance, but then it moved onto full-fledged affairs, like with Frank."

Teresa felt like someone had thrown cold water onto her face. A full-fledged affair? Teresa had never thought of it like that, but yes, of course it was. *Who am I kidding?*

"Can I ask you a question? Why do you stay with him?" Teresa tipped her drink to her lips.

"My parents would never speak to me if I got a divorce. Appearances and all." Joanie waved her hand as if the matter were something everyone would agree with.

"Is that the only reason? What about the kids?" Teresa lowered her voice. "And money? Doesn't Henry have a great job?"

"Sure, all that too," Joanie said, flailing a dismissive hand in the air, causing a strand of hair to come out of her ponytail. Looking at the loose strand, Teresa suddenly felt sad. And alone. More alone than ever. Here she was, talking to the woman married to the man her husband was sleeping with—the one person who knew exactly what she was feeling—yet she didn't feel any connection to her. No kindred-spirits kind of thing. This woman was a stranger. Teresa realized she'd never truly known Joanie. Their couples friendship had been surface level, born out of proximity. Joanie had known for a long time what was really going on and had never thought to reach out to Teresa. She wasn't Teresa's ally. Far from it.

A sense of righteousness rose in Teresa. "Frank is a good father—and even husband, in his own way. There are no rules for this. None. I guess we're just making it up as we go along."

Joanie turned and looked at Teresa with sadness, defeat, and even some hatred in her eyes. "Then I guess we're the ones who're trapped, aren't we?"

Chapter Eighteen
LENA - LOS ANGELES, CA
July 2015

I sat at the banquet table, chewing on the rubbery chicken I'd expected to eat when I promised Marcus I would attend this event in his place. The food was awful. No one came to the LA Bar Association dinner for the cuisine—they came for the networking. But I wasn't much in the mood for networking and found myself alone at the table with only one other woman seated a few chairs away. Everyone else at our table was in the restroom, networking at other tables, or mingling by the bar. She made eye contact, and we smiled at each other. She then moved to the seat next to me.

"I may as well come sit next to you since we're the only two here." Gesturing to her name tag, she said, "Hi, I'm Kate Haynes." She thrust out her hand, grinning.

I shook it. "Nice to meet you. I'm Lena Antinori," I said, gesturing to the name tag stuck onto my chest.

"Fabulous name. Italian?"

I smiled and nodded.

"Nice to meet you, too, Lena. What firm?" she asked.

"Not with a firm. I'm with the US Attorney's Office, Civil Rights Division, for Central California."

"Oh." She pulled her head back in surprise and lifted her eyebrows. "Very cool."

I laughed. "It is, actually. I love it."

"Well, it's refreshing to meet a lawyer who loves what she does. Few of us left." She snickered. "I'm a tax attorney. And most people, including lawyers, hear that and think 'Boring.' But I love it. It's like a big maze I get to figure out. I'm a numbers person and a problem solver, so it's perfect for me."

"Good for you," I said and meant it.

She was right. There were so many miserable lawyers stuck in dissatisfying careers, trapped because of high student loans or a sense that they owed the profession a chance after spending so many years training for it. And here were the two of us, happy in our unique roles.

"What's your position there?" she asked.

"I'm one of the two deputy attorneys. We handle discrimination claims, such as age, gender, disability, sexual orientation, race. You know—the protected classes."

"I'm impressed. Big fan of civil rights, here. Born and bred in the Midwest to parents who were 1960s hippies. You know the type." She laughed good-naturedly.

We chatted about various subjects. I found her very easy to talk to and learned we had some shared interests and were only a few years apart in age. She'd just started running after years of doing yoga. I told her I was the opposite—a longtime runner who was trying to force myself to do yoga.

"I'm hoping yoga will help me relax more, teach me how to breathe properly. I'm a tad high-strung." I smiled, embarrassed to admit the truth so quickly to someone I'd just met. But conversation with Kate was effortless compared to other people I'd met over the years at these shindigs. Her authenticity was refreshing.

She laughed heartily, throwing her head back. "Too funny. I wish I could say my motives were that deep. I'm taking up running because

I need to ward off the butt spread that seems to have crept up on me the past few years."

I laughed too. She was a hoot.

Kate continued. "But my moms warn me it's a lost cause. They say, welcome to the midforties, my dear."

I stopped, my antennae raised. *Did she just say "moms"? As in, plural? Could she mean...?*

I jerked my head up and gaped at her. "You said 'moms,' didn't you?"

Kate smiled. "Yes, I did. It's a long story, but the short version is my mother is a lesbian. She came out when I was in high school and actually fell in love with another mother in our town. They left their husbands for each other, so it was quite the scandal. They're both named Marie, and they're still together to this day. I call them either my moms or the Maries."

I was dumbstruck, trying to process what she said. I hadn't met anyone who had a gay or lesbian parent. Well, at least none I knew of. And Kate's mother had come out when Kate was in high school. We seemed to be about the same age, so that might mean our parents were contemporaries. I realized I was staring at Kate and still hadn't said a word.

"It's okay," Kate said gently as if I needed reassuring. "We're all doing really well, and I'm very open about it. They've been forgiven for their indiscretions."

I sputtered over my words. "Oh, I'm sorry. I'm... I'm just a little in shock."

"Yes, I know it can be very shocking for people. It's certainly an unusual background," Kate added, lifting her eyebrows again while a playful smile spread across her lips. She seemed so at ease with this conversation.

I looked pointedly at Kate, and then the words fell out of my mouth. "Not as unusual as you might think. My father is gay. He came out when I was in middle school."

"Wow," Kate said, eyes wide. "That's incredible."

I nodded vigorously. "Yes, it is. What are the chances?"

"I don't know," Kate said. "Well, I do some volunteer accounting work for a nonprofit organization that specializes in children of gay and lesbian parents and families with same-sex partners. So I'm familiar with statistics and percentages. Plus, like I said, I'm a numbers person. But I'll tell you what—I don't meet many people my age with a gay or lesbian parent. Or at least many who admit it."

Heat rose in my neck and face. "I rarely admit it. In fact... I've hardly told anyone besides my husband." This revelation made me tingle. This closely held secret that I'd guarded for so long... I thought of all the people I hadn't told. Not my high school friends, as most were too sheltered or judgmental—though some might have cheered me on and been in my corner—nor my college roommate, who probably would have been supportive. And not even my colleagues at work, most of whom were allies and advocates of the LGBTQ community.

Kate leaned back in her chair and looked at me carefully. "Well, I'm honored. I've never actually kept it a secret myself. I felt like there were enough secrets and hiding to last a lifetime. So I decided to just be very open about it."

I nodded. "My brother was the same way. He told a few of his closest friends, and if they were okay with it, great. If they weren't, then he figured he didn't want them in his life." I shook my head, remembering how angry my mom had been. "My mother wasn't happy about that. She wanted us to keep it quiet. I can't say I blame her, given all the circumstances and the era." I didn't need to rattle the issues off for Kate, sure that she was familiar with them—societal stigma, religious doctrine, lack of legal protections.

Kate frowned. "That's tough. I'm sure she did what she thought was best. People have different ways of dealing with it. There's no one right path. Being the spouse or kid of a closeted gay or lesbian parent doesn't come with a rule book. Especially back in those days."

I felt my emotions rise to the surface. "She basically instituted an Antinori gag order. We all abided by it out of respect for her."

Kate studied me. "Lena, I'm glad you told me. It must be very lonely not really having anyone in your life you can confide in besides your family."

I felt wetness on my cheeks and quickly lifted my hand to wipe my tears. "I'm sorry," I whispered.

"Please don't be sorry. I'm so glad we met. I think this is going to be the beginning of a very special friendship. We have lots of other things in common—our legal careers, our ages, and apparently, attempting to learn a new form of exercise and failing at it miserably." She smiled. "But our shared experience about our parents is something special."

The rush of affection I felt for someone I'd just met surprised me. I didn't realize I needed this so badly—to meet someone around my age with a closeted gay parent who came out when they were a kid. It felt strangely like peering at a mirror image of myself.

As I opened the door, a thrilled Atticus greeted me, wagging his tail so forcefully it could do damage. The house smelled delicious, and I heard notes of jazz playing. Kevin was humming along, busy at the stove. I put down my bag, kicked off my shoes, and gave Atticus a few pets.

"Hey, babe," Kevin said as I walked over and gave him a kiss hello.

The scent of him, warm and familiar, sent pleasure signals to my brain. I leaned into him, nuzzling his neck, breathing him in. He swept away a curl that had fallen on my face. I had the kind of curly hair that looked great one day and horrible the next. In New York, I often looked like the character Roseanne Roseannadanna from *Saturday Night Live*. But fortunately, in the dry heat of California, most days were good-hair days—one of the many reasons I was happy that I'd met Kevin after I moved out to the West Coast.

He held out a spoon. "Taste this."

I licked the spoon to taste whatever deliciousness he'd been cooking up. "Mmm, that's so good." I hummed with pleasure.

Kevin turned off the burner under the pan. "All ready to go. That's the extra sauce for the stuffed mushrooms. Your mom's recipe, of course." He smiled brightly as he gathered our plates and started serving dinner.

"Yum. I love her stuffed-mushrooms recipe. And you make it so well."

"I do now. Didn't go so well the first time around." He chortled.

"Oh, I remember." A bubble of laughter rose in my chest, warm and expansive, as I recalled the burnt mushroom dish. It was our first Thanksgiving as a married couple, and he'd been eager to show off his culinary talents to my mom and her boyfriend, Larry. He was so nervous because I'd bragged about what a superb cook my mom was. And he screwed it up. Burnt to a crisp. But she ate it—every bite. And when he was cleaning up the kitchen, she came in and even had the good grace to tell him she'd burned it also the first time she made it. Kevin had said it was so sweet of her to eat the dish anyway and not embarrass him.

As we walked outside to eat in the garden, I sighed contentedly, remembering that visit. It had been a special one for Mom and me. I'd been so excited and proud to show her the house. We gave her and Larry the grand tour, pointing out the renovations we'd done and the gardens we'd planted.

"Oh, Lena, this is beautiful," my mom cooed.

I felt swathed in her love and approval. As monumental as it was that I owned a home with my husband—something my parents could never afford—it felt like her blessing wasn't just for the house but for my entire life in California. I knew it had been hard for her to say goodbye to me when I left New York.

New York, New York. What a love-hate relationship I had with it. I missed it but also felt like I'd escaped something I'd outgrown that didn't serve me anymore. I'd felt myself exhale when I moved to California in 1995. *Ah, yes. Now my life can begin*—as if it hadn't started yet. I felt strange sometimes about moving to the place in the country where my father lived—almost like I was cheating on Mom. Deep down, I worried Mom felt like I'd chosen my dad.

When I first moved, I remember her saying, "I love your father, but I don't know how you can live out there when he's just all... out!"

I'd tried to assuage her worry by telling her he kept a lower profile than she realized. My dad might be free to live his life, but I didn't have to rub my mom's face in it, sharing all the gory details. I'd held back to protect her, sure. But it made me simmer beneath the surface, as I sometimes felt more like my father's daughter than I cared to admit. Old habits died hard indeed.

Kevin raised his glass of rosé. "Cheers," he said, pulling me out of my memories. We tapped glasses.

"So, I met someone," I said.

"Oh really?" He smirked. "Do I need to kick his ass?" Kevin wasn't really the jealous type, fortunately, but he did like to tease when he thought there was something he should be jealous about.

"Her," I corrected. "And no, you don't need to kick her ass. Her name is Kate. She's a tax attorney. We sat together at the bar thingy last night. I really liked her. We may go to yoga class together. She's apparently very good at it."

"Cool. You said you've been wanting to do more yoga."

"She just took up running. So I may try to drag her on one of my runs too."

"Poor woman," Kevin said, shaking his head and smirking. "*Drag* is the operative word in that sentence. She doesn't know what she's in for. You're not the right match for a newbie runner."

"Hey, I can slow down," I said, pouting.

"Yeah, right. I'll believe it when I see it."

"So... we have something else in common—Kate and I."

"Oh yeah, what's that?"

"She has a lesbian mother who came out when she was in high school. Left the family for the mother of another kid in their town." I sipped my rosé, hiding behind my wineglass.

I was curious to see how Kevin would react. My family was not like other families. I knew that even growing up. And now I'd met someone who reflected my atypical background.

"Wow..." Kevin dragged out the word. "How did that come up?"

"She just told me. Explained it all so calmly. Didn't seem to have any discomfort. It was kind of... neat. I've never met someone so open like that about such an unusual background. I mean, nowadays maybe, sure. But she's my age. Things were different back then."

"Did you tell her?" Kevin asked.

I knew that was what he would want to know. He always encouraged me to be more open about my dad. I resisted, of course. He never pushed me, but I knew he didn't want me to feel so twisted up about my past. Now I was telling him that someone else had a similar family dynamic to mine, and she didn't pack it away like a shameful secret.

I raised my finger to my lips and felt myself attempting to bite a nail then quickly caught myself and placed my hand back around my wineglass. *No, I will not start biting my nails again.* I made a mental note to call my local salon and schedule a gel manicure, which had kept the biting at bay ever since I graduated from law school.

I inhaled deeply. "Actually, I did tell her. There was no one else at the table at that point, and I found myself opening up. I mean, if anyone understands, it's her. It felt good. Kind of cathartic." I felt like a kid who'd just gotten an unexpected A on a test at school and was bashfully sharing her score. I wasn't looking for approval exactly, but I had a feeling Kevin would be proud of me.

"Wow, I'm surprised. I mean, good for you. I'm glad you did. But I'm still surprised. Maybe you're becoming more open to talking about it. Maybe this is a good sign."

"Maybe," I said, careful not to make any promises. I'd spent much of my childhood, and my young adulthood, defined by this one fact—that I was the daughter of a gay father—yet as much as it defined me, I still hid it. It would never be something I shared with everyone. Kate was unique, and I wanted Kevin to understand that. "I think it has more to do with Kate than me. She was so open about it. I think it made me feel safe to tell her. Like we were in a little cocoon."

"That makes sense. Either way, I'm glad you confided in her, Lena. I think it's going to be helpful for you to have a friend with such a similar background."

"Yeah, I think so too." I shifted in my seat and then shifted gears, done with this topic for the time being. "Thanks again for making the stuffed mushrooms. You know I love them."

"You're welcome."

"You cooked, so I'll clean up," I said, reiterating our long-standing arrangement. I rose from the table, grabbing my plate.

"Thanks," Kevin said, kissing me as I leaned over to stack his plate on top of mine. "I'm going to sit out here a little while longer and knock out some email. It's so nice out."

"Good idea." I headed into the kitchen.

I loaded the plates into the dishwasher, put the pots and pans in the sink, and started scrubbing away. I noticed my wedding ring gleaming through the suds. Our wedding had been a great day. But of course, there'd been drama. With the Antinori family, there always was. Deciding where to hold the wedding was more difficult than I expected. I loved the idea of a California wedding but worried that my extended family wouldn't be able to attend with the distance and expense involved. In the end, Kevin and I decided on a beach wedding in California followed by a large Italian-style party in New York before heading to Europe for our honeymoon in Madeira.

My parents were excited about the wedding and getting along well in the months leading up to it. I grappled with the tradition of the father walking the bride down the aisle and giving her away. It seemed so old-fashioned. Besides, I felt like my mom had been the one to raise me. My dad just hadn't been there as much as she had, and I felt as if asking him to be the one to walk me down the aisle would be a slap in the face for her. I couldn't help thinking my mother belonged by my side too. In the end, I had them walk me down the aisle together, and it felt right.

Then there was the matter of whether my dad would bring his boyfriend to the wedding as his plus-one. Kevin, of course, knew about my dad by that point, but few other people did, including his parents, who we didn't tell until after we'd been married for a few years. Our wedding list included extended family members, friends, and work colleagues.

When I asked my mom for advice, she made her position crystal clear. "Don't let your father ruin the most important day of your life. This isn't his coming-out party, for God's sake. It's your wedding!"

I'd told my dad it would be best if his boyfriend didn't come with him because I didn't want his relationship to be the focus of the wedding—for him to essentially out himself to anyone who still didn't know he was gay. Remembering this filled me with regret and an overwhelming sense of sadness that my dad had needed to hide who he was on one of the most important days of my life. Sometimes agreeing to live the same lie made a family a family. We excelled at burying the truth and all its inconveniences.

Chapter Nineteen
FRANK - NEW ROCHELLE, NY
1979

Frank and Henry made plans to meet at the boat that evening after work. Frank knew something was up just by the way Henry had acted on the phone. He seemed guarded, as if he was holding back something, or perhaps Joanie had been in earshot. Frank had a sinking feeling in his gut. He knew Henry was getting impatient and wanted them to come out. Frank wished he could get on board. He didn't want to lose Henry. But he also didn't want to lose Teresa and the kids—his family.

Frank watched Henry's familiar, confident stride as he walked down the dock. Henry stepped onto the boat and said hello to Frank, greeting him with a distance that made Frank nervous. He reminded himself they still had to be careful when docked at the boat club—play the charade of two good friends getting together.

They left the marina and headed out to open water. Once they reached a small inlet with more privacy near Glen Island, Frank slowed the boat down and cut the engine. He turned to Henry and looked at him pleadingly. "Talk to me."

Henry didn't hold back. That wasn't their style. They didn't play games with each other. There was enough lying in their lives.

Henry looked Frank in the eye, unflinching. "It's time, Frank. I'm ready to fully come out. To leave Joanie. And I want you with me. Which means you have to tell Teresa... everything."

Frank sucked in a sharp breath.

"She deserves to know, Frank," Henry said.

Frank stared at Henry, his mouth agape. He couldn't believe it. Of all people, Henry was lecturing him about being truthful with Teresa. Henry, who was just as much a guilty party as he was—who was the reason for his guilt, for God's sake. Frank would decide exactly what Teresa needed to know and when. She was his wife, dammit. He didn't need anyone else telling him how to handle his marriage. He already had enough guilt, thank you very much, without Henry constantly reminding him of it. Although he recognized Henry's attempts to be helpful, they often came across as bordering on threats—like Henry would reveal his secret if Frank didn't come out soon.

"Stay out of it," he said with a growl to his voice, which surprised him.

He was so confused. On the one hand, he felt like he had to defend Teresa and his marriage. Yet this was Henry. His Henry, who wanted him to be free to be himself for his own sake but also so they could be together.

But can we? Frank was wrestling with feelings of guilt and sin and wasn't sure he could ever break free of them and be himself.

Henry softened his voice. "I think Lena may suspect something, based on how she acted on the boat on Saturday. I wouldn't be surprised if she tells her mother. Do you really want Teresa to find out that way?"

"No, of course not." Frank shook his head, confused. "I don't know what that was on the boat the other day. I've thought about it a lot since then. But let's not overreact. Lena's only nine years old, for Christ's sake. I doubt she thinks we're lovers. She probably..."

Frank couldn't put into words his garbled thoughts, not sure what exactly *had* happened with Lena. She'd seemed surprised when she came out of the cabin and saw them. *But will she really jump to the conclusion that I'm gay? Will she even know what that is at such a young age?*

"She's pretty damn precocious, Frank—you know that. She may not know exactly what she saw, but I wouldn't put it past her to be suspicious."

Frank nodded. Even if Lena couldn't define it, he wouldn't be shocked if she thought something was amiss with him and Henry. And that made him feel so many competing emotions—petrified, heartbroken, guilt ridden. His daughter might have unintentionally seen him for who he was—someone deceiving his family time and time again.

Frank put his hands over his face and blew out a long breath as he slumped down against the boat seat, feeling it hold him up. "I don't know. I can't wrap my head around all this. Teresa wants us to be more of a family. And I do too. I want my family." He hesitated. Then he looked up at Henry and whispered, "But I also want you. I love you."

"I love you too. You know I do. But I can't do this any longer, Frank. I need to be the real me—inside and out. No more hiding."

Frank didn't know if Henry was extremely brave or stupid and naive. But he was jealous—so jealous. He was jealous of Henry's ability to break free from his self-imposed jail. Jealous of the man Henry would be with once he fully came out. Because Frank could already see it wouldn't be him. He couldn't leave Teresa. He wasn't ready for the change Henry described, because as tempting as it sounded, he would have to give up his family. And just the thought of losing them made him feel physically ill. He'd known this choice would come—Henry or his family. And he had a feeling which he would choose. By the look on his face, so did Henry.

"You're not ready? You're not leaving her?" Henry gazed at him, waiting.

Frank shook his head. He felt tangled in a web. He could either deny who he really was or live a life he couldn't share with his family. It was impossible to reconcile what he felt and who he was with what was expected of him.

Henry gave a long sad sigh that said so much. "Okay. I had a feeling. And now I know."

"I hate this. I want to be with you. I do. But I hate what being with you makes me."

"Oh, Frank, stop it. You're so brainwashed. There's nothing wrong with you! Goddamn Catholic church. I swear, you kill me sometimes. You really do."

"It's not just my religion. It's everything. Our entire society." Frank shook his head. "I'm sorry. But I'm not where you are. Maybe I'll get there someday. But not yet."

"You know what this means?" Henry asked, sadness blanketing his features.

Frank knew. It meant they were over. His heart already hurt thinking about it. He nodded.

"You break my heart, Frank Antinori. You really do. I think I always knew you would." Henry's voice shook, and Frank's eyes filled with tears. Henry plopped down next to him and intertwined his hand with Frank's. "Now what do we do?" He kissed Frank gently on the lips and then gave him a small, pouty smile.

"Don't let go? Keep going on as we were? Love each other?" Frank said.

Henry shook his head. "I don't think so. I think we both know that isn't the best thing for us." Henry looked away, and they were both silent for a while. Then he turned back as though he'd just received a phone call with the answer. "I'll always be your friend. I can support you. But I can't go on as we have been. I need to be out." He gave Frank's hand a squeeze. "You aren't ready yet. I am. I have to do this before I chicken out. It won't be easy. I'll pave the way. You won't be too far behind. I know it. I can't promise that I'll wait for you. But I can promise I'll be there always." He stared at Frank expectantly.

Frank had known this day would come, could see it looming on the horizon. His love affair with Henry had always come with an expiration date. He couldn't expect Henry to wait for him. Besides, he didn't know if he'd ever have the guts to follow in Henry's footsteps and fully come out, because that would mean losing his family. And he couldn't bear that. But losing Henry—the first man he'd ever loved, his world for so many years, the one he could truly be himself with... he might not survive that.

Frank felt like his insides were burning. He worried he'd be physically sick and almost doubled over in pain. He knew he was doing the right thing by setting Henry free—by choosing Teresa and their beautiful children and not turning his back on them. But it also devastated him. Frank felt like a caged bird peering out between the bars, watching another bird fly away, free at last.

Chapter Twenty
TERESA - JOHNSTON, NY
1979

Teresa swallowed hard, her heart ricocheting against the walls of her chest. She was sitting on the edge of their bed, and Frank was in the doorway. He looked hesitant, keeping some distance between them.

"Teresa, what's going on?" he asked, leaning against the door.

The kids were downstairs, listening to music. Teresa could hear the Pink Floyd song "Comfortably Numb" wafting up the stairs and couldn't help thinking that was exactly how she felt. Like she was drifting through her life. Numb. But she didn't want to be numb anymore, dammit. She was anything but comfortable. She needed to confront Frank once and for all. Teresa had to summon the courage because once this was out in the open, there was no going back. Now that she knew there were lies sitting just beneath the surface of her marriage, she wanted to know them all, no matter how much it might hurt. Every single one. Lies, even small ones, piled up until they eventually toppled over.

"Frank, that's a good question to start with. What's going on with you? Really going on? And please don't lie to me. I know something isn't... right."

Frank shifted his eyes to the side as if he was deciding which way he wanted to go—to deny it or come clean. She was afraid he would say the thing she feared the most. *If he says it, does that mean I'll have to leave him? Or will he want to leave me?* She wondered if there was a way for them to stay a family for the kids.

Teresa stood up and took a step toward Frank. She nodded, encouraging him to speak up. She needed to hear every word of what he had to say. If she didn't, she would talk herself out of believing it. And as much as it hurt like hell—as if someone was punching her in the stomach repeatedly—she needed to hear it to convince herself that what she'd suspected for so long was real. Even if it would tear them apart.

"There's nothing wrong, Teresa. I've got a lot going on with work."

Frank had chosen denial. She wouldn't accept it. Not this time.

"No, Frank, that's not it, and you know it." She stared at him, and this time, he met her gaze and didn't look away.

"What more do you want from me?" There was an edge to his voice—a defensiveness. He stepped into the room, pointing at her. "I provide a good life for you and the kids. If not for my hustling, you and the kids would have nothing. You'd be just another Italian girl from the West End of New Rochelle, living next door to her mama with a drunk of a father. And all you do is nag me and act ungrateful while getting fatter and fatter."

Teresa sucked in her breath and took a step back, feeling for the bed behind her to steady herself. She felt dizzy. She couldn't believe it. Frank was going on the attack. It was so unlike him.

She took a few deep breaths to gather herself then stood back up, facing Frank directly. "How dare you! I'm the glue that holds this family together. I take care of the kids, the house, and more, while you go gallivanting with who knows who, doing who knows what. I may be an uneducated West End Italian girl, but I'm no idiot, Frank. I know what's going on."

She felt the deep disappointment that comes from being intentionally wounded in one's most vulnerable place by the person one used to trust.

"So you won't give it up, this life—going out constantly, leaving me and the kids all alone? Making a fool out of me? You think people don't know what's going on, Frank? Who do you think you're kidding?"

Frank glared at her, his hands fisted, a strange glint in his eyes, like a bull ready to charge. He'd never been aggressive physically, but then again, she'd never confronted him so squarely. But he didn't move closer to her. Instead, he collapsed onto the bed, leaned forward, put his face in his hands, and started sobbing. He looked young and lonely and vulnerable, like a boy who'd just watched his beloved dog get hit by a car.

"I'm sorry, Teresa. You know I didn't mean what I said. I'm sorry."

Half of Teresa wanted to gather him in her arms. The other half wanted to batter him with her fists. She stood there, paralyzed, letting the two sides battle it out. Deep in her gut, she hurt for him. This was her husband, and she could see that he was devastated. But her heart was breaking for herself and for Anthony and Lena. She was feeling stronger and stronger in her conviction that she deserved more. She deserved to be someone's priority, not to be caught up in his confusion. If Frank being who he really was meant they had to be apart, she was coming to terms with that.

But as the minutes flew by, sobs racking Frank's body, Teresa's own body lost tension. She deflated—however unwillingly. She'd never seen him cry like this. What pain he must be in. What horrible, harrowing pain.

He looked up at her, his face twisted in torment, and she realized she was crying too. Fat tears escaped her eyes and made their way down her cheeks. She walked over to Frank, put her hand on his shoulder, and pulled his head into her stomach. He wrapped his arms around her waist, burrowing his head into the extra flesh around her midsection.

She stroked his hair and said, "Shhh, shhh" over and over, torn between feeling a maternal need to comfort her sobbing husband and awkwardness at doing so.

In her heart, she knew that if Frank could change, he would have. He wasn't doing it for sport, but because it was who he was. And no amount of love she could give him could change that. Frank was broken inside, and all her love couldn't fix it. Nothing could fix it. He would constantly tread water, trying to keep his head above the surface so he wouldn't get pulled down under. And for years, she'd been holding onto him with one hand on him, in the water, and one hand on the shore. And she didn't even know how to swim. Yet here she was, the lifeboat that kept them both afloat. Well, it might be time to let go. Frank would either go under or drift out to sea without her, but Teresa needed to stop trying to swim and plant herself firmly on the ground. Anthony and Lena needed her to be strong. They would need her even more if she and Frank parted and the reason for it got out.

Teresa untangled herself from Frank and left him in their bedroom to gather himself. It was a long time before he emerged. When he did, he joined her in the upstairs hall bathroom and looked her straight in the eye, putting his hand over hers.

"Teresa, my God. What you must think of me. You're so strong. I'd never survive what you're going through. And it's killing me because I'm the one causing it. You're my best friend, and I haven't been able to talk to you about... things. So many things. I've distanced myself from you, thinking I was protecting you. Please forgive me. I love you. I can't stand that I'm hurting you."

She pulled her hand back and crossed her arms. "Frank, decide what it is you want."

"I want my family. I don't want to lose you." Frank exhaled deeply and ran his hands through his hair, a gesture she'd loved since the first time they'd met.

How hard she'd fallen for Frank. Like jumping off a cliff. Nothing could have kept her from leaping. And the memory of that time, when she'd felt so much promise in her heart, made her cry again. Teresa couldn't stop the tears. *Stupid heart. Doesn't it know he hasn't really been yours to cry over for a long time now?*

Frank reached over and wrapped her hand in his.

"We'll figure it out, Frank. I don't know what that means just yet, but we will. But you have to be honest with me. That's all I ask for now."

He kissed the back of her hand. "Okay, you want the truth?" Frank shook his head and then nodded sharply as if convincing himself to continue. He let out a ragged breath. "It's over. I swear. That other thing..." He waved his hand. "I ended it. No more, Teresa. I promise."

She felt relief wash over her, mixed with utter exhaustion. She and Frank were tired and worn. Their ruts were so deeply cut into the road that she wasn't sure they could steer themselves anyplace new.

"You're really going to be able to do that, Frank?" She didn't know how realistic that was. She wasn't the one struggling with this.

"Yes. I can. I will." Then he added, "I don't want our family to end. I couldn't bear it."

She nodded and looked out the window at the trees swaying in the wind, which seemed to echo how she felt. Unsteady. Then she turned back to Frank. "Well, I couldn't bear it if you started doing this again. I love you. I love our family, but I can't take living a lie anymore, Frank. If anything happens again, I don't think I could take it. Do you understand what I'm saying? What I mean?"

She couldn't speak the words aloud—*I would leave you.* But they were there between them.

"It won't happen, Teresa. I won't let it," Frank said.

Their marriage had come to this—her begging her husband not to have an affair with a man. It wasn't the type of love story she'd envisioned years before when their relationship held so much promise. Teresa couldn't help wondering if theirs was becoming what some people called a marriage of convenience. She didn't want that. That was not why she'd gotten married. But so many women she knew were trapped in inconvenient, or even dangerous, marriages to men who were drunks, drug addicts, physically abusive, or just nasty. By comparison, Frank's attraction to men didn't seem so horrible.

She thought of Joanie and how reconciled she was to the situation. She'd given up and let it go on right under her nose, giving tacit permission. Teresa didn't want to become a mirror image of that—a sad, defeated woman, allowing herself to live a lie because she didn't have the courage to leave.

She remembered Joanie's words: "Then I guess we're the ones who're trapped, aren't we?"

Teresa shuddered. She couldn't let that happen.

Chapter Twenty-One
LENA - RANCHO PALOS VERDES, CA
July 2015

My dad grinned at me in the parking lot of the Terranea Resort, where we'd just met with the wedding coordinator to go over the menu. And by going over the menu, I meant we tasted almost every dish.

"Well, that worked out well," my dad said. "We don't even need to eat dinner now."

"We chowed down," I agreed. "Glad you like the menu."

"Love it. Love everything about this place. The wedding is going to be fabulous." He smiled at me. "Thank you."

"You're welcome," I said quickly, brushing it off.

I didn't want brownie points for planning this wedding. The whole concept of me as wedding planner for my father's second wedding still wasn't sitting right with me. I didn't love the idea of him getting married again. It brought up so many issues from my past. But this wedding was moving forward with or without me, and I'd thrown myself into my responsibilities.

Over the last few weeks, I'd secured this site for the ceremony and reception and booked a local officiant who specialized in LGBTQ weddings. I'd been planning on getting the invitation de-signed by a local print shop when my father informed me that Oliver wanted to design it himself. Fine with me—that was one less thing to do. Oliver was a graphic designer, so that was right up his alley.

"I wish Oliver could've been here." My dad had explained earlier that Oliver's cousin had a two-hour layover in LA. They hadn't seen each other in years, so Oliver was trusting Dad on the menu.

"He'll love it," I said.

"We visited together last week so he could see it again. He remembered it from when we came here a few years ago with you and Kevin. He loved every part of it." My dad swept his hand over the expansive view of the ocean.

I followed his gesture, taking in the beautiful scene. The reception would be outdoors on the patio, complete with a pergola covered in grapevines, a bubbling fountain, twinkling lights after dark, and tons of gorgeous potted plants brimming over with color. It reminded me of a winery in Tuscany, one of my favorite places in the world. Heck, it made me want to marry Kevin all over again.

I mentally checked my wedding-planning to-do list. Only a few more things left. The officiant had emailed to ask for insight into my dad and Oliver so she could personalize the service. How could I explain to her how different this man was from the dad I grew up with—how calm, happy, and settled he was with Oliver?

Living with my father when I was growing up had been like riding a roller coaster. Exciting, turbulent, and a little scary. He could be attentive and affectionate, calling me by my pet name, Cricket, giving me his big smile, and making me feel so special. But he could also be dark and withdrawn, with long, uncomfortable silences punctuated with little tsks to show he was both bored and disapproving. At those times, we walked on eggshells, unsure of how to act and afraid we would set off his temper. I would enter a room he was in and pause just inside the doorway, trying to gauge the temperature of the room. We all did this a lot. We paused for a beat to sniff out Dad's mood and figure out who we needed to be so as not to set him off. Sometimes we could sense his state of mind as soon as we got near him. Other times, we had to tiptoe around, waiting to see if he would reveal himself.

I could never fully understand what would make him unhappy. In the evenings, when he came home for dinner—if he came home for dinner at all—we waited to see what kind of mood he was in when he walked through the door. Would he flash that big smile, singing, "I'm home!" and give us a squeeze? Or would he sullenly walk in the door and look at us with a defeated look, remembering he was still playing the role of a typical suburban husband married to a woman with kids?

On weekends, if we went out for a family drive, we would sit in silence, not saying a word for fear he would fly off the handle. He would impatiently fiddle with the radio dial, trying to find a good song, hitting upon static in between stations, getting frustrated and visibly mad at the radio and often cursing at it as if the radio had an agenda. Then an opera song would come on or a tune he loved, and he would start humming along, a smile spreading across his face. There was no predictability, no way of knowing which version of Dad we were going to get. He was a paradox that swung from brusque aloofness to soulful warmth and affection.

With the benefit of hindsight, it was easy to psychoanalyze him. He was constantly fighting with himself, worrying others would discover his secret and his world would come crashing down around him, while also yearning to be free. His inner struggle often manifested in tantrums. And we were paying for his silence daily.

My dad's voice broke through my thoughts. "Oh, that's Henry calling. I'm going to pick it up and say hi. I texted him about the wedding, but we haven't had a chance to chat with him about it yet."

Just great. I loved that my dad and Henry had stayed friends for a lifetime—that they had such a special bond. But sometimes it was still hard for me not to focus on how they'd begun.

"I'll switch to FaceTime and show him this place and the view. He'll love it. You know our favorite place in the world is on the water."

That I did. All too well. They'd practically lived on that boat when I was a kid. And their time on it hadn't always been innocent. Far from it. I shuddered as I remembered one time in particular. *Don't think of that now.*

I heard Henry's voice over my dad's phone, reminding me to focus on the present. "Frank, you old fart, you're finally doing it. I'm proud of you. Took you long enough."

"Hey, I just never found the right guy. Now I have," my dad said, beaming.

"Ouch. I could be offended by that, you know," Henry said.

I swallowed a lump in my throat. *Water under the bridge, as they say.* But it still hurt sometimes. This was the man my father cheated on my mother with.

"I couldn't catch up to you, Henry. You moved too fast for me," my dad said, matching Henry's banter. It amazed me how easily they could tease about it all, not only because they must have hurt each other but because they also hurt everyone around them. It didn't seem like a laughing matter. But maybe humor was their way of dealing with what they'd done.

"Yeah, yeah," Henry said. "I know. I'm just teasing you, old friend. Lena, I see he's got you planning this event. He's a lucky guy. Wish my kids were that involved in my life. But hey, you can't always get what you want."

I pressed my lips together and looked away at the ocean. I remembered Henry's two kids—a boy and girl, just like Anthony and me but older. Spoiled brats. And his ex-wife, Joanie. So beautiful but always distant. I wondered if that had been her way of dealing with the situation. Once Henry and Joanie split up, the kids had turned their backs on him, refusing to see him. He'd told my dad how he threw money at them to buy their affection. They would take the money and still snub him. Back then, I envied them. Mom insisted Anthony and I continue a relationship with Dad, so we did. But God, balancing that ten-ton weight on our shoulders, accepting him while keeping up the pretense in front of everyone else, had been a heavy load to bear.

I took my eyes off the ocean and looked back at my dad, who was eager, waiting for my reply. "Yeah, well, someone's got to make sure this thing is a classy event," I teased back, deciding I might as well play along.

"Good for you," Henry said.

My dad squeezed my hand. "I'm a lucky man. Both my kids will be by my side, and my grandkids. Anthony and Donna are coming out with Christopher and Ella," my dad said to Henry on FaceTime, but he was looking directly at me, gratitude on his face.

"That you are, old man. And I'll be there too. Wouldn't miss it for the world," Henry said.

"Thanks, Henry. Means a lot to me you'll be there."

"All right, now, don't go getting all mushy on me."

My dad laughed. "Shut up. Just get your ass out here, okay? I'll email you the invitation once we finalize it. Oliver's designing it, so it's going to be gorgeous."

"Can't wait to see it," Henry said. "Say hi to Oliver for me. Bye, Lena."

"Bye, Henry," I said.

"Talk to you soon," my dad said and hung up.

As we sat staring at the gorgeous views of the ocean, my dad sighed. "Sure beats an attic apartment on the third floor with a view obscured by a fire escape."

"Sure does. But we moved up from there," I said, referring to the duplex home we rented in Johnston.

"Yeah, it was an upgrade." He paused. "But I didn't get to live there very long. Kind of a shame."

And whose fault is that? I thought.

But I held back. I had an ambivalent relationship with our Johnston house, which we'd moved to when I was nine years old. I loved the house itself, which had felt like such a step up from what we'd moved away from. My father was doing well enough in his job that we could rent a house. He was so excited to show us, like a little kid with a new toy. In retrospect, it almost seemed like he was trying to convince himself that a change of scenery would somehow fix us. I'd hoped we'd be happy there. But it would prove to be the scene of one of the worst moments of my life.

I drove home from Terranea with the roof down on my Fiat. The breeze felt refreshing. I caught glimpses of the ocean from the highway. Snippets of the evening with my dad played over in my mind, one phrase getting caught in a loop—"You know our favorite place in the world is on the water," he'd said, referring to him and Henry. And like a gravitational pull, my thoughts wandered back to a particular Saturday afternoon that was etched in my memory.

Anthony and I had been out on the boat with Dad and Henry along with Henry's two kids—the moms having stayed at home "to give the ladies a break," I recall my dad saying. We'd anchored in Manhasset Bay, and Anthony was frolicking in the water with Henry's kids, diving off the deck on the back of the boat over and over. I'd had enough swimming for the time being and went down below into the cabin to read a Judy Blume book. After a while, I came back out to the deck area to head into the water again because it was so hot out. I saw my dad and Henry laughing, their heads together, with Henry's hand on my dad's arm. My father was beaming at Henry—the kind of smile when you had a secret—looking like someone I didn't even recognize. I felt shell-shocked, my head buzzing. I stood frozen in place, not daring to walk any farther onto the deck. They must have heard me because I saw my dad flinch and jerk his arm away from under Henry's hand. My dad cleared his throat and looked out at the kids swimming in the water. Henry looked momentarily startled and then also looked out at the water, avoiding making any eye contact with my father, acting nonchalant.

The moment had passed. But I knew what I'd seen. It had never occurred to me before to think of my father as a man with desires. Like all kids, I preferred—despite my very existence—not to think of my parents as sexual beings. But I started thinking of all the times I'd seen my dad and Henry together. There was something about the way my dad's body relaxed around Henry. A familiarity to his movements. An excitement in his voice when he'd speak about Henry. An easy banter between them. They seemed to orbit each other.

I felt like I was piecing something together. The late evenings home from work... my dad always wanting to go out on the boat with Henry. Fury rose like bile in my throat. *What exactly is he hiding? And how can he be so deceitful?*

After that day, I kept my distance from my dad at home. I ignored him and responded to his questions with simply yes or no. I felt like everything was unbalanced—like the world I knew had somehow tilted on its axis.

And the worst part was that I didn't know what to do with this information. I didn't want to tell my mom. My kind, loving mom.

When we got home from the boat that night, she greeted us, grabbing our wet towels to put in the laundry. "Did you have a good time?"

When I looked at her, my heart skipped a beat. I wanted to ask her about what I'd seen on the boat that afternoon and what it meant. But I didn't know how to phrase it.

"Yeah, it was nice out," I eked out, safely referring to the weather.

I turned away from my mom's gaze before she could read my face, wanting to go back and erase what I'd seen. I had the strange sense that I shouldn't share information about my father's behavior on the boat with my mother, and I hated keeping something from her. I felt a heaviness as I trudged off toward my room. The situation was too big for my nine-year-old self to navigate.

I saw Anthony walking ahead of me, heading into his bedroom.

"Anthony, wait up." I followed him in and shut the door behind me.

"What's up?" he asked.

I studied his face. He'd been playing in the water earlier that day, oblivious to the scene I'd witnessed between our dad and Henry.

"Do you think there's something... different about Dad?" I asked.

"Different in what way? What do you mean?" Anthony sounded annoyed, like he wanted to get on with settling in.

I didn't know how to explain it to Anthony—this hunch that started as a terrible seed and had grown into an invasive vine, threatening to take over. I opened my mouth but said nothing.

"Lena, what do you mean by 'different'?" he asked impatiently.

I hesitated, my dread rising. I wasn't sure I wanted to bring Anthony into this. Dad was Anthony's hero. I didn't want to say anything to tarnish that when I wasn't even exactly sure what was going on.

"Nothing really," I said, trying to backtrack. "I just think he's been acting a little strange for a while now, don't you?"

"Not really." He shrugged. "Seems kind of the same to me."

I nodded nervously. "Okay, I'm sure it's nothing. Don't worry," I lied. Little did I know it would be the first of many lies and my future modus operandi. I would become my parents' daughter—a master of deceit.

It wasn't until four years later, at thirteen years old, during a human sexuality class at school, that I finally had a context for what I saw and could connect the dots. We covered homosexuality, which was taught as a cautionary taboo subject. And it was like a lightbulb exploded in my brain. That was what my father and Henry were. Now I had a name for it and a framework to comprehend more fully what I'd witnessed. And it confirmed all my fears—that this was bad, something to be ashamed of, to be kept secret.

Chapter Twenty-Two
FRANK - JOHNSTON, NY
1983

Frank walked into his favorite bakery to buy a pastry and a cup of tea—a ritual he enjoyed about once a week. While waiting for his turn to order, he noticed a man in a white chef's hat putting cannoli into the front case from a big metal tray. The man wore a white coat with the words *Ricky - Pastry Chef* embroidered on the chest. He looked up and locked his chocolate-colored eyes with Frank's, and Frank felt a bolt of electricity course through his veins. He was mesmerized.

Frank must have been staring, because Ricky gave him a sly smile and then turned away, looking back down at the tray. That smile told Frank everything he wanted to know—Ricky liked how Frank was staring and was interested too.

Frank wanted him—instantly.

But he'd made a promise, to Teresa and himself, that he wouldn't have another affair. And for the past four years, Frank had stayed true to that promise. He'd tried to make things work with Teresa, dancing around the truth, the two of them not asking or telling each other too much in order to keep the peace, even having sex occasionally. He and Teresa were living in a ceasefire, a sort of limbo where they weren't miserable but also weren't truly happy.

Ricky left the front counter and went back to the kitchen, out of sight. Frank put in his order then sipped his tea and ate his pastry at one of the café tables, hoping to get another glimpse of Ricky. But it wasn't his lucky day. Or maybe it was, given that this was one of the first times Frank had seriously felt himself weak not only in the knees but also in his resolve to stay loyal to his marriage.

As much as Frank had missed Henry since their breakup, he felt relieved that there were no dalliances to hide or secrets to keep track of. Plus, the AIDS crisis had hit the gay community with a vengeance, adding yet another reason for Frank to not stray outside the safety of his marriage. Frank swore off gay bars, not wanting to take the chance of meeting someone. He hunkered down at work at the Cadillac dealership and the boat club and tried not to go out in the evenings and on weekends to the Village or any other places that might tempt him. What he didn't expect was that the local bakery would be a temptation.

Frank tried to put the exchange out of his mind over the ensuing week but obsessed over different scenarios in which he approached Ricky and asked him out. He stopped by the bakery more often over the next few weeks, hoping to catch Ricky out front, filling the cases. When he did, there were always other customers around. He had to be careful about how he approached Ricky. Frank was still a married man. Eventually, he got his chance early one Friday morning, about a month later, when he walked in and saw Ricky out front again, filling the cases, with no one else in the bakery. Frank leaned over the counter and tried to keep his voice low.

"Hello there. It's good to see you. Every time I come in, this place is so busy. I never have the chance to say hi."

Ricky looked up, a small smile playing on his lips. "To me?" he asked coyly.

Frank pointed at him. "Yeah, you. Who else do you think I mean?" He gave a small laugh.

Ricky looked around then back at Frank. "I know you meant me." He giggled.

Frank loved the sound of it. He also loved Ricky's Spanish accent and wondered where he was from originally. He wanted to know everything about the man.

"Hey, what're you doing tomorrow night?" Frank asked.

Ricky shrugged, putting more pastries in the case. "Depends on what you want to do." He looked back up at Frank and batted his eyelashes.

Frank moved in closer, leaning on the counter. "Whatever you want," he whispered.

Ricky clucked his tongue. "Well, then, I may just have to say yes."

"You'd better. How about I pick you up at eight? Here, write your address." He gestured to the notepad for taking orders, on the counter.

Ricky grabbed a pen from his pocket and scribbled down his address and phone number. He ripped the top sheet off and handed it to Frank. "Don't be late, okay?"

Frank laughed. "No, never."

"What do I wear?" Ricky asked, hands on his hips.

Frank raised his eyebrows and tilted his head to the side, eyeing Ricky. "You look great in a chef's jacket and hat, so I can only imagine how good you'll look in regular clothes."

Ricky swatted his hand at Frank. "Of course I'll wear regular clothes. But I need to have an idea what I'm dressing for, okay? Oh, and the name of the person I'm going out with."

"The name's Frank. And we're going to the Village. Dinner first. Then maybe a club."

Ricky's eyes widened. "Ooh, maybe some dancing?"

"Do you like to dance?" *Please let him be a fabulous dancer.*

"Oh yes, I love to dance. These Puerto Rican hips can move, baby. Wait until you see." Ricky shook his hips slightly for effect.

Puerto Rico. So that's where he's from. Frank had never been there, and his mind conjured up swaying palm trees on beaches with Spanish music playing in the background and Ricky dancing on the beach.

"I'm looking forward to it—trust me," Frank said, feeling his stomach lurch excitedly.

"Great. Then I'll see you tomorrow night at eight o'clock sharp."

"See you then." Frank tapped the counter and turned to leave.

"Oh, and, Frank?" Ricky called.

Frank loved hearing his name in Ricky's accent, with the rolled *r* making it sound so much more sensual. He turned back around, facing Ricky.

"Took you long enough," Ricky said.

Frank laughed and broke into a big smile.

On that first date, they were driving into the city, and another driver cut Frank off on the highway. Ricky gestured to the car, speaking in rapid-fire Spanish.

Frank smiled. "Whoa, listen to you. My God, you sound like Ricky Ricardo," referring to the character on the television show *I Love Lucy.*

To which Ricky replied, "Um, no, he's Cuban!"

"So what? Same thing."

"Oh no, it isn't," Ricky said, snapping his fingers, mock glaring at Frank.

Frank leaned his head back and laughed. Ricky had so much fire in him. Frank adored that.

He fell hard for Ricky, who wound up smashing every one of Frank's self-imposed rules. Frank had never felt such an attraction to anyone in his life. He walked around work during the day, charged up, all his senses heightened. He wanted to know Ricky completely.

The first time he touched Ricky, he actually gasped. It was weeks later, at the end of their third date. They went back to Ricky's place, a small apartment in the same neighborhood as the bakery. Pressed body to body, Frank lost all reason. Good God, he'd never felt such desire. He'd loved being with Henry, who would always hold a special place as the first man Frank had ever been with. But this? Never this. With Ricky, he felt like he was one half of a whole. Like he'd found the missing piece of the puzzle.

Afterward, naked and breathless, side by side in the bed, Frank wanted to feel guilt, regret, or even surprise at what had just happened. But all he felt was an overwhelming sense of relief. And he knew, as of that moment, there was no going back. Frank had stepped out of one existence and into another. He was sure Ricky would be his undoing.

Chapter Twenty-Three
TERESA - NEW ROCHELLE, NY
1983

Teresa sat by her mother's hospital bed, listening to the hum of the machines hooked up to Rosa to handle her breathing. Rosa was now what people called a vegetable. Teresa cringed at the word. It didn't describe her beautiful mother.

Teresa had become so consumed with raising her children and navigating a difficult marriage that she hadn't seen her mother as much as she would have liked in recent years. There were frequent phone calls, and she tried to take the kids to see their *nonna* from time to time, but she wished she'd tried harder. Regret tugged at her. But as Teresa looked at her dear mother, the regret faded away. Rosa knew how much Teresa loved her. She was a sweet, forgiving woman, often to a fault, putting up with her husband's drinking and bullying and her son Marco's drug addiction and dependency. Teresa was grateful her older brother, Sal, had never caused Rosa any heartache—well, other than moving away, of course. She'd been in touch with him constantly for the last two weeks, giving him updates on Rosa's condition. Teresa dreaded calling him once Rosa passed, knowing it would make this nightmare even more real. And Marco—she didn't even want to think about what a mess he would be.

She took Rosa's hand and spoke to her, unsure if Rosa could hear her. "Okay, Ma. If you need to go, I understand. I don't want you to. I'll miss you so much. I don't want to be here without you. But if you can't find your way back, if it's too hard, then go toward the light." Teresa broke down, sobbing, and clung to her mother's frail, limp hand. She lingered there for a while, kissing her mother's hand over and over and rubbing it against her cheek.

The last two weeks had felt like an eternity. They'd been excruciating. It had all happened so fast. Rosa had collapsed at home, and when she arrived at New Rochelle Hospital, tests revealed that an aneurysm had burst in her brain, causing her to go into a coma. Teresa prayed to Mother Mary, Jesus, God, the Holy Spirit, and any other celestial being who would listen. *Please, I'm not ready. I can't lose my mother.* But she knew she had to let go, and it tore her apart inside.

Rosa passed away minutes later, as if she'd been waiting for her daughter to give her permission. Teresa breathed deeply, putting her head between her legs to ward off the feeling that she might faint. Her mother was gone at only sixty-six years old. And Teresa was thirty-two—too young to be left with no parents in the world. Her father, Sergio, had died years before, and now Teresa was officially an orphan.

"I know you'll be fine without me," she imagined her mother saying. Teresa patted her mother's motionless hand gently and lovingly and tried to convince herself this was true.

Teresa needed to get some air. She went out to the nurse's station to let them know her mother had passed. The head nurse immediately jumped into motion. She came around the counter and placed her hand gently on Teresa's shoulder. "I am so sorry for your loss."

Teresa knew the nurse must say those words constantly, but they sounded genuine. She felt the tears flowing down her cheeks and was grateful for this kind woman who'd taken such good care of her mother the last two weeks.

"Thank you so much," she whispered. "I need a little break. If my husband comes, please let him know what happened and that I stepped outside for a little while." She knew Frank was on his way to the hospital after work.

"Sure thing, dear. We'll take care of things for your mother. Take your time, and come back up when you're ready."

Teresa rode the elevator down to the ground level, feeling claustrophobic in the small space, like she was suffocating. She felt an overwhelming need to escape to the outdoors and be in nature. As she walked out into the blinding sunlight, she couldn't help but find it strange that her mother had passed away but the sun continued to shine. She walked around the perimeter of the parking lot, stretching her legs, cramped from sitting in a hospital chair for so many hours.

Then she caught sight of Frank's car, parked in a remote spot along the edge of the lot. *Oh, thank goodness, he's here.* She breathed a sigh of relief that she wouldn't be alone anymore.

She walked closer to the car, approaching Frank's driver's-side window. And then she stopped short, like she'd hit a brick wall. For there was Frank, leaning over the passenger seat, smiling, his arm on the shoulder of a man she'd never seen before—a man who was smiling back at Frank, one hand cupping the back of Frank's neck. In a flash, the features of the man impressed themselves upon Teresa's consciousness, like acid eating away at a photograph—the brown eyes, the thick dark lashes, the curl of hair that swooped down onto his forehead. And she knew immediately that he was Frank's lover.

A thousand questions competed for Teresa's attention: *Who is he? Where did they meet? When did Frank start seeing him? How long has it been going on? Why is he doing this again? Is it serious?* The questions bounced from one side of her brain to another like a pinball machine. She felt nauseated. At that moment, Frank looked up through the window, and an expression of horror and guilt crossed his face. She turned and ran.

Behind her, Frank screamed, "Teresa!"

"No" was all she got out. It sounded garbled, like she was underwater.

Don't turn around. She wouldn't, couldn't. All she wanted was to escape this pain. She'd just lost her mother and couldn't take any more. This revelation felt like a whole separate loss as she accepted the truth that Frank would never change. That he couldn't. That the moments of hope she'd clung to over the last few years during their ceasefire were like little life rafts—memories of who they'd once been.

Teresa reached the hospital, burst through the main doors, and hit the elevator button as if her house was on fire and she was trying to escape the flames. She felt like the doors were opening in slow motion. She stepped inside and turned to face Frank, hitting the button for the third floor. He reached his hand out to stop the doors from closing.

"Teresa, I'm so sorry. I didn't intend for you to find out like this."

That was when she felt it. Rage. It boiled up from within and burst through her like a tsunami. She spit out her words. "How dare you, Frank? Bringing him here, of all places."

The elevator starting chiming as Frank continued to hold the door open. "He was just going to wait in the car, not come in. I—"

"You know what, Frank? Stay with your fucking boyfriend. I don't want you upstairs. You don't deserve to say goodbye to my mother. You're too late anyway. She died a little while ago." An involuntary wail escaped her, tears threatening to overtake her.

"Oh my God, Teresa, I'm so sorry," Frank said, reaching out his other hand to touch her, but she flinched back. "Truly I am. Your mother was such a sweet woman—a saint."

"Yes, Frank, she was a saint for putting up with my father, and I'm realizing I'm taking after her in more ways than one. Get out of my sight!" Her voice was like venom dripping with tears, spittle, and years of frustration.

Teresa shoved his arm away from the elevator doors, and they closed. Frank stood in shock as he disappeared behind them.

ACT 3: THE TRUTH SHALL SET YOU FREE

Chapter Twenty-Four
LENA - LOS ANGELES, CA
August 2015

I stared down at the cake my colleagues had ordered with Way to Go! blazoned across the top. I was basking in the win's glow. It felt so good to have the Hawke Health Care case behind me—like I was coming down from balancing on a high wire.

I grabbed one more piece of cake and accepted congratulatory high fives from a few more colleagues as I headed out of the conference room.

"And where do you think you're going?" Marcus asked.

"To my office. I feel so behind from that damn trial. Thought I'd go catch up on some things before the weekend."

The grueling trial had gone on for weeks. In the end, we'd not only won but had also entered a consent decree to ensure system-wide changes that would positively affect all female physicians who worked for Hawke. This was everything we'd hoped for and more, helping topple the long-standing inequity that Hawke had allowed to fester over many years.

He shook his head. "Nope. You're taking the afternoon off." He pointed his finger at me and lifted his eyebrows. I opened my mouth to speak, but he cut me off. "I'm serious. Get out of here. That's an order."

I smiled, nodding. "Okay, I will. Thank you."

"You deserve it. Well done, counselor. Seriously." He clapped me on the shoulder. "That was some amazing work. You should be proud of yourself. I know I am."

A warm feeling spread through my insides. I couldn't help reacting to Marcus's praise. His opinion meant so much to me. I worried that I actually might be blushing, which was not my typical response. I ducked out before saying something corny and making a fool of myself.

I hoped it would be smooth sailing from now until my dad's wedding. Other than a quick business trip to San Francisco, nothing on my agenda would take up that much mental space. I was looking forward to a less stressful month ahead.

To kick it off, Kevin and I were going to dinner that night to celebrate the win. And the next day, I was meeting up with Kate in person for the first time since the bar association dinner the previous month. We'd emailed back and forth, texted, and spoken on the phone a few times, but this was the first time our schedules matched up.

I went to my office to grab my laptop. I quickly scanned my email and saw a new message from my dad with the subject line, *Mock-up of wedding invitation*. I opened it and saw an image of an envelope with the names Magdalena Antinori and Kevin Ryan in a beautiful calligraphy font. I smiled and clicked the digital envelope to open the wedding invitation.

Frank and Oliver are pleased to invite you to their wedding ceremony and reception on the 17th of October, 2015, at Terranea Resort in Rancho Palos Verdes.

Beneath the fancy black font was a silhouette of two grooms in tuxedos with matching red pocket squares. The image was simple and elegant, and I felt myself getting excited about the wedding for the first time. But the moment quickly passed as I heard footsteps in the hallway and reflexively closed the digital wedding invitation.

I glanced over my shoulder toward the door, hoping no one had walked by and seen the screen. Toby came into view, slowing down near my open door. Of all people, he would probably be totally accepting of me having a gay father. I pictured telling him and the two of us bonding over it and then caught myself. For God's sake, this wasn't show-and-tell in elementary school. And work certainly wasn't the time or place to have an intimate conversation with Toby. Besides, I hardly knew him. I'd just divulged my secret to Kate after not sharing my family history with almost anyone. That was enough. Gay people had always been there, and it was wonderful that they didn't have to hide as much anymore. But I'd lived a private life and planned to keep it that way. I didn't enjoy being the center of attention with personal stuff. Accolades for my career? Fine. My personal business? Off-limits.

"Hi, Lena. Great work on that case. I hope to get to work with you on the next one. Can I make a formal request?" he asked, grinning.

"Thank you. Yes, let's do it. Next case, you're on the team. I'll call first dibs on you, okay?"

"Sounds good," he said, saluting casually then continuing down the hallway.

Suddenly, I felt guilty for slamming my laptop shut and worrying about someone at work seeing my father and Oliver's beautiful wedding invitation. I didn't need to hide this from them. They were lawyers specializing in employment law, and I couldn't think of any who'd ever given me the impression they were homophobic.

I realized with a jolt that I'd been lying about my behavior, just like my dad had lied about his for years. Even my mom had lied by staying in the marriage and not disclosing the truth after she knew about my dad. We were a family of liars and hypocrites. When would it end?

People talked about straddling two worlds, but I'd never achieved that perfect balance. It was like living my life inside a masquerade ball—carefully holding up a mask to shield my identity. It took so much work.

What would it be like to drop the mask?

I was always eavesdropping on a quarrel between internal opposing voices. One voice was the attorney. It remained skeptical, only revealing facts when absolutely necessary. It didn't play its hand until the odds of winning were high. The other was a voice I hardly ever heard, of someone who wanted to throw strategy out the window. Who yearned to be free. To no longer hide. "Wait!" it cried. "Don't run away. Don't be afraid."

As I walked to my car, I thought about heading home to unwind for a few hours before meeting Kevin for dinner. But then I glimpsed my hands holding the steering wheel and knew exactly what to do. In the last two months between prepping for the trial and Dad's big day, I'd lost my battle with my former nasty habit and had bitten my fingernails to the quick. The state of my hands was embarrassing. I needed a set of acrylic tips stat. This would be the perfect opportunity to get them done. The salon I typically went to near my house was tiny and booked up far in advance. It would be a mob scene on a Friday afternoon, with everyone gearing up for weekend plans.

I checked Yelp and found a salon a few miles away that got excellent reviews, so I headed there. When I walked in, I was happy it was clean and didn't smell of nail polish toxins like some salons did. I looked around and saw some women getting pedicures down the line of chairs, most on their smart phones or reading a magazine and one who looked like she'd fallen asleep. No one was getting a manicure at the moment, and I hoped that meant I didn't have to wait.

A technician with big red hair, glasses, and a pink smock approached me. "Can I help you, sweetie?"

"Yes, I'd like a set of acrylics, please."

"Sure, seventy-five dollars for a full set, 'kay?"

"That's fine, thanks," I said, making a mental note to add this to the other costs of planning this wedding. My nails had been gorgeous a few months back. Nothing like massive amounts of stress to bring back a nasty childhood habit I thought I'd left in the rearview mirror, along with other parts of my past.

"Pick out a color in that basket and then take a seat at the first station, hon. I'll be right over," the technician said.

I smiled, went over to the basket, and picked out a gorgeous burgundy called You Had Me at Merlot. I loved the movie *Jerry Maguire*, and I also loved wine. *Score.*

I sat down and started chitchatting with the technician, whose name tag read Diane. She looked like a Diane. She seemed funny and warm, and I liked her instantly.

The doorbell jingled. Diane looked up and didn't look pleased. She pursed her lips and tightened her jaw. "Can I help you?"

Someone behind me said, "Yes, I'd like to get a manicure, please." The voice sounded like a woman's, but I was pretty sure it was a man with a feminine voice.

Diane hesitated and looked back down as if she needed to give my nails immediate attention. *Why is she stalling and not giving this person her full attention?* I was uncomfortable knowing she was ignoring him. I looked at her intently and nodded to convey that she should turn back to the person at the door.

After what seemed like an interminable amount of time, she finally spoke. "Oh, I'm sorry. I'm fully booked this afternoon. I don't have time for a walk-in." She said all of this without looking up.

I shifted in my seat. Something told me she was lying—call it the lawyer in me or intuition, but I was getting the definite impression that Diane didn't want to do this person's nails.

I finally turned around to look at the person by the door, doing so slowly and nonchalantly, with a smile on my face. I saw a man in a beautiful, bright poncho, high-heeled boots, and a perfectly made-up face. Only his nails weren't picture perfect, with chipped purple polish past its prime. He desperately needed a manicure. That I could see.

"Oh, that's too bad," he said, sounding disappointed but also annoyed. He didn't budge from where he stood. He lifted one finger to his mouth and bit the edge of his cuticle. "I really could use a manicure. I can wait—that's no problem."

"No, that won't work. I don't have any openings today, I'm afraid." This time, Diane looked up and stared right at him, unwavering, and it startled me to see that she looked downright mean. Her entire face had transformed into something malevolent. Not at all friendly.

"I see," the man by the door said. I could hear frustration and resignation in his voice.

He sighed heavily and clicked his tongue like a teacher would at a student who'd stepped out of line. Then he looked at me inquisitively, cocking his head, resembling a dog being asked a question. I sat there, dumbfounded, glued to my seat, unable to move a muscle or utter a word. I wanted to scream at Diane, "Are you kidding me?" But I didn't. I wanted to say, "I'm sorry" to him. Despite that, I said nothing. I gave him a small sympathetic smile, like you would to the last kid left on the playground who didn't get selected to play on anyone's team.

Then I slowly turned back around and faced Diane. I heard the bell jingle again, and the door closed with a thud. The salon seemed so quiet even though the background music still played.

Diane tsk-tsked. "I'm not doing his nails—no, sir." She wasn't really addressing me in particular, but there was no one else in earshot.

I couldn't help myself. "Why?" I asked, already regretting where this was heading but letting myself get sucked in.

"You know. Because he's one of them."

One of them. I knew that was what was going on but had thought she would use some other sorry excuse. Instead, she'd said it as plainly as could be.

"What do you mean, 'one of them'?" I wanted her to spell it out. To say it out loud. I had to hear it.

"You know... a fairy."

Wow. She'd said it so matter-of-factly, like she was giving me the score of a baseball game.

Heat crept up my neck and into my face. Beads of sweat broke out on my upper lip, and I felt my heart rate speed up. I was afraid one of my panic attacks was coming on. Thank God I was already sitting down. *Breathe, Lena, breathe.* I counted to myself: *One one thousand, two one thousand, three one thousand.* I was relieved to feel my breathing steady.

I knew I should just leave it alone. I wasn't at work—no longer on the clock. But I couldn't help myself. "Listen, what you just did—refusing to serve someone because of who they are—that's illegal."

Diane kept buffing my nails and took her sweet time responding. "What're you, a lawyer or something?"

"Yes, as a matter of fact, I am."

"Well, this is a small establishment. Privately owned. We can serve who we want, okay?"

"No, actually, you can't. There's a state law in place that forbids not serving a customer who's part of a protected class. And sexual orientation is one of those."

She shifted in her seat, looking uncomfortable. *Good. That makes two of us.* She chewed on her lip. We were both silent for a beat.

"Hmm, well, okay, then. I guess now I know," she said perfunctorily.

Her response wasn't an apology for what she'd done. Or the epithet she'd spewed. I wanted to demand more. To make her take back what she'd done, what she'd said. To force her to stuff her homophobia down her throat.

I thought of the look on the man's face—defeated. It reminded me of the look on my dad's crumpled face when he'd told me years before that he was gay—the way his shoulders had sagged like he was the child and I the parent—humiliated and belittled by merely being who he was. I thought of all the times he'd been made to feel like a freak just because he loved someone like I loved Kevin. I sat there, dumbstruck, unable to take this woman to task, wondering where the lawyer who spun words for a living had gone.

Diane changed the subject with a wave of her hand as if she were dismissing what just happened as not important enough to even continue talking about. She started blabbering about a television talk show she loved and one guest who'd been on it that morning. I didn't pay any attention. I was totally inside my head, having a debate over what I should have said while the man was in the doorway, how I could have handled the entire situation better, and what a coward I was.

After a few minutes, the fog in my head lifted, and I stared at Diane's red hair, so sad that I was afraid I would cry right there. I knew exactly what I wanted to say now. It came to me way too late. What I wanted to say was "That could be my father. I am the daughter of a gay man, and I definitely won't be getting my nails done here. You just lost a customer. Be careful of what you say... you never know who's sitting across from you." But I didn't say any of that. Not a word.

I was ashamed of myself. I'd missed an opportunity to stand up not just for the gay man in the doorway, or gay men in general, but for my dad in particular. But I didn't stand up. I just sat there.

Chapter Twenty-Five
TERESA - JOHNSTON, NY
1983

Teresa saw the car in front of her momentarily inch forward and took her foot briefly off the brake to follow suit. She was trying to snap out of the funk she'd been in since Rosa's death. That night, she'd picked Lena up from track practice, but she wasn't in any mood to cook so was at McDonald's, in line at the drive-through. She had no interest in going inside and being around strangers. She looked over at Lena, who appeared lost in thought.

Teresa's thoughts wandered to Frank, who took up so much space in her mind even though she'd ignored him in the weeks since her mother had died, only speaking to him in cryptic sentences when absolutely necessary.

He tried to engage her when they were alone, making excuses for his behavior. "It's not what you think. It doesn't mean anything. I won't see him anymore. I slipped up, but it won't happen again."

Lies and more lies but no apologies. *Is this how it ends—sixteen years of marriage dismissed with a few angry words and a closed elevator door?*

Teresa knew in her heart that figuring this out would be insurmountable. Her patience was as brittle and thin as a sheet of ice ready to melt. Frank would never change. She could never make him change. The situation with Frank had stripped away all her innocence, and the only answer that kept coming to her was *Get out*. But then this voice in her head would reply, *Easier said than done*.

Some couples divorced and survived it. It didn't look easy. She'd have to get a full-time job. Frank would have to pay child support, and they'd have to set up a visitation schedule for Anthony and Lena.

She cringed, realizing she'd be a divorcée. Many married people viewed divorce as a communicable disease. It branded a woman as someone who couldn't make her marriage work and was now prowling after other women's husbands to steal them away so she'd have a man again to provide for her and her children. *Jesus*.

Even worse, not only couldn't she get her marriage to work, but she couldn't even get her husband to want to be with a woman, or at least not with her. People would view her as a total failure. A dread filled her, seeping through her blood like an injection of ice water.

He should leave. I should have kicked him out years ago. It wasn't enough anymore that they had children together. Teresa didn't want Anthony and Lena to be children of divorce but worried about hurting them more by staying in a sham of a marriage. She didn't want them to see her resentment and anger and wonder why she'd allowed it to go on so long.

She pulled up to the drive-through window and ordered a Big Mac for Anthony, a Quarter Pounder for herself, and a small hamburger and fries for Lena.

"Can we pull over and eat it here? I don't think I can wait until we get home. I'm so hungry," Lena whined.

"Sure," Teresa said.

Anthony wouldn't be home from his wrestling tournament for another hour. Once they got their order, Teresa pulled into a parking spot, and they began to eat. Lena attacked her food with gusto, shoveling french fries in her mouth.

"Slow down," Teresa admonished. "You'll get sick if you eat so fast. You should have a snack before track practice. It isn't good to be this hungry."

Lena nodded, smiling while chewing. She swallowed. "Good idea. I swear Coach is trying to kill us at practice."

Teresa laughed and leaned back in her seat, enjoying her food at a slower pace. She glanced to the right and saw two men walking across the back of the parking lot, holding hands. Teresa felt flushed. She glanced over at Lena to see if she'd noticed them. Lena was eating her hamburger, looking down at her lap. She glanced up at Teresa and instantly turned toward the two men as if Teresa had been pointing that way with a neon sign that read, Look to Your Right.

Lena stopped eating, watching the men intently. One of them leaned over and kissed the other full on the mouth. Fear gripped Teresa as she watched her daughter observe the scene. She tried to swallow the last bite of food she'd taken, but it felt like a ball in her mouth.

Lena turned to Teresa and whispered, "Mom? I think I know what Dad is."

"What? What do you mean, what he is?"

Of course, Teresa knew exactly what Lena meant. But she was shocked.

Lena looked at her sheepishly. "Do you think Dad likes men... sort of, he *like* likes them?"

Teresa sat, dumbfounded, not trusting herself to speak. She busied herself by wiping her mouth with a napkin, stalling for time. Then she reached for Lena's hand.

"I think some of Dad's friends are... more than friends," Lena continued.

Teresa squeezed her hand hard, willing her to go on.

"Like Henry. I saw them on the boat a few years ago and wondered about them." Lena's eyes looked like big glassy orbs as tears built up but didn't flow.

"Oh, Lena, honey..." Teresa soothed. "I'm so sorry. I wish you'd come to me."

"I wanted to tell you—honestly, I did. But I was scared."

"Scared of telling me? You know you can tell me anything."

Lena wailed, letting the sobs escape. "No, Mom, I was scared of being right. About what it would mean. About hurting you."

"Sweetheart, what did you see that made you wonder about them? It's okay. You can tell me now."

Lena looked out the window as if the past lay there, off in the distance. "It's hard to explain. It was just a moment, but I felt like I caught them together. They looked like... a couple."

Teresa stroked Lena's hand. "It breaks my heart that you were scared. You must have felt so alone."

"I tried talking to Anthony, but he didn't think anything was wrong. So I started doubting myself. But then we had that sex ed class in school this semester, 'member?" She hiccupped as another sob escaped. "And we learned about... homosexuality. And I knew I'd been right."

Lena started sobbing harder, and Teresa hugged her, stroking her hair and whispering, "Shh, it's okay, Lena. It's okay."

"No, it's not, Mom. I know what Dad is. He's one of them." Lena was breathing fast, and Teresa could feel her trembling. Her forehead was sweating, and her sobs morphed into choking.

"Lena, calm down, sweetie. You're making me nervous."

Lena frenetically shook her hands. "I feel strange. My heart is going too fast. I feel like I can't breathe."

"Breathe, Lena, now. Breathe slowly with me." Teresa rubbed Lena's back. *What is happening?* She breathed deeply in and out, and Lena mimicked her. "That's it. In... and out. In... and out."

A minute later, which felt excruciatingly long to Teresa, Lena's breathing had stabilized. Her face was pale, but Teresa was relieved that overall, Lena was noticeably calmer.

"Lena, listen to me." Teresa grabbed a napkin from the pile and gently wiped her daughter's tear-strewn face. "Thank you for telling me. I'm sorry you had to carry that for so long by yourself. I love you. We'll talk more about this—I promise. But for now, let's go home. I want you to rest and stay calm, you hear me? You scared the hell out of me just now." Teresa caught a sob in her own throat and hugged Lena firmly.

For a while, Teresa had sensed that her daughter knew what was going on but hoped she didn't know the extent of it. Teresa wanted to protect her. So she'd lied to Lena about Frank's late nights and absences over the years, providing cover for his indiscretions. Now the harsh reality dawned on her: she'd been teaching Lena how to lie as well. To be a liar. And here was her thirteen-year-old daughter, telling her she knew exactly what was going on, and all Teresa could think was *Who in the world did we think we were fooling?*

Teresa felt heavy with the weight of lies. There were so many layers.

When they got home, Lena went straight upstairs to her room, and Teresa knew what she was doing. She was writing in that diary of hers. Teresa often wondered what she put in there. She was the one to give Lena her first journal. She'd wanted Lena to have a place to write out her emotions, the way Teresa had with her journals over the years. She realized that the thing to do at the moment was to give Lena the space to let her thoughts flow. This was one way she saw herself in her daughter—the place they felt most comfortable telling the truth was to a blank page. They both held so much in and didn't share with others... and then it spilled out on paper.

With their dog, Libby, in her arms, Teresa shuffled upstairs to her bedroom. She gingerly opened her nightstand and pulled out her journal, knowing she would find the entry in blue ink with the words she'd written on the night her mother died. She reached for those words now, grasping at the truth.

This wasn't all in her head. It wasn't just a bad dream she could wake up from. It was a reality. And she'd finally come to terms with it. And that meant she had to let Frank go. Teresa was already lonely with Frank. Now she needed to learn how to be alone without him.

She flipped through the pages with shaking hands until she saw the entry. There it was, taunting her, reminding her she was making the right decision even though it was killing her inside.

That night, when she'd arrived home from the hospital, she'd come to a conclusion that became the turning point of her marriage and life. She'd known about her husband years before, but until she wrote it down with her own hand, it hadn't seemed real. Now as she stared at those words, it was all too real. For there they were, calling her out, no longer letting her stay in denial—the words she'd never fully spoken out loud.

My husband is gay.

A few nights later, Teresa was busy making one of her mother's favorite meals for dinner, *pasta e piselli*. It was the kids' last day of school, and she always made this for them to start the summer. She didn't want to disappoint them. Plus, she was a ball of nerves, and cooking usually calmed her down. But not that night.

Frank was late getting home for dinner—again. And this time, she didn't have to wonder where he was. She knew. She now had a picture in her mind of what Frank's lies looked like. Frank was with the guy she'd seen in his car in the parking lot of the hospital. His boyfriend. She'd been such a fool. Well, she was done being a fool. No more.

Tonight would change everything—her marriage, her family, her kids, and her life. She was going to ask Frank to leave. No, not ask. Demand. It was time. She'd had enough.

Frank sauntered in a half hour later and washed up at the sink. He looked so at ease, unperturbed that he'd made them all wait. Teresa called Anthony and Lena to the table as she brought over the serving bowl heaped with pasta.

"Kids, time to eat—c'mon."

Anthony scurried to the table and plopped down in a chair. "It's about time. I'm starving."

She turned to Frank. "Yes, it *is* about time. Why are you late? I told you we were eating at six tonight."

Teresa knew the answer but wanted him to have the courage to say it—to say anything other than the crap he'd been feeding her for years. He'd say nothing close to the truth—she knew that. But it didn't stop her from chiding him. She was fed up. Their marriage had been nothing but lies. Years of them.

"I was at the boatyard. I told you that," he replied.

Lame excuses, like always. And the kids sat there listening to them and watching her accept them. She couldn't take it anymore. Her pulse throbbed in her temples, and she felt like her head was going to explode. All the years of pent-up frustration and disappointment threatened to break the surface.

"No, you most certainly did not."

"Well, I thought I did. Either way, I was at the boatyard. That's it."

She fumed at his dismissive tone. "That's not it, Frank, and we both know it. There's a lot more going on, isn't there?"

He stared at her, a frightened look in his eyes. "Teresa, what are you doing? Stop with the theatrics."

She was tired of being made a fool, like she was insane for imagining what was really going on. Something inside Teresa broke loose.

She grabbed her plate of spaghetti and peas and hurled it in Frank's direction. He crouched down, hands over his head to protect himself, and it hit the wall with so much force it surprised her it didn't break through. She saw the incredulous look on his face, like he was dealing with a madwoman and didn't recognize her.

"Theatrics? Oh, that's a good one. These are your theatrics, Frank."

He stood, gripping the sides of the table. "Don't be hysterical, Teresa. Nothing's going on."

There was a time when she would have bought it—when she'd wanted nothing more than to accept his excuses, to keep loving him, to not lose him for good. But that time had long passed. Memories flooded Teresa's mind: Frank's late nights, her emotional overeating, his flirting with Henry, seeing him with his lover in the car right after losing her mother. All that was bad enough. And then on top of it, to find out Lena had suspected for years and kept it hidden. What a burden that must have been.

"Why don't we talk about the real subject, Frank? The one we keep avoiding."

She hadn't planned to say anything in front of the kids. She'd envisioned confronting Frank in private later, after dinner—just the two of them having it out. But she'd be damned if she would let him continue to paint the picture of her as the crazed wife with a wild imagination, when they both knew that was a complete farce.

Frank's lips quivered, and he glanced nervously around the room, like an animal backed into a corner. "Teresa, please, that's enough." His eyes softened, pleading with her silently to stop, to keep his secrets, to continue buying his lies.

No more. I'm done.

"Yes, it is. Enough is enough, Frank. You aren't fooling anyone anymore. Your own daughter knows what's going on—a thirteen-year-old."

Frank turned frantically to Lena, who looked like she was trying to make herself disappear. Anthony stopped eating, his face in shock, trying to register what was happening.

Teresa then heard herself say the words she should have had the courage to say years ago. "Get out, Frank. Get out of this house now."

Anthony jolted upright and cried, "What do you mean, get out?"

"I mean, I want your father to leave," Teresa said calmly.

Frank didn't budge or move a muscle. "Teresa, please stop. Let's talk about this later. Alone." He was trying to talk his way out of this, the way he always did.

Stay strong. You need to do this. For yourself and for the kids. Anthony would be heartbroken, but the best thing for him wasn't for her to continue this charade. And Lena knew exactly what was going on. Teresa wouldn't force her daughter to live a lie any longer.

"No, Frank. No more talking. We've lived with this secret long enough. I'm not doing this anymore. I'm done."

She hurled the entire serving bowl across the table. She watched it crack against the wall, spilling the precious food she'd taken so much time to prepare, the bowl now in pieces, ruined. She didn't care. It was inconsequential. Leftover debris from her failed marriage.

Teresa glared at Frank, who looked defeated, sinking back in his chair. She clenched her jaw. He was the one who'd broken his promise not to begin another affair. He was the one who should leave. But he just sat there while she blew up in front of their kids, throwing plates. And as he did, she felt an overwhelming sense of claustrophobia. She couldn't stand another minute in his presence, living this lie. She had to escape, to get out of there.

"If you won't leave, I will." The words were out of her mouth before she'd processed what she was saying. She didn't have time to second-guess her next move.

As if her body had a mind of its own, she felt herself get up from the table, go into the kitchen, grab her purse and keys, and head for the back door.

"Mom, no! Don't go!" Lena cried. Her frightened voice broke Teresa's heart. She hoped Lena and Anthony could forgive her someday.

Teresa turned the knob on the back door, opened it, and stepped outside. She marched to her car, flung open the door, and sat in the driver's seat, hands trembling as she tried to put the key in the ignition. Her mind raced, thoughts tumbling over each other. *What have I done? Where will I go? How long will I stay away? Am I prepared to come back and kick him out? What if he won't leave? And how could I leave my kids behind?*

Teresa shook her head, forcing those thoughts to take a back seat. She couldn't deal with them at the moment. All she knew was that she couldn't go back inside. She needed to get away. She started the engine, took one quick glance back at the house with her fractured family still inside, and drove away.

Chapter Twenty-Six
LENA - SEAL BEACH, CA
August 2015

I jumped in my Fiat to head to Seal Beach, where Kate lived with her husband and two teenage girls. I adored that town and knew it well because Kevin had lived there before we married. We spent a lot of time there while dating, so it was a happy place to revisit. Plus, it was on the ocean, which always blissed me out. *Like father, like daughter.*

The plan was to take a yoga class at Kate's favorite studio, followed by brunch at the Crema Cafe, one of Kevin's and my favorite former spots.

Kate reminded me by text, *Self-care is a must. Smiley face emoji.*

I promised to decompress and recharge, adding that I hoped not to injure myself. Plus, I'd made her swear she would go for a run with me next weekend as payback.

I'm looking forward to that, I thought deviously.

It was a gorgeous morning devoid of the marine layer of fog that usually engulfed the Los Angeles area in the early hours of the day. The convertible top was down, and I pulled my hair back in a ponytail so it wouldn't be a tangled mess when I arrived. I was glad Kevin had a softball game with his work league that morning so I didn't feel bad cutting out on him.

I chuckled, remembering his comment as I left: "Have fun with your new best friend."

Yoga was harder than I expected. Not the actual poses. I was flexible thanks to good dance genes and training. It was the deep-breathing technique that proved difficult.

"Don't worry," Kate whispered, "you'll get the ujjayi breathing eventually. It takes a lot of practice."

"That's if I don't faint trying," I said, trying to sound self-deprecating instead of self-conscious.

She laughed and then caught herself and made a serious face to cover up, which made me laugh. We were acting like two high school girls.

"Sorry," I stage whispered. "I promise not to get you kicked out of your favorite studio." I put my finger to my lips and made the universal shush-mouth shape.

She widened her eyes and said quietly, "Me? It's you. Stop making me laugh."

I smiled and went back to trying to do whatever the hell that deep-breathing technique was called. Man, I missed running.

When class ended, we freshened up and headed to the café, where we ate scones, sipped cappuccinos, and shared tales of our legal careers, trying to one-up each other with who had the better war story. She was as intrigued by my legal career as I was by hers. And we could have gone on like that for hours, I suspected.

But what I really wanted to talk about was our family backgrounds—specifically, my gay father and her lesbian mother. My heart fluttered. I broached the subject gingerly. "So, I was thinking about our upbringing and how amazing it is that we have something so unusual in common. I'd love to know more about your experience with it all."

Kate smiled. "I was wondering when you'd get around to asking about that."

"Am I that obvious?" I asked, feeling exposed.

"Not at all. I figured we'd talk about it. I just didn't want to push after seeing how hard it was for you to talk about it when we met."

"Thank you. I appreciate that. But I'm actually curious. I find myself thinking of so many questions to ask you, but I don't want to annoy you. I mean, you're not some specimen to dissect. I just don't really have anyone else with firsthand knowledge to talk to about it with, except my brother."

She nodded. "I would love to tell you about my experience and ask you more about yours, if you're open to it, of course. And I can share more about other people who have LGBTQ parents too. Remember, I'm involved with that nonprofit group I told you about. They're called COLAGE—Children of Lesbians and Gays Everywhere."

"Wow, how is it I've never even heard of them and I work in the discrimination field?" I felt kind of stupid for admitting that.

"I don't think it's strange you haven't heard of them until now. They're not humongous, and unless someone tells you about them or you do an online search using those types of keywords, I don't think they'd come across your radar. They're not a legal-advocacy group technically. More of a support organization."

"Got it. Well, I'd like to know more about them for sure. Kind of fascinating that there's an entire group of people... like us. But I'd like to start by talking about our own backgrounds first. Is that okay?"

"Absolutely. Ask me anything. Seriously. I think it'll be good for both of us."

Kate was being kind. It was blatantly obvious that she was way further along in her journey of being the daughter of an LGBTQ parent than I was. Heck, if I were being honest, I wasn't even sure I'd taken the first sure steps. If this were the infamous Yellow Brick Road, she was in Oz and I was still dealing with the aftershock of the initial tornado.

"How about another cappuccino?" I asked. "On me. I have a feeling this could take a while."

"You got it. Order away, and then fire away. Let's do this."

I got us two more cappuccinos and brought them back to the table. Fortified with more caffeine, I swallowed, took a deep breath, and dove in. "Did your mother know before or after she married your father?"

"Oh, she knew," Kate said. "She hid it when she married my father. Besides, she really wanted kids, and let's face it, that was the safest and surest way to do that back then. When she told my father she was leaving him for Marie, he was devastated—embarrassed, humiliated, and a little depressed. But eventually... he bounced back. He remarried a few years later, and I have a wonderful stepmother and two stepbrothers. Funny, now I have three moms." She laughed. "What about your parents?"

"My father grew up Catholic, and you know what that means. It was off-limits." I thought about my next statement before voicing it. "I think he also really loved my mother."

Kate nodded. "I think my mother loved my father, too, and I'm sure that made it harder to leave, besides what an enormous risk it was for her to come out."

I sighed and took a sip to wet my dry mouth and stall for a moment. "My mom said she knew about my dad for years. She denied it, hid it, then finally decided she deserved better—to be with someone who wanted to be with her unconditionally and faithfully. I think she also wanted my father to be able to fully be himself."

"What a gift she gave both of them. She sounds very brave."

I nodded, and my eyes filled with tears, but I held them back. "Yes," I whispered. "A gift he may not have deserved as he cheated on her so many times."

"I understand," Kate said. "It's hard to forget the pain of that betrayal, no matter how much you want to. It's even harder when it's wrapped up in someone's closeted sexual identity. You don't want to blame them for trying to be who they really are, but you also don't want to excuse harmful behavior. There's so much to untangle and process."

I stared at her, a bit in awe of how she was giving voice to thoughts that had plagued me over the years. My God, did she get it. It felt like she was peering inside my head.

"When did you know?" I asked. That was the most pressing question on my mind, probably because I'd known for so long and hidden it.

"I didn't know until my mother made her big announcement when I was sixteen. Maybe I should have seen breadcrumbs or clues, but I didn't until after the fact. What about you?"

"I knew from a very young age. Nine, if you can believe it. But I didn't tell anyone for years. I was confused and didn't want it to be true. I finally told my mom what I suspected when I was thirteen. A few days later, she kicked my dad out. I somewhat blamed myself for their breakup, although my mom told me she'd caught my dad having yet another affair with a man a few weeks before. She swore my revelation was merely the last straw and not the main reason for her decision." My voice quivered, and I took another sip of coffee. "Wow, I've never told anyone all of that except Kevin."

Kate leaned across the table and squeezed my hand, smiling supportively. "Thanks for confiding in me. It's not easy being queer spawn."

"Queer spawn?" I repeated with a note of distaste. I didn't like the sound of that phrase. It reminded me of *devil's spawn*—not a good association.

"Yup, that's what we're called," Kate said, amused. "And by the look on your face, I can tell you hate the term." She laughed good-naturedly. "I did, too, when I first heard it. But it's what the community has chosen to call itself. Kids of LGBT parents are sort of betwixt and between, not quite members of the LGBTQ community and not quite typical kids with straight parents either. So they came up with a term that uniquely defines them and use it in an empowering way."

"Huh," I said, turning the phrase over in my mind. "I don't see myself feeling comfortable using it. But good to know it exists so I'm not totally clueless."

"Lena, you're not clueless at all. You've lived this. You're one of us."

One of us. I felt a glow spread within me. I couldn't help thinking Kevin might have been onto something this morning. Kate might just be my new best friend after all. And there were other Kates out there—an untapped community of us. A heaviness I didn't know I'd been carrying slowly lifted. Holding onto my secret all these years had become a way of life. It was surreal to share with Kate so openly about things I typically deemed off-limits, too private. As if something was being released. If I'd had someone like her on my side to confide in years ago, maybe things would have been different.

Chapter Twenty-Seven
TERESA - JOHNSTON, NY
1983

Teresa took a sip of white wine and glanced at the suitcase on the floor, filled with Frank's clothes. She sat in their bedroom, waiting for Frank to come home from work. A strange sense of calm came over her, and she didn't know if she should attribute it to the wine, which she so rarely drank, or the fact that she was as ready as she'd ever be for this confrontation.

For three long days while she camped out at her cousin Ronnie's house away from her home and family, Teresa had thought about what it would be like to be divorced and raising her children alone. She no longer had any immediate family to help—her parents were gone, her brother Sal lived far away, and her brother Marco could barely take care of himself. Sure, she had Ronnie, but she couldn't expect her cousin to support her financially or take her and the kids in if she couldn't make it on her own.

Teresa realized that between saving her marriage or saving her children, there was no competition. She would choose her kids without hesitation. She loved them more than anyone or anything in the world—more than life itself. And now she needed to protect them. They would be okay as long as she was with them. The three of them would survive this.

She heard Frank's footsteps approaching, and in a moment, there he was, standing in the doorway. She watched Frank's tears fall as he took in the scene and felt it all dissolving, his tears washing away everything in their life. Everything being diluted until nothing was left except a bare patch of dirt that used to be her marriage and her life. And she stood on it alone. Anger rose in her throat, anger that felt like a fire that just had oil poured on it. She wanted to slap him.

"You lied to me about everything!" she wailed.

"You're right. I've wanted to tell you, but I couldn't. I was so afraid. Because I'm..." Frank stopped, clamped his hand over his mouth, and shook his head like he couldn't say it out loud.

"You're a homosexual," Teresa finished his sentence. "You have sex with men."

Frank contorted his face as if he were in pain. But he looked up at Teresa and slowly nodded. He stood to reach for her, but Teresa put her hand out to stop him, to keep the distance between them, and walked to the door.

She turned around and looked at him. "Don't. Not yet. I'm not ready. Leave me alone right now."

He sat back down on the bed, crumpled, and put his hands in his lap, looking like he didn't know what to do with them. "I'm sorry," he whispered.

Teresa closed the bedroom door behind her, went into the hall bathroom, and splashed water on her face. She then sat on the toilet with her head in her hands, inhaling deep breaths. She tried to reconcile her anger with her stubborn love for Frank, a love that still lingered. It wasn't the same love that she'd always had for him. It had morphed into something different. Less of a romantic love, and more of a familial kind. It almost felt protective, similar to an emotion she would feel for another family member, like her brother or one of her children.

This is so goddamned confusing.

She shuddered as she realized she was worried about what would happen to Frank. The ugly words people would use to describe him—*fag, fairy, homo*. To have to keep a secret like that must be... lonely.

And now there was this epidemic going around, killing gay men. *Will he be able to stay safe?* No, she couldn't go there. It was too much. She had so many questions she wanted to ask him, yet a big part of her didn't want to know the answers.

Looking back, she realized there'd been signs during the early years of their marriage, and even before, that she might have seen if she'd known enough to look. Teresa examined Frank's past behavior through a new lens—one with no filters blocking the truth. The way Frank had looked at anyone, man or woman, who was extremely attractive. The way he would hold his stare, following their body as they moved, appreciating their beauty as if it was a work of art that he couldn't take his eyes off of. She would often get jealous, thinking that he was leering at other women. Now she realized he didn't discriminate—his gaze would linger on other men as well. Maybe he'd done that with women as a way of overcompensating so he wouldn't be outed. She thought about how he often wanted to go to Greenwich Village, a well-known gay enclave, and drive around, and about all the male "friends" he'd become extremely close to, sharing sideways glances with them like they were privy to an inside joke. She would have to recast all her memories.

The fact that Frank had been lying about who he was—unable, perhaps, even to be honest with himself—was deeply disturbing. *What must his life have been like growing up? How did he feel all those years during our dating and marriage?*

She left the bathroom and slowly opened their bedroom door. Frank was sitting on the edge of the bed where she'd left him.

"How long have you known that you... prefer men?"

"I don't know. Maybe always?" Frank hesitated, looking at Teresa, but she nodded for him to go on. "Somewhere deep down, I think I always knew. I wasn't sure. I thought maybe it was a phase or something that would go away in time. But it didn't."

"No, it certainly didn't," Teresa said.

Frank put his head down, looking as if he were trying to make himself disappear.

"Did you ever try to tell anyone?" Teresa asked.

"No, not really. My mother walked in once when I was studying with my friend Eddie from high school. We weren't even doing anything. I was just standing near him and maybe had my arm on his shoulder. What I can remember is that I felt like I'd been caught doing something wrong, because I knew what I was thinking and feeling inside. And it was like that was being broadcast out loud." Frank stopped and took a deep breath. "She looked so shocked and mad. She told him to go home and glared at me. I knew she disapproved. I hadn't even really acted on it yet, but I realized it would be very wrong in her eyes to do that. So I kept it a secret, trying to bury it, willing it to go away."

She took his hand. "Oh, Frank. I'm so sorry. For me, of course. For the kids. But also..." She whispered, "For you." She hesitated. "But why did you marry me?"

"Because I loved you, Teresa. I still do. I don't want you to think I don't love you..."

"I know you love me. It's hard to make sense of all this. But that much, I know."

"Good. Never doubt that for a second. I may have lied about many things, but loving you has never been one of them. I'll take care of you and the kids always. I'm not sure what that will look like, but I promise you I will. You're my family."

Teresa felt defeated. She was so tired. It was all too much to bear.

Chapter Twenty-Eight
FRANK - JOHNSTON, NY
1983

The feeling of finally telling Teresa the truth was hard to describe. It was like he'd reverted back to some essential version of himself—one he'd put aside years before when he fell in love with Teresa and thought marrying her would be enough and would somehow fix him.

But he refused to look at their marriage, their life together, and the children they'd created as a mistake. Who else would have stood by him so fiercely? Teresa loved him despite his flaws—had committed her life to him. She was way better than he deserved. She was the best thing in his life, the glue that held them together. And now he felt that glue pulling away from him like it had lost its stickiness.

Frank thought back to when he and Teresa honeymooned in Quebec City. He remembered the night they went ice skating at the rink overlooking the St. Lawrence River, twirling in circles, giggling like kids, stopping to hug and kiss. Then they went back to the hotel and slept together for the first time. And afterward, he was satisfied knowing he would only be with her, a woman, for the rest of his life.

The innocent young woman he'd met and fallen in love with all those years ago was gone. He'd underestimated her and, at times, seen her as an obstacle to be navigated. But she was far from that. She was his lifeline, his confidante, and his friend. The best friend he'd ever had. And he really did love her.

Damn it all. You're the love of my life, Teresa. You're just the wrong gender.

F rank walked into Lena's room and sat on the edge of her bed. Lena looked up at him and then right back down at the book she was reading. Frank gently placed his hand on the book and waited until she met his eyes.

"Lena, I need to talk to you. I'm going to talk to your brother, also, but I wanted to talk to you first." He hesitated, running his hands through his hair. "I know you have some questions... that you're confused." He'd been dreading this conversation but knew his children had to hear this from him directly.

Lena nodded and didn't say a word but kept her gaze on him. Frank realized his daughter wanted the truth. She deserved it.

"There's something I need to tell you. Um... part of the reason your mom and I have been fighting so much lately..." Frank swallowed hard. "Lena, I'm different from many other men. I like... other men the way most men like women. I've kept it hidden from you and Anthony because... because I didn't want you to know that about me. I really didn't want you to know that about me. But you have to know. You deserve to know."

"I already know," she whispered. "I've known for a while now, Dad." She bit her bottom lip.

He took a deep breath and blew out the air slowly to steady himself. *So it's true.* Teresa had confided in him that Lena had suspected for years. Henry had worried that Lena had caught them in an intimate moment on the boat a few summers earlier. Frank could only imagine how confused she must have felt. Frank could see Lena's eyes filling with tears, hurt and pain etched on her face. He could also see a stiffness in her jaw, a lift of her head—anger and defiance. He had put all of it there. Frank's eyes filled up with tears as well.

He gently touched Lena's cheek. "I'm sorry, Cricket. I never meant to hurt you or disappoint you. Or your mother or brother. I can't help it. It's just who I am. I fought it for a long time, but I can't anymore. And I can't ask your mother to keep such a big secret anymore. It isn't fair to her. I have to be honest with you all. You deserve it."

Lena reached out suddenly and hugged Frank hard, throwing her arms around him and burrowing her head in his neck and crying. They sat there for a long time, entwined. Frank held onto Lena tightly, his arms wrapped around her and his hands pressed against her back.

"I love you," he whispered into her hair.

Lena nodded but said nothing. That was okay. Frank knew she loved him but needed time and was angry and confused. For now, this was enough.

Frank left Lena's room and paused at the top of the stairs. He planned to talk to Anthony next. But first, he needed to take a moment to gather himself. This truth telling was exhausting. As he sat on the top step, he felt a jab from the keys in his pocket—he hadn't even put them down on the counter when he got home, as if he'd known that he wouldn't be staying.

Frank knocked softly on his parents' front door. "Ma, Pa, it's me, Frank. Let me in."

His father opened the door with a startled look on his face. "Frank, what are you doing here? We didn't expect you. Come in, come in. Are Teresa and the kids with you?"

"No," Frank said. "They're not. In fact, I need to talk to both of you about that... about my family. It's important."

His mother came into the kitchen as Enzo led Frank down the front hallway. She read Frank's face immediately and already knew something was wrong. He could see it in her eyes.

Frank knew they would have a hard time receiving and processing the blow he was going to deal them. But it had to be done. Frank thought of his parents leaving Italy for a totally unknown new world. They must have been eager and anxious for their new life in America. They'd had to start over in a place where they knew hardly anyone and didn't speak the language. What a risk. In a strange way, this gave him strength. If they could start a new life, he could too. They would be offended if they knew he was comparing coming out as a gay man to their leaving the Old Country to come to the United States. But to him, it wasn't so different.

"I have something to tell you, and it's not easy," Frank said.

"Oh my God, Frank, what's wrong? Are you sick? What about the kids?" Eva asked nervously.

"No one's sick, Ma. I promise."

"Then what?" Eva asked.

"It's about me. I'm... gay. Fought it for a long time, but I can't anymore. I've been hiding for too long. Teresa knows. Well, she's known for a while, actually. I'm not sure what's going to happen, but I don't think we can stay together anymore. It's not fair to either of us or the kids."

Eva stared at Frank, her mouth hanging open, as if he'd just told her she couldn't talk. Enzo shifted uncomfortably and leaned against a kitchen chair, like he needed it for support.

"How does this happen? I don't understand. You've always liked girls. You're married to a woman." Eva pointed at Frank, scolding him.

"I don't know, Ma. Some people are just born this way."

"You weren't born this way, Frank. I delivered you from my body. You were a normal, healthy boy. Trust me."

"Yes, I was a normal healthy boy who happens to be gay."

"Well, you weren't always that way," Eva declared.

"Actually, Ma, I think I was. I had a feeling I was different. I didn't want to be. It wasn't... easy." Frank sighed and looked pointedly at his mother. "C'mon, Ma. You knew. Don't pretend you didn't suspect. You were onto me. Remember that time with Eddie in high school? Nothing happened, but I wanted it to, and you knew it."

Enzo looked shocked. "I never heard any of this." He looked from Frank to Eva, a puzzled expression on his face. "Eva, you knew? Why didn't you ever say anything to me?"

"I thought it was just a phase. That it would pass." Eva waved her hand dismissively like she could wipe away Frank's gayness with a swipe.

Frank shook his head vehemently. "Well, it didn't. And I can't hide it any longer. I am who I am."

His father walked over and put his hand on Frank's shoulder. "So... now... you're sure?"

Frank looked up at him and nodded solemnly. "I'm positive now. I could never be sure in the past. I was with Teresa and hadn't really acted on my... interests. But now that I have, I know I'm gay."

Enzo nodded back and squeezed Frank's shoulder. He looked deep in thought.

Eva jumped up, flailing her arms in big, sweeping arcs. "Why, Frank, why? Where did I go wrong? How could you do this to me?" She paced back and forth, sobbing like Frank had told her he had a terminal illness.

"I didn't mean to hurt anyone. It just happened. Ma, you think you're upset about this? Think about Teresa and the kids."

"I am thinking about them, Frank. A lot. And you. What kind of life are you going to have like this? Certainly not *normale*."

"I don't want normal, Ma. I want to be me!" Frank realized he was yelling and put his fist to his mouth to stop himself.

Enzo turned to Eva. "*Basta*. Enough, Eva."

His voice shook with force, which surprised Frank. His father almost never raised his voice to his mother or told her what to do. Eva retreated to the chair in the room's corner, looking forlorn.

Enzo then turned back to Frank, his hand still on his shoulder. "I love you. You're my son. That's all I care about." Enzo took a beat. "Besides, if people are born this way, it sure doesn't seem like something you can control. Or that you or anyone else should be blamed for. It shouldn't tear families apart."

Enzo looked over at Eva intently, waiting for her to say something. But she just sat there, crumpled in the chair, silently weeping.

Frank reached up and grabbed his father's hand. He couldn't bring himself to speak. *He accepts me for who I am. For what I am.* A flood of relief washed over him. He was in awe of his father, this man who could show him so much empathy and forgiveness. Frank knew he would forever be grateful to him.

Chapter Twenty-Nine
LENA - ORANGE, CA
August 2015

"Easy, killer," I said. "Save some for the whales."

"I could drink a gallon of water. What're you trying to do—kill me?" Kate glared at me in mock horror.

My eyes narrowed jokingly. She snorted, laughing over the rim of her water glass.

Kate and I were back at it a week later. But this time, it was my turn to torture her. It was Saturday morning, postrun. We sat at an outdoor table at the Filling Station Cafe, a few blocks from my house, having brunch. Kate had inhaled several glasses of water in record time.

"I'm starving," she said. "We must have burned a thousand calories on that run."

"We barely ran three miles," I teased.

The server came over and poured us both steaming mugs of coffee. After Kate ordered way too much food for two people, we relaxed back in our chairs. I stretched out my legs, enjoying the feeling of postrun endorphins working their magic.

She put down her coffee mug and looked at me, her expression growing serious. "Lena, so I've been thinking. You know how I mentioned I'm involved with COLAGE? I serve as one of their board members. I think you should get involved. I bet you'd love the group and get a lot out of it."

I nodded, suspecting there was more. I could hear it in her voice.

"So, I just found out that the keynote speaker for an event they're holding in the LA area in October had to back out, and they need to fill the spot."

I pursed my lips together and waited. *No, she couldn't mean...*

"I think you'd be perfect for it."

"Me? Be the keynote speaker?" I shook my head as if this was the most asinine idea I'd ever heard. "What in the hell would I talk about? I don't even know the group."

"I was thinking about it," Kate said, excited. "You can talk about the legal landscape for sexual orientation discrimination. That's something you know a ton about. It's timely and interesting—and would be a safe way to approach this."

Safe? What a strange comment. Like I needed a strategy for something I had absolutely no intention of doing.

"Kate, I'm not going to be their keynote speaker. I wouldn't feel comfortable."

"Why? You're an expert on this kind of law, Lena. It's a perfect solution. You talk about some cool recent cases, strides made, areas that still need attention. They learn and get inspired. Win-win."

"I've got enough going on. I'm planning my dad's wedding, which is in two months, remember? This would just add to my stress right now. No thanks."

"It would actually be the week after the wedding. And you don't have to do much prep at all. Just an outline of some legal points you could probably recite with your eyes closed. Think about it, okay? For me?" Kate looked at me pleadingly, and I had the feeling this was more than just a favor. "And I think it would be good for you."

There it was. The truth. She thought she was helping me. *Seriously? Not helping,* I wanted to scream. I shifted uncomfortably in my seat.

"Lena, I know it's bold, but I feel like it's meant to be. We met for a reason. I can't help thinking that your struggle with coming out will resonate."

"My what? Kate, in case you haven't noticed, I don't need to come out—I'm not gay." I glared at her. "My dad came out years ago. I'm fine with it. I just don't need to scream it at the top of my lungs."

"You know what I mean. At least, I think you do." Now she looked uncomfortable too.

Good, that makes two of us, I thought.

She leaned forward. "Children of LGBTQ parents need to come out too. We often hide who we are as much as our parents do."

So that's what she meant. I cringed, imagining standing up publicly in front of a bunch of strangers, claiming my status as the daughter of a gay parent, like some kind of poster child.

"Just tell me you'll consider it," she said.

I remained silent. Stubborn to the core. That was the Italian in me.

"Okay, okay, I'll stop pushing. I know I'm not your therapist." Kate flashed a nervous smile.

Yeah, I stayed away from therapists for a reason. Many reasons actually: my mother's insistence we could take care of things ourselves and should not air our dirty laundry, the guidance counselor's admonition to keep my family secret quiet, our desire to not get my father fired or thrown in jail. Besides, I'd had my journal growing up, which I used to say was like therapy—much closer to the truth than I cared to admit.

Kate sure had some nerve psychoanalyzing me. But I was afraid she might be right. I'd never thought of it quite that way before—that I was the one who needed to come out and was still allowing my past to define my present and future. By hiding, I was giving so much power to those old wounds—the hurt little girl still held sway over me. I was the one who wasn't free. I envied Kate. Sure, she had overstepped. But that didn't make her entirely wrong.

"Come on, Lena. I just ran—what, a half marathon?—for you. The least you could do is help me with this," Kate said teasingly.

"A half marathon? That was barely a five K," I replied, feeling lighter.

"I'll tell you what. For now, agree to it only as a lawyer who works in this area. Don't worry about the personal side, okay? The board would be thrilled to have a replacement who can cover an interesting topic related to this group."

I shook my head, not committing but feeling my anger dissipate. I took in a huge breath of air and let it out slowly. "I'll think about it." I shrugged.

Kate pounced. "Thank you so much, Lena. Truly. I hope you agree to do it. If you do, I'll support you in any way I can. Do an email introduction to the board members and help you outline your speech—whatever you need. And of course, I'll introduce you at the event before you go on stage. And cheer you on from the front row."

"Okay, okay," I said, wanting this line of conversation to end.

"'Okay,' you'll think about it, or 'okay,' you'll do it and take me up on my offer to help?" She looked at me expectantly, a twinkle in her eye.

"The latter," I said, annoyed but already forgiving her.

As I waved goodbye a little while later, I felt a strange mix of fear and excitement, like a train had just left the station and was careening down the tracks, full speed ahead, with me on board, regardless of whether I wanted to be.

"You're perfect for that speech, Lena. I don't think you have to prep for it." Kevin and I were on our patio, eating breakfast the next morning, and I'd just finished rehashing the details of my conversation with Kate. "Just be yourself. How many people—let alone lawyers—have close personal experience with the topic the way you do? Kate chose you for a reason."

I looked away. *I know why she chose me. That's what's stressing me out.* I thought of Kate's words again. *Your struggle with coming out.*

"Plus, you hardly ever talk about that aspect of your family or your background in public," Kevin continued. "Probably because many people wouldn't get it. This group certainly will. You'll be in good company, Lena. And I'll come if you want me to be there." He grabbed my hand and squeezed it.

"I'm not planning to share my personal story about my father. I made that clear to Kate. Just the legal stuff."

Kevin pulled back, looking disappointed. "Well, I think you should reconsider. If there's ever a group to share your story with, it's this one, Lena. Give it some thought. I think it's time."

It's time? My personal story didn't come with a sell-by date. I knew I could speak to almost any group in my role as a discrimination lawyer. But to tell a bunch of strangers—even ones with something truly unusual in common with me—about my deepest, darkest family secret that I'd hardly shared with anyone? That seemed over the top. I never intended to become the spokesperson for children of gay parents.

"I don't know. I'll think about it," I said, ready to stop talking about this.

I felt like I was in a trance. All I could focus on was the idea of standing in front of a large group of strangers in a very public setting, sharing something I typically kept private. In my mind's eye, I was already up on that stage, staring at an audience of expectant faces—and it terrified me.

Then I thought of another expectant audience, albeit a much smaller one, and remembered something I had to do for my dad and Oliver's wedding.

"Ugh," I moaned.

"What?" Kevin asked. "Am I pushing too much?"

"No, it's not that. I need to email the wedding officiant some details about my dad and Oliver. She wants me to share some tidbits about them so she can personalize the ceremony. I was supposed to do it earlier this week, but with everything going on with work lately, I forgot."

"Do it tomorrow," Kevin suggested.

"I could, but I'd rather just do it now and get it over with. Plus, you know me... I hate to be late for anything."

"Okay. It shouldn't take too long, right? Just send some fun anecdotes about them—how they met, what they like to do, stuff like that. I bet you'll be surprised how easy it is once you sit down and put your mind to it."

"Maybe I'll look through some photos for inspiration. That'll help me jot down some ideas for her."

I went to our home office and fired up our sleeping iMac. I opened the Family folder in my digital photo library and looked through some pictures from the last few years of outings with my dad and Oliver. Boating adventures, check. Dinners at their favorite restaurants, check. Classic cars, check. Lots of beach shots, check. The opera, check.

As I scrolled through the photos, I saw some albums with the names of former family occasions and older dates. I opened a few, and a kaleidoscope of memories hit me—Mom at Shore Beach with toddler versions of me and Anthony playing in the sand. Mom and me at my sweet-sixteen party and then again at my law school graduation. They triggered a painful longing, a sense of sheer abandonment I'd only felt two other times in my life—the first on the heels of the Great Spaghetti-and-Peas Incident.

As if that tragic incident weren't bad enough, in the aftermath, my mother had walked out on us. That description of events was shocking to think of now because it made her seem like the one at fault, like she'd failed us by utterly deserting us. That couldn't have been further from the truth.

Yet the fact remained that she'd left and not just for a few hours—for three long days. Dad told us we had to go to school and he had to go to work and Mom would come home when she was ready. I couldn't focus on school. I felt as if my entire world were crumbling and I was looking at it through a strange murky lens. My mind kept drifting back to the scene in the dining room. I knew nothing would ever be the same again for our family. And I worried it was partly my fault.

After school on the second day, the phone rang, and I prayed it was her. I ran across the kitchen to pick up the receiver, petrified if I didn't get to it quickly enough, it would stop ringing.

"Hello?" I answered.

"Lena, honey, it's Mom."

Relief flooded through me upon hearing her voice. "Mom..." I slumped down on the linoleum floor, cradling the phone to my neck, and started crying immediately.

"It's okay, sweetie. How're you doing?"

"Not good, Mom. I miss you."

"I miss you too. And your brother."

"Where are you?"

"I'm at Ronnie's house. I needed some time to think."

I felt both comforted and angry that my mom had been at a place I knew so well. She was within reach yet felt so far away.

"When're you coming home?" I asked.

"Soon. I'm not ready to come back just yet. But within a day or two—I promise."

"Can I come there and see you? I can get a friend's mother to drop me off maybe."

"No, sweetie. And please don't tell your father where I am. I want to be alone right now."

"Okay. But, Mom... you have to... you have to leave Dad."

There, I'd said it—the thought that had been going through my mind ever since my mom picked up that plate of spaghetti and peas and threw it against the wall. It was as if the crash had woken all of us up to the reality of what was really going on.

"I don't blame Dad for... for being what he is." I could hear her breathing softly into the phone, listening intently like she always did. I could picture her face as she thought about what I was saying. It gave me the courage to continue. "But you have to leave him, Mom."

"Lena, it's complicated. I'll be home soon. Please tell your brother I called and that I love him and will see him soon, but don't tell him where I am. He'll be tempted to tell your father."

I nodded even though she couldn't see me. "Okay. I'll tell him you called but not where you are." I didn't want to hang up.

"I'll see you soon, honey. I love you."

"I love you, Mom." I sobbed on the last word and slowly hung up. My tears dripped onto the linoleum, where our dog, Libby, licked them up. I grabbed her and pulled her into a hug, smelling her fur and missing Mom something awful.

The next day, I came home from school and saw my mom's Cadillac in the driveway. I raced into the house and heard a sound coming from my parents' bedroom—the *click-click* of the suitcase latches opening then a thud as the lid hit the floor. Barging into the room, I found my mom calmly packing my dad's things, with a glass of wine in her hand. I couldn't remember my mother ever drinking wine or liquor in our house. The most I'd ever seen her drink was a sip of wine at my grandparents' house during a holiday dinner.

"Are you kicking Dad out finally?" I was so relieved that she was packing his things and not her own. I didn't feel the least bit guilty that I'd picked a side and stood firmly in my mother's corner.

She nodded then turned back around and kept packing. My stomach fluttered with nerves, but I was reassured. Mom was back to stay.

When my dad came home a few hours later, he walked in wearing a somber expression and headed straight upstairs to my parents' bedroom, barely looking at Anthony and me as he passed us in the living room. I went up to my room and tried to read a book in bed. But I couldn't focus. I heard voices and muffled sobs for what seemed like hours. Eventually, my dad appeared in the doorway. He sat on the edge of my bed, and then, incredibly, told me the truth. My father came out to me when I was thirteen years old. To this day, I was still a bit in shock that he'd done that.

After my father left my room, he went downstairs to speak to Anthony. Then I heard him cross the first floor to the back door and close it. The sound of my dad's car as it pulled out of the driveway then sped away had a ring of finality. Silence settled over the house like a cloak. When the three of us sat down for dinner later that night, my dad's absence was noticeably different. This time, it didn't feel like he was late coming home from work. It felt as if he'd never been there. Already, my dad seemed like a different person—someone I'd known once a long time ago.

And here I was, all these years later, sending insider information to the wedding officiant so my dad could tie the knot with someone else. I was grateful that my dad and I had grown closer over the years. But I also felt like a traitor. I had to reconcile my acceptance of my father for who he fully was with my deep allegiance to my mother.

Why does being a pivotal part of my father's wedding, a joyous occasion, make me feel like I'm taking sides, even after all this time? I felt like we were still playing some decades-long game, and I didn't know which team to root for.

Chapter Thirty
TERESA - JOHNSTON, NY
1983

"Well, what do you think?" Frank asked. He'd called Teresa to see if he could get the kids this weekend and take them out on the boat. Without her, of course.

"I'll ask them later when they get home from after-school activities," she said, already knowing how they would react. Anthony would immediately say yes, wide-eyed and excited to see his father, while Lena would shrug and say she was too busy with schoolwork and other activities. The kids had made it abundantly clear how they felt about their father's departure from their home—her son was heartbroken and her daughter relieved.

Teresa thought back to the day, three months ago, when she'd asked Frank to leave. She'd come downstairs after an hour of sitting in her bedroom, crying her eyes out. Anthony was in the living room, eyes red and puffy from crying and mouth puckered as if he were sucking on something sour. Teresa wanted to reach out and stroke his hair and tell him she hadn't meant for any of this to happen. She could see the questions in his eyes.

"It's your fault! You made him like this. You're too fat!" Anthony screamed.

Teresa stepped back, feeling like someone had punched her. Anthony's face was red, eyes glaring, arms akimbo. Pain oozed out of her son, and Teresa could barely keep herself steady under the onslaught. Anthony was hurting just as much as she was—maybe more because he clearly had seen none of this coming.

"How could you let this happen? Why did you make Dad go?" Anthony wailed.

Ah, yes—there it is. Anthony had always been Daddy's boy, which had been adorable when he was a child. But it became less endearing as Anthony grew older and forgave Frank for every misstep while blaming Teresa for everything. It didn't matter that Frank was a flirt, embarrassed Teresa in public, left her alone night after night, and was unfaithful. Anthony didn't see any of that. He only saw his father, the hero. So Teresa could understand why Anthony, in his furious defense of his father, came at her.

"I hate you!" he screamed, running past her into his room and slamming the door.

Teresa moved toward his room, ready to go after him, and then stopped. She slumped down in the chair in the living room, depleted. Anthony spent so much time with his father at the boat, while Lena spent most of her time with Teresa, doing errands and visiting family on weekends. Teresa could see the split now, and it all made sense. Lena was thinking of Teresa, alone all these years, crawling into an empty bed while Frank was in some man's bed across town. For Anthony, the view was very different.

Teresa had to decide how much she should tell Anthony. The gory details of the illicit affairs behind Teresa's back, on their own boat and who knows where else—what toll would that take on her son? She didn't want to turn Anthony against Frank. But damn if she was going to take all the blame for what had happened here.

Teresa knew what she needed to give Anthony was time. And love. She could do that. She hoped he would come around and see what was really going on. His father wasn't the hero Anthony thought he was. And she wasn't the evil villain.

Frank's voice brought her back to their conversation. "Okay, thanks for asking them."

He was trying to be conciliatory these days, gingerly approaching sticky subjects. They were both navigating this new arrangement, and the results were clumsy, like toddlers learning how to walk, constantly in danger of toppling over. She was still in shock at all this and wondered if Frank was too. She knew she'd done the right thing by standing up for herself and asking him to leave. But that didn't make it easy.

One difficult subject was that they needed to discuss money. Teresa stared at the pile of unopened bills spread on the counter, dreading what she'd discover when she opened them. She'd always worried about money. Watching her family barely squeak by during her childhood had left her with a nagging sense of scarcity. It was like a disease that had spread through her, coursing through her veins, staying with her into adulthood. Over the years of their marriage, she and Frank had gotten by, but she still carefully watched what she spent and made decisions with finances in mind.

With Frank no longer living under the same roof, she felt that old worry growing even stronger. She needed to get a job soon but was overwhelmed just thinking of where to start. Next week, she would make a plan. *One thing at a time.*

"Frank, we need to talk about money. Now that you've rented a place, there'll be two rents to cover."

"I can manage it, Teresa. The place isn't expensive. It's kind of a dump. I'll land somewhere better, but for now, it's fine. I don't want to bring the kids there just yet, though. That's why I want to take them to the boat, instead, this weekend."

Teresa pictured herself in their very early years, sitting on the back deck of Frank's boat, staring out at the water. She saw the whitecaps pop up and break the surface and then disappear. She'd never be able to look at the ocean without thinking of Frank. It was one of hundreds of triggers that conjured him in her mind. She had these moments often. They were tied to certain songs, foods, phrases, and views. Even a smell could trigger a splintery recollection. She'd have to learn to live with them, like learning to live with a limp or low-grade pain.

The envelope of time was swallowing her. She wondered if she hadn't already adjusted, however slightly, to Frank's absence. How quickly the mind accommodated itself, even in such tiny increments. Perhaps after a series of shocks, the body acclimated itself, each subsequent shock bringing less impact. First, she'd lost her mother, then Frank. So much loss.

Sometimes Teresa felt like life was just a series of obstacle courses. It reminded her of Lena running the hurdles on the track. She would go around and around in a circle, gearing up to jump over a hurdle only to come down and get ready to jump over the next one—again and again and again.

"Also, if I come to get the kids this weekend, I can look at that leak in the bathroom," Frank said, jolting her out of her thoughts. "Anthony told me it's still acting up."

She didn't know if she wanted to see Frank or if she could handle it. She hadn't set eyes on him since he'd left. *Will he look different? What if he looks happier, more carefree?* She sighed. That was what she should want for him, of course. And for herself—for both of them to be happy without the other. But it still hurt.

Teresa missed Frank. No, not really Frank himself but what he used to do for her. She realized how much she'd taken all the little things he did for granted. Not that she didn't appreciate him—she did. But it wasn't until those things stopped that she understood what a good provider he was. If her car broke or the oil needed to be changed, all she had to do was mention it to Frank, and he would take care of it. If her brother Marco had gone on a bender and needed to be picked up at three in the morning on a street corner, all she had to do was hang up and let Frank know, and he would put on his pants, get the address, and head out. No questions asked. He was a doer. Frank got things done. So even though he might not always have been emotionally present during their marriage, she missed the practicality of him. She wasn't making excuses for herself. She'd obviously stayed in the marriage way too long. But she was slowly figuring out why and forgiving herself for it. The only people who could truly understand a marriage—or any relationship—were the ones in it.

"Has enough time passed?" Frank whispered, and Teresa realized she'd been silent a while.

She wondered exactly how much time would be enough. "Honestly, Frank, I'm not even sure how to answer that."

"Okay," he said, tiptoeing around the awkwardness of the situation. "I won't push. When you're ready to see me, let me know."

"I will. I just need more time." She hesitated, unsure whether she wanted to share any more with him. Or whether he deserved it. But there had been too many lies for too long. Now was the time for honesty. "It's hard for me, Frank. I'm here alone. And you have everything you wanted."

"No, not everything. I don't have my family. And I don't mean only the kids. I mean you, too, Teresa. You're the mother of my children. I don't want us to be like strangers."

"I don't either, Frank," she whispered, trying to keep her emotions at bay. "But I also know we can't be what we used to be. It wasn't good for any of us. Not for me, not for you, and not for the kids."

Teresa took a deep breath and slowly let it out. She could survive this. She could survive most things. The most important thing was her children. That was what she needed to focus on. The rest was just details.

She looked up at the clock. The kids would be home soon from after-school activities. "Frank, I have to go. I promise I'll talk to the kids about this weekend on the boat, okay? And let's talk again in a few days after I've had a chance to go through more of the bills and discuss finances."

"Okay. Thanks, Teresa. I'll talk to you soon."

She hung up, closed her eyes, and rubbed her temples. A few minutes later, she heard a noise on the back steps and then Anthony saying, "Bye, Mrs. Knight."

The kids were being dropped off by a neighborhood friend's mother.

"What's for dinner?" Anthony asked as he burst through the back door. He was all sweaty, Teresa noticed, remembering that he'd had lacrosse practice after school. He would be hungry. Starving. And although she usually loved cooking, she just didn't have the motivation for it these days like she used to. They were only missing one person at the table, the one who'd hardly ever been home for dinner anyway when he'd lived with them. Yet Teresa felt Frank's absence palpably, like the table had shrunk since he left.

She sighed and turned to Anthony. "Shit on a shingle is what's for dinner." The words were out of her mouth before she even knew she'd said them.

"Gross," Lena said, walking into the kitchen, crinkling her nose as if she actually smelled feces. "Mom! What in the world?" Lena looked at Teresa with a mixture of disgust and amusement.

Anthony laughed and shrugged. "Sounds good to me."

"Of course you would think it sounds good. You're disgusting!" Lena hit him on the arm playfully.

"Well, if you prefer, we can have marinated moose cock. That's a specialty of the house."

They both stared at her wide-eyed. Anthony exclaimed, "Wow, Mom, listen to you. What a mouth!"

Teresa was tired of holding back her thoughts. Her mother's death and Frank leaving had killed her inner censor. And she wasn't apologizing for it. She knew it was inappropriate to talk like this in front of her kids—to her kids, actually. But she didn't care. She was sick of being the well-behaved parent, always playing it safe. If she wanted to curse, she would.

"I don't know what that tastes like, but it sounds good to me." Lena giggled, and Teresa could tell she was playing along.

"You're cool, Mom," Anthony said, wrapping his arms around her and giving her a hug.

She was so relieved that he'd seemed less angry with her the last few weeks.

"Yes, I suppose I am," she said, squeezing him and smiling.

She then walked over to the refrigerator to see what she could throw together for dinner as Lena opened the cabinet to set the table. Teresa realized with a sense of pleasure that she was happy to cook dinner for just the three of them. She needed to get used to it. She *was* used to it. It had always been the three of them over the years. Now it was just more official. *The three musketeers.*

Chapter Thirty-One
FRANK - PELHAM, NY
1984

F rank looked out the window again to see if Teresa had pulled up with the kids. Anthony and Lena were visiting him and Ricky in their new apartment this weekend for the first time. Teresa had offered to drop them off, which surprised Frank, but he didn't question it. Maybe she wanted to see where he lived to make sure it was a safe neighborhood. Or maybe she was genuinely worried about this next step for the kids and thought her driving them would make them less anxious. Frank had agreed to drive them home on Sunday. He checked his watch. They'd arrive any minute.

He turned to look at Ricky in the kitchen, dressed to the nines in all black, fussing over everything. Frank wasn't the only one who was a bundle of nerves. Ricky had cooked up a storm and baked a delicious dessert called tembleque, a Puerto Rican pudding with coconut milk he hoped the kids would love. He put fresh sheets on the bed in the guest room for Lena and laid out ones next to the couch for Anthony. Frank watched Ricky primp and prep and knew he would continue doing so until the kids walked through the door.

"Relax. Everything will be fine," he said, unsure whether he was trying to convince Ricky or himself.

"I know, I know. I just want it to be perfect," Ricky said, flashing a megawatt smile.

Frank and Ricky kept a low profile, going to places where no one would be likely to recognize them and only hanging out with gay friends in private or at gay clubs. This was the first time Frank was intentionally permitting his two worlds to collide. When Frank and Teresa first separated, he'd moved into a tiny basement apartment in the Bronx—alone. It wasn't his first-choice location, but it was affordable. Plus, the landlord didn't live on the premises, which meant fewer questions about Frank's most frequent visitor, Ricky. Frank didn't want to live with Ricky initially, but as time passed, he decided it was time for him and Ricky to move in together, so they searched for a place less cramped and depressing. They found a garden apartment in the town of Pelham, with its own private entrance in the back, and Frank was relieved that it didn't come with nosy neighbors. Eventually, he'd gotten up the nerve to ask Teresa if the kids could come visit him and Ricky for the weekend, and she'd consented.

"Hey, remember, this isn't my coming-out party. We still need to stay below the radar. I promised Teresa I wouldn't make the kids feel uncomfortable. I'll be introducing you as my friend, and there'll be no public displays of affection."

Ricky nodded, agreeing to adhere to this list of rules that forced them to live double lives. Frank might have come out when he left home, but it was only a soft outing.

Frank saw Teresa's car pull up and opened the front door. The kids jumped out and grabbed their bags.

Teresa lowered her window and called, "Have a good time, you guys."

He waved to her, feeling awkward, like he'd never waved at someone before. His hands were sweaty and felt heavy. She waved back and pulled away from the curb. He watched her go and felt a moment of melancholy, as if he'd forgotten the words to a favorite song.

"Come in, come in," Frank said, welcoming the kids and gesturing them inside.

They walked into the apartment, and Ricky looked at them sheepishly. He was leaning against the couch. Frank couldn't help thinking it looked like the couch was holding him up.

"Hi, Anthony. Hi, Lena," Ricky said, and it came out too eager—loud and forced.

"Hey," Anthony said.

Lena pursed her lips and grumbled, "Hi," sounding like she wished she were somewhere else.

Ricky took their backpacks, told them to make themselves comfortable at the kitchen table, and asked what they wanted to drink. He went to the fridge to get them sodas. Lena grimaced as she sat down at the table and looked around. She wore a nice sweater with a skirt, tights, and boots. Her hair was long and feathered back like the *Charlie's Angels* actresses all the kids adored. She had her legs crossed and her hands folded in her lap. She looked like a stranger in some ways. His little girl had grown up.

His mind wandered back to the time he'd taught her how to dance the Latin hustle. At eight years old, she already had rhythm, moving her slender hips to the beat. He remembered how her long dark hair had whipped around her diminutive frame as he drew her close and spun her away, and she'd broken into giggles every time she looked over at Teresa or Anthony, the makeshift audience, who were snapping their fingers to the music.

He peered into Lena's dark-blue eyes now, trying to find her there. But he'd looked away too long, and his Cricket had vanished. In her place stood a teenager who wanted to be left alone. Frank could already feel her fighting to break away, like a puppy wriggling to get out of the too-tight grasp of an overeager child.

Ricky came over with the kids' sodas and handed one to Lena. "Here you go," he said, and Lena grabbed it, not saying thank you.

She wasn't being friendly to Ricky, as if she wanted to either make him feel uncomfortable or start a fight. Her aloof—borderline rude—behavior continued throughout dinner and dessert. Frank didn't like this at all. She had an outright attitude.

He decided to confront her. "Lena, hey, cut it out."

"What?" she asked, looking at him defiantly. "Cut what out?"

"You know what I'm talking about. I don't like your behavior. The way you're treating Ricky."

Ricky patted his hand, clearly embarrassed. "Frank, it's fine. She's fine. Don't." He looked at Frank pleadingly.

"It's not fine. She knows what I'm talking about, and I want it to stop." He looked at Lena. "When you're here, I want you to treat Ricky with respect. You hear me? This is bullshit, Lena." Frank was getting upset.

"Oh yeah?" Lena said, like it was a challenge. She stood up and backed away from the table. "Well, then, maybe I just won't come here. How's that?"

Frank didn't know what to say. There were so many responses coming to his brain, but he couldn't form the words. Ricky was oozing discomfort. Anthony was squirming in his seat, trying not to make eye contact. Frank wondered if he would side with his sister and turn his back on Frank. No—he knew Anthony wouldn't do that. The boy wanted to be here—with Frank.

Frank turned back to Lena, afraid he'd say something he'd regret. So he said nothing. Instead, he slammed his hand down on the table. Anthony and Ricky jumped, startled. Not Lena. She was already sashaying down the hall toward the guest room.

Frank got up, but Ricky grabbed his arm. "No, Frank. Let her go. Give her some space, some time. Please."

Frank sat back down. He heard the guest room door slam. "God dammit!" he screamed.

He wanted to run after her, fling open the door, and have it out with her. But he didn't. He sat at the table, trying to calm down. Maybe Ricky was right. Lena needed space and time. He hoped he could give her that. He'd caused this mess, and she was angry and hurt. But he didn't want to allow her to misbehave. *Where do I draw the line?* There was no rule book for this.

Later that night, Frank was in their bedroom, pacing at the foot of the bed. He ran his hands through his hair. "Man, I can't believe this. That didn't go at all how I wanted it to. I lost my cool."

Ricky came over and put his arm around Frank's shoulder. "Hey, *querido,*" he cooed, "it's okay. She'll come around. Talk to her in the morning."

Frank sighed heavily. "I don't know what to do. I really don't." He shook his head. "Teresa always knew how to act in these situations. She'd say the right thing."

Ricky sat down on the edge of the bed and stared at him. "Oh my God. You miss Teresa. I'm so sorry, honey, but I'm never going to be her."

Frank grabbed Ricky by the shoulders and pulled him toward him until their foreheads touched. "I'm sorry. Forgive me. I love you—I do. But yes, I miss her."

The next morning, he called Teresa. "Lena doesn't want to be here."

"She said that?" Teresa asked.

"No, but she was acting like it. She was being... she wasn't very nice to Ricky. She left the table and slammed the door to the guest bedroom and didn't come out for the rest of the night."

"Aha..." Teresa said. "You're surprised?"

Frank sighed. "Not really. I just don't know what to do."

"Honestly, Frank? You caused all of this. What did you expect? For God's sake, you amaze me. You want everything to go your way.

You change the kids' entire lives, and you expect them to just jump on board with no issues?"

"I know, I know," he said, burying his head in his hands as he cradled the phone against his neck.

"Give her time. She needs you to be there for her and to step up. Get involved in her hobbies. She spent her entire childhood watching you go to the boat with your friends or with Anthony. Now you have this apartment and new boyfriend and life, and you again expect her to fit into it, to accept it. It's always about you. Try to meet her on her terms and in her places. For once."

Frank was quiet. She was right.

"Thank you," he whispered. "I appreciate your help. I really do. And I hear you."

"I hope so, Frank. Otherwise, you may lose her."

Frank vowed not to let that happen.

Chapter Thirty-Two
LENA - ORANGE, CA
August 2015

"Ugh, I give up," I said, pushing aside the deposition binder I'd been staring at for the last ten minutes.

Kevin, who'd been engrossed in one of his geeky tech projects for Disney, peeked out from behind his laptop and gave me a sympathetic look. "Maybe take a break."

"Maybe," I said, not sure if that would solve the problem. "I'll go get us more coffee. Be right back."

We were having coffee and croissants on the back patio, both—unfortunately—working on a perfect summer morning. I was prepping for an upcoming deposition for a disability discrimination case. I typically enjoyed deposition prep, as this was the stage when the opponent was finally forced to show their cards. The discovery phase was frequently a jumble of documents meant to overwhelm and confuse more than shed light. In contrast, the deposition let me spot the chinks in the armor, determine where the hidden agenda was, and build strategy. It was the stage that helped solve the mystery of the case.

But I couldn't focus. My mind kept wandering, inventorying all the items for the wedding on a constant loop. Plus, there was the COLAGE speech looming over me only days after the wedding. I planned to draft a keynote focused on legal issues having to do with the LGBTQ community. I knew that content so well and could recite it in my sleep, yet the speech wasn't sitting right with me.

I went into the kitchen, filled our coffee cups, and placed them on a tray. On the way back outside, I grabbed the notebook I'd been using for wedding planning, which was sitting in the breakfast nook. After plopping back down at the table, I handed Kevin his coffee and opened up the notebook. I reviewed the guest list, making note of some RSVPs that had recently come back by email. I stared at Henry's name and thought back to how long he and my dad had been friends—and how their relationship had begun.

"Did I ever tell you that Henry was my father's first lover?"

Kevin hastily chewed and swallowed the colossal piece of croissant he'd just shoved into his mouth. "Um, no, you didn't tell me that. I knew they went way back and were both gay. I don't think I ever realized they were a couple."

"Yup, they were secret lovers. Had an affair behind their wives' backs. This was before my dad came out. When I was a kid."

"Wow. That must have sucked. But he didn't stay with Henry, right? You told me he lived with some guy you despised when he first moved out. What was his name again?"

"Ricky," I said. "Yeah, I wasn't a fan."

Wow, I hadn't thought of Ricky in years, probably because I tried desperately to push him and that time out of my mind. It might have been an auspicious time for my dad, but it wasn't for me.

When my parents split up, I had questions. Unfortunately, my dad didn't have answers. He was like a sick-in-love teenager, behaving in the tremendously irritating way most people did when they had their first love. He had that puppy dog look on his face, laughed at pretty much everything Ricky said—even if it wasn't funny—was overly attentive to him, and was so darn happy in a way I hadn't seen him in a long time. Probably ever.

I wished I could report that in those early years of my parents' separation, I was kind and patient—or at least accepting and tolerant—of my father's new life and of Ricky. Instead, I fumed with jealousy and anger. Dad's new boyfriend became the distillation of all my hurt. The knowledge that Ricky was someone whose company Dad preferred over ours only made things worse. Feeling ill at ease and displaced, I often resisted seeing my dad on his scheduled weekends, citing teenage commitments—track practice and meets, theater rehearsals and shows, and hanging out with friends. I was punishing my dad and relishing it.

It didn't help that Ricky felt so foreign to us, with his high-pitched soft voice and black eyeliner. Anthony and I didn't see the appeal of this man who'd moved in with our dad within a year of my parents' split, decorating their apartment with lush curtains, throw pillows, bed linens, and knickknacks that, to us, only exhibited his bad taste. Even my dad didn't seem enamored by all the changes—I caught him rolling his eyes when Ricky put the frilly place mats on the table before we ate dinner. Maybe my dad hoped those hideous-looking place mats were just temporary. Well, I hoped Ricky was temporary.

While my dad was busy playing house with Ricky, my mom took care of us and tried to make sense of her new normal, a state she didn't create and had no choice but to endure. Everything my mom expected—everything she'd been told to want—had exploded in her face in the most embarrassing manner possible. She'd been betrayed, cheated on, and made a fool of. She was alone and the subject of gossip. Her not-quite ex-husband would sometimes arrive at the door, tearfully apologizing and confessing his longing for his family while also claiming to be the happiest he'd ever been. She had one kid in the throes of adolescence and very much taking out the loss of what he considered to be his heroic father on her. And she had me, a bundle of competing emotions, trying to make sense of it all and failing miserably.

Was I sad at the time? Sure. But mostly, I was angry. And then my anger made me feel guilty. If my father had cheated on my mother with another woman, I'd have had every right to scream bloody murder, take her side, and roar at my father. But because he was gay, I felt like I was supposed to be understanding and compassionate. As a teenager, I couldn't muster those emotions lying below the surface. There were too many other emotions strangling them.

Dad and Ricky's relationship eventually faded away, becoming another inadvertent casualty. *Good riddance.* A long line of boyfriends replaced him—until Oliver came along, fortunately putting an end to my father's serial dating. The only other steady man in my father's life had always been Henry. After his breakup with Ricky, my dad reached out to Henry for support, and they kept their promise to be lifelong friends.

Kevin leaned over and took a sip of my coffee, his cup apparently already empty. I slapped his hand playfully. "Hey, you stealer. Leave me the last sip."

"That's what you get for letting your mind wander who knows where. You snooze, you lose."

I smiled, realizing I'd been deep in thought. "I was remembering how tough it was after my parents split up and my dad was with Ricky." I looked down at my chocolate croissant. "Although... he worked at a bakery. Man, could he make some amazing desserts. That was his only saving grace." I gave Kevin a sly smile.

"That was ages ago," Kevin said soothingly. "Your dad has come a long way. You all have. Try not to think of that old stuff now, 'kay?" I nodded, and Kevin kissed my forehead. "Besides, we all know the way to your heart is through chocolate, so he got that part right."

I smirked, put a forkful of the delicious pastry in my mouth, and let it melt on my tongue—along with the past.

Chapter Thirty-Three
TERESA - JOHNSTON, NY
1985

Teresa kicked off her flats and dropped her pocketbook and keys on the counter. She glanced at the clock on the stove. Five thirty. The kids were at friends' houses for dinner, and Ronnie would be here any minute, so the two women would have the place to themselves for a few hours. Fortunately, Ronnie said she'd pick up takeout on the way over.

"Knock, knock." Ronnie stood at the screen door, plastic bags of Styrofoam containers in her hands. "I come bearing the best of Carmelina's," she said, referring to one of Teresa's favorite restaurants in New Rochelle.

Teresa opened the door and took one bag out of her hands. "Hey, you," she said, kissing her cousin on the cheek. "You're a godsend. I miss that place. Please tell me you got the *mozzarella en carrozza*?"

"Hon, of course I did. Who in their right mind would go to Carmelina's without getting that dish? A crazy person, that's who." Ronnie cackled, dumped the other bag on the counter, and pulled Teresa into a big hug. She let go and stepped back, arms outstretched. "Let me look at you. You know what you look like? A survivor, that's what. I swear, every time I see you, you look stronger and stronger." She nodded approvingly.

Teresa laughed and hit her gently on the arm. "Stop it."

"I'm serious. You're doing really great, Teresa, you hear me?"

"Thank you. You know what? I am doing better. Day by day. When Frank left, I didn't think I could go on. I didn't even think I could sleep in our bed alone. But I did it. And I'm still doing it. And each day, there's a new thing that I learn to do on my own or get through without him. I'm figuring it out."

Ronnie squeezed Teresa's arm. "Life, apparently, goes on. You know what this means? You're going to be okay, sweetie. You're moving on."

Teresa smiled, grateful for her cousin's constant support since the separation. What a long two years it had been.

"So, how's the new job going? Good?" Ronnie served hearty plates of food for the both of them.

Teresa had enrolled in a class in advanced typing and Gregg shorthand. She did really well in the class and had heard from the instructor that a nearby children's hospital had an opening in the psychology department. For as long as she could remember, Teresa had dreamed of being a psychologist. She loved the idea of studying people and helping patients overcome their problems. Teresa submitted an application, put on one of her favorite outfits for the interview, and landed the job. She felt like she was truly contributing and knew the doctors and researchers valued her work. They started giving her more responsibility, and she even got a raise after being there only a short amount of time. She now made $2.90 per hour. With a forty-hour workweek, that was $116 per week. It felt like a lot of money to make on her own.

"The job is great." She nodded, chewing her mozzarella. "Hmm," she moaned appreciatively and pointed to her plate. "And so is this."

"I'm glad it's working out so well. I'm proud of you. And now that you have some more money coming in, maybe it's time to hire that lawyer and get a divorce."

Teresa's stomach flip-flopped at the mention of divorce. She still couldn't wrap her head around getting an actual divorce. She hated the idea of it, considering the time and attention it would take to unravel the marriage and life she'd spent years building up and living. A divorce was a kind of messy, prolonged death. And expensive to boot.

It would be easier if Frank had died. She could have mourned him and not hated him as much as she did at times. Time would freeze, and she could remember him and their marriage as they'd been before everything imploded. She felt horrible for thinking this, but she couldn't help herself. If he'd died, she would have been a widow with all the privileges and pity that went along with that title and role. Instead, she was just a scorned woman with a soon-to-be ex-husband and no "other woman" to blame.

"I don't know... I'm not sure I'm ready for that yet. Soon, but not yet."

Ronnie nodded. "I know you're nervous about it, but it's not as bad as it used to be. Heck, I've paved the way for you."

"I know I shouldn't, but I still hate what others will think." Teresa didn't like admitting this, even to Ronnie.

"Screw them. Let them worry about their own friggin' lives. Goddamn busybodies."

Teresa knew the neighbors had whispered how she was separated with two kids and a husband who had cheated on her. *If they only knew the truth, they would have had even more to gossip about.* Never mind. She couldn't do anything but continue to improve her situation little by little.

One way of improving her situation in the eyes of others would be to get an annulment. But that cost much more money than she'd expected—money she didn't have lying around, ready to hand over to the Catholic church so they could declare that her marriage was a sham and needed to be stricken from the record. She also hated the idea that an annulment meant her marriage had never truly existed as far as the church was concerned. It wiped the slate clean. That would mean, by extension, that her children were bastards, born out of wedlock. She refused to do that.

Teresa thought of Anthony and Lena. *How could anything that produced such beautiful children be invalid?*

She needed to get a divorce at some point, but she dreaded the finality of it. The severity. So for now, she would stay in this limbo period, a wife with no husband and the mother of children whose father didn't live with his family—alone but trying to graduate to independent.

A few months later, Teresa attended a community event for the hospital where she worked. She sat at the table with colleagues from her department, including the psychologists, who always treated her with respect even though she was merely the secretary. They insisted she use the hospital's car service, which made her feel important as she sat in the back seat, being driven to and from events by a professional driver.

That night, her ride home was a driver named Larry, who seemed to be behind the wheel frequently when she used the car service. He was easy to talk to, and she'd learned they had some things in common, including being Italian American and having failed marriages.

At a red light, while they were deep in conversation, Teresa looked at Larry's reflection in the rearview mirror and realized, with a start, that she found him attractive. She hadn't looked at a man that way—physically, romantically—in a very long time. The spark of attraction excited her but also made her self-conscious. She hoped she wasn't noticeably blushing.

Larry was talking about getting through his difficult divorce. "I'm not sure I would've made it through that first year after my separation without talking to people who'd been there. It's true what they say, you know—divorce, in some ways, is worse than death. It's a horrible thing to say, but it's the honest-to-God truth. You're stuck being connected to this person because you have kids with them, and yet all you want to do is cut off all ties. It would've been better if they just didn't exist anymore."

Teresa sucked in a breath. No one had ever said that to her before. And here was Larry, telling her he'd felt the same way about his ex-wife right after his separation. It validated everything Teresa had felt at that delicate time.

She met Larry's eyes in the rearview mirror. "Yes, exactly. That's exactly how I felt too. And I never said it to anyone because I thought it was..."

"Messed up?"

"Yes. And I guess it is. But it's how I felt. And it's good to know someone else felt the same way."

Larry fixed his gaze on her in the mirror, and she felt his eyes boring into her. She glanced away, embarrassed by his direct stare, but then forced herself to look back. He was still staring at her, and a smile formed at the corners of his lips. Before she could change her mind and start censoring her behavior, she smiled back. She hoped her smile conveyed everything she felt: *I'm scared. Don't hurt me. I want to love again, but I don't know if I can trust. Be gentle with me. Love me. Adore me. Don't leave me.*

Chapter Thirty-Four
FRANK - JOHNSTON, NY
1985

Frank drove to Teresa's house on Christmas morning, singing along with Nat King Cole about tiny tots with their eyes all aglow. He thought of his kids—no longer tots—and their Christmas-morning routine, which comprised eating breakfast in their pajamas while opening their presents. His gifts were all wrapped and ready to go in a bag in the back seat. He parked the car and looked up at the house, seeing the Christmas-tree lights twinkling even in the daylight.

He rang the bell. Anthony opened the door and beamed when he saw his father. "Hi, Dad!"

"Hey, kiddo. Merry Christmas." Frank leaned over and gave him a hug. Anthony's hair smelled like baby shampoo. Frank laughed to himself. His son was a teenager, and his hair still smelled like a baby.

"Who is it, Anthony?" Teresa called from inside.

"It's Dad," Anthony answered.

"What? What's he doing here?" Teresa asked.

Frank froze in place. That wasn't what he'd hoped to hear.

"He came to see us for Christmas," Anthony answered, not taking his eyes off Frank and looking at him questioningly as if he wanted to know if that was the correct answer.

Frank heard rustling inside, and then Teresa appeared at the door, shooing Anthony back and blocking Frank's view into the house. "Frank, you can't just show up like this. It's Christmas. We talked about this. It's my holiday with the kids."

Over the last two years, Frank and Teresa had been flexible about the holidays, splitting them up or alternating. This year, Frank was getting the kids on Christmas night, and the plan was for them to stay over and spend the following day with him, as he had off work. Today was Teresa's time with them, but he'd wanted to surprise them with his gifts this morning. *Is that a crime?*

"I know, but I missed them. I wanted to see them. And you. I brought presents," he said, gesturing to the bag in his hands.

Anthony's eyes twinkled with delight. *Such a kid.*

"No, Frank. That's not how this works. You're interrupting my holiday. You can't just mosey on over because you miss the kids. Sorry, but that's unacceptable. And..." She looked back into the house.

"And what?" Frank asked, ignoring the rest of her comments. Now he was curious. *Is someone in there?*

"I have company," Teresa said matter-of-factly, standing up straighter and looking defiant.

"Company? What does that mean?" She was hiding something, and Frank wanted to know what. No, he had to know.

"My friend... Larry is here. He's spending Christmas with us."

"Oh. And who is Larry?" Frank asked in an accusatory tone.

"None of your business," Teresa snapped, raising her voice and stepping out onto the landing. Frank could still see Anthony's head peeping out, curious as ever. "He's my boyfriend." She looked Frank directly in the eye.

Frank had known this day would come at some point, but that didn't mean he was ready for it. "Your boyfriend? Spending Christmas with my wife and kids?"

"I'm not your wife anymore, Frank."

"Technically, you are. We haven't finalized the divorce yet."

Teresa had started the process a few months before, which Frank knew had been a long time coming, but it still stung.

"Seriously? I haven't been your wife for years, Frank. You can't just decide we're still technically married when it's convenient for you. You have no say in what I do or who I see."

Frank slammed his hand into the door. Teresa and Anthony both jumped back.

"Frank!" Teresa screamed.

In a moment, a large man was standing in the doorway, placing his hand on Teresa's shoulder. "Is everything okay, Teresa?"

The man didn't look at Frank, instead keeping his eyes glued on Teresa. But Frank couldn't turn away. He was staring at him—this man who was dating *his* wife and spending the holiday with *his* children. He had a thick mane of brown hair and a trim mustache and was neatly dressed in slacks, shoes, and a button-down shirt. He was tall—and stocky. He made an imposing figure, standing next to Teresa, claiming her.

"Son of a bitch," Frank muttered.

Larry turned and looked at him directly. His face was calm but serious. "I think you should leave."

Frank felt his anger rise a notch higher. This bastard was telling him what to do. He couldn't believe the nerve.

"Yes, Frank, I need you to leave. You can give the kids their gifts when they come to your apartment later tonight for your scheduled visit," Teresa said in an even tone.

Who is this woman? Frank thought. She seemed so different. He didn't like it at all. Not one bit.

"Fine. I'll leave. But this is bullshit. Absolute bullshit." He turned to go, thought about it again, and then dropped the bag of gifts at his feet on the landing. "I want my kids to open their fucking Christmas gifts on Christmas morning. Is that too much to ask? I'm leaving these here. The least you can do is bring them into the house and put them under the tree."

He knew he had no right to be angry and was being unreasonable, but he couldn't help himself. His feeling of propriety was strong. *That's my wife and kids in there, dammit. No matter what.*

Chapter Thirty-Five
LENA - ORANGE, CA
August 2015

I sipped my coffee and marveled at Atticus, splayed on the grass, legs spread, ample belly exposed to the sky. He groaned in pleasure, a ball underneath his back while he rocked back and forth, giving himself a massage.

Smart dog. I could sit here all day and watch him, but knew I should get a move on. Kevin was playing in a double-header softball game with his league, and I had the place to myself. My plan was to get caught up on work stuff.

My phone chimed, and I groaned, hoping it wasn't said work stuff interrupting me on a Sunday. I was relieved to see a text from my niece, Ella. Our text exchanges were always a highlight of my week.

Aunt Lena, I can't wait to see you for the wedding. Less than two months! It's getting closer. I'm so excited. I got a new dress. Mom took me to Forever 21. Here's a photo. Do you like it?

I beamed, looking at the selfie of my niece looking oh-so-pretty in a peach dress that set off the natural highlights in her hair.

Oh, I love it! And I can't wait to see you too. It's going to be a great time. Hey, what's Christopher planning to wear? Think you can get him in a suit? My nephew was seventeen and not one to get dressed up.

She replied with a laughing emoji and then followed it up with, *I don't think he has a choice. Dad told him it was a suit or else. So they went shopping too. Chris is so tall now he doesn't fit into his old one.*

I figured, I wrote back. *I'm sure he'll look great!*

I can't wait to see Grandpa and Oliver all dressed up as the grooms! Do you think they'll wear rainbow bow ties? She sent emojis of two men wearing tuxedos, along with the Pride flag.

I hearted her text. I remembered Ella adding a rainbow flag to her Facebook profile photo when the Supreme Court decision was announced earlier that summer. *Yeah, I'm sure they'll be looking very dapper. But not sure if they'll do the rainbow bowtie theme. Ha ha.*

My friends at school said they should! They think I'm the coolest kid for having a grandfather who is gay and getting married to his partner. LOL.

Boy, had times changed. I envied the freedom my niece felt to go to high school and reveal the news of her grandfather's upcoming nuptials, knowing her friends would be supportive, treating it like a badge of honor. Good for her. Definitely not how things had been when I was a kid, that was for sure.

You ARE the coolest kid! At least to me. I added a heart emoji.

Aww, thanks Auntie Lena. Three dots appeared—she was typing more. *Okay, gotta run and finish a school project. Tell Uncle Kevin I said hi. Love you!*

Love you too. Good luck with the project! I smiled and shook my head, in awe of how open my niece was about her grandfather.

When my parents separated, I'd been trying to figure out a way through the messiness of the situation. It was the 1980s, when half the student body of Johnston looked like the kids in a sleek Benetton ad and the other half like they were playing a part in the rough-and-tumble movie *The Outsiders*. The preppy aesthetic ruled, and the rich kids got the popular vote, with their college sweatshirts collected from fall tours of Ivy League schools, BMWs handed to them on their sixteenth birthday, stashes of marijuana and cocaine they could afford to purchase, and houses in the rich part of town with sweeping lawns, in-ground pools, and parents who were conveniently never home when a party occurred over the weekend. With my divorced parents, single mother shacking up with her boyfriend in a rental in the working-class part of town, hand-me-down clothes, and old-jalopy American-made used cars, I wasn't exactly part of the ruling class.

So when Jessica Mitchell, one of the most popular and wealthy girls, invited me over on a Tuesday to hang out at her house after school and stay for dinner, I said an emphatic yes. In this two-person play, Jessica was a Benetton kid, and I was clearly cast in the role of the outsider. Mom was due to pick me up, but she got stuck working late. Her boyfriend, Larry, had his bowling league on Thursday nights, so he couldn't come. And Anthony, who'd just gotten a used car, was at his girlfriend's house. By process of elimination, Mom sent Dad to come get me. And that would have been a nonissue, but my father showed up with Ricky, who was so obviously... out. I hated when my dad showed up places with him. Eventually, Mom would prohibit my dad from bringing Ricky anyplace where Anthony and I could bump into people we knew. But on this occasion, that rule wasn't yet in effect.

When I opened Jessica's front door to leave, there was my dad standing outside his car on the driver's side, waving, with Ricky standing next to him, resembling the musician Prince. He wore black leather pants, boots with small heels, a bright-purple button-up shirt, and fingerless gloves. His thick brown hair was wavy, with a curl dipping over one eye, and he wore a heavy layer of eyeliner visible even from many feet away. I wanted to crawl under a rock.

"Who's that?" Jessica asked.

I knew who she was referring to but answered, "My father."

"No, the other guy." I looked out at Ricky like I didn't know who he was. "Oh, I think he's one of my dad's friends from work." I shrugged, acting like it was no big deal.

She looked out again, examining Ricky like she'd been assigned to write a report on him. "He looks…"

I held my breath, waiting for the rest of her sentence. Dreading it.

"Weird." She sniffed the air like a hound dog who'd caught a scent.

"He's fine. They're not close friends. I don't know why my dad brought him. Probably giving him a ride or something." I looked out at my dad and put up a finger, gesturing I'd be there in a minute. He nodded.

Jessica looked from my dad to Ricky and then back to me. "Whatever. Okay, see you tomorrow."

"Bye," I said, heading down the walkway, relieved that was the end of that.

But it wasn't. The next day, Jessica approached me between classes in a hallway that wasn't heavily trafficked. "Hey. Listen, Lena, I have to tell you something, but don't be mad, okay?"

I flinched, worried about what was coming.

"After you left last night, my parents said they don't want me to be friends with you."

"Why?" I asked, not liking where this might be heading. But needing her to spell it out. A glutton for punishment.

She looked around to make sure no one was in earshot and then back at me. "My parents were watching from the family room window when your dad and that guy picked you up. They said your dad's friend looked like… a faggot. And maybe your dad is too. So they don't want me to hang out with you."

I took a step back. *Wow, her parents were snooping? Bunch of busybody snobs.* "And you're gonna just go along with that?" No questions, no conversation, no explanation, no defense permitted to be asserted. I was guilty by association.

"What am I supposed to do, Lena? They're my parents," she said, flailing her arms at her sides. "Besides, he looked like a homo. It's kind of weird that your dad hangs out with him. Made me wonder if maybe your dad is one too." She held up her head, proud of her announcement, taking a stand.

I felt a rage buried deep inside me unleash itself. And the target of all that rage stood before me as Jessica. Her outstretched chin protruded from her neck, eyes defiant, judging, mocking. My hand soared through the air and hit Jessica's cheekbone with a slap that reverberated through the empty hallway.

"Don't you dare call my father that, you hear me? If I hear you say anything like that ever again, to me or anyone else, I'll beat the living shit out of you." My eyes burned and nostrils flared. I felt possessed.

Jessica held her hand to her cheek, tears welling up in her eyes. She looked truly frightened. I didn't care. I wanted to hit her again and stepped toward her with my arm raised. She cowered, dropping to the floor and letting out a bloodcurdling scream. It stopped me in my tracks. I drew my arm back, looked at her with disgust, and marched down the hall away from her. I looked back before I turned the corner and saw her curled up in a fetal position, crumpled on the floor like a discarded mop.

In the end, Jessica opened her mouth again—she marched to the principal's office and announced that I'd smacked her in the face. Thank goodness she didn't divulge the reason for our fight. The principal then dragged my mom to school. And the following day, I took an enormous leap of faith to confide in the guidance counselor—only to be shut down. The counselor confirmed my worst fears—that kids my age, and even adults, couldn't be expected to handle our family secret.

I could still see the counselor's face, full of concern, after I'd spilled the beans. "Oh, sweetie," she'd said, her voice laced with pity I didn't want. "I think your mother's right, and this is something that should just stay within your family. Kids can be really cruel, and what happened with your friend Jessica is probably just going to be the tip of the iceberg." She hesitated. "It's also a difficult time right now. With..." She waved her hand and pursed her lips. "You know, with this 'illness' going around. I think if you want to have a much better experience in high school, you should keep this quiet. It's nobody's business, after all."

If the guidance counselor was right, and what happened was the shape of things to come, I didn't want to divulge my family secret ever again.

ACT 4: A COMING OUT OF A DIFFERENT KIND

Chapter Thirty-Six
LENA - WEST HOLLYWOOD, CA
September 2015

"**D**id you get the mock-up of the wedding invitation Oliver designed? Isn't it gorgeous?" my dad excitedly asked as soon as the four of us sat down for dinner at a swanky new Vietnamese restaurant in West Hollywood that he and Oliver had been dying to try.

"Yes, it's beautiful," I said, smiling.

The two of them looking like little kids beaming with pleasure at their creation.

"Yeah, Oliver, good job." Kevin glanced at me and back to my dad. "Hey, did Lena tell you she was asked to give the keynote speech at the annual COLAGE conference this fall, a few days after your wedding?"

Oh no. Why did he have to bring it up? I tried to telekinetically communicate *Please don't* to him, but he wasn't getting the message.

"What's that?" my father asked.

"It's a national organization that specializes in offering education, awareness, and support to children and adult children of lesbian and gay parents."

I was impressed by how closely Kevin had paid attention when I'd told him about it. *Or did he pull up their website?* Maybe he was more curious than he let on.

"They asked her to speak about some of the legal issues. But one of the board members has become her friend and also encouraged her to speak as an adult child of a gay parent. Isn't that cool?" Kevin beamed.

I could tell that he not only meant well but was also genuinely proud of me, as if this was some type of award I'd won.

My father looked over at me. He appeared cautious, like he was trying to read me. "Wow, that's cool. Are you ready for it?"

I couldn't tell if he meant the speech itself or the possible revealing of my deepest secret—and his—to a vast audience.

"Not yet." And then I added hastily, "But I will be."

My dad nodded.

Oliver grabbed his arm and squeezed it. "Frank, this is wonderful, isn't it? We should go hear her speech and take photos."

I shifted in my seat, realizing I was nervous about them being there. My father and his newly minted husband would be front and center, cheering me on. There was no hiding.

Desperate, I changed the subject. "Did I tell you I'm heading to San Francisco next week for work? I'll be there for three days. Bummer that Kevin can't come with me. His team has a huge project going on at Disney. I'll actually have some free time when I'm not presenting at the conference. I'd love to do some sightseeing in the City by the Bay. Every time I go there for business, it's a quick in and out. I'm dying to visit Alcatraz Island. The tour is supposed to be really moving." I couldn't shut up. But this topic felt a lot safer than that goddamn speech.

"Hey, why don't I come with you?" my dad said. "I love San Francisco and haven't been there in years. It would be fun to spend some time together and do some sightseeing. I've always wanted to see Alcatraz as well. Plus, Oliver also has a major work project next week. You wouldn't mind if I joined her, honey?" He looked at his partner expectantly.

Oliver shook his head. "Not at all."

"Really? You've never been to Alcatraz either?" I asked.

"Nope. I've been to the city a few times but never did that tour," my father said.

"What a great idea," Kevin chimed in. "You two should go. Can you get the time off on such short notice, Frank?"

My dad waved his hand. "Yeah, that shouldn't be a problem. I'm the manager and have a good team. Besides, I have so much vacation time accumulated."

I thought about it, analyzing the logistics. Even if my flight wound up being full, my dad could easily find another flight from one of the Los Angeles area airports to San Francisco. It was a quick trip. And I would still have to check online and see if there were tickets left for Alcatraz. But that was all doable. *Why not?*

"Okay," I heard myself saying. "Let's do it."

Apparently, I was going to San Francisco with my father. My family had taken a few vacations before my parents split up, but I'd never been away with just my father—not as a child and certainly not as an adult.

When I mentioned I'd be staying at the hotel where the conference was being held in Union Square, he asked if I would be open to staying someplace else.

"What'd you have in mind?" I asked.

"My friends know this great inn in the Castro. They stayed there last year and loved it."

"The Castro? Isn't that the gay area?" I asked, raising my eyebrows.

"Yes, it is. It's nice. I think you'd like it. Plus, it's got some history that may interest you. We can go to Harvey Milk Plaza and walk around."

I processed his comment. My dad wanted to show me the gay area and to experience the culture together. *This should be interesting.*

A wave of excitement rippled through my body. I had a feeling this trip would be more than a visit to a former prison on an island.

Chapter Thirty-Seven

FRANK - PELHAM, NY

1987

F rank hummed along to Puccini's "Nessun Dorma," one of his favorite opera arias, feeling like a kid who got out of school early. He'd worked a lot of overtime lately to make extra money, so his boss had given him the afternoon off. It was Wednesday and Ricky's day off at the bakery. Frank planned to head home, change his clothes, grab Ricky, and take the boat out for a spin with him, something they never got to do on a weekday.

He pulled into the driveway and saw a station wagon parked nearby in one of the visitor spots for their apartment complex. Frank didn't know who it belonged to. He entered the apartment and called out for Ricky. No answer.

"Ricky?"

Still no answer. He heard music coming from the bedroom. Frank opened the bedroom door, and there was Ricky, in bed with a man.

Frank stood in the doorway, his mind racing. *No, no, no. Not Ricky. What in the world? Why? Who?*

He grabbed the guy and lifted him out of the bed, disgusted to see his naked body, knowing it had just been touching Ricky. The guy tried to pull himself away. Frank punched with all his strength, landing his fist somewhere on the guy's face. The guy stumbled back, losing his balance, then righted himself. He grabbed his clothes and ran out the door. Frank tracked him with his eyes, feeling like a madman. If he'd had a gun, he definitely would have pulled the trigger.

He turned around and saw Ricky, still in the bed, the covers now pulled up to his neck, shielding his body from view. How many times had Frank seen him naked? That was his body to touch, to make love to, not some stranger's.

"Get up!" Frank yelled.

Ricky cowered under the covers, as if the comforter would bring him some protection. "No, Frank, you're crazy right now. I'm not getting out of this bed until you leave the room."

"Who is he?" Frank yelled. "I want to know who he is. I will kill that motherfucker, you hear me?" His chest burned. "How long, Ricky?"

"How long what?"

"Don't fuck with me! How long has this been going on?" Frank moved closer to the bed, and Ricky shifted farther under the covers. *Goddamn coward.*

"A few months," Ricky whimpered. "He's a pharmacist. That's how I met him. At the drugstore. His wife and kids don't know he's gay. I'm sorry, Frank. I'm—"

"Shut up." Frank put his fist up and moved toward Ricky. Then he stopped. He wouldn't hit him. Couldn't. He was furious, but he was also heartbroken.

"His wife and kids don't know he's gay," Frank repeated. And then he laughed. It sounded maniacal. "Well, isn't that familiar. Is that your thing, Ricky—you get them while they're still married and show them what it's like on the other side? Does that make you feel useful—to fuck the guys who haven't had the guts to come out yet?"

His voice dripped with sarcasm and exhaustion. And suddenly, that was what Frank felt. Utter exhaustion.

"I lost my wife and kids. My family. For this." He gestured at the room, the bed, at Ricky. "For you. For us. I loved you." His face contorted, but he wouldn't let the tears come out. "I did this to Teresa. Oh my God, so many times. I did this." He shook his head. "Maybe this is my punishment. I don't know. Because now I know how she felt. And it's..."

He stopped. He couldn't put into words the disappointment, the pain, the betrayal. The way it had wiped out all his hopes for their future together in the single moment when he saw Ricky with that man.

"Get out. Now. I mean it. I'm going out on the back patio for ten minutes, and when I come back in, I expect you and all your things to be gone. Do you understand?"

Ricky nodded solemnly.

"And never come back. Ever."

When Frank came back into the apartment, Ricky wasn't there. Frank broke down and cried, the force of the wails threatening to overtake him. So many losses. If this was cosmic payback for the way he'd betrayed Teresa, he deserved it.

Frank picked up the phone and dialed Teresa's number. He couldn't believe he was calling her, of all people. The betrayer reaching out to the betrayed. Yet somehow, he knew she wouldn't turn her back on him.

He heard her voice on the other end of the phone say hello, and it sounded like home.

"Teresa, it's me. I... I..." Frank whispered.

He couldn't continue. *What can I say? "My boyfriend cheated on me, and my world feels like it's falling apart, and now I know what you must have felt every time I betrayed you"?*

Frank felt foolish. He had no right to call her and expect her to console him. That wasn't her role anymore.

"Frank? What's wrong?" Teresa asked.

Frank sighed and slumped to the floor, cradling the phone in the crook of his neck. "I'm a mess, Teresa." He shook his head. "I'm the one who caused all this. I set all this in motion." He gasped. "I'm so sorry." The tears flowed, and he couldn't keep his voice steady.

"Frank, what happened? Talk to me." Her voice was soft.

So he told her. He droned on and on, sitting on the floor of his apartment—the one that he'd just kicked his boyfriend out of—telling his ex-wife, whom he'd betrayed repeatedly, about how he was just betrayed and that he now knew what that had felt like for her.

He went further, admitting he was jealous of her new relationship with Larry even though he knew he didn't have a right to be. He told her all the thoughts and fears swirling around in his mind. And she listened. Teresa remained calm, offering words of support. But when he told her he missed his kids and feared they would turn their backs on him the way Henry's kids had, he heard her voice change and felt a shift in her demeanor.

"Frank, if you don't want to lose your kids forever, you've got to change. I told you that years ago when you asked for my advice. Especially with Lena. Anthony's already coming around. He's making his way back to you. And I'm sure that's partly because you make more of an effort with him. I know it's easier with him being out of the police academy and Lena being busy at college. But that's really just an excuse. This has been going on a while, Frank, between you and Lena. You've always spent more time with Anthony. And Lena strayed even further from you during her teenage years. I watched it happen and tried to step in when I could, but now it's really up to you. You need to show up for both your kids, Frank. Make it a point to spend as much time with Lena as you do with Anthony. Try to let her really know you. Let her in. If you don't want to lose her, give her your presence, which, honestly, was sorely lacking when she was a kid."

Frank understood that Teresa was handing him a gift—the gift of truth, something he hadn't given her for many, many years. He felt unworthy of it but grateful.

"Thank you. I will. I promise," he said and meant it. He was ready to be the father he needed to be, at all costs. It was time to put his kids first.

"Okay," she said with a note of finality. "I'll let you go for now." She hesitated. "Frank, I'm sorry about... you know. But I'm glad we talked."

"Me too," he said. "Thank you for being there."

"Uh-huh," she said. "Bye, Frank."

He heard the phone click and placed it back on the receiver. Frank was heartbroken over what had happened with Ricky but also felt a renewed sense of hope. He had needed to talk to Teresa in order to move forward. He still needed her in his life. It was so much better with her in it. She was his anchor, and he felt afloat without her.

Chapter Thirty-Eight
FRANK - BRONX, NY
1988

F rank parked in the visitor spot in front of Lena's residence hall on the Rose Hill campus of Fordham University. He stopped at the resident assistant's desk and gave his name, showing his identification as required. He liked that the college had such strict security. It made him feel better about Lena living here. Not that he didn't trust her. She had a rebellious streak, sure, but she also had a good head on her shoulders and took her studies seriously.

The RA buzzed him in, and he walked to suite 4A and knocked. No answer. He knocked again. "Lena, it's me, Dad." He heard some rustling inside and a groan.

What the hell?

"Lena, open up. It's Dad. Come on."

"It's open." Lena sounded far away, like she was in an echo chamber.

He opened the main door to the suite and walked into the shared living room. He could see Lena's bedroom beyond that, with the door open and her suitcases and clothes hamper packed up, ready to go home for the winter break. She shared a double bedroom with a roommate, and two other girls shared the other double.

Not a bad setup for a group of college kids.

"I'm in here." Her voice was hoarse, like she'd been using it too much or was exhausted. It was coming from the bathroom. The door was open, so he walked in, and there she was, sitting on the floor, leaning against the toilet.

"What the hell? Are you sick?" Frank asked.

"Kind of. Well, not exactly. I'm... hungover." She looked at him with sheepish eyes, pleading with him not to be angry.

Well, this is something new. Frank had never known Lena to drink. But she was in college, after all, and he supposed college kids drank.

She looked horrible. Her hair was a ratty mess, mascara running down her face, and her cheeks had tear stains on them. *Man, that must have been some night.*

"What happened?" He had an idea, but he wanted to hear it.

"Ugh. I drank wine coolers, and then some idiot made vodka drinks, and I had some of those too. They don't mix. At all. I felt so sick, and nothing would make it go away. Nothing except vomiting. And you know how much I hate to vomit." Lena looked at him as if trying to figure something out. "At least I *think* you know how much I hate to vomit. Mom knows. I can't really do it. Never have been able to. Well, I guess I physically can. But it's rare, and I have to be really sick. Which I am." She stopped and took a deep breath as if she were trying to gain strength. She moaned. "Mom is going to kill me..." She looked at him pitifully.

"Let's get you up off the floor, cleaned up, and changed. You can't go home like this. You're a mess. Are you feeling better now, at least? Please don't tell me you slept here, leaning against the toilet, all night long."

He went over and slowly helped her up. She gave him a small smile. As pathetic as she looked and as much as he should have been mad at her, he smiled back. She was his little girl. Yet she was so fiercely independent. So smart. But she was still capable of making a mess—one he'd walked into and now had to help her with. He could do that.

"I didn't want to throw up in bed. That's gross and dangerous," Lena said, always the reasonable one even when she was dealing with her own inappropriate drunken behavior.

"Do you feel well enough to take a shower? I can start bringing your bags to the car."

She nodded. "Yeah, I can do that." She looked around as if surveying what it would take to get into the shower.

"Come on. Get going. You'll feel better once you've cleaned up."

She nodded again and this time looked more confident. "You're right." She grabbed a towel and hung it on the hook outside the shower door. She turned back to him. "Thanks, Dad. I appreciate you not being mad about this. I already feel like shit, and trust me, I've learned my lesson the hard way. Never again. I'll be more careful about what I drink and how much."

"I know." Frank was sure she would never do this again. One thing he knew Lena could do was learn. "And I won't tell your mother. She doesn't have to know. Unless you want to tell her, of course. I know you pretty much tell her everything." He snickered.

"I may tell her at some point. No, I will. But not right now. I don't want her to worry while I'm home for the holiday break."

"Sounds good to me. It'll be our secret."

She looked at him, her eyebrows knitted, and he couldn't read her expression. He wasn't sure if she was happy that he was going to keep her brief night of debauchery in confidence or if there was something else on her mind. She turned around and headed to the shower, and he stepped out into the living room to give her some privacy and closed the door behind him.

A little while later, they packed the car up with her things and were on their way, sitting side by side on the front seat. Lena leaned her head against the window, subdued. Definitely not her energetic self.

That's what she gets for drinking herself sick. He turned on the CD player, and the entrancing music of the aria "Un bel dí, vedremo," from the opera *Madama Butterfly*, filled the car.

Frank hummed along for a few bars before turning to Lena. "You know my mother had an issue with alcohol for a while, right?"

"Yes, I know." Lena shifted her body toward him, taking her head off the window. "How bad was it? Was she an alcoholic?"

"I think so. My father was certainly worried and made sure she got help and stopped drinking. He was so good about it. But that was his way, as you know. She was a forceful person, so it wasn't easy. She resisted at first but eventually agreed to get help."

"A strong personality, Dad?" She snickered. "That's an understatement. Your mom was a force to be reckoned with. She scared me often." Lena winced.

Frank laughed. "Yeah, she could be scary. But she meant well. She loved her family and could come across as... well, let's just say that no one wanted to cross her."

Lena gave him a small smile and gazed off into the distance as they headed up the Bronx River Parkway. She looked deep in thought. Lena favored Frank's father and felt intimidated by his mother, never really connecting with her the way she did with Enzo. That didn't surprise him. Eva was a complex woman. She could be overbearing, and Frank often felt like she was inspecting him through a microscope. Yet Lena often reminded him of his mother. Not that she had an iron fist like Eva, but she was so feisty and strong-willed. Maybe that would serve her well in life. He hoped so.

"You hungry? Feeling well enough to eat?" he asked, knowing they would pass one of his favorite diners on the way home.

"Not sure if I can eat yet."

"C'mon, you got to eat. Trust me—you'll feel better. Let's stop at the Highway Diner."

She broke into a big smile. "Oh, I love that place. Okay, maybe I'll get something small instead of my typical triple decker sandwich."

They got settled into a booth at the diner and ordered their lunches. Lena looked through the songs on the jukebox and stopped at one. She peered at him. "Mom loves that song."

"Which one?"

"'The First Time Ever I Saw Your Face,' by Roberta Flack."

Frank got warm and clammy. "It was one of our songs." He felt himself choking up and swallowed.

Lena reached across the table and grabbed his hand. "I like knowing that the two of you had songs together once upon a time."

He looked deep into her eyes and found an empathy there he'd never seen before. He lifted her hand to his lips and lightly kissed the back of it. She smiled warmly, her dark-blue eyes twinkling—his father's eyes. It was always such a shock to see them reflected in Lena's face. Just maybe, his Cricket was making her way back to him.

Chapter Thirty-Nine
LENA - SAN FRANCISCO, CA
September 2015

My dad and I flew together a week later from LAX to SFO and took a taxi to the Willow House Inn, which was smack in the middle of the Castro. After checking us in, they gave us keys to our suite, which had two separate bedrooms and a shared bathroom. We entered the suite, looked at each other, and smiled. The bright bedroom had a queen-size bed with a willow wood headboard, two large windows, an armoire, a pair of oversized armchairs, and a dresser with sherry, glasses, and chocolates waiting for us. We set down our luggage and walked into a smaller but equally charming bedroom with a queen bed, a small nightstand, a large willow wood chair, and even more windows.

"I'll take this room," my dad said, putting his jacket down on the chair.

"You sure?"

"Yeah. You take the other bedroom so you're closer to the bathroom to get ready for your conference in the morning."

"Okay, that makes sense. Thanks."

We settled in, unpacked our suitcases, freshened up in the bathroom, and then headed out for dinner. The owners of the inn, a gay couple, recommended a restaurant down the street. After dinner, we started walking back to the inn, and my dad looked over at a club with music pouring out of its doors and a black-velvet rope entrance. The bouncer made eye contact with my dad, who nodded and smiled back.

My dad bumped my shoulder, pushing me toward the door. "Let's go."

"Where? There?" I whipped my head around, pointing to the nightclub, even though I knew what he meant.

"Yeah," he said, grinning like a little kid. "I want to check it out."

"I'm too old to go to a club," I protested. *Is he kidding me?* I didn't go to clubs anymore. And even if I did, I wouldn't go with my father.

"If you're too old, then I'm ancient." He laughed. "Come on. It'll be fun. We can dance."

He knew how to get me. The ability to kill it on a dance floor was one thing I'd inherited from him. I looked longingly down the street toward our inn. Then I looked back at the club and gave a small shrug. *What the hell?*

He grabbed my arm and steered me toward the entrance. The bouncer greeted us with a smile and nodded at my dad again. It was like they spoke the same language.

He then turned to me. "ID, please, miss."

"ID? Miss? Why, thank you," I said, acting as if his job requirement were flattery.

He examined my license and handed it back to me. "Have fun."

He winked at my dad, and at that moment, it hit me that this was a gay club. Of course. We were in the Castro.

We walked in, and it took my eyes a few minutes to adjust to the dark, bluish-tinted lighting. There were lots of men at the bar, standing around and drinking. Men of every size, in various forms of dress—and some undress—packed the dance floor, shaking, moving, and gyrating like one gigantic mass. I was the only woman in the entire place, from what I could see. That made me feel kind of special in a bizarre way, like I was being granted admission to a private club.

"Come on, let's go." Dad grabbed my arm and led me onto the dance floor. "I love this song," he said, shaking his hips to the beat. It was "Enjoy the Silence," by Depeche Mode—a throwback to the '90s. I loved it too.

I was nervous. Even though I loved to be in the spotlight—performing in high school theater and now in the courtroom with a judge or jury and spectators—I felt very much on display.

"Relax," my dad whispered into my ear and then pulled his face back so he could look at me.

He was smiling, and I realized he didn't mean it to reprimand me. He was trying to put me at ease. I looked around again and noticed that everyone was dancing, laughing, and very much enjoying themselves. No one seemed to notice me or care that I was the only woman there.

I felt my shoulders relax, and I started swaying to the music. We were moving in rhythm, shaking our hips in time to the beat, showing off our fancy dance moves. We were smiling, clapping our hands, and laughing so hard sometimes that we would throw our heads back.

"Woo! I love this. Beautiful. Dancing with my baby girl." My dad grabbed me, and we started dancing as a couple, doing the moves of the Latin hustle that he'd taught me when I was a little girl. My body knew exactly what to do even though it hadn't danced these steps in ages.

The song ended, and we stayed on the dance floor for the next. And the next. And the next. We took a break to get some drinks and then went back out. A man walked over to us, smiling, and whispered something to my dad. The music was too loud for me to hear what he said.

My dad motioned to me. "That's my daughter." He smiled proudly.

"Your daughter?" the guy asked, nodding approvingly. "Well, well. That's cool." He raised his drink, saluting me.

I waved, laughing.

A few other guys came over, probably friends with the first one. They were all chatting with the guy who had first approached us, smiling at my dad and me. Some were even waving and saying things like, "Aww, dad and daughter—that's so sweet. Look at them. Damn, they can dance. Oh my God, I love this. How cool."

My dad was in his element, dancing and enjoying himself. He looked so happy. And I realized it wasn't only because he was in a gay club, where he could be himself. It was also because he was there with me. We'd never been dancing at a gay club before. My father was showing me who he was and wanted me to experience it with him.

I realized he was such a risk taker, a fact I hadn't fully grasped when I was younger. His entire life was a risk. Yet he really didn't seem to care what others thought of him. Or maybe it was more that he *couldn't* care if he was to live the life he chose.

We said goodbye to the guys, who patted us on the back, wishing us well. As we walked back to the inn, the music and excitement of the club faded behind us, and we fell into a comfortable pace, leisurely strolling side by side. My dad hooked his arm with mine, and we walked in contented silence for a few city blocks. We approached Harvey Milk Plaza, with the Rainbow Flag bathed in moonlight. Milk was also a New Yorker and would have been about my father's age had his life not been tragically cut short at the age of forty-eight.

I glanced at my dad and felt goose bumps spread across my skin.

He squeezed my arm. "I'm glad we're here together, seeing this."

"Me too," I said, realizing how fortunate I was that my father was standing next to me, alive and healthy. He'd never been injured or killed in a police raid or gay-bashing incident and had made it through the AIDS epidemic. Now he was about to marry his partner and declare his love for him publicly. What a journey. Tears welled in my eyes.

"Tell me your story," I blurted. "I'm ready to hear it. *Your* story." It felt like I'd longed to say this for years, even if I hadn't been fully aware of it.

My dad raised his eyebrows. "What do you want to know?"

"Everything. When did you know? What was it like for you? Were you ever with a man before Mom? I'm ready to hear it all. To listen."

I wanted to know his story completely. I now understood that fear of the unknown had led me to stifle my father's voice. *What if it's worse than what I already know? What if there were other ways he betrayed Mom?* I'd held back out of loyalty to her and an uneasy sense that by permitting him to talk about his indiscretions, I approved of them. Well, that was not how it worked. His perspective deserved my full attention, which had to be better than years of burying my curiosity and replacing it with circumspection and anger.

"Okay," he said, "I will. Let's go back to the inn and talk there, all right?"

I nodded, and we continued our trek back.

O nce back in our suite, I poured us each a small glass of sherry and handed one to my father, along with some chocolates. He sat in one armchair, and I plopped down in the other, folding my legs under me.

I grinned. "I've never had sherry before."

"Me neither," he said, smiling.

"Really? Well, here's to firsts." I raised my glass.

He hesitated, his glass suspended in front of him, and then said, "Yes, to firsts. I'll drink to that." I knew he didn't mean merely sherry.

My dad took a deep breath and looked like he was gathering himself. It felt like we were diving into the ocean, and once we broke the surface, there was no going back. He needed to be honest with me. I deserved it. So did he.

"I think I always knew deep down that I was gay." He took a moment. "I'd never been with a man before I married your mother, although I wanted to once when I was a teenager. But I knew it wasn't an acceptable choice back then. My family was traditional, as you know." He spoke calmly, but I sensed he was trying to contain a tide of emotions. "And Catholic, of course. The times were a lot less tolerant. Not that they're perfect now, by any means."

He took a sip of his sherry. I did the same and immediately felt a wave of warmth flow through my body. Damn, that stuff was potent. No wonder the glasses were so tiny.

"I didn't come out to my parents until after your mom and I split up. My mother didn't take it well. She acted like my life was over or she was being accused of having raised me wrong. So dramatic." He rolled his eyes. "But my dad? He was amazing." My father shook his head, an incredulous look on his face. "So supportive. Even put my mom in her place." He laughed, and I smiled.

"And then there was your mom." He sighed. "I don't need to tell you how amazing she was through it all. You were there." He breathed in deeply and then exhaled meditatively, like he was releasing the past. "When I met her, I thought everything would be okay. I hoped I could... I don't know, pack it away. Bury it. Besides, I loved your mom and knew I wanted a family. I wanted children."

I'd never heard my father say he wanted kids—that he'd intentionally chosen us. I wondered what his life might have looked like if he'd been born ten, twenty, or thirty years later. *Would he have ever been with my mom at all?* A tiny gasp escaped me as I realized the reality of that alternate universe—it would erase me. I trembled at the thought that I never would have been born.

"We dated and then married, and for a short while, we were happy." He smiled warmly and closed his eyes. I imagined he was seeing the two of them back then. "We had Anthony and you, and we were a family. And I tried to convince myself that was enough." He hesitated. "Then I realized I wasn't really me—the real me underneath it all. And that's when it all fell apart. But it's also when it all came together, if that makes sense."

I nodded, finally seeing my dad for who he truly was—a man who'd tried to persuade everyone, including himself, that he could shoehorn himself into a so-called traditional marriage and life. All the while, a fundamental part of him had refused to stop yearning for the life he knew could be his if he just had the guts to reach out and grasp it. But doing so meant he would forever mourn the family he'd left behind. I thought of the way he'd stepped into his new life once he allowed himself to do so. It was still shocking sometimes. Most people didn't know who they were and paid close attention to what everyone else wanted for them—who everyone told them they were. Yet he decided not to live life through the filter of others' eyes, and he created his own version.

My father's voice brought my focus back to the present. "Did I ever tell you about the recurring nightmare I had when I first moved to LA?"

I shook my head.

"It was when I first came out from New York. I was staying with a friend in West Hollywood while looking for a place to live. I woke up in the middle of the night to the entire building shaking. No, not the building. The earth beneath it. Scared the shit out of me. I panicked and ran out of his apartment in my underwear. It passed quickly, and when my friend came out to check on me, he laughed because it was such a minor tremor. But I wasn't laughing. It spooked me. Never felt anything like it."

My dad looked at me. I nodded, encouraging him to continue.

"After the earthquake, I kept having nightmares, experiencing it all over again. And I would see this girl and boy crying, stuck in the middle of the earthquake, buildings crumbling around them."

He stopped again and put his fist to his mouth. I could see that he was trying to keep himself from crying. I grabbed his hand and held it tight, letting him know I was right there.

"I would try to get to them, to help them. And when I finally reached them and could see their faces... every time, it startled me to discover they were you and Anthony."

I looked at him, my heartbeat quickening. My dad had been worried about us. His nightmare was clearly a metaphor for our family and what happened to us. We'd experienced an earthquake of immense proportions.

"Dad." My voice was soft. "I don't like that you had those nightmares. But if I'm being honest, I'm glad you were worried about us."

"Always," he whispered, and tears pooled in the corners of his eyes.

He wiped away a tear and summoned the courage to continue. "For years, I felt like I was in the middle of an earthquake. But we're out of the epicenter." He attempted a weak smile. "Sure, there've been some aftershocks. But we made it through."

He squeezed my hand, brought it to his lips, and kissed it. "It means a lot to me. Your support. I know it wasn't always easy for you. Or for Anthony. And Mom, of course." He looked away then turned back to me. "I miss her. Part of me wishes she could come to the wedding. Isn't that weird?" He shook his head.

"No, not weird at all. I miss her so much. It feels strange that she somehow won't be a part of it. She would be happy for you, you know?"

"I know." He smiled. Sadness and happiness took turns crossing his face. "What matters to me is that you and Anthony will be there, not just happy for me but accepting me."

"Of course we do, always."

"Not always." He hesitated, staring at me. "Even after you accepted me, you were still ashamed of me. And you know it. I mean, c'mon, Lena, you told no one." He turned away but didn't look mad.

He was right. I'd been ashamed of my upbringing. It seemed stupid now. I couldn't change where I came from or what I'd been through, so why should I be ashamed of what had made me the person I was? That would be like being ashamed of myself. *No, thank you.*

"Maybe I was ashamed," I admitted, "but I'm not anymore."

He smiled that big, beautiful Frank smile I would bet had made my mom's stomach flip-flop all those years ago when they met.

"That's my Cricket," he said. "You're my daughter, too, you know. Never forget that."

I'd kept so many things from my father because I thought my role as an adult was to be supportive and empathetic and to let the past lie. Maybe I should have allowed myself some righteous anger at all the things he'd missed. The school plays, athletic events, teacher conferences, and countless nights he hadn't been there when I went to bed. I'd never really confronted him about his absence. We'd never had a knock-down, drag-out fight about it. It had lived hidden inside me, that anger, not announcing itself even to me—except as a vague ache that came and went, ebbed and flowed over the years.

I realized that this was one benefit of time and life lived. If you were lucky, all that old stuff worked itself out. Like a rotary telephone cord that had gotten stretched and knotted, and then one day you took the time to uncoil it and get all the knots out, allowing the heavy headset to hang while the cord morphed back into shape. You could see that some knots had left their mark and some stretches were still in the cord, but overall, it was intact.

Chapter Forty
TERESA - ORANGE, CA
1997

Teresa tied her robe tightly around the waist and leaned back in the Adirondack chair. She looked out over the backyard of Lena and Kevin's bungalow and let out a contented sigh. Teresa and Frank could never afford to buy a house, and she and Larry still only rented their place. She loved how her daughter owned not just a house but also the land it sat on—the gardens, the trees, everything. It had an orange tree in the yard. An actual orange tree. The concept was so foreign to Teresa that she felt like she'd been transported to a different country. She smelled something divine and wondered which plant it was. They were so different from the ones on the East Coast.

"What's that amazing smell?" she asked Lena, who'd come outside to join her on the patio.

"Star jasmine. Isn't it heavenly?" Lena said, handing Teresa a mug of tea.

"Thanks, sweetie," Teresa said, grabbing the mug. "Yes, it's amazing. I love it."

Lena sat down next to her and smiled as she looked out over the garden. "I'm so glad you're here, Mom." She grasped Teresa's hand and squeezed it.

"Me too," Teresa said, stroking Lena's hand.

She saw the pearl ring on her daughter's hand and smiled. Teresa had given her mother's pearl ring to Lena as her law school graduation gift. She remembered watching Lena cross the stage to receive her diploma and proudly thinking, *My daughter is going to be a lawyer* for the umpteenth time.

Teresa looked down at the framed wedding photo of Lena and Kevin that she'd found on display in the living room and brought to the patio. The couple was peering out from a vintage Rolls Royce.

Lena looked over. "Oh, that wedding photo cracks me up."

"Why?"

"Because we were like two little kids in that Rolls Royce. We felt so spoiled, the two of us, riding in luxury like old-fashioned movie stars. I remember turning to Kevin when we got in and saying, 'You don't know how cool it is that I'm even sitting in this car. A Rolls freaking Royce! I grew up on the west end of New Rochelle in a tiny attic apartment.'" Lena grinned.

Teresa smiled. "What did Kevin say?"

"He said, 'Well, look at you now, baby.' We did a champagne toast and then kissed. That's when the photographer snapped this photo."

"Lena, I'm thrilled you have a good marriage, especially after what I went through with your father. You and Kevin seem to have a great relationship. Romance, friendship, support. And loyalty, which is something I always wanted for you."

"And most importantly, he isn't gay!" Lena blurted. They both laughed. "I'm also happy for you, Mom, to have found love again with Larry. He's such a good guy, and you deserve all the happiness he brings you. He adores you, you know. Even if you won't let him make an honest woman out of you and marry him."

"I've had enough of marriage for one lifetime, thank you very much. I have no problem living happily in sin for the rest of my life."

Teresa smiled. Larry always let her know how he was feeling and how much he cared for her and made her feel loved. But it went beyond that. She felt desired. He couldn't get enough of her. He didn't mind the extra weight she carried on her frame. In fact, she thought he might find her more attractive because of it. He flirted with her, coming up with excuses to nuzzle her. And she basked in the attention.

She and Frank had married so young, and their relationship had soured so quickly. Frank's get-it-done attitude helped her feel safe when she was a young bride. And she stayed with him because he showed love through everyday gestures, which made her feel well taken care of. But Teresa had realized she deserved a partner who would be emotionally and physically there for her. She hadn't been sure if that was even an option.

Fortunately, she'd found that in Larry. Maybe he didn't change her oil for her, but he was so attentive in other ways—and those ways mattered a lot to Teresa.

Chapter Forty-One
LENA - ORANGE, CA
September 2015

I woke up the Saturday morning after returning from San Francisco, harnessed Atticus, and hit the neighborhood streets for a run. I'd missed several days because of the early meeting times of the conference. As I ran, I thought of my time with my dad in the City by the Bay. I pictured him dancing at the gay club, so free, so happy, and so proud to show me his world, and then our heart-to-heart at the inn when I finally got to hear his story from his perspective. It made me realize that there was a piece of my mom's story I hadn't yet explored. The last journal she'd kept—the one she'd filled during her battle with cancer—I'd never found the strength to read, so I'd let it linger for years. I would periodically take it out, thinking I was ready to peer inside, but would find it too painful and place it back.

Well, it was time to be brave. I wanted to understand both my parents' complete stories. I remembered the day I heard the word *cancer* in the same sentence as my mother's name. It was October 25, 2008, and I'd been standing in a sterile room at Sloan Kettering, staring at the doctor who'd just uttered that one paltry word that would change everything.

"Teresa, I'm so sorry." The oncologist looked at my mother, his eyes soft and earnest. "Your pancreatic cancer is inoperable, incurable. We'll provide treatment to prolong your life as much as possible and keep you comfortable, but this is terminal. I am truly sorry."

The realization hit me like a knife to the heart. My mother was going to die. Soon. The news was so devastating that all I could do was grip the counter as if it was the only thing tethering me to the earth. I wanted to howl and scream. I felt like I would choke as I tried to stifle anything from coming out of my mouth. My stomach churned, and I felt dizzy. I was overcome with homesickness, not for a place but for the life I'd just had before the diagnosis. I was going to have to live the rest of my life without my mom in it. I couldn't fathom that. I felt completely dislocated, unmoored, drifting out to sea. What would it be like to be a motherless daughter? I felt so out of control, emotions flooding me and threatening to take over.

As soon as we left the hospital that day, I requested a leave of absence from my job, and fortunately, Marcus granted it. I temporarily moved back to New York, securing a short-term rental right near my mom and Larry's apartment. What we sadly thought would be a few months turned into a year and a half as my mom held on longer than expected—a blessing and a curse, as it gave me more time with her but meant she was suffering as the cancer slowly killed her. Kevin was supportive, visiting when he could and patiently waiting for me to come back home to California for short stints to get more clothes and check in on my life then return to New York. I was there every step of the way for my mom's medical treatment and helped her see every specialist possible. Doing something, anything—researching online, making phone calls, organizing her paperwork—made me feel less helpless. It was the only way I could cope with such momentous news. But it still didn't mask the fact that I was losing my mom as she was losing her battle with the disease.

What made it even harder was that she could read me so well. I could never hide from her. It was like she knew everything that crossed my mind. My mother's intuition was so strong that I would swear sometimes she was psychic. It took me years to realize that what I thought was her predicting the future was really her uncanny, deep knowledge of me.

I'd never forget when she said, "Sweetie, this is killing me literally, but it's also killing you emotionally because you can't put your hands inside my body and take out the cancer. Please come to terms with the fact that I'm at peace with this, and just be there with me and stop trying to fight."

So reluctantly, I did. I thought of the time after I'd taken her to chemo and she was resting in bed and I crawled in next to her. We lay there on our sides, facing each other, looking into each other's eyes. We said nothing aloud. Our lips never moved, but our eyes said so much.

I love you. I will always love you.
I know.
I wish I could make this better.
I know.
You are my life.
I know.
Please go on loving me after I'm gone.
I will.
Thank you.
Thank you.

Chapter Forty-Two
TERESA - JOHNSTON, NY
2009

Teresa gazed out the window at the golden leaves on the beautiful maple tree in the front yard. Autumn had always been her favorite time of year. She loved to watch the trees display their change of colors throughout the season before dropping their leaves altogether for the winter. She couldn't believe a year had passed since her diagnosis. She'd watched the leaves fall then blinked, and here they were, dying off again.

She thought back to this time last year, when she'd been sitting in a state of shock in the waiting room of an oncologist's office, seeking a second opinion. Lena, by her side, was sipping a cup of coffee from the vending machine. They were alone for a few minutes while Larry and Anthony parked the car.

Lena grabbed her hand and squeezed it. "Are you afraid?" she asked sheepishly.

"Of dying? Yes, of course. But I'm more afraid of suffering while I'm still living—of what's coming and how bad it might be. I don't want to be in pain," Teresa admitted.

"We won't let that happen. We'll talk to your doctors about pain management and make sure they have a plan in place. I can't change your diagnosis, but I'll be with you every step of the way and make sure that you get the best treatment possible," Lena assured her. "Let's sit down after this first appointment and have lunch nearby. We can come up with a treatment plan. I can do some advance research, and we can set up appointments for later this week."

Lena had that determined look on her face that Teresa recognized. She'd seen it in her daughter's eyes many times over the years. Lena always loved a project she could sink her teeth into. Part of the reason she was successful wasn't just that she was a talented lawyer, with the smarts to back it up, but also because she was a doer—she got shit done.

Teresa's illness had become Lena's project over the last twelve months. Teresa was grateful for this daughter of hers who took matters into her own hands. Larry was there, literally holding Teresa's hand every step of the way, and she loved him for it. But Lena did the hard work of research and phone calls, had the tough conversations with the doctors, took notes, asked questions, and was the advocate Teresa needed and didn't have the mental strength to take on herself.

But Teresa was dying. And although she didn't want Lena to give up on her, she needed Lena to know that she couldn't save her. It was so typical of Lena to think she could somehow change the course of Teresa's terminal illness—that with sheer force of will, she could make anything happen, including miracles. She never gave up. She was so strong-willed. Teresa loved her daughter's tenacity. Even so, no amount of getting shit done could change this terminal diagnosis.

Teresa glanced back at the brightly colored leaves out her bedroom window. Larry had left for work, and Lena was at the pharmacy, picking up Teresa's latest prescriptions and doing a quick food shopping on the way back to the house. Teresa was alone, except for her beloved dog, Allie, who was curled up against her in bed. She stared down at the journal she'd been keeping during the long, grueling months of chemo and radiation. She'd wanted to write a long passage while she had the apartment to herself, but it exhausted her just thinking about putting so many words on paper. She realized she'd only written one brief paragraph. It stared up at her: *It's been a good life. I wish it were longer. I thought I'd have more time. There are things I still want to do. I would have liked to dance more. I never got to see the Grand Canyon. But I've loved every minute I've had.*

The love she felt here in this life was so strong that she had to believe she would get to take it somewhere or carry it forward. Yet she also had doubts. Teresa wondered if there was, in fact, no afterlife at all. Maybe when a person died, they just ceased to exist. Maybe they didn't even know they were dead. Like eternally sleeping. She shivered. What a sad thought. So final. But even the thought that there might be nothing ahead didn't diminish life itself. It almost raised the present to divine status. Like life was the heaven. If that were true, it didn't matter where she was going or what would happen to her soul after she died.

Maybe God was life itself. The feel of her mother's soft skin against her when she was a little girl, the cries of her babies when they were born, Anthony's crooked smile and look of awe when he learned something new, Lena's deep concentration when she was reading a book, the love and admiration in Larry's eyes... the laughter, the tears, the sound of the rain hitting the ground, the flowers growing in the yard, a fresh fig right off the tree. Maybe that was the divine, not some afterlife that no one had ever debriefed. God was in every one of those moments. Why did this life have to be merely a stepping stone for the next one? Teresa felt like she'd been seeing the face of God for sixty years in the faces of everyone she loved. In nature, music, and art. Why couldn't it be that her entire existence had been an exercise in the divine?

If someone could hear her thoughts, they would think she was being blasphemous. Yet it wasn't disbelief coursing through her. Far from it. It was the utter belief that the Holy Spirit had touched her while she was here on earth. She didn't need to be certain that there was a heaven to feel she'd glimpsed the divine. The Catholic church had taught her to look ahead constantly at what was waiting after death. She didn't want to look ahead. She wanted to look back at her life and seek out God's touch while she was here. Blasphemous would be having missed God the entire time she was alive because she didn't trust that he'd show up for her until the afterlife.

Teresa knew that loss, hurt, and pain were an integral part of life. She'd experienced them enough in her lifetime to know this with absolute certainty. She thought back to her early years with Frank. She'd loved him. Then she'd gotten used to him, and he became her family. Then she was suspicious of him and became disappointed in him. And then, after all the betrayal, the separation, and the divorce, she hated him. But eventually, she'd forgiven him, and the love glowed again, reminding her it had always been there, deep inside.

Life was also filled with things so achingly beautiful—her children, Anthony and Lena, whom she loved with all her motherly heart. And then she'd been blessed with two grandchildren, whom she cherished. It broke her heart that she wouldn't have more time with Christopher and Ella and would be deprived of watching them grow up. And then there was Larry, a man who'd given her years of constant attention and affection. She would forever be grateful that they'd found each other and she'd had a second chance at love with such a loyal and caring romantic partner.

And now she had this thing in her body, growing inside her, slowly taking her life. Teresa was so tired that it depleted her just to get up from bed and go to the bathroom or the kitchen. She'd imagined her life would last a lot longer than sixty years and had pictured getting old, like many of her great-aunts. Now Teresa would be lucky if she lived beyond a year.

She heard the front door open, and then Lena putting the groceries away. A few minutes later, she entered the bedroom and looked surprised to find Teresa awake.

"I thought you were sleeping," said Lena, her voice soft. "I was just going to sit here with you for a bit while you slept. But since you're awake, I wanted to tell you about some places I found that are doing experimental treatments..."

"Shhh, sweetie, not now, okay?" Teresa said.

Lena nodded, but Teresa could tell she didn't want to let it—or *her*—go. Teresa reached out. Lena took her hand and moved closer. Teresa gestured for her to lie down next to her on the bed. Lena complied, letting out a huge breath as if she'd been holding it in for several minutes or even hours.

"I want to talk to you about something, honey," Teresa said. "It's important. It won't be easy for either of us, but it's time."

Lena nodded again, and this time, it was more deliberate. Teresa could see that she had her full attention.

"I don't consider myself a loyal Catholic anymore. I don't know what I believe in. Still, I think there is a God. I've decided I want to be cremated. I don't want to be buried underground. I don't want to be trapped. I want to be free. That way, it will be easier for my soul to leave my body and go where it needs to go." Teresa took a deep breath.

"I want a memorial service, not a traditional Italian Catholic wake," she continued. "I hate the idea of my body being displayed in a coffin for all to gawk at with viewing hours where everyone cries and talks in hushed tones. I want a gathering of friends and family. Have it at the community center Larry and I go to often, where everyone is welcome. Display photos of me with my loved ones, and have people tell stories and share funny memories. I don't want it to be a sad occasion."

"I understand," Lena said. "I do. You want it to be a celebration of your life."

"Yes, exactly." Teresa smiled. "And, Lena... I'd like to donate my organs if they're, well, able to be donated." She grimaced, and Lena grabbed her hand and squeezed it.

"Okay, Mom. I'll help you with that. I like that idea."

Lena's lips broke into a small sad pout, and she started to cry. Teresa reached out and gently touched her daughter's face and smoothed back her dark hair. Lena took Teresa's hand and cupped it against her cheek. Teresa wiped away some of Lena's tears then took her daughter's hand and put it on her pillow. They lay like that for what seemed like a long time. Neither of them said a word, yet that conversation was one of their best. Teresa silently conveyed all her love to Lena. There was nothing left to say, not because they were alone in their grief but because they were together in it, as if they were one person instead of two.

Chapter Forty-Three
LENA - ORANGE, CA
October 2015

I returned from my run and saw a note from Kevin that he'd gone to the farmer's market to get some fresh bread, fruits, and veggies and would be back in about an hour. I went into my closet, reached up to the top shelf, and brought down the hat box where I stored my mother's cards, letters, and journals. I brought it to the breakfast nook, made a cup of herbal tea, and sat down. Atticus grunted under the table, thumping his tail against the floor lazily, comforted by my presence above him. I pulled out one of my mom's cards.

There was her signature line: *Love, as always, Mom.* She ended all her notes and cards to me that way. It gave me a familiar lurch in my stomach, like I'd just ridden a roller coaster.

I opened her last journal, full of her beautiful handwriting, and had a rush of emotion, looking at the familiar shapes created by her long fingers. I flipped through the pages and saw an entry that made me catch my breath. I started reading.

March 3, 2010

Frank just visited me in hospice, and I need to write this down before I forget it, because it was one of the best exchanges we've ever had. Long overdue. My darling Larry gave us some privacy, shaking Frank's hand on the way out of the room. What a gem.

I haven't seen Frank since Lena and Kevin's wedding fourteen years ago. And then, there he was, standing in the doorway, his familiar—and I have to admit, still handsome—face looking at me, flooded with emotion. In some ways, it felt like I'd seen him just yesterday. It was Frank—I knew him intimately.

I wanted to tell him how I felt all these years later. Now that time was running out for me. I don't think I'd ever told him that I forgive him. So I did. I knew he loved me and couldn't help who he was—who he is. I'm glad we were both able to move forward and find happiness, eventually. It meant so much to me that we remained connected, and I know it meant the world to the kids. We loved them enough to put them first. I'm proud of us for that.

I'd never heard my mom say these exact words. She felt empathy for my father. She forgave him. Such simple words, really, when you thought about it. It brought me relief to read that my mother had forgiven my father. Had I? I thought so. But I wondered if fully forgiving my father meant betraying my mother, the woman who'd fed and clothed us, protected us, and had always been there for us. I continued reading.

And Frank finally went on record, saying he was sorry, taking the blame for what happened to us. It broke my heart when he told me that the tragedy of his life was not only being in the closet but also hurting the people he loved the most by coming out of that closet. He was sorry for all we went through.

While he sat there on the edge of my bed, apologizing for the past, I realized something important. The fact that he was gay didn't ruin my life. In the long run, his being who he needed to be made me stronger. It forced me to get a job, be a good role model for the kids, and put myself first. It wasn't easy, but I did it. Frank told me that when he looks at Anthony and Lena, he thinks I should take a bow. That I did one hell of a job as their mother. I waited years to hear Frank admit that I'd ba-

sically raised the kids alone. Yet hearing it didn't feel like a victory. Just the reality of a messy, but beautiful, life.

Frank cried tears for himself and tears for me as he knows I don't have much time. At one point, he gently kissed my cheek. It'd been many years since I'd felt his touch, and it was comforting and familiar. He confided in me that I was the love of his life but just the wrong gender. That made me cry. What a pair—the two of us, crying together all these years later for what once was, and wasn't.

At one point, Frank stared out the window, looking like he was stalling for time. I think he was afraid to say goodbye, knowing it would be our last time together. In that moment, I saw the very best version of him, at the helm of our first boat, the Horizon, sunglasses on, wind whipping at his hair—which he still had back then. I remembered him saying, "We're tied to the ocean, all of us. Our bodies have the same percentage of salt as the sea. Saltwater is in our sweat and our tears. It's a part of us."

As Frank stood at my hospital room window, I thought to myself, no regrets. We were a part of each other, like the salt of the ocean that he described. I couldn't erase that history. Suppose we'd never met. In that alternate world, there might have been no Frank and Teresa, none of the countless hours we'd spent together, the shared memories. No Anthony and Lena. And my life would've looked entirely different. As I thought of that, I realized that even now, I wouldn't choose differently than I did. I wouldn't change a thing.

I tasted my salty tears as they streamed down my face. I could picture the two of them together in my mom's hospice room, healing the long rift between them while her body couldn't heal itself. It broke my heart but also brought me solace.

I reached the last paragraph of the entry.

After Frank left, I reflected on all we'd been through as a family. I was so worried about what others thought. Consumed by fear. So much so that I forced all of us to stay in that same closet Frank had been trying to break out of. And for that, more than anything, I was sorry.

I gasped. She was sorry for prolonging the secrecy and lies. She'd taken some of the blame. *Oh, Mom.* I took in big gulps of air to steady myself.

My mother's love for her children was fierce, and that had translated into wanting to protect us—first, from the truth, then once we knew it, from the truth getting out. Keeping everything a secret at all costs was her way of sheltering us. But it had also caused us to hide in fear, often living a double life.

I realized with a sharp pang that there was more forgiving that needed to be done. I had to forgive my mother. But how did you forgive someone you revered, who struggled and sacrificed for you, and who you missed so much that your heart hurt? A sob escaped my throat.

My mother had passed away sixteen terribly long-suffering months after her diagnosis—months that felt excruciatingly slow yet flew by much too quickly. After she died, I searched and searched for the perfect words to include in my eulogy at her memorial service. When I came across a quote by William Shakespeare, goose bumps rose along my arms, and my heart pumped wildly in my chest: *The breaking of so great a thing should make a greater crack...*

My heart cleaved into two parts, before and after. I kept going back to the thought that my mom was gone, as if I needed to be reminded of it repeatedly or I would forget and think I'd dreamt it all. It struck me how unfair and strange it was that the earth would keep on turning without my mother in it. It seemed inappropriate for the light to be so bright and the sky to be so blue. I found myself relieved when a cloud drifted over the sun and the sky turned from blue to silver to gray in the fading light. All I could think was *I'm never really saying goodbye.*

Some people said the first days after death were the hardest. I disagreed. Those first few days after my mother died, I was numb. That was how I could plan a memorial service down to every detail and sort through all her belongings—donating some, saving some, and purging others. The numbness was like a morphine drip keeping the pain at bay and my head hazy.

After her memorial service, I returned to California and threw myself into my work, a positive distraction from the reality that my mom was gone. And then it hit me like a ton of bricks, the pain so powerful I wondered if I would survive. The grip that grief had on me was suffocating and made even breathing feel agonizing. Kevin had hovered over me for weeks, trying to soothe me as I fell apart.

Now here I was, five years later, staring down at her final journal—at her words that she'd taken the time to capture. That were important to her. That freed her—and freed all of us.

I ran my hands across the page, caressing her handwriting. "I forgive you, Mom," I whispered. "I know you did it out of love. You tried your best. You just wanted to protect us. Thank you."

I turned the page, and the remainder of her journal was tragically blank—a visual reminder of the years she'd lost. The entry I'd just read was the last time she wrote in her journal—the last record of her thoughts and feelings. I gently closed her journal and held it close to my heart.

The door to the garage opened, and Kevin entered the kitchen, carrying bags of goodies from the farmer's market. He placed them on the counter, took one look at me, and quickly rushed over. I must have looked like a hot mess from all the crying I'd been doing while reading my mom's journal.

"Are you okay? What happened?"

"I'm okay. Just sad. I've been... reminiscing about my family." My face contorted. I started crying again, my body heaving though no sound coming out—an ugly cry I couldn't stop until it had had its way with me.

Kevin hugged me. "Oh, Lena. Wow, you're really upset. Let it out." He rocked me as I cried, shushing me gently.

Atticus tried to wedge himself between the two of us, licking repeatedly, which he did when one of us was distraught.

"It's okay, boy."

Atticus wormed his way closer and licked my cheek.

"Hey, big guy," I said, trying to soothe him.

He was so intuitive—an old soul stuck in a dog. That thought dislodged a memory of the time when I was eight and got in hot water with the nuns in CCD religion class for refusing to believe that dogs didn't have souls and wouldn't go to Heaven. The nuns had wanted my mom to punish me. Boy, were they surprised when she took my side, agreeing that dogs most certainly had souls and would go to Heaven. *What a mama.*

"The last few months have been hard on you," Kevin whispered. "No matter how happy you are for your dad, I know it's strange for you that he's getting married again."

I felt guilty because he was right. "Planning my dad's wedding all these months took me back. Made me keep revisiting the past in a lot of ways. My parents, the way they fell apart." I stopped, trying to keep myself from crying again, my emotions surfacing. Kevin listened in his quiet way, eyes locked on me, not interrupting. "It still feels a little like I'm betraying my mom, even though that's silly. I can't help thinking of what she went through. I think of my parents on their wedding day all those years ago, and it just makes me... sad."

I pictured the photos of my mom and dad at the altar the day they got married at St. Bartholomew Church. They were so young and looked innocent and hopeful. *Did they know they'd fall apart someday? Did my father have an idea he would betray my mother in order to be himself? Had she any inkling that the happy marriage she envisioned would crumble?*

"I had a feeling." Kevin hugged me harder and stroked the back of my hair, running a strand through his fingers. "If you weren't a little sad about your parents now that your dad is tying the knot again, I would think you were in denial."

Kevin nailed it. I was mourning the demise of my parents' marriage all these years later. I needed to take a mental snapshot of the two of them—the younger versions of Frank and Teresa, when they were happy and in love—and hold on to it. And then put away the rest. What came after was painful, but that wasn't the entire story of who they were.

"Thank you for understanding," I said, giving him a weak smile. I wiped my eyes and grabbed for a tissue to blow my nose.

Kevin took in the table, which was littered with the remnants of my earlier trip down memory lane. "Hey, what's all this?" he asked, gesturing to my mom's cards, letters, and journal.

"Oh, I finally read my mother's journal this morning. The one she kept when she was sick," I said, and his eyes widened. "It was calling me. I felt ready after all these years. Especially after my dad and I had our bonding session in San Francisco and he told me his story. I wanted to find out the rest of hers, you know? And here's the thing. She forgave him, Kevin—she really did—for what he did to her, to all of us. And deep down, I'm not surprised. My mother tried not to make us hate our father."

"Because that's not who she was. She didn't want you and your brother to hate your dad—or who he was."

"But she made us keep it a secret. That she did." I hesitated, knowing I had to tell him the rest. "And this is the part of her journal that really surprised me. My mom regretted that. She recognized that she was acting out of fear because of the times and that it forced us all to live a double life. She was sorry for that." I leaned into him, and he put his arm around me.

"She was doing what she thought was best with an unusual and difficult situation. She wanted to protect you and Anthony. And herself. It couldn't have been easy for her."

"No, it wasn't."

"They had tough choices—both of them. They did what they thought was right. And now... you have the choice to continue that legacy of secrecy or free yourself from holding that all in."

I thought of how the parental relationship might be the most fundamental and powerful one a person has. It was probably the greatest single influence on a person's outlook and who they became. Most of us spent our lives either trying to live up to our parents' ideals or actively rebelling against them.

"You mean I don't need to keep being the former me—trying to fix everything—all while holding back a dam of lies and omissions?" I oozed sarcasm.

Kevin smiled tenderly, and my face crumpled as I felt the sobs returning. I buried my head in his neck while the tears flowed. He held me, rubbing my shoulders in a soothing back-and-forth rhythm.

He lifted my face gently. "Lena, you don't have to be like them. You can make a different choice."

Kevin was right. I didn't have to be like my mother. But it hurt so much. I felt like I was betraying her.

"I always admired your mother. She was a strong woman in so many ways. More than just what happened with your father." He let that sit between us for a moment. "You take after her. You're also strong. And you're more than what happened with your family."

"Thank you," I said, managing a small smile. "And I know one choice I never have to second-guess." I kissed him on the lips then rubbed his nose with mine. "I married the right person."

Chapter Forty-Four
LENA - RANCHO PALOS VERDES, CA
October 2015

I couldn't believe that after months of preparation and anticipation, the wedding day was finally here. I looked in the mirror and took stock of my outfit and jewelry: a purple dress because that was my mom's favorite color, the earrings she'd given me on my wedding day, my wedding ring, Mom's pearl ring, and the bracelet Kevin had gifted me on our fifteenth wedding anniversary.

"You okay in there?" Kevin appeared in the bedroom doorway.

I smiled at him through the mirror. He looked so handsome in his olive-green suit, the one he knew I loved that set off the flecks of gold in his amber eyes.

"I'm going to take Atticus for a walk before we leave. I made some coffee. Anthony's having some now. Donna and the kids are still getting dressed. They may be a while. He said he'll wait for them and drive over in the rental car so you and I can get there early and check on things before the ceremony begins."

"Okay, thanks, hon. I'll be out in a minute," I said, smoothing the front of my dress. A few minutes later, I walked into the kitchen area and saw my brother sitting at the island, sipping coffee.

"Ready?" he asked.

I nodded and caught sight of his purple tie.

He looked down at it and then back up at me and smirked. "Do you like it?"

"For Mom?"

He smiled. "Her favorite." He looked me up and down. "Love your purple dress."

I hugged him, and my eyes teared. "Don't make me cry. I'll have to do my makeup over."

Anthony laughed.

"Is it strange that we both wore her favorite color to our father's second wedding?" I asked, slipping onto the stool beside him.

Anthony shrugged. "Nope. Not at all. Not for us." There it was—that nonchalant attitude.

"I wanted her with me today. I miss her," I whispered.

"Me too. But she's here. She wouldn't miss it." Anthony wove his arm around my waist and pulled me into him.

I rested my head on his shoulder. My big bro. He was my oldest ally, my other half. Without him, I was less defined. Less myself. Lena without Anthony was like a brain without a heart. A yin without a yang. It was the two of us against the world. And once Anthony came to his senses and stopped blaming Mom for our parents' split, it became the three of us against the world. The three musketeers, she'd called us.

I looked at my big brother, so handsome in his suit. "Anthony, I want to ask you a question."

"Sure, shoot," he said.

I smiled to myself. That was a typical Anthony response. He had such a straight-shooter, no-nonsense style. I found it refreshing. I always knew where I stood with him.

"I've been asked to give a speech to an organization in LA in a few days. They want me to talk about LGBTQ law. It's an organization for people with gay and lesbian parents."

He nodded, taking in what I was saying.

"I made friends with a woman who does some volunteer work for them and serves on their board. She recommended me."

"Sounds like it's right up your alley," Anthony said matter-of-factly.

"Yes, it is. I can talk about how far the law has come and how much progress still needs to be made. Discuss some test cases." I saw Anthony glance at my hands, which I was nervously wringing. He had that police officer's instinct, looking for the tell.

"So, what's the problem?" Anthony asked. "You said you wanted to ask me something."

"My friend Kate, the one on the board, she thinks I should add in a bit about my personal story. About Dad. That he's gay." I hesitated. "Kevin thinks so too."

"What do *you* think?" Anthony sipped his coffee, but his eyes never left mine.

"I'm torn. I don't want that to pull focus from the talk. I want to share what's going on with the legal landscape. That's an important topic."

"It is." Anthony put his coffee cup down and swung his stool to face me directly. "But, Lena, don't you think the fact that you have a gay father is also important to share with this group? There're many lawyers who can talk about this stuff, but how many of them have an actual gay parent and know about this personally? Few, I bet."

"I guess," I said, unconvinced but wondering if he had a point.

"I think it'd be strange if you didn't share it with this group. You're one of them. Sure, you're a lawyer who knows a lot about this area. But what makes you uniquely qualified to speak to this group is that you walk in their shoes. You've got street cred. Instant connection."

I turned away as tears pricked my eyes. I put my hand up to my mouth to stop myself from sobbing. Anthony reached out and touched my arm. I put my other hand around his fingers and squeezed, nodding to signify that I was okay but needed a moment.

"Lena, look at me," Anthony said. I turned back toward him, sniffling to clear my nose. "If you don't want to talk about it, don't. But the question then is, why? That's what you should ask yourself."

"I know," I whispered. Then the words poured out of me like a fire hydrant had burst open. "I've held it in for so long, never talking about it with people. You, sure. Kevin, Dad—yes. But not... people. Keeping the secret has become a part of me. Like a habit I can't break..."

He shook his head. "I think you have to add your personal story in. If not, you look... fake." He threw up his hands. "That's what I think. If you don't talk about it to this group, it's like you're hiding something. Of all people, these aren't the ones you should hide from."

I nodded slowly, knowing I would tell someone else the same thing. *You have a connection with these folks. Why wouldn't you highlight that?*

"Honestly, Lena, you shouldn't be hiding at all," he continued. "Look at what you do for a living. It's a big part of your career. But you also live it personally. And that's the part you keep hidden. I've always found that strange. You'll talk about your cases, the people you represent. Those people are fair game. But about your own father, you're close-lipped. Why are you so passionate about helping gay people but won't admit that your father is one?" He looked me straight in the eye. I knew him well enough to know he wasn't mad at me. But he was challenging me for sure. "And don't say, 'It's nobody's business,' or 'I'm a private person.' I don't buy it. You're afraid to say the truth out loud. It still feels taboo to you. And it's okay. I'm not judging you. I just think it's time you get past this." He shrugged.

I breathed in deeply, processing everything he said. "Thank you," I said, the tears flowing freely now. "I think I knew the answer, but I wanted your opinion. I know what I have to do. I'm petrified, but I think you're right."

He hugged me and then pulled back. "It's time, Lena."

I sat there, replaying our conversation, while Anthony enjoyed his morning coffee, looking relaxed. I couldn't help hoping my big brother's carefree attitude—and courage—would rub off on me.

We arrived at the Terranea Resort and walked to the area over-looking the ocean, where the ceremony would take place. There was a beautiful trellis made of intertwined vines and bougainvillea flowers, creating an arch that framed the blue of the sky and sea. Waves lapped against the rocks below, and the sun stretched its rays down to meet the water in the distance.

"Wow, what a spot," Kevin said, echoing my thoughts.

I caught sight of my dad and Oliver, looking debonair in their suits, with matching red boutonnieres and bow ties. I gave them each a kiss on the cheek. "Love the look. So matchy-matchy."

My dad laughed and gestured to Oliver. "His idea. I just follow orders."

Oliver grinned broadly, hooking his arm through my dad's.

We checked in with the staff and the officiant to make sure everything was in order. I saw Anthony and his family walking over from the parking lot and waved at them. Ella waved back excitedly. When they reached us, they hugged my dad and Oliver one at a time, switching partners like in a country line dance.

They made an impressive lot, all decked out for the occasion, Anthony and Christopher in dark suits and ties and Ella in the peach dress I'd seen in her text, which looked even better in person. Donna wore a floral sundress and a wide-brimmed hat.

I gestured to it. "Nice touch."

She curtsied teasingly.

Anthony clapped my dad on the back. "You look good. How're you doing? Nervous?"

"Nah. Nothing to be nervous about. I've got everything I want." Dad winked at Oliver. "Especially now that you're all here." He gestured to us—his family.

Other guests started arriving and mingling. A radiant feeling enveloped me as I watched them greeting the soon-to-be-married couple. My dad and Oliver seemed inseparable, never straying far from each other.

A half hour later, the officiant announced that the ceremony would begin. "All of Me," by John Legend—my dad and Oliver's song—played while they walked over to join the officiant at the wedding arch. She instructed us to make a semicircle around my dad and Oliver. I looked at the intimate group of people here to celebrate with them. Anthony, Donna, Christopher, and Ella were present, of course. Henry had come without a date, claiming he wanted to fully focus on my dad's big day and not have to babysit a plus-one who didn't know anyone else. My dad and Oliver's close friends in the LA area, some straight, some gay, were all happy to be included, as well as a few of my father's work colleagues who had become like family to him over the years. What a far cry from years before when we'd had to hide who he was and worried about him getting fired.

Dad and Oliver held hands, stared into each other's eyes as the officiant spoke about the two of them, her words made more meaningful by the insider info I had provided. When she mentioned the hobbies my dad and Oliver enjoyed, some of their favorite songs, and a few funny anecdotes, Kevin squeezed my hand and smiled at me. I squeezed back, glancing at him sideways and trying not to get too emotional.

No such luck. A tear slipped down my cheek, and as I wiped it away, I noticed others also shedding happy tears. What a triumphant day—a chance for my dad to declare his love for Oliver publicly, a man who I felt was a good match for him after so many failed relationships. I thought of how he and my mom had failed at marriage, but it hadn't exactly been a failed relationship.

We'd reached the ring-exchange part of the ceremony. I loved the rings they chose—a modern two-tone band with silver edging and an inlay of black in the center. My dad took Oliver's left hand, repeating after the officiant, "With this ring I pledge my love to you," with a quiver in his voice.

Oliver reached over with his right hand and rubbed my dad's shoulder. My dad nodded, signaling that he could hold it together. He placed the ring on Oliver's finger and then brought Oliver's hand up to his lips and kissed it.

"Not yet, Frank. No kissing until I say so," the officiant said.

We all laughed, and my dad looked like a kid who'd been able to sneak a cookie from the jar before dinner.

"Now we'll perform the ribbon ceremony," the officiant announced. "Frank and Oliver will pass around a ribbon, and each person will hold it and share a wish for the grooms and then pass the ribbon on to the next person. That way, all the friends and family members here will have a hand in shaping who the grooms will become as a married couple."

I'd never seen this tradition. I leaned in closer, curious to hear what kind of sentiment each person would share. They ranged from humorous—"I wish for you a private chef because neither of you is a good cook!"—to heartfelt, "May your love shine as brightly as the sun."

My dad's face grew more expressive and emotional with each passing of the ribbon. He reminded me of a peacock, feathers splayed in their glory. He seemed to expand, buoyed by the words of love and support directed at him and Oliver.

When the ribbon reached me, I said, "I hope you always have laughter to accompany you and love to guide you. And that you continue to choose each other every day."

My dad wiped a tear and blew me a kiss. I caught it and placed it in my heart.

The ribbon arrived at the end of the circle of guests. The officiant looked around expectantly and then turned to my dad and Oliver. "I now present to you the married couple, Frank and Oliver." We all started clapping. The officiant's voice broke through the applause. "And now you may kiss your groom!" My dad and Oliver kissed and embraced, holding each other for a long time, while we clapped and cheered—the sounds of our revelry blending with the crash of the ocean waves to create a symphony of celebration.

After the ceremony, the photographer gathered us for a group photo. At first, everyone acted as expected, grinning at the camera. But then Oliver and my dad struck various poses, and others started doing the same. It became a goofy ham-it-up fest, with people sticking out their tongues and making jazz hands.

The staff then directed the group to the reception on the patio. My dad and Oliver stayed behind so the photographer could take photos of just the two of them. I grabbed my phone from my purse and snapped a picture of them silhouetted against the sea, kissing.

The dinner reception had a romantic setting with twinkling lights, a bubbling fountain, grapevines on a pergola, and terra-cotta pots framing the patio. Once my dad and Oliver joined us, Anthony kicked off the toasts to the happy couple. I'd asked him to go first, thinking it was appropriate, given that he was the oldest. Plus, I knew it would buy me some time and allay my nerves.

"Hello, everyone. I'm Frank's son, Anthony, although I think you all know that," he said, looking around at the expectant faces.

"I'm not one to make long, fancy speeches, so I'll keep this brief. We're here to celebrate my father and Oliver's special day, one I know my dad has fought for a long time. It's been a journey for him to get here, and I'm glad he's arrived. And with someone as great as Oliver." Anthony raised his glass and looked pointedly at my dad and Oliver. "So let's raise our glasses to Frank and Oliver and toast their arrival at their destination. Cheers."

Guests repeated "Cheers" throughout the room and took sips of prosecco. My dad and Oliver beamed as Anthony walked over and hugged them.

And then it was my turn. *Yikes.* I'd planned to keep my toast short, also, thinking about what I was going to say that morning as I was getting dressed.

I stood up and began. "Thank you for coming to help us cele-brate my dad and Oliver's big day. I'm Lena—Frank's daughter, unof-ficial wedding planner, and sort of best man." That got a few laughs. I smiled. "I know it means the world to them you're here. They want-ed to be surrounded by people who love and support them, and that means all of you. Please join me in toasting the grooms. Love is love," I said, ending with the popular refrain of same-sex-marriage propo-nents. I raised my glass and took a hearty sip of prosecco.

I sat down, glad to have that behind me. Then I heard someone else tapping a glass. Henry stood.

Well, well. Is he going to give a toast? As I was ruminating about whether that was appropriate, he began talking. *No stopping him now.*

"Hey, folks. I'm Henry. You could say I'm a best man too." He snickered. "Let's face it. A man can never have too many best men! I'm Frank's longtime friend—someone who's been on this journey with him since way back when. I can't tell you how much joy it gives me to see Frank marry Oliver, his partner, lover, and friend." My dad and Oliver wore big smiles and held hands. "I wouldn't have missed this day for anything. Frank, here's to you, buddy. I love ya. Cheers!"

Everyone raised their glasses one last time and drank to the newlyweds.

The evening flew by with dinner and dancing. After the servers cleared the main course, Ella sat down next to me. "They're so cute, aren't they?" she cooed, eyes glowing.

I loved seeing how much it thrilled my niece to be a part of this celebration. I looked around, trying to locate the happy couple, and spotted them standing hand in hand, talking to friends at a nearby table.

"Yup, they really are," I agreed, laughing to myself that a fifteen-year-old was using the term *cute* to describe a couple decades older than she was.

"I can't wait for the wedding cake. It looks so good. Did you see it?" she asked.

I looked over at the corner of the patio where the wedding cake sat, looking resplendent with fresh flowers on top. "Yes, I even tasted it."

Her eyes widened. "You snuck a piece?"

"No, silly. Although that would be pretty funny, actually. Your grandpa and I came here to sample the menu a few months ago, and they let us taste a few kinds of cake. We chose the chocolate ganache one."

"Well, duh," she said, eyebrows raised. "Because chocolate is the best."

"You're right about that, my girl," I said, holding up my champagne flute in a toast.

"Hey, speaking of sneaking..." She looked around quickly. "Can I have a sip?" She nodded at my prosecco.

"Sure. It's a special occasion, isn't it? Have at it. But just a sip." I handed her my glass and watched her take a gulp.

She smiled, licking her lips. "I like the bubbles," she said, giggling.

Ella got up to take her seat as they were serving the wedding cake. I looked down at my plate and admired the chocolate concoction. I took my first bite. Melt-in-your-mouth delicious.

I looked around and saw Henry with his hand on my dad's shoulder, leaning in, the two of them laughing. Henry was still so darn handsome, just like my father. They had aged well. I remembered what they'd looked like when I was a kid and thought about what a striking couple they must have made. That caught me by surprise. Over the years, when I thought of my dad and Henry, it had always been with a hint of anger and shame, linked to my dad's betrayal of my mother. But Henry and my dad were so much more than the scene that the little-girl version of me had witnessed on the boat. They'd been friends for over forty years, even after their inauspicious beginning. I let that really soak in. Not many people had a taboo affair, broke up, and then didn't just remain cordial but became life-long best friends. It really was extraordinary.

Henry caught me watching him and smiled. He walked over and sat down in the vacant seat next to me. "Hey, Lena. Thought I'd say hello for a sec." He looked around and smiled. "Beautiful place. Fabulous wedding. You did a great job. Your father is so happy."

"Thanks. He is happy." I added, "And he's so glad you came."

"Of course I came. It's a big deal. A milestone. And I've been there for them all—good and bad. The worst was the heartache of losing friends to AIDS." He stopped and shook his head. "Then he met Oliver. Thank goodness." He looked over at my dad, who was saying hello to friends at a nearby table, an arm around Oliver's waist, pulling him close. "He deserves some happiness."

It was jarring to hear Henry mention my dad losing friends to AIDS. It brought me back to a dark Broadway theater in 1996, when I'd been visiting New York after being out in California for a year. I was attempting to spend more time with my dad, so I'd accepted an invitation to see a Broadway musical with him, Henry, and their friends.

"Remember when we went to see *Rent*?" I asked.

"Oh yeah, I remember that. What a show. Beautiful but heartbreaking. I remember your dad having a hard time after. He said, 'I finally come out, and that's the exact time in history when this insidious disease comes along to wipe us out?' It almost felt like bad karma to him. You know, he always had that Catholic guilt going on about being gay. He couldn't shake the feeling that he was being punished or something."

"That's so sad. I don't think he ever really told me that." I thought back to conversations I'd had with my dad over the years.

"I know he tells you a lot. He trusts you. But he's also tried to spare you, you know?" Care showed in Henry's eyes.

"What are you two talking about over here?" My dad grinned and put his arm around Henry and me from behind.

"Heavy stuff, actually," Henry said. "We were talking about when we went to see *Rent* on Broadway. Remember that? And that got me thinking of friends we lost to AIDS."

"Ah," my dad said, nodding. "Yes, there are some friends who should be here today." He stared intently at one spot as if he could see their ghosts right beside him. Then he looked at me. "And you know what? I was with them both in the hospital when they died. One was my friend Luke, only twenty-eight years old. A baby. His body swelled up like a balloon. He suffered so much." His eyes flooded with tears, like puddles of water. "My other friend, Matteas, was older but still only forty-three. His family wouldn't come to the hospital to see him when he was dying. Those motherfuckers left him there alone. So I went. I held his hand as he took his last breath. I'll never forget it." He swiped at his eyes.

"Sorry, Frank. Enough of this downer talk. Let's toast." Henry grabbed the nearest glass of wine, probably Kevin's discarded one, and held it up. "To friends who couldn't be here with us today."

"*Salute*," my dad said, grabbing a water glass to join in the toast.

"I'll drink to that," I said, tapping their glasses with my prosecco.

That night in 1996, watching *Rent*, I hadn't entirely understood the brave choice my father and his friends had made in coming out. I'd mostly thought of the impact my father's choice had on my mother, Anthony, and me. But now I could move that to the side, like opening a curtain to peer through the window. And what I witnessed on the other side was my dad's struggle.

Oliver and Anthony walked over to join us. "Hey, do I see another toast happening? What're we drinking to?"

"We were toasting my friends who are no longer with us—Luke and Matteas—and wishing they were here," my dad said.

"Cheers to that," Anthony said, and Oliver lifted his glass too.

"Ooh, I have an idea!" My dad ran over to the DJ, whispered something in his ear, then came back and grabbed Oliver's hand. "Come on," he said, gesturing for the rest of us to follow. "Let's dance. This was one of their favorite songs. I love it!"

I heard the first few notes of the disco song "Don't Leave Me This Way," by Thelma Houston. My dad hit the dance floor, snapping his fingers and moving his hips, singing along to the words, with Oliver by his side, swaying to the beat. Anthony, Henry, and I joined them. The next thing I knew, everyone was flooding the dance floor, losing themselves to the music and the moment.

FINALE

Chapter Forty-Five
LENA - LOS ANGELES, CA
October 2015

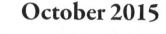

I stepped onto the stage and walked toward the podium, smiling at Kate, who'd just introduced me. In the last few days, I'd frantically reworked the speech, and now that I was here, I was afraid I wouldn't be able to get through it. I touched my mom's pearl ring for good luck.

I looked out into the audience and caught sight of Kevin, handsome and supportive, smiling at me. And there was my dad with Oliver at his side, the two of them beaming. *No turning back.* This was my story. And it was high time I fully owned it in all its flawed truth and beauty.

I'd always guarded the different parts of my life from each other. If I could keep them in isolation from each other, nothing could ever hurt me as deeply again. I built a quiet construction of separate rooms, like protective compartments, around me. But most of the time, I felt alone in the center of that house. The trip to San Francisco with my father had flung open the front door. And then reading my mother's journal, with its implicit permission to stop hiding, had knocked down the walls.

"Good evening. My name is Lena Antinori, and I'm a deputy US attorney for civil rights. I spend my days trying cases for marginalized groups, including the LGBTQ community."

I spent the next ten minutes giving them an update on federal and state LGBTQ rights law, outlining its bracing contradictions of idealism and pain. I described how the glimmers of hope when legal battles were won and progress was made were pitted against the glaring recognition that the war continued to wage.

With the legal recap behind me, I shifted gears. *Now for the hard part.* I was diving off a cliff—petrified but exhilarated. I took an audible breath amplified by the microphone. "I wrote my speech for this event over a month ago. That comes as no surprise to those who know me well. I'm quite the planner." Some light laughter came from the audience. "I intended to *only* talk to you about the legal landscape. But that's not solely why I'm here."

The audience seemed to realize something was up. There was a change in the air.

"What most people don't know about me, including even those I work with, is that I'm the daughter of a gay father. That statement isn't something I typically share in casual conversation. In fact, for much of my life, I've hidden that truth. Or maybe *hidden* is too strong a word. Let's say I didn't freely divulge it." I tried to smile, but my face felt plastic, like it might crack.

I looked at my work colleagues—Marcus, Brad, and Toby, and his partner, David, seated together in the audience. I'd invited them in the last few days, after I revised the speech. I'd been hiding in plain sight all these years. Now it seemed so misguided to have kept this vital part of my background from people who dedicated their careers to ensure acceptance and equality for others.

Juggling my private life as the child of a gay parent and my professional identity as an advocate for marginalized individuals had been exhausting and, I was convinced, had eroded parts of me. Children of so-called normal parents didn't bear that burden. The world didn't require them to shape-shift in order to survive.

I wanted to heal the gaping wound of society that forced my father, and by extension our entire family, to live a lie, and by not coming out about being the daughter of a gay parent, I wasn't the advocate I claimed to be. My silence all these years had made me complicit. It was time to trade my privacy for transparency.

I took another deep breath, pulled my shoulders back, and stood up taller. "I'm here as one of you. The child of a gay parent. That's what COLAGE is all about, and I realize that's really why I've been invited to speak. Not just for my legal work." I looked at Kate, who was seated in the front row, smiling at me.

"So many of us go through life with our stories hidden, feeling ashamed or afraid when our whole truth doesn't live up to some established ideal. We grow up with messages that tell us there's only one way to be a family, a couple, a daughter, a member of society. That if we don't experience love in a certain way, or our parents don't, we don't belong. Until someone dares to tell that story differently. For years now, I've dared to tell my clients' stories but not my own."

I cleared my throat. The audience members watched me intently, some leaning forward in their seats, a few nodding, inaudibly encouraging me to go on. I realized my pause had lasted a long time.

"And so I stand before you today, admitting that I've rewritten this entire speech in the last few days. I'm finally ready to talk about my journey as the child of a gay parent. This is my coming-out story. Because as much as I thought I was supportive of my father years ago, I realize that I've been a hypocrite. And as children of LGBTQ parents, it's our responsibility to come out too."

The audience applauded, and I stopped to take a moment. My eyes met my dad's, and I saw a spark of pride in them. I swallowed. I couldn't stop, or I would lose it.

"It took me a long time to arrive here. I'm not talking about LA traffic, which I'm sure you hit on your way here, or the many years of legal training required for me to achieve my current position. The first gay person I ever loved broke my heart, and it took me many years to forgive him. Only then could I accept him."

These were not new thoughts. They were a version of what I'd been thinking for years but had never actually said out loud—until now, in front of an auditorium full of mostly strangers.

"I was thirteen years old when my parents separated in 1983 and my father officially came out. Yet it would be years and years before I could freely tell anyone outside my family about my father and who he really was—before I could take all that hurt and anger and embarrassment and weave it into my story. I would take steps in the right direction but would often fall short of fully owning it. I'd get on my soapbox about civil rights issues and even sexual orientation discrimination but not come clean that I had a gay father. Sometimes I'd even say I had gay 'family members' or that my father was 'seeing someone,' but not who exactly. I was constantly playing the pronoun game, skirting the issue. The wounds of homophobia are like tentacles, their grip on not only the gay person but also on their children."

I swallowed and licked my lips, which suddenly felt bone-dry.

"Growing up with a gay parent when homosexuality was not only not as acceptable as it is today but abhorred as an abomination of nature and religion, and downright illegal in some states, is an experience that has left me profoundly changed. I wouldn't be who I am today without the fierce, unconditional love of my mother. I also wouldn't be who I am without the risk-taking bravery my father exhibited."

I glanced down at my notes and then back at the audience.

"Was it easy for my dad as a gay man? Not at all. He experienced so much loss: the loss of friends and family members who turned their backs on him, his fear of losing his job, and the worst kind of loss—several of his friends dying from AIDS. Was it easy for my mom, who was besotted with my father only to realize that the thing that was keeping them apart was sexual orientation and that she needed to let him go? Absolutely not.

"In time, a clearer picture of myself emerged from my upbringing with these two people, as flawed and authentic as they were. I realized I was now a piece of the story too. As my story took shape, I sought to understand how they revealed different parts of themselves by looking closely at how they had loved each other, however imperfectly."

My childhood, the events of my past, rushed at me like a wave crashing onto the shore. Everything looked crystal clear, each memory a piece of the puzzle that fit in exactly as it should and brought me to this moment, right here on this stage.

"Sometimes it only becomes clear what something's really about later on, when time and life and memory have done their filtering and perspective has brought things into focus. My father lived his life on his own terms. It's taken me a long time to realize I actually admire him for that. They weren't always terms I agreed with. I certainly didn't like what his terms were doing to our family. But I realize now that he needed to be true to himself, even if that meant losing everything. As much as things were lost, things were gained too. Because in the end, I gained my real father. Not the one he thought he had to be."

I hadn't fully accepted that truth until this moment.

"And it means the world to me that he's here today, listening to me claim my truth. Even better, he's sitting beside his new husband." I gestured to my dad and Oliver, who were smiling radiantly.

I locked eyes with my dad as the group vigorously applauded. He smiled and grabbed Oliver's hand. They held their hands up for the audience to see.

"Thank you all for listening. For being brave. For coming out as the children of LGBTQ parents and for being willing to be the real you, no matter what."

I took a deep breath. I'd done it.

I kept my eyes on my dad, and he wiped his eyes and nodded, just the slightest dip of his head. Then he did something that was so quintessentially him. He let out one of his ear-piercing whistles. The whole place erupted in laughter and then lots of whooping. I threw my head back and laughed, tears in my eyes.

As I looked out at the audience, all the faces receded into the background, and all I could see was my mom sitting in the last row, beaming her big, beautiful, slightly crooked smile, eyes twinkling, hands clapping. She mouthed, "I love you."

I mouthed back, "I love you too, Mom, always," and took a bow.

THE END

AUTHOR'S NOTE

When I sat down to write the author's note to explain the story behind this novel, I had to take a deep breath first, as I knew it would be personal. This is the book of my heart. The one I've written and rewritten. And although it was a beast at times, it felt important to write.

Writers of fiction are often asked, "How much of this book is real?" Every writer's answer is different, and the author's note is the hallowed place where we get to explain how we departed from the factual record. This book contains fragments of the truth filtered through the lens of fiction. The most important truth at the heart of this novel is that I'm the daughter of a gay father who came out in 1979 after being married to my mother for fourteen years. I'm so proud of my father and his journey to becoming who he truly is. But this isn't my family's story. Once I decided to create fictional characters, dialogue, and scenes, the writing flowed, and the story took on a life of its own.

One thing that is not fictional is the food at the center of this book, specifically spaghetti and peas, which led indirectly to this novel. It made me think about the emotional weight carried by recipes and how sometimes they define significant aspects of our upbringing, forever linked to a familial event.

Writing a novel is like making Italian gravy (otherwise known as pasta sauce to non-Italians!). The base includes fresh tomatoes, always. Nothing else will do. Add to that garlic, olive oil, basil, oregano, parsley, onion, salt, pepper, and the all-important Italian meats. Then you let it simmer for hours until not only your kitchen but your entire house smells absolutely delicious.

It's the same with the fictionalization of a true story. You start with the "truth" based on personal experiences and those of people around you who you've had the pleasure of knowing. Those could be derived from real-life events, childhood memories, journal entries, interviews with family members, or a reaction to a family photo. Then, on top of those, you layer imagined conversations you weren't around for, characters and events you never planned on inserting into the novel but that barged their way in, and lots of pretend anecdotes that want to get in on the action. The ingredients blend, forming a gravy that might have started with the base of truth but now is entirely a work of fiction. You let it marinate until the novel is ready, and hopefully, the finished product is delicious.

As I wrote this novel, a lifetime of fleeting impressions helped me to develop the fictional characters and scenarios that appear in these pages. The scenes from New Rochelle and Long Island Sound reflect some of the geography and history of the area where my parents, grandparents, and great-grandparents lived when they emigrated from Italy. The town of Harrison in Westchester County, NY, where I grew up, inspired the fictional town of Johnston, where Lena and her family lived. Sights mentioned in both towns are based on a mix of actual and invented locations.

Many of the characters in this novel are people who do not quite fit into the boxes that others have set up for them. They struggle against stereotypes and the lives that other people expect them to lead based on gender, culture, sexual orientation, or religion. Their difficulties are both universal and specific to the times and places in which they live. This book took on a subject that is so necessary yet, sadly, still controversial in some circles—a closeted gay man, a family struggling with balancing the truth against maintaining privacy, the ripple effect of secrets, and unconditional love of all kinds.

Even fictional stories typically contain emotional truths. I wrote this book as someone with a vested interest in making the world a safer, more inclusive place for LGBTQ individuals and their family members and children. I wanted to show that although we have come a long way in some respects, we also have a long way to go. History repeats itself, and the current backlash of anti-LGBTQ laws sweeping some parts of the US places us squarely back to the times when the Antinori family had to hide their secret. I hope Lena, Frank, and Teresa's journey can be educational. But more importantly, I hope it inspires compassion.

Although Lena's story strays from my own, we share the identity of being the child of a gay parent. *Everything We Thought Was True* is told from the perspective of "queerspawn"—the children who have always been in the shadows of the coming-out experience of their LGBTQ parents. Stefan Lynch, a cofounder of COLAGE, coined that term as an empowering way to take back the word *queer*, which was formerly used in a pejorative manner. While writing this book, I conducted detailed research on adult children of LGBTQ parents, and LGBTQ parents themselves, who were now out and proud but had lived a portion of their life closeted. My research included reading articles and books, watching films and television series, volunteering for an LGBTQ organization, and following blogs, podcasts, and social media groups. I realized that my experience was only a tiny fraction of the larger umbrella of LGBTQ families' experiences. While specific conflicts experienced by the novel's characters were fictional, they drew inspiration from real-life examples of what various LGBTQ families went through between the 1960s and present day.

If you are interested in learning more, I recommend starting with these compassionate organizations: COLAGE, Family Equality, and the Queerspawn Resource Project.

There is no singular queerspawn experience. There are moving memoirs that offer different but fascinating insights into this identity, including *Affliction: Growing Up With a Closeted Gay Dad* by Laura Hall, *Ashes to Ink* by Lisa Lucca, *The Family Outing* by Jessi Hempel, and *Fairyland: A Memoir of My Father* by Alysia Abbott, as well as the young adult novel, *This Terrible True Thing* by Jenny Laden. There are also excellent films and documentaries, such as *Uncle Frank* and *Nuclear Family*. All these works do an outstanding job of bringing to life some nuances of the experience of being the child of an LGBTQ parent, including capturing the sense of dual identity that many queerspawn individuals have felt. This list is not exhaustive, and I encourage readers to continue their own exploration. The Queerspawn Resource Project curates an ever-growing list that centers the experiences of people with LGBTQ parents and caregivers at QueerspawnResource.org.

Below, I've composed an LGBTQ history timeline to help readers better understand how this novel frames itself against the larger backdrop of LGBTQ rights and history. You can find additional resources by visiting my website at LisaMontanaroWrites.com.

Writing this book has been one of the most challenging, yet rewarding, experiences of my life. I hope this book impacts you—by entertaining you, providing an escape, educating you, or changing the way you see and interact with the world. We are all a beautiful collage, comprised of the things we've experienced throughout our lives, both light and dark. My deepest wish is that after reading this book, others will be inspired to speak their truths too—and come out in their own ways.

LGBTQ History Timeline

- 1940s: The Lavender Scare – the practice of mass dismissal from government service of LGBTQ individuals based on their being an alleged national-security risk and communist sympathizers.
- 1950s: McCarthyism – the political repression and persecution of individuals, including those in the LGBTQ community, based on alleged communist leanings, spearheaded by US Senator Joseph McCarthy.
- 1959: First gay uprising on Main Street in Los Angeles when police attempt to arrest individuals for attending a gay meeting at a Cooper Do-Nuts café.
- 1962: Illinois is the first US state to remove sodomy law and behavior by "consenting adults in private" from its criminal code.
- 1966: Compton Cafeteria Riot in San Francisco – a riot and protest following a police raid at a popular gathering spot for the LGBTQ community.
- 1969: Stonewall Uprising – a series of demonstrations by members of the gay community in response to a violent police raid at the Stonewall Inn in Greenwich Village, NY. The riots are widely regarded as a pivotal moment that brought about significant changes in the gay-liberation movement and the twentieth-century fight for LGBTQ rights in the US.
- 1970: Inaugural Gay Pride Week. A year after the

Stonewall Uprising, to mark the anniversary, the first gay pride marches took place in Chicago, Los Angeles, New York, and San Francisco.

- 1973: An unresolved arson fire at the Upstairs Lounge gay bar in New Orleans kills thirty-two people and injures fifteen more and is the worst mass murder of gay Americans until 2016.
- 1977: Harvey Milk becomes the first openly gay person to be elected to public office in California but tragically gets assassinated less than a year later in 1978.
- 1978: Gilbert Baker creates the rainbow flag as a symbol for the gay-liberation movement, and it flies during the San Francisco Pride Parade.
- 1980: An antigay shooting at the Ramrod Bar, a popular gay spot in Greenwich Village, NY, featured in the Village People's "YMCA" music video, kills two men and injures six more.
- 1982: HIV is first identified.
- 1983: Rock Hudson dies of AIDS.
- 1985: The first memorial to the Nazis' gay victims is unveiled at Neuengamme concentration camp.
- 1987: The American Psychiatric Association removes homosexuality and sexual orientation disturbance from its official list of psychiatric disorders.
- 1990: The World Health Organization removes homosexuality from its classification of diseases.
- 1996: *Rent* opens on Broadway and features gay characters living with, and dying from, AIDS.
- 1994: The US military's "Don't Ask, Don't Tell" policy takes effect, banning openly LGBTQ individuals from military service and creating a culture of secrecy and closeted existence for nonheterosexual people.

- 1995: The Dachau Memorial Museum installs a pink-triangle plaque to commemorate the suffering of LGBTQ individuals by the Nazis during WWII.
- 1997: Ellen DeGeneres comes out, and so does the character based on her, making that television show the first to feature a lesbian or gay lead character, only to be cancelled by the network a year later.
- 1998: The hate crime murder of Matthew Shepard. Two men brutally beat Matthew Shepard—a gay Laramie, Wyoming, college student—tie him to a fence, and leave him overnight. He dies six days later.
- 1998: Executive Order 13087 from President Bill Clinton prohibits discrimination based on sexual orientation in the workplace. However, it does not extend to the military.
- 2003: The US Supreme Court overturns sodomy laws, proclaiming rights to privacy and decriminalizing homosexual behavior.
- 2004: The first legal same-sex marriage ceremony in the US takes place on February 12, 2004, when mayor of San Francisco Gavin Newsom orders city hall to issue marriage licenses to same-sex couples. On May 17, 2004, Massachusetts becomes the first US state to recognize same-sex marriage.
- 2009: Congress passes the Matthew Shepard and James Byrd Jr. Hate Crimes Prevention Act, signed into law by President Barack Obama.
- 2010: The Netherlands becomes the first country to legalize same-sex marriage.
- 2011: The US military repeals the "Don't Ask Don't Tell" policy.
- 2013: The Supreme Court strikes down the Defense of Marriage Act and rules that California's Proposition 8 ban

on same-sex marriage is unconstitutional, making California the thirteenth state where same-sex couples can marry.

- 2015: The Supreme Court strikes down all state bans on same-sex marriage, legalizing it in all fifty states and requiring states to honor out-of-state marriage licenses.
- 2016: A mass shooting at Pulse, a gay nightclub in Orlando, Florida, kills forty-nine people and wounds fifty-three more and is the deadliest attack on an LGBTQ gathering in history.
- 2020: The Supreme Court extends protection to LGBTQ individuals against employment discrimination in the private sector.
- 2021: Pete Buttigieg is sworn in as the US Secretary of Transportation, becoming the first openly gay member of the US Cabinet.
- 2022: Florida Governor Ron DeSantis signs the Parental Rights in Education Act, commonly known as the "Don't Say Gay" law, prohibiting classroom instruction and discussion about sexual orientation and gender identity in schools, as well as expanding book-banning procedures and censoring health curriculum and instruction. The law prevents students from talking about their LGBTQ family members and LGBTQ history, creating a chilling effect and promoting a culture of fear and silence. Other states use the Florida law as a template to pass prohibitions on classroom instruction and discussion on gender identity or sexual orientation, including Alabama, Arkansas, Indiana, Iowa, Kentucky, and North Carolina.
- 2024: The settlement of a lawsuit brought by Equality Florida and other advocacy groups clarifies that Florida's Don't Say Gay Law doesn't prohibit discussing LGBTQ

people as long as it's not part of formal school instruction.

ACKNOWLEDGEMENTS

This book was inspired by a family and created by a village. The life coach and author Martha Beck coined the phrase *believing eyes* to capture the concept of surrounding yourself with people who believe in your vision. I will forever be grateful to those who believed in this novel and were essential in getting it out into the world. They are my believing eyes. I could not have asked for better champions of me or this book.

Thanks to Erica Lucke Dean and Streetlight Graphics for the classy book cover design, Rashida Breen for formatting, and Casey Dembowski for helping to nail down the title.

To Lynn McNamee of Red Adept Publishing, thank you for believing in this manuscript and helping to bring this story into the world. To Angie Lovell, I was in awe of your amazing content editing, which helped shape this story into a more beautiful version of itself. Your belief in this book and guidance on how to strengthen it were invaluable. To Sarah Carleton, thank you for your keen eye for line editing. You helped polish the manuscript to a fine sheen.

I'm grateful to my early draft reader and amazing sister-in-law, Betsy Hulsebosch, for assisting me with bringing the story to a whole new level by asking all the right questions. Your decades in publishing were of immense value to me! To my WFWA mentor, Christine Adler, thank you for seeing the potential in the early stages of this project and encouraging me to continue. To book coach Lidija Hilje, much appreciation for deep-level feedback that was both big picture and eagle-eye detailed and helped me craft the book into a better version. To beta readers Melissa Naatz, Mary Pat Smith, Pamela Thompson, Alan Winnikoff, and Kelly Hartog, sincere gratitude for pushing me to go deeper. To author friends Elaine Stock, Rachel Stone, Julie Mayerson Brown, Barbara Conrey, Gabi Coatsworth, Sharon Kurtzman, and Linda Rosen, many thanks for your assistance with aspects of the publishing process. Hats off to Ann Bremer, who couldn't have been a better writing and critique partner nor a more supportive friend. Ann deserves a trophy for listening to me talk endlessly about this book for years and for reading draft after draft.

I was fortunate to have, as a beta reader, Dr. Ali Dubin, a marriage and family therapist who published her doctoral thesis on disenfranchised grief and treating the family system when one person comes out as LGBTQ. Society doesn't acknowledge disenfranchised grief as legitimate, so individuals often keep it a secret, causing ripple effects in families for generations. When she put a term to the festering wound that forces Lena to keep the family secret well into adulthood, it was indeed like putting a name to a face. Ironically, Ali and I met after I wrote this manuscript and added COLAGE as the organization that Lena gets involved with in Los Angeles. Imagine my surprise when Ali shared that she was one of the original founders and codirectors of the first iteration of COLAGE in, of all places, Los Angeles. It felt like art imitating life and then life imitating art. Call it kismet—she was meant to be part of this book's journey into the world.

To COLAGE, which welcomed me into its inclusive community and made me feel seen. Thank you! Much appreciation to Miranda McLaughlin Wise for first introducing me to COLAGE. When someone says to the daughter of an LGBTQ parent, "My dads," your antennae go up, and you realize you've found a kindred spirit. Same thing for my friend Kim Sumner-Mayer, except she uttered, "My moms." Warmest thanks to Kim, who inspired the character of Lena's new BFF, Kate.

They say one should keep good company as a writer. In that area, I am truly blessed. Thank you to my amazing writing community who kept me going through this solitary endeavor—Women's Fiction Writers Association (shout-out to the Writing Date Inmates and Historical Fiction Affinity Group), Ink Tank, TGIF Rogue Writers, and the Red Adept Publishing Authors and Mentors. These amazing writers cheered me on, inspired me, held my hand through insecure moments, listened to me vent, were patient with me as I wrote and revised over several years, and helped me improve my writing at every turn. I wish I had room to list every one of you by name, but please know I see you!

Props to my local Davis Writer Pals—Robin Dragoo, Mary Pat Smith, and Lally Pia—who provided moral support, feedback, and life-sustaining amounts of food and tea to help make this novel happen and, when reinforcements were needed or milestone celebrations in order, prosecco.

Attending writer events helped me to hone my writing chops, shape this novel, and connect with truly fabulous supportive writers, especially the Northern California Writers' Retreat, San Francisco Writers Conference, Women's Fiction Writers Association annual retreats and tenth-anniversary conference, and the Writer Unboxed Unconference.

To those who promote books and the readers who read them, I would not be living this dream without you. I am particularly grateful for the online groups Great Thoughts Great Readers, Bookish Road Trip, Readers Coffeehouse, A Novel Bee, Women Writers Women's Books, and I Like Big Books.

Deepest gratitude to my uncle Maurice Barone for gifting me my first journal when I was eight years old. Little did we know it would create a lifelong love affair with journaling and writing. Look what you started! A heartfelt nod to my uncle Joe Barone, who loved to read and always had a book in his hand. I hope you're enjoying some Stephen King novels in heaven!

Thank you to my high school English teacher, Joseph McLaughlin, who sadly passed away before this novel published. He ignited my love of words, poetry, reading, writing, literature, and world travel—and inspired me to spend a few years teaching high school English at the NY School for the Deaf while putting myself through law school, which made me appreciate him as a teacher even more!

Enthusiastic gratitude to my friends April Welch, Mandy Bota, and Cheryl Friscia for being this book's midwives and listening to me continually talk about it as I "birthed" it. They never let me give up—even when I sometimes wanted to!—and made sure this story made its way into the world.

Thank you to my beloved friend Linda Marino Spilka, who cheered me on even as she was undergoing treatment for cancer. I miss her terribly and am grateful for the years of beautiful friendship. She was the sister I had never had. Lin, I did it!

Thanks to my aunts, uncles, cousins, in-laws, and friends who encouraged me relentlessly, even as the contents of this book remained a complete mystery to many of you as I worked on it. Big hugs to my sister-in-law Danette Montanaro, and nephew and niece Joseph Montanaro and Angelle Montanaro—love you!

Furry-baby mama love to my canine mascots—little Jerry, the sweetest, scruffiest terrier mix, who kept me company through years of writing before he passed over the Rainbow Bridge, and to Naya, who gladly took up his post and kept the dog bed warm during my marathon writing sessions.

A passionate thank-you to my husband, Sean Hulsebosch, who was my rock through every moment of this journey. His patience and understanding as I spent hours writing in solitude, attending writer retreats far from home, or holed up at the local Starbucks with my writers' group was a true gift. Throughout the long and winding road of this novel, he never once doubted its future. He celebrated with me during my triumphs and comforted me with every disappointment along the way to publication. He took part in countless brainstorming sessions and made me laugh when I needed to keep a sense of humor. His love of story and stint as a filmmaker in his twenties proved to be instrumental in helping me develop the narrative. He provided an audience of one and offered spot-on feedback as I did the final oral read-through of the manuscript. I will cherish that collaboration and always remember how he fell in love with the Antinori family, shedding tears for them and rooting for them. Thank you for always believing in me, encouraging my creative side, and allowing me to mine my life for stories—even though they sometimes include you, and you're such a private person!

And last, but certainly not least, deeply felt thanks to my parents, Joseph and Carol Montanaro, and my brother, Michael Montanaro. They are the real people who inspired this book. To my brother, thank you for being a supportive big brother and sounding board. Heartfelt thanks to my father for sharing honestly and bravely about his life and for being so encouraging of this passion project. He's always marched to the beat of his own drum and taught me to be my own person. Love you to the moon and back, Dad. Deepest gratitude to my mother for always keeping me tied to my Italian roots and for being a constant cheerleader at every stage of my life. She passed away before I wrote this book but was with me for every page. My love for her is immeasurable. Writing this book was a way of keeping her with me and honoring her struggles and triumphs. I miss you, Mom, and know you're smiling down on me and this book.

Mille Grazie!!

About the Author

Lisa Montanaro has a unique background, having traveled the path of a performer who didn't want to be a "starving actress." After saying no to Broadway, she worked as an instructor of high school deaf students to put herself through law school and practiced employment law for a decade. She then defected from her legal career and started her productivity consulting business on the heels of the September 11 tragedy.

Lisa has been keeping a journal, by longhand, since she was eight years old. She is the author of countless nonfiction articles and blog posts. She has served as webinar host for the Women's Fiction Writers Association (WFWA) since 2019 and as a passionate member of its Diversity and Inclusion committee since 2018. Lisa is also a facilitator of the Retro COLAGE group, which is made up of mature-aged adult children of LGBTQ parents. She is the proud daughter of a gay father.

A native New Yorker, Lisa has called California home since 2012. There, she savors life with her veterinarian husband and their spoiled rescue mutts. In addition to being a writer, Lisa is a community theater geek, avid cyclist, world traveler, dedicated gardener, and wine lover.

Read more at https://lisamontanarowrites.com.

About the Publisher

Dear Reader,

We hope you enjoyed this book. Please consider leaving a review on your favorite book site.

Visit https://RedAdeptPublishing.com to see our entire catalogue.

Check out our app for short stories, articles, and interviews. You'll also be notified of future releases and special sales.

Made in the USA
Monee, IL
28 December 2024

72263874R00204